THE CHILDREN'S WARD

The Children's Ward

Howard L. Weiner, M.D.

G. P. PUTNAM'S SONS
NEW YORK

Library of Congress Cataloging in Publication Data

Weiner, Howard
    The children's ward.

    I. Title.
PZ4.W422358Ch 1980   [PS3573.E3933]   813'.54   80-16365
ISBN 0-399-12509-4

Printed in the United States of America

To my dear parents

SUNDAY

The door to the emergency ward sung open. A visibly distressed couple burst in, the man cradling a small boy in his arms.

The boy was not half asleep, as he might have been, awakened on an early Sunday morning by his father. He was not sitting on his father's forearm either, legs dangling, hands around father's neck and head bobbing as he viewed the world from father's shoulder. And he was not struggling to be put down, so he might investigate the surroundings on his own. But the child was struggling. His legs and arms were stiff, his back arched and his eyes rolled up so they appeared predominantly white. Then his eyes darted to the left. The left side of his body began to shake violently. Soon the right side shook as well and his entire body trembled in a massive convulsion.

"Call the neurology resident," the head nurse ordered as she hurriedly led the father and son into room 7 of the emergency ward.

Almost immediately a flurry of activity surrounded the boy. His pajamas were torn from him as the pediatric house officer searched for a vein to start an IV. One nurse tried to measure blood pressure while another attached oxygen tubing to the boy's nose and attempted to place an airway between his teeth.

The pattern of the convulsion now became rhythmical, the boy's extremities flexed and extended and his head jerked to the left. His eyes darted in the same direction, returning toward midline only to be driven left again and again.

Dennis Balsiger stood in the room almost unnoticed and watched the scene. It was not the first time. Although the horror he felt when he witnessed his son's first convulsion didn't touch him at this particular moment, he felt terrible.

He watched the pediatric resident manage to start an IV, then fill a syringe with Valium and slowly inject it. Within seconds, BJ's eyes stopped darting, then they rolled up and out; the nurse pushed the small boy's eyelids closed. BJ's arms and legs were now still, his mouth hung open, and the blue color of his lips that always frightened his parents when he had a convulsion turned pink.

Florence Balsiger sat on a chair in the emergency ward of New York's Children's Hospital and thought of all the chairs in emergency wards that she had occupied. Although she had become relatively immune to the fear that had once gripped her when BJ convulsed, she was now afraid for another reason. The new medicine that had been working so well seemed to have failed.

In another part of the hospital multiple shrill "beeps" disturbed the quiet. Dr. Alex Licata pressed the tiny button on his beeper and it obliged him by stopping the noise. He walked to the nearest nurses' station, dialed 6060 and waited for the page operator to answer.

"Dr. Licata, neurology, answering a page."

"3448 emergency ward," came the reply.

When he called the emergency ward, he was greeted by the pediatric resident.

"We have a four-and-a-half-year-old boy who just came in with a generalized seizure; I stopped it with IV Valium and he's sleeping now. Anything you want us to do before you arrive?"

"Is he a known seizure patient?"

"I haven't spoken to the family yet, but he has a hospital record number. The old chart should be here when you arrive."

"If the parents say he's taking medication, draw blood for anticonvulsant levels. I'll be right there."

For Alex Licata, the week was starting one day early, but Alex didn't mind. After all, he was a doctor and though he didn't like Sunday duty, he loved neurology. As the neurology chief resident at Children's Hospital, he would in the course of the week orchestrate the care of children on the ward, be the first to examine children in the emergency ward, and all the while, he would teach the interns and medical students who were rotating through the neurology service. Every week had more than its share of challenges. The week would challenge Alex with the myriad of neurologic illnesses that only a mother such as nature could ever bestow on her children. But even more, this week would challenge Alex in a personal way, not only in terms of his family, but in terms of his profession as well.

Sunday morning is usually quiet at Children's Hospital, and this Sunday was no exception. The five-minute walk from division 17 to the emergency ward— downstairs, through corridors, and downstairs again—was punctuated only by a few exhausted hellos and the sound of Alex's reflex hammer occasionally touching the wall as he passed. He thought of a boy's stick clicking on a picket fence and smiled to himself. It was not unusual for him to be called for a child with a convulsion. It was a journey he had made many times in his three years of residency.

He walked into the emergency ward and looked for the parents of his patient. They were obvious. Only one couple sat amid the empty chairs that would be filled later. He nodded, knowing he soon would be talking to them. They watched him go by, another doctor wearing white pants and a white jacket.

"The boy with the convulsion is in room seven," the nurse said, but she hadn't completed her sentence before Alex was in the room looking at the boy.

"How's he doing?" he asked the nurse.

"He stopped seizing after I gave him Valium," she replied. "His parents woke up at six-thirty and heard noises coming from

9

his room; they found him convulsing. The chart's come up, it's on the desk out front. It's a thick one."

Alex Licata looked briefly at the small figure, then walked out to the front desk and checked the boy's hospital chart. It was an inch and a half thick. On the cover it said: *Brian James Balsiger 52091, Volume II of III.* The final entry was a year and a half old, dating from BJ's last visit to the seizure clinic. Alex leafed through the chart of a child with an uncontrollable seizure disorder. There were pink brainwave, or EEG, reports—all abnormal. There were innumerable laboratory tests and clinic notes. Each clinic note began with a long list of BJ's anticonvulsants and ended with a plan to add a new anticonvulsant, drop an old one or change doses. Alex skipped back to the first clinic notes and then followed the course of BJ's treatments from ages three to four. The early anticonvulsants were virtually identical with the most recent, eighteen months of anticonvulsant manipulation had merely come full circle. He glanced again at the cover of Volume II, then asked the secretary to get Volume III.

He walked back to the waiting area and introduced himself to BJ's parents. "I'm Dr. Licata from neurology," he told the couple. "Before we talk in detail, could you tell me what medication your son is taking?"

Florence Balsiger recited the names of five medicines. Alex made sure the boy's blood had been sent for the appropriate tests, then sat down with Dennis and Florence Balsiger.

In most encounters with children's parents, Alex was the one most experienced in the doctor-parent interview. This was not true for BJ's mother and father; they had invested many hours talking to doctors. Although it hadn't brought a cure for BJ's convulsions, it gave them experience at interviewing, experience often greater than the doctor's. They could tell how much the doctor speaking to them knew about epilepsy. Often they guided the interview to ensure the right questions were asked. It soon became clear that Alex was knowledgeable about epilepsy. Alex, in turn, recognized parents who had spent most of their son's life explaining to doctors about his problem.

"Exactly what happened this morning?"

"About six-thirty I heard noises in BJ's room," Mrs. Balsiger

10

began. "He was grunting and frothing at the mouth. His left arm and leg were shaking and he looked to the left. I called to him, but he didn't answer. I placed his head on my lap; after a minute the shaking stopped and he fell asleep. He lost control of his urine and feces, all over the bed."

"He didn't have a convulsion for over a week," her husband added, "and we thought the new medicine was helping. When I came into the room, my wife was cleaning the bed. BJ started again. The same pattern, eyes and head turned to the left, left body shaking. Then it began to involve the right side and he had difficulty breathing. That scared us. When the second seizure was over, we brought him to the hospital. He had two more in the car."

Alex looked at their faces. The woman was about thirty, her face was plain, framed by short, straight, brown hair. There was a visible space between her front teeth. When she spoke, dimples appeared in her cheeks. It was strange, despite a distraught face, the dimples made her seem happy. Her husband's face was rugged, weatherbeaten. There were deep furrows on his forehead and a trace of acne splashed across his nose and cheeks. Pale blue eyes and large white teeth flashed when he spoke. He was very intense.

Next, Alex began the long and often painful process of recreating the boy's medical history; first, questions about recent months, then a return to birth and careful documentation of a story that filled three volumes of hospital charts.

Florence Balsiger's pregnancy was uneventful. BJ was a six-pound-ten-ounce term baby. The delivery was normal; mother and child left the hospital on time. BJ smiled at three months, sat up at six, and at ten months stood up and cruised around the house. Florence even thought he said "mama" a few times. The first page of his hospital chart was written when BJ was eleven months old, he convulsed on the living room rug while his parents watched television. It took months for Dennis and Florence Balsiger to accept the picture of BJ's first convulsion. The young infant cried out and fell. Spasm after spasm rippled his body while his parents struggled with him. BJ seized continuously and his mother was certain her son would die. Fifteen minutes later, in room 7 of the emergency ward at Children's

11

Hospital, BJ received his first injection of anticonvulsants. The injection brought quiet to a trembling body.

His first hospital admission was routine. Skull films were normal and there were only mild abnormalities on the EEG. Blood and urine tests were normal. The boy was started on phenobarbital and the seizures stopped.

Alex made notes on what would be the next pages of the chart as he listened for clues that might explain BJ's subsequent stormy course.

"What happened after the first hospital admission?"

The mother continued. "He did well until he was a year and a half. He was walking and understood a few words. But then he started having strange episodes; he would be walking and suddenly would fall to the floor. First I thought he was tripping but it happened too frequently. Funny, it didn't bother him; he stood up and started off again. I became worried when he fell and had a short convulsion, his arms and legs stiffened, eyes rolled back. We brought him to seizure clinic."

Florence paused. She seemed to be viewing the scene of BJ falling to the floor. Her husband reacted to the pause as if it were a cue in the script of a play and continued the story.

"The doctor in the seizure clinic told us the falling episodes were seizures and added Dilantin to the phenobarbital. It didn't help, only made BJ unsteady," Mrs. Balsiger began. "The episodes and short convulsions increased in frequency. I remember calling the hospital that month—increase the Dilantin, lower the phenobarbital; bring him in for a blood test; lower the Dilantin, increase the phenobarbital. Finally, BJ was readmitted to the hospital."

Alex scanned the typewritten summary of BJ's second hospital admission, then turned to the second sheet. "Discharge Diagnosis: mixed seizure disorder. Medication: Dilantin, phenobarbital, Zarontin. Prognosis: Good. Follow-up: Seizure clinic in one month." During that admission BJ was assigned to Nolan Magness, then a first-year neurology resident who had followed BJ for the remaining three years of his residency. Nolan was still in New York, doing research in neurochemistry. Alex knew him well and made a mental note to call Nolan later that day.

"What happened after the second admission?"

Dennis Balsiger continued. "The Zarontin helped the falling spells, but he was still unsteady. It was summertime and when he was outside we had to watch him carefully. He didn't do well. Then, the frequency of his seizures increased."

"Do you want to see the chart of his convulsions?" Florence blurted out. She seemed to remember the clinic appointment with Dr. Magness in the fall of BJ's second year. "It's very important," Nolan Magness had said, "to document exactly the frequency and character of BJ's seizures. It's the only way to know if the medication is helping." BJ's mother accepted the task. As with most things that related to BJ's illness she had no choice. By recording each spell, Florence Balsiger detached herself one tiny step from being the mother of her son. She was now chronicler, scribe, doctor's assistant. She did a good job. She had collected forty-one charts; each represented one month. The chart was like a calendar, and under each day, she wrote a comment—"No spells, groggy today, three drop attacks, a large convulsion, called Dr. Magness, increased medication, decreased medication, started new medication, stopped medication." She handed Alex Licata the most recent chart. Florence Balsiger kept no chart as a mother, only as chronicler. The mother's chart would have read, *Poor BJ, why us? Won't he ever be well? Should we have another child? Does Dennis think it's my fault? I can't take it anymore. . . .*

"Dr. Licata, the boy is waking up," BJ's nurse said. "Do you want to see him?"

"Absolutely," Alex said. He left BJ Balsiger, age one and a half, and examined the boy of four. He was moaning and occasionally moved his arms and legs. Alex called to him; there was no response. He lifted the boy's eyelids—pupils were two millimeters and reacted to light. A pinch on the shoulder brought a more forceful groan and an attempt by the opposite hand to remove the painful stimulus. Reflexes were equal, both toes were abnormally extensor.

"Give him sixty milligrams of phenobarbital intramuscularly," Alex told the nurse, then returned to continue his interview with BJ's parents.

Florence and Dennis Balsiger watched as the white pants and jacket approached them. Alex was stocky. The white hospital clothes fitted tightly, and a bulge was beginning to develop above his belt. He wore gold, wire-rimmed glasses that sat on a broad nose. His features were coarse, a peasant's face topped by brown hair that was never in place. His best feature was a gentle smile. He didn't look like a doctor.

"He's coming out of it," Alex said, comforting the parents with his smile. "I gave him extra medication."

By now, Alex had worked his way to the middle of Volume I, which dealt with BJ at two years old. Florence Balsiger's charts had provided Nolan Magness with a rational basis for manipulating BJ's medication, but that hadn't helped the seizures. In the summer of BJ's second year, he was admitted to the hospital for the third time. BJ was investigated extensively: a repeat spinal tap, special blood and urine studies, a CAT scan, arteriography to outline the blood vessels in his brain, and even pneumoencephalography to outline the cavities of the brain with air. All tests were negative. Again, the only abnormal study was the EEG, which still indicated underlying seizure activity.

Several months later BJ's parents discovered he was not developing normally. Previously they had suspected he might be slow, but had no other children to measure BJ against. Psychological testing was ordered and it showed that BJ was functioning at the level of a two-year-old, one year behind.

A flood of questions poured from the pages of Florence Balsiger's unwritten charts, only now they were verbalized. Was BJ retarded? Why isn't he developing normally? Were the convulsions responsible? Could anything be done?

Nolan Magness's clinic notes reflected the change. After commenting on the mechanics of BJ's convulsions, notes about Dennis and Florence Balsiger's questions, fears, and at times their misconceptions appeared. It was difficult to give answers when there were none.

Nolan Magness had frankly confessed to the parents that he didn't know why BJ had seizures. There was no evidence of a brain tumor. BJ's slow development was common in children with uncontrollable convulsions. There were no new tests to try. All he could do was adjust anticonvulsants until the proper combination was found. Was there a combination that could control BJ's convulsions? He didn't know.

Alex finished Volume I and picked up Volume II, knowing what to expect. The medication on the first and last pages of the chart were identical despite multiple changes on the intervening pages; the first and last pages attested to the futility of the changes. In the middle of Volume II, BJ was admitted to the hospital for the fourth time. Now three and a half, he was placed on a special diet that sometimes helped severe seizure disorders.

"Did the diet help?" Alex asked.

"He did better initially," the mother said, "but then was the same."

Alex glanced at the record of BJ's fourth admission; the boy was hospitalized for an entire month. It took a week on the special diet before the appropriate changes took place in BJ's body chemistry. Alex leafed through countless urine and blood tests, dietitian's and nurse's notes, and a graph that recorded the frequency of the boy's convulsions. He found nothing to add to Florence Balsiger's simple statement, "Better initially, but basically unchanged."

Volume III, when it appeared, turned out to be relatively thin; there had been no subsequent hospital admissions for BJ until this morning. By now, Nolan Magness had completed his residency and his handwriting was replaced by that of a seizure clinic doctor who had tried new medications unfamiliar even to Alex. The drugs were seldom used because of their toxicity, and were so experimental that they were listed only by number. Luckily, BJ hadn't experienced side effects from the medications, but his seizures hadn't improved. If anything, they had merely changed character.

"In the last nine months his convulsions have been different," Florence Balsiger volunteered. "Often he just stares. Sometimes he picks at his shirt over and over; he doesn't hear me while he's doing it and afterwards he's groggy and sleeps. Once he walked in circles, then sat in a chair and slept. I didn't even know these were seizures until the seizure clinic doctor told me. Today's the first time in three months he's had a major convulsion."

Alex knew what she was describing—temporal lobe seizures or psychomotor epilepsy. The most recent EEG confirmed it. He read the last clinic note and found that the new medication

15

BJ's parents spoke about was a recently approved drug for use in severe epilepsy. It didn't help BJ.

The history-taking over; Alex asked questions about BJ's general health, allergies, and family illnesses. He saved the most painful part of the interview for the last. He tried as gently as possible to assess BJ's level of development. Although his tone was gentle, the words asked a harsh question.

"He's done better the past few months," the father said. "He can say his ABCs now."

"He could do that last year," Florence said. "It's much more difficult for him now."

"You forget the new medication," Dennis argued. "It's made his speech slurred."

"His walking and running is the same," Florence Balsiger continued. "Of course, he doesn't play with children his age."

"He can't even keep up with children in his special school," the father admitted.

"He's so dopey from the medication, Dennis, how can he improve?"

"But he needs it for his convulsions."

Alex watched their faces. The man's eyes were hollow, tired of an oft-repeated conversation. His wife's dimples had somehow disappeared; not even the false appearance of joviality. They knew as well as Alex that BJ at four and a half was functioning at a three year old level.

"We'll keep him here at the hospital," Alex said. "I want to observe any other major convulsions he might have and check anticonvulsant levels; he'll go through X-ray and then to the neurology ward, division seventeen."

"How long will he be here?" the father asked.

"I can't tell."

"Why's he had a major convulsion when he was doing better?" the mother wondered.

"We'll watch blood levels of anticonvulsants and recheck his EEG," Alex repeated.

"Any new tests planned?" the father asked.

"Or new medications you'll try?" the mother added.

"Not at this time."

The barrage of questions stopped. Then the mother asked quietly. "What's going to happen to him?"

The young doctor moved the thin third volume between his fingers, avoiding their gaze. Finally he looked up. "Mr. Balsiger, go to the admitting office. Mrs. Balsiger, stay with BJ for his X-ray. I'll be here all afternoon. We'll talk later."

Alex couldn't answer the last question. Saying nothing was better than "I don't know." To Dennis and Florence Balsiger both were the same. They had heard them many times.

Division 17 is the combined neurology-neurosurgery floor at Children's Hospital. There are approximately twenty-five children on the ward. Diseases of the brain and spinal cord are not bound by age: on division 17 there are newborn infants, toddlers, kindergarten, and school age children, budding adolescents and veteran teenagers ready to enter adulthood. Many have bandages on their heads; They've had operations. Some wear football helmets in case they convulse and fall. Older children wheel younger children around in carts and feed them dinner. Toys litter the hallway and improbable friendships are made. The noise of the ward invariably contains the cry of an infant. Some children are too ill to participate in the animation of the ward, and they form the still life, sitting listlessly in a cart or lying expressionless in bed.

Although many children have seizure disorders, not all do; there are always children on neurosurgery having shunts put in place to bypass blocked brain cavities. There are children with headaches, children with infections of the brain, and children with brain tumors. It is not a happy ward.

Alex Licata stepped into division 17 and greeted the nurse. "I admitted a four-and-a-half-year-old boy with convulsions from the emergency ward. He's stable, there shouldn't be any problems."

"I know, BJ Balsiger," the nurse said. "He's been here before."

It was late morning. The ward was quieter than it would be twenty-four hours later, and there were no seriously ill children that needed Alex's attention. As he walked through a ward often

17

filled with children whose seizures were difficult to control, Alex knew that convulsions were the most treatable illness seen by the pediatric neurologist. Then he contrasted BJ Balsiger with the many children whose convulsions were easily controlled by a single medication. He thought of those epileptics who had been ostracized by society in the times before anticonvulsants. Famous figures in history had had epilepsy—Dostoyevsky, Julius Caesar, Napoleon. Then Alex remembered his own eyeglasses; in Roman times, myopia alone would have limited him to a place in a slave galley.

Alex was uncomfortable with BJ Balsiger; there was no obvious solution to the boy's uncontrollable seizures, and a doctor had to "feel comfortable" with his diagnosis and treatment. If there was no physician anxiety, nothing more needed to be done. If the doctor was uncomfortable—more tests, consultation, different treatment. In fact, doctors could be classified by the appropriateness of their anxiety. Those who felt comfortable with a patient when they shouldn't were incomplete in their diagnostic testing, falsely secure, often unknowledgeable, and dangerous. Those who rarely felt comfortable performed too many tests, also were unknowledgeable, and although not overtly dangerous, failed to provide the security needed by patient and family. After all, if the body's metabolism was predicated on a delicate balance, it was only logical that the same apply to the self-appointed guardian of that mean. Doctors had a phrase for it—clinical judgment.

Alex had good clinical judgment. It built slowly during his training, two years in pediatrics and three years in neurology. But it was also something he had, a natural. Medical educators tried to teach clinical judgment, but there was no formula. Yet, if one doctor worked with another who had good clinical judgment, it sometimes rubbed off. As the chief neurology resident at Children's Hospital, this is what made Alex a good teacher. He knew how to care for patients, he was anxious and comfortable at the right times, and, by working with him, students, interns, and residents learned.

Alex always wanted to be a doctor, a chance to be more than his parents. More than a secretary and more than a salesman. It was a chance to help people, to build one's ego, to be productive, and to be somebody. He was nearing the end of his training and he had achieved his goal. Yet, the excitement of being a doctor was now blunted by the hours, the routine. Alex often felt he only watched a disease progress rather than alter its course. Though he was a good doctor, one with good clinical judgment, he didn't belong in the world of academic medicine, the world of research and the laboratory, the world where a doctor might achieve fame, discover the cure for a disease, get his name in the papers. He was more than his parents but would never be more than a good doctor. It was enough, but Alex hadn't realized it.

Alex picked up the telephone and called Nolan Magness.

"Hello, Nolan. Why are you home on Sunday?"

"It's raining outside," came the logical reply.

Alex hadn't noticed. "I admitted an old patient of yours to division seventeen. BJ Balsiger."

"Anything new or just more problems with convulsions?"

"Just convulsions."

Nolan Magness was pursuing a career in academic medicine. Nine months out of his neurology residency, he was working in a neurochemistry lab. Alex had always suspected he was a better clinician than Nolan, that Nolan seemed more interested in test tubes than patients, but could find nothing wrong in Nolan's handling of BJ.

"Poor child," Nolan continued. "I'm glad I don't follow him anymore. There was nothing more to offer and he wasn't getting better. The parents are really being hurt by the illness. He's their only child."

"Why don't they have another?"

"They're afraid," Nolan said. "I'm not surprised that BJ's back again. I could never keep him out of the hospital."

"He had a major convulsion this morning," Alex told him. "It was a focal seizure which started on the left side and drove his eyes to the left."

"God, I hope you can do something for him, Alex. Do you want me to talk with the parents?"

"Maybe later in the week. Any ideas?"

"If the convulsion was focal and we've no new medication to offer, maybe he should have repeat studies."

"I was thinking the same. Probably a CAT Scan, then arteriography.

"I did those when he was three and they were normal. But it couldn't hurt to do them again," Nolan said.

"So how's the neurochemistry lab treating you?"

"Good. I'm getting my feet wet."

"Miss the wards?"

"Probably not as much as you would. By the way, what are you doing at the end of this year?"

"Private practice," Alex said.

"They sure could use you at the medical center, Alex. They need someone to teach patient care."

"I'd only stay in academic medicine if I had a lab interest," Alex said. "I can take care of patients in practice and teach part time at a medical school. Clinicians are second-class citizens in academic medicine."

"Not always, Alex."

"I didn't say it should be that way, Nolan. I'm saying that's how it is."

Nolan began to tell Alex about his lab work, but Alex wasn't listening. If I'm a good clinician, Alex thought, why couldn't I be a good researcher as well? I could discover a drug that would cure the epilepsy of children like BJ Balsiger and take care of the kids at the same time. All I would need is a few years in the laboratory, a chance to fiddle with the test tubes and publish papers. Alex knew there was no advancement in academic medicine without publishing papers, and one didn't publish many papers by talking to the parents of children with epilepsy.

"When will I see you, Alex?" Nolan asked, and upon hearing his name, Alex realized he was in the midst of a telephone conversation.

"Probably this week when you visit BJ," Alex said as he imagined Nolan standing in a room with thousands of test tubes and hundreds of scientific papers that he had written. "I'll call you in the lab, Nolan."

"Have a nice day, Alex."

"Sure," Alex said dryly. "You too."

* * *

It was late afternoon on division 17. Alex was checking lab slips and X-ray reports and leafing through the daily progress notes. He came across the medical student's writeup on a child admitted for ataxia—difficulty with gait. It was a female medical student named Casey, and Alex liked having her on the service. She was smart. Her writeup was long and encompassed five sheets. Both sides of each sheet were filled, the pages were neat, the writing legible. In fact, Casey had used two colors to make the organization easy to follow. Her writeup represented two hours of interview with parents and child plus one hour to perform the examination, thirty minutes to arrange the notes, two hours of reading in the library, and one hour to transcribe the information onto the five hospital sheets.

Although it had taken Casey over six hours to prepare the writeup, Alex could have done the entire operation in an hour, including transcribing, but excluding research time in the library. Even so, Casey had missed two major points in the history and had not carried out one important part of the examination. Still, her work was more than adequate, and Alex wrote "excellent workup" at the end of her five-page note, then jotted down what she had missed. Casey was clearly one of the better students rotating through neurology, and Alex looked forward to teaching her during her month on the neurology service.

He smiled to himself, remembering his own writeups from student days. He knew how Casey was approaching patients, following a set scheme, asking all the questions, giving all answers equal weight. She had not yet learned which leads to follow, which questions to pursue, which to drop. She was afraid of missing something and not totally certain of her observations; she was slow to integrate positive findings or to discard negative ones. In the end, her diagnoses were based on textbook cases, not firsthand experience; half her diagnoses didn't apply and the other half weren't sufficiently developed.

Time would change her rigid approach. As Casey saw more patients and began her internship, she would confront problems she had seen before. Time spent with the patient would be shorter, there would be more depth to her view of a problem, more refinement in her diagnoses. Her writing would change too—less neat, harder to read—the product of too many hours

21

writing and too many times writing the same words over and over. Abbreviations would creep in, ends of the words would disappear. People didn't realize that even doctors known for their illegibility began their careers as neat and legible scribes.

Alex left the nurses' station and stopped in on BJ. The boy was sleeping quietly, and had had no more convulsions since admission to the hospital. Alex adjusted the dosage of the anti-convulsants, then spoke briefly to BJ's parents, who seemed considerably less apprehensive. Now that BJ was in the hospital, they no longer feared that something might happen at home for which they would blame themselves. And of course there was always the hope that perhaps in the hospital something new would be discovered—a clue, a new observation, a different medicine, a solution to their problem.

Alex glanced at his watch and realized it was time to call home. "Hi, Mellissa, just checking in. How are the girls?"

"Fine. Elizabeth is playing next door and Kristen is here with me."

"Are you coming to the hospital for supper?"

"What time is it now?"

"Five, but I can eat anytime."

"How about six o'clock? I'll meet you at the main entrance . . . are you busy?"

"Not too bad. I just admitted a boy from the emergency ward with convulsions. It's a difficult case."

"Is he all right?"

"I won't know for a few days. See you at supper."

Mellissa was a pretty woman. Her straight blonde hair framed a lovely face composed of striking green eyes, full lips and teeth any movie star would have been happy to have. Her figure more than pleased him, though Mellissa complained her breasts were too big and that two children hadn't helped. Compared to Mellissa, Alex was plain. His stocky figure was an inch shorter than hers. But his coarse features and broad face were deceiving. A gentle smile was part of his gentle manner. People liked to talk with Alex. He was quick, humorous, and didn't threaten.

22

Mellissa fell in love with a gentle personality; Alex fell in love with a pretty girl.

Theirs was an improbable marriage. Mellissa was the only child of a general practitioner in a small Connecticut town, and she grew up resenting the hours her father took from the family to give to his patients. She had met Alex when they were in college, but his medical aspirations hadn't bothered her because she didn't think he would get into medical school.

Alex didn't realize how strong her feelings against doctors were until he was accepted at the Boston University Medical School and she broke off the relationship. There were many others anxious to court her. However, a year later, it became apparent that Alex loved medicine more than Mellissa hated it and that she wasn't satisfied with her new suitors. They moved to New York, when Alex was accepted in the neurology training program at New York's Children's Hospital.

Mellissa had worked for an advertising firm for the two years before she became pregnant with Elizabeth. Now that Elizabeth was almost four and Kristen, twenty-one months, Mellissa was getting anxious to return to work.

They were still in love, though five years of internship and residency was beginning to show. Mellissa was less patient with Alex at home and less tolerant of his time at the hospital. He forgot how boring it was for Mellissa to spend the day with two young children. More time together was needed to strengthen the relationship; other marriages like theirs had already broken.

Mellissa sat with Alex in the hospital cafeteria while the girls played on the bicycle merry-go-round in the lobby.

"When are you on next week?" Mellissa asked.

"Tuesday."

"And you're off for the weekend?"

"Yes. Maybe we can go on a trip."

"How about the ocean?" she asked.

"It'll be chilly, but we can walk on the beach."

Alex spoke methodically. For someone who listened so closely to what parents said and how they said it, he was surprisingly indifferent to Mellissa. Maybe he was resting from the rigors of interacting with parents, or maybe he felt he knew Mellissa, so he didn't have to pay attention. No need to prove himself to his wife.

"How'd you like to live in Texas?" he asked casually.

"I wouldn't."

"There's a great opportunity for a pediatric neurologist in Dallas."

"Not interested."

"Two other pediatricians in the group, affiliation with the university, and full partnership in two years."

"Have they run out of children in New England?"

"Only sick ones," Alex laughed. "I'm still checking out a place in Connecticut and the offer in Maine."

Mellissa refused to live far from her family; there was really nothing to discuss. Alex's mother lived in Chicago with his older sister. His father had been dead for five years.

"When will you be coming home?"

"Probably after ten."

"I guess I'll wash my hair tonight."

"Take money from the bank today?" he asked.

"Today's Sunday, Alex," Mellissa said, a tone of resignation in her voice.

"I can get some tomorrow; I have to deposit my check anyway." He didn't seem to hear her answer.

Mellissa gathered her two children and walked the three blocks back to the apartment complex where many interns and residents lived. For Alex, living so close to the hospital meant night call at home; for Mellissa, it meant not sleeping alone. But for her it also meant being confined with two young children in a small apartment on the fourteenth floor.

Alex was alone again in the hospital. Mellissa's visit was nothing more than a forced break in his hospital rhythm, a rhythm he regained with ease as he walked down the hospital corridor. Alex came alive as he took a clipped packet of twenty 3 x 5 cards from his shirt pocket. Each card was stamped with the hospital plate of a patient, all were arranged in alphabetical order according to the child's last name, and each contained clinical observations and lab data relating to the case. Alex couldn't function without his walking file. He reviewed it to pick a case for grand rounds, triumphantly read the hospital number to X-ray or lab control when told they couldn't proceed without the hospital number, and did a reasonably complete job of monitoring the progress of children in the hospital without having to resort to hospital charts.

Sifting the cards, Alex mentally reviewed the cases on the ward and children he had been asked to consult on in the hospital. He removed the cards of two children discharged on Friday and of one who had died on Saturday.

As he put a blank card on top, the quiet of the corridor was interrupted by four shrill beeps. Alex stepped into the nearest nurses' station and called the page operator.

The word "beeper" was an appropriate term for the tiny box that tied Alex to the hospital; that's all it did—beep. There were certain things to know about the beeper. Never wear it while doing a spinal tap; sterile gloves prohibited turning it off. It could be set off voluntarily by shutting it, then turning it on again, a convenient way to legitimately leave a boring conference or the professor's rounds. Finally, if it didn't beep for over an hour, the batteries were dead. As Alex unconsciously fingered the top of his beeper, he heard the page operator tell him to call division 10, the newborn nursery.

If there were few seriously ill children on division 17, there were many, including the premmies, in the newborn nursery. They lay in plastic incubators that kept temperature optimal, two holes in the side of each box providing entry for hands that were almost as large as the infant. Most infants had exchanged the umbilical cord that connected them to their mother's placenta when they curled in her womb for an umbilical catheter that connected them to an intravenous bottle as they rested in the incubator. Some wore eyepatches to protect their eyes from a special light that burned excessive yellow from their jaundiced skin. Others were connected to heart monitors and proclaimed their existence 120 times a minute with a beep. In the midst of the five tiny beeping hearts, a doctor often didn't hear his own beeper go off.

As he entered the nursery to evaluate a newborn infant with convulsions, Alex knew he would be confronted with a different

25

clinical picture than that of BJ Balsiger. Since the brain of a newborn is only partially developed, the convulsions of a newborn are different. Rather than massive spasms, a newborn's convulsion may only be minor twitching of an extremity, or turning of the hand in a strange posture, or nothing more than a subtle interruption of breathing. Alex came to see Baby Girl Carlson, so new, she hadn't yet been named. She was fifteen hours old.

Baby Girl Carlson was a large girl and her birth had been difficult. Even though it was her mother's fourth delivery, labor had lasted over twenty hours. Five hours after the birth, a nurse noticed that the baby's right arm was twitching. A doctor confirmed the observation and the infant was transferred to Children's Hospital. The twitching had continued intermittently for the next ten hours, but as Alex approached her incubator, the infant lay still.

A neurologic exam is usually involved and complex, but in the newborn, the brain, although already unique, imparts nothing more than the reflex behavior of an animal, and this is what Alex came to check. First he studied the baby. She didn't move one side more than the other or show any evidence of seizure activity. Then he banged the top of the incubator and she startled. Both hands shot up as if to grab an imaginary ball on her chest. It was the Moro reflex, and Alex called it normal. He lifted the cover of the incubator and took the baby into his hands to see how she felt. This part of the exam couldn't be quantified. Alex had learned it by a very straightforward method; he had held many normal infants. Baby Girl Carlson felt normal. Her muscle tone was good and she was not too floppy. She responded normally when Alex's tiny reflex hammer struck her knees, then Alex held open her crying eyes and examined her retina and optic nerve.

Next came transillumination. A nurse carried the baby into a dark closet and Alex applied a flashlight to the baby's head. What a refined test, Alex thought as he watched for areas of the skull that might light up. Light doesn't pass through brain, but a large collection of fluid might turn the skull into an orange globe. Normal.

Back in the nursery, Alex tested the infant's brain in three additional ways. First, he measured it. A tape measure around the head effectively measured the size of what was inside. Too small, not enough brain. Too big, probably an excess collection of fluid inside. Baby Girl Carlson's head circumference was normal. Second, he felt it. The skull is open in babies, and one can feel for the brain. Parents call the opening the baby's "soft spot"; doctors call it the anterior fontanelle. It felt normal to Alex; it wasn't bulging. Third, he tapped it, like checking a watermelon. If there was an excess collection of fluid or raised intracranial pressure, it would sound hollow, the "cracked pot" sound. The sound made by Alex's finger on the side of the skull was normal. Three more refined tests, Alex thought to himself, as he placed the baby back in the incubator.

"What do you think?" the pediatric intern working in the nursery asked as Alex thumbed through the baby's chart.

"She looks good and her exam's normal. Have you started her on any medication?"

"Phenobarbital. Her calcium and glucose are normal."

"All there is to do now is a spinal tap."

"Stay and help," the intern, said. "We're short one nurse."

The brain is bathed in fluid; it actually floats in the skull. This makes it lighter than the two and a half pounds it weighs. The same fluid bathes the spinal cord and is crystal clear, like water. If there is infection or bleeding it shows in the cerebrospinal fluid.

Alex returned the baby to the fetal position. The bony prominences in her lower back protruded even more as the pediatric intern cleaned the area, first with brown and then with a clear solution. Next the intern advanced a very tiny needle just over his thumb, which he had placed on one of the baby's prominences for a marker. He pulled back the stylet that fitted into the needle and waited for fluid.

"I'm in," he announced as the first drops fell into a plastic test tube.

Nice job, Alex thought as he struggled to see the fluid.

Pink.

Alex waited. Pink meant blood, but sometimes it was only bleeding caused by the needle and after a few drops the fluid cleared.

27

Still pink.

"Looks like she's bled," the intern said.

"Right, but we'll have to spin it down."

They took one tube of the fluid to the laboratory and centrifuged it.

Yellow.

With the blood forming a red dot on the bottom of the tube, the fluid was still not clear. No question now. Baby Girl Carlson indeed had bled.

"It's probably a subarachnoid hemorrhage," Alex said as they returned to the nursery. "The baby looks too good for bleeding into the brain. She'll probably do all right, but we'll know more after an EEG tomorrow. I'd continue with the anticonvulsants."

"Do you want to talk to the father? He's waiting outside the nursery."

Mr. Carlson was the thirty-five-year-old father of two other girls and a boy. He was a man not frightened by illnesses in children, having learned during the preceding ten years that although children often became very sick, they usually got well. Up until now he had been lucky.

"I'm Dr. Licata, from neurology," Alex greeted him. "I've just seen your daughter."

"How's she doing?"

"Over the past ten hours she's had convulsions. We've done a spinal tap and it shows bleeding inside her head." Alex watched his face for a reaction that didn't appear. "The bleeding is most probably related to her size and your wife's difficult delivery." Still no reaction. "We've started medication to control the convulsions."

"I understand."

He couldn't possibly understand, Alex thought, translating Mr. Carlson's comment as, "I'm listening."

"Have any other children in your family been seriously ill?" Alex asked. "Anyone with convulsions?"

"They're all fairly healthy. The usual illnesses children get—chickenpox, measles, colds. My eldest girl broke her leg and was in a cast for three months; she's fine now. Actually, my boy had a convulsion; it was with a high fever, but he's never had another one."

"What type of work do you do?"

"I own a restaurant."

"Does your wife work?"

"Not with three children."

Although many people were frightened by convulsions, Baby Girl Carlson's father apparently wasn't one of them. His experience with illnesses had always had a happy ending. What's more, Alex was sure that Mr. Carlson didn't mind the children when they were sick. That was his wife's job.

Alex spoke through him to the wife, who would soon be questioning her husband about their new daughter. "Your daughter's examination is normal and I find no evidence of brain damage." Alex was not certain Mr. Carlson had thought about brain damage, and felt it prudent to plant the thought in his mind. "We'll do a brainwave test tomorrow and then I'll have more information. Do you have any questions?"

"Not really," Baby Girl Carlson's father said. "But what should I tell my wife?"

Alex smiled. Mr. Carlson was satisfied, but somehow knew his wife wouldn't be. "Tell her not to worry, her daughter will probably be all right. I'll be happy to talk with her on the phone tomorrow after the EEG."

A quick handshake and Alex wrote a note on Baby Girl Carlson's chart.

It was 9:30. Division 17 was quiet. Parents and visitors had gone, lights were turned out, and the children put to bed. Alex figured he could be home by ten as he'd promised Mellissa, even allowing for a brief stop at BJ's room.

"How's he doing?" Alex asked a nurse who happened to be in BJ's room.

"Fine. He's slept most of the day, but we woke him for supper and he ate a little. He's taking his medication orally." The nurse studied the medication cards on her chart and the tiny cups with different-colored pills. "His parents seemed quite worried," she added as an afterthought. "They stayed in his room all day and called the nurses several times for trivial things."

"I know."

Did one of the other nurses tell you?"

"No, but I'm not surprised. I spent time with them in the

emergency ward. They have an enormous problem on their hands."

"What's going to happen?"

"I don't know." Alex had no better answer for the nurse than he did for the parents.

He gently jostled the boy to rouse him for what seemed to be in a light sleep. BJ was moving both arms and legs well. Alex lifted each eyelid and glanced at the pupils, then checked the reflexes and stroked the soles of the boy's feet. The left big toe went up, the right down. In the emergency ward both had gone up. There was something abnormal about the right side of BJ's brain.

"Does he have a fever?"

"No."

"Laboratory tests back yet?"

"They're probably at the desk, waiting for the secretary to put them in the chart."

Alex checked the lab slips, then wrote a note in BJ's chart. "March 12, 9:40 P.M. Patient resting quietly. No further seizures. Exam is normal apart from left upgoing toe. Dilantin and phenobarb levels a bit low—dosages increased. No evidence for intercurrent infection or metabolic factors to account for today's convulsion. Will have to decide on investigations to carry out. Scheduled for EEG and repeat blood levels of anticonvulsants tomorrow."

As he left the room, Alex knew that by morning BJ would be awake and he would meet the boy. He looked forward to it.

One last call to division 10 revealed that Baby Girl Carlson had had intermittent tremulousness, which the nurses weren't sure were seizures, although Alex knew they probably were. Nevertheless, the infant was better, feeding well, and had no overt seizures.

Finally, a call home. The telephone rang eight times before Mellissa finally picked up.

"Sorry, I didn't hear the phone—I'm under the hair dryer."

"Are the girls asleep?"

"Yes."

"I'm on my way home. See you in a few minutes."

The night was pleasantly warm for late March in New York, not humid as it would be in the summer. Alex walked among the

30

blocks of medical buildings that included four major hospitals, a medical school, a school of public health, a school of pharmacy, and even a hospital for animals, where he had once gone on "neurology rounds." He entered his apartment building, which formed one of the newest and cleanest of blocks, and waited for the elevator to pull him to the fourteenth floor.

Mellissa had just finished the tedious process of drying her hair. She always did it when Alex was on duty, since she didn't want to take away time they might have together. Often, however, time together was spent separately—Alex reading and filing articles from medical journals, Mellissa doing chores in the apartment, reading, or at times painting. When they were alone, they liked to talk—it was always the same topics: where he was going to practice, how life would be when he was no longer a resident, money, and the children. They seldom said anything that hadn't been said before, but enjoyed talking nevertheless—it was ritual more than communication.

Mellissa looked very pretty with her clean blonde hair. She didn't expect much from Alex on the night he was on duty, but she thought she might as well look nice. Alex noticed. The wife he had not seen when they ate supper together in the hospital cafeteria now caught his eye. It wasn't something that usually happened. Alex kissed Mellissa in more than a perfunctory manner and picked up the telephone.

"Hello, page operator—this is Dr. Licata, neurology. I'm off my beeper. I'll be at my home phone. Not urology, neurology. That's right."

"I know the instrument you play best, Alex."

"What's that?"

"The telephone."

Alex smiled. Mellissa poured coffee, then joined him. Alex's hand fingered the now bare spot on his belt where the beeper attached. Even though he was connected to the hospital by telephone, not wearing the beeper made him feel a bit freer.

"It'll be over soon, Mellissa," Alex said as the conversational ritual began.

"Yes, but you'll always be a doctor—with patients and the hospital and medical journals and rounds on weekends and the telephone."

"But I won't always be a resident and someday I'll make a

31

reasonable amount of money," Alex said reflexively. But the ritualistic words, spoken many times, now seemed somehow hollow and out of tune.

Alex was not interested in the conversational ritual. Tonight it would bring him no solace, and besides, he knew all the questions and their answers. One subject the ritual did not contain was the possibility of his doing research after his residency. Alex knew Mellissa would never accept another period of training, and as he looked at his wife, he was not certain he wanted it either. Actually, at this moment, he knew exactly what he wanted. It wasn't clinical neurology and it wasn't research. He wanted to escape backward in time, escape into his wife's arms. After all, his beeper was not attached to his belt, and Mellissa's hair was so shiny. Mellissa sensed something in the way Alex looked at her. She knew Alex's love for neurology was strong. Even at home, as he pored over journal articles or prepared a case for presentation in the hospital, Mellissa could feel herself intruding on his medicine. But tonight Alex seemed free of medicine, free of a mistress he carried on with openly in front of his wife. . . .

The phone rang.

Alex looked at his wife apologetically. "It's probably my mother calling from Chicago."

"I'll bet you ten dollars it's not!" Mellissa shot back.

He picked up the telephone without responding to her challenge; he wouldn't take a losing bet.

It was the hospital. "Yes, this is Dr. Licata."

"It's an outside call, Dr. Licata—4217. Shall I connect you?" At least the call was not from the emergency ward, which meant going into the hospital but it was also not from division 17, which usually meant only giving a medication order over the telephone.

"Here is Dr. Licata. Go ahead, please," the operator said.

"This is Dr. Licata," Alex began. "Can I help you?"

"Yes. My name is Mrs. Danville and my son Arthur is followed in the seizure clinic. He's all out of his medication and I don't know what to do." Alex sat down and nodded to Mellissa. It was OK, he wouldn't have to leave.

"Which doctor follows him?" he asked the mother.

32

"Dr. Barnes."

"Why don't you call him tomorrow morning?"

"He's on vacation and if I don't give Arthur his medication, he might have a convulsion."

"When was his last convulsion, Mrs. Danville?"

"Two years ago."

"How old is he?"

"Ten."

Alex didn't know why she hadn't waited until the morning to call, but could imagine her fear of convulsions, especially since her son hadn't had one in two years. The medication was vital to her, though Alex knew that one missed dose would have no effect on the boy's seizure control. Rather than tell her not to worry, Alex tried to solve the problem. "I can do one of two things, Mrs. Danville. I can call a pharmacy that's open tonight or you can pick up medication at the emergency ward."

"My pharmacy's not open now. Could you call the pharmacy in the morning?"

"Sure. You know, Mrs. Danville, nothing will happen if your son misses one dose of his medicine."

"I know, Dr. Barnes always tells me that, but I'm terrified of him going into another convulsion. Thank you very much, doctor, and I'm sorry to bother you."

Alex took the 3 x 5 cards from his white jacket and clipped a piece of paper with the pharmacy's number on the front so he would see it first thing in the morning.

Then he walked over to Mellissa and put his hands on her shoulders.

Mellissa put her hands on his.

"I love you," he said.

She gave his hands a squeeze.

"I'm sorry I'm a doctor, Mellissa, but I wanted to be one."

"Kiss me," was her only reply.

Alex took her into his arms and pressed his lips to hers. As his hands moved under her blouse, and onto the warm skin of her back he remembered the first time they had made love. It had been in a place where they couldn't get undressed, and so they had loved each other on the floor with all their clothes on.

Those memories made their embrace even sweeter, and their

33

kisses seemed more passionate than they had for a long time. Now, to make up for that first time when they couldn't take their clothes off, Alex and Mellissa undressed each other slowly, sensuously, until they lay naked in full light on the living room floor. By now Alex was miles from the hospital.

"The children," Mellissa whispered.

"They're asleep."

"I know, but they could wake up."

Alex obliged by carrying Mellissa into their bedroom and locking the door. He laid her down gently and was bending over her when the phone rang.

"Shit," Alex said, deciding to ignore it.

It continued to ring.

"You'd better answer it, Alex." A pause. Then, with a big smile, Mellissa added, "It's probably your mother from Chicago."

"Shit," he repeated, straightening up to lift the receiver. "Maybe if I'm lucky it'll be an obscene phone call." It was the hospital. "It's the emergency ward, Dr. Licata—3448. Shall I connect you?"

"Do I have a choice?" he mumbled.

"What was that, Dr. Licata?"

"Never mind, connect me!"

Alex sat naked on the bed, listening to the intern, as Mellissa lay beside him, gently stroking his back.

"Alex, I have a five-year-old girl down here who had a convulsion earlier this evening. She was seen at another hospital and a doctor sent her over with a note for admission to neurology for a workup."

"Is she all right now?"

"She's been fine since her convulsion. The seizure didn't last long."

"Anything abnormal on her exam?"

"No, to my exam she is perfect neurologically."

"What was the convulsion like?"

"It sounds generalized, both arms and legs going, no focal features."

"Has she ever had seizures before?"

34

"No."

"Is she developmentally normal for her age?"

"Yes, but I think she's in a special school for children with behavior problems."

Alex's sexual excitement was gone as he sat on the bed to begin negotiations with the pediatric house officer in the emergency ward. Mellissa lay contentedly in the dark. The phone call didn't upset her as much as it did Alex. She was actually happy.

"Start her on medication, schedule her for an EEG and an appointment at the seizure clinic," Alex was saying. "There is no reason to admit her to the hospital."

"This mother won't leave without seeing a neurologist," came the reply.

"Tell me the truth, do you honestly think I need to come down and see the kid?"

"No."

"Do you feel comfortable discharging her without my examination?"

"Yes."

"Then tell the mother you talked to the neurologist and he recommends against admitting her child to the hospital. We'll schedule her for some tests and see her in clinic. Give her my name and tell her to call me if any problems develop."

"Hold on while I check with her," the house officer said.

There were only three situations that would have forced Alex away from his wife and into the emergency ward: if, after hearing the problem, he felt he had to see the case personally; if the doctor in the emergency ward requested his presence; and if the parent or patient demanded to see a neurologist. Although some doctors didn't feel bound by patients' demands, Alex did. Points one and two were settled, but now he had to win point three.

The pediatric house officer returned to the phone. "Alex, this mother's a problem. There's no way you're not going to examine her child. You'll have enough trouble keeping the kid out of the hospital."

Alex was beaten and he was angry—angry with the mother,

35

angry with the outside doctor who had sent the child with a note for admission, and angry with himself for somehow being trapped by circumstances.

"I'll be there in about fifteen minutes," he grumbled. The pediatric house officer felt no sympathy for Alex, for although he would come merely to satisfy the mother, after thirty minutes in the emergency ward, Alex would be back in bed. The pediatric house officer had to stay up all night seeing cases in the emergency ward, and he envied the consultant's position.

"It looks like I have to go in, Mellissa. I'm sorry. Some crazy mother I have to comfort." He kissed her lightly, then began dressing.

Mellissa didn't mind. Even though they had been interrupted, she had won. Alex's display of affection and the reaffirmation that their bond was still viable was more important than a lost orgasm. She didn't feel any more sympathy for Alex than the pediatric house officer in the emergency ward. It was his problem, and there was a certain paradoxical justice—medicine usually diluted their marriage at her expense—in this instance, it was at Alex's.

Alex put the wire frames back on his nose, forced his paunchy body into the clothes he had worn all day, attached the beeper to his belt, and spoke to the page operator so she wouldn't call and wake Mellissa. Then he kissed Mellissa and rode the elevator down to the first floor. It was a different doctor that threaded his way among the giant blocks that stood in the middle of the night. He was upset and tired. If he had been going to see a true neurologic emergency he wouldn't have minded, but to go in at night only to satisfy a mother was a nuisance. Subconsciously he tried to remain half awake so he could easily fall back to sleep when he returned. He was not the doctor a mother would have wanted to examine her child. Intellectually, Alex knew he was in the wrong frame of mind. But he couldn't break it.

11:30 P.M. The emergency ward was quiet. There had just been a change of nurses, and the pediatric house officer had four children to see. Even though he didn't really care, he halfheartedly apologized to Alex.

Alex looked at the scribbled note from the referring doctor. It said the child had had a convulsion and needed to be sent to

36

Children's Hospital for immediate admission. What a buffoon! Alex thought. Doesn't he know there's no need to admit a simple convulsion to the hospital?

Alex was expressing the dichotomy between private physician and university physician in its ugliest form. Too often, the doctor associated with a large academic center was critical of practicing physicians in the community. There were reasons. Complicated cases, or patients doing poorly, were referred to academic centers. More time was available for patients in an academic setting, away from the scheduling demands of the practicing physician. In private practice it was possible to become isolated from the latest medical thinking. Nevertheless, the academic center itself was faulty—too big, too impersonal, and some of the doctors were more interested in research than patients. Furthermore most academic centers were inefficient. One place was not intrinsically better than the other. Although there were unique problems best handled in an academic center, most illnesses could be handled equally well in both settings. In the end, patient care depended on the doctor; there were good doctors and bad doctors in both environments. At that particular moment Alex was a bad doctor.

Alex walked into the room and greeted the mother.

"Hello, I'm Dr. Licata from neurology. What's the problem?"

Alex's greeting set the tone for the encounter. "What's the problem?" implied he was bothered. It was a question that challenged, not one that put at ease or showed interest. He could have said "How's your girl doing?" or "Could you tell me what happened tonight?" He sounded more like a policeman challenging a suspicious loiterer than a doctor.

The girl's mother was not insensitive to his greeting and challenged back, "As you can see from the doctor's note, she's had a convulsion and needs to be admitted to the hospital."

Unless there was a dramatic finding, Alex had already decided the girl would not be admitted to the hospital. He began with routine questions, but only half listened to the answers.

"Has she ever had convulsions before?"

"No."

"What was the convulsion like tonight?" The mother

described the convulsion in a very excited manner, but it didn't excite Alex.

"How is she doing in school?"

"OK. She attends a special school for slow learners." It was an answer that deserved more questions, but rather than asking them, Alex tried to push the answer aside. "But she's doing all right in her classes?"

"Yes," came the forced reply.

Alex looked at the girl, an eight-year-old, sitting quietly next to her mother. Seeing the girl woke him up a little, and he asked her her name. She told him her name was Heather Papineau. He smiled at her as he lifted her onto the examination table. Her exam was normal, though Alex had to repeat parts of it because he had been sloppy. He reviewed the case briefly in his mind—still no reason to admit the child.

"Your child's exam is normal and she doesn't need hospital admission," Alex said. He didn't console and he didn't explain. He announced his conclusion victoriously, as if the mother and child were guilty of the entire episode.

"But the other doctor said she needed to come into the hospital," the mother protested.

"I know. But all she needs is medication to prevent another attack, an appointment for a brainwave test, and a seizure clinic visit."

"Doctor, there are some questions I'd like to ask you."

"You'll be able to get your questions answered in the seizure clinic." Alex was at his lowest. Refusing to listen.

Heather Papineau's mother may not have known much about medicine, but she knew what to do when the service was bad.

"Is there another doctor I could talk to?"

The question startled Alex. It was one he was almost never asked. The question didn't make him angry. It woke him up. He tried to gain back the ground he had lost in his haste.

"Perhaps I could help with some of the questions you have, Mrs. Papineau," he said gently.

"My child's had a convulsion and you just want to send her out," the mother said, now somewhat frantic. She hadn't registered Alex's conciliatory tone.

He persisted.

"What were the things you wanted to ask?"

Heather's mother seemed to hear Alex the second time and said tentatively, "Well, what's this medication?"

As he began patiently to explain, Mrs. Papineau started to relax—she was now talking to another doctor. They spoke for twenty minutes.

Although the overt hostility between Alex and Mrs. Papineau had dissipated, the girl's mother left the emergency ward with reservations about the care her daughter had received. Alex was certain he hadn't made a wrong decision, but knew he had not been a good doctor. It bothered him. As he walked outside between the giant blocks, he blamed himself and he blamed a system, one that had made him vulnerable. In the past, medicine had been all-encompassing. Tonight, when he began to move away from it, he had let his guard down too much. The elevator pulled him up into a bed where Mellissa was soundly asleep. Alex had not been successful in his attempt to remain only half awake. It took over an hour for him to fall asleep. Moreover, the events of the evening would haunt him in the coming week.

MONDAY

Monday comes to the hospital like a parent who's been away and returns to take charge again. The weekend is forgotten. For those who didn't work on Saturday or Sunday, the reality of the hospital offers a sharp contrast to a world where people are healthy. To those who did work, the change is equally dramatic, for the machinery of the hospital that was turned off over the weekend is now running. All labs are open, and any test, not just emergency ones, can be performed. The radiology department is bursting with technicians, doctors, and children lined up for a picture; complicated X-rays are feasible. The operating room is full. Nuclear medicine, the EEG lab, pathology, social service, the gift shop, and the appointment desk are functioning. Even the man outside on the corner of Lexington Avenue is back selling balloons and toys at inflated prices; soon, after March has warmed into April and May, he will sell ice cream as well.

Alex climbed two flights of stairs and walked onto division 17, in front of the nurses' station. People poured into the small area from the three corridors that intersected at the desk: children, parents, nurses, nurse's aides, hospital messengers, escorts, volunteers, lab personnel, social workers, dieticians, and doctors. Alex made his way behind the station and glanced at the clock: 7:45. Picking up the phone, he checked his beeper with the page operator while he sifted through the 3 x 5 cards in his shirt pocket. He saw the reminder he'd left for himself and called a pharmacy to order the medication he'd discussed with the distraught mother on the phone the night before.

Sunday stood out clearly in Alex's mind: BJ Balsiger, his talk with Nolan Magness, Baby Girl Carlson, the abortive attempt to make love with his wife, and Heather Papineau's mother in the emergency ward. His fellow residents would ask Alex about his day on call, but would only listen superficially. If he had had an easy time, they would be envious, comparing it to their difficult night duties. If Alex had had a rough day, they would sympathize, but inwardly would be pleased it hadn't been they. Alex knew. He felt the same way.

Before rounds started, Alex checked BJ Balsiger. The boy had had no more seizures and sat in bed playing with a toy.

At eight o'clock, Alex gathered people for rounds. There was the first-year neurology resident, Mort Corning, enthusiastic, aggressive, eager to work but sometimes forgetting to think. He went by the name "Mo," and unfortunately for him was not related to the family that had made a fortune selling cookware. Jim Wellander was the pediatric resident, rotating for a month on the neurology service; a good pediatrician but cynical about neurology, considering it a specialty that could diagnose esoteric diseases but then have no effective therapy.

Mo Corning and Jim Wellander were a study in contrasts. Mo was big, even fat, with a round face and balding head. Jim was thin and viewed the world from a narrow face, behind horn-rimmed glasses. Jim was smarter than Mo, but Mo, despite his size, was more energetic than Jim. Jim felt he could teach Mo more about pediatrics than Mo could teach him about neurology. Neither was married and both were in their first year of residency. Jim was an athlete, and when there was time, he and Alex played squash at the nearby medical school courts. Mo was an enthused freshman neurologist, his pockets always stuffed with articles to be read and cards with drawings of various pathways in the brain.

A medical student, Casey Lilstrom, was also rotating through the neurology service. This was the second week of her two-week rotation, and it was her writeup that had caught Alex's attention the day before. At first glance, Casey was a plain girl, with a thin, angular face and slight body. She wore no makeup, and her brown hair was pulled back and fastened at the nape of her neck with a brown leather pin. But her face could be pretty if one stared into it; the straight lines of her jaw complemented high cheekbones, and her brown eyes came to life as they stared back at you. She was an intense student, bright and interested. One day she would be a fine doctor.

Louise Kidner, the head nurse on division 17, was in her late thirties, a tall, awkwardly built woman with bright red hair. Unlike many nurses, she was not bothered by a role that made her subservient to the doctor. She did not want the responsibility that accompanied decision-making, but worked hard and often knew more about the children on the ward than the doctors.

Today, Louise, along with a dietician and two people from physical therapy, would be joining Alex, Mo, Jim, and Casey for morning rounds.

A doctor's rounds should have a single purpose: patient care. For the child who is old enough and well enough, it is a chance to communicate with the doctor. For the doctor, it is the opportunity to observe, diagnose, and plan. But at the Children's Hospital in New York, or in any university teaching hospital, rounds had multiple purposes, all of which Alex was aware of as he pushed the chart rack down the corridor. Rather than playing one instrument, for him, leading rounds was an orchestration.

Other doctors on Alex's rounds judged him not only by the way he handled patients, but by how interesting rounds were and by how much they themselves learned. Alex taught on different levels: to Casey, who supposedly knew least, he tried to impart the basic tenets of patient care and to explain the medications used on the neurological service. Jim Wellander, the pediatrician, knew how to take care of patients, but he needed to be taught neurology. Mo Corning, the first-year neurology resident, had to be taught neurology, but at a higher level than Jim. Louise Kidner, like most nurses, was rarely

43

taught directly: she had to ask questions. Any teaching directed to the dietician or physical therapists was purely gratis.

Teaching meant asking direct questions: What were the five causes of a symptom? What was the dosage of a medication? What was the anatomy of a particular tract in the brain? Teaching meant demanding someone examine a child on rounds and give an evaluation. Teaching meant asking someone else to teach; the boundaries between chief resident, student, pediatrician, neurology resident, nurse, dietician, and physical therapist were often artificial.

In addition to teaching and patient care, Alex had to make sure rounds finished on time. Invariably, children seen first received more time and attention; because of this, each day rounds began on a different part of the ward.

Today they started with BJ Balsiger.

BJ sat in a crib with both side railings up. He was too old to be in a crib, but required it as protection against seizures. Alex walked to the side of the crib and let the railing down while the others formed a half-circle around the bed.

It must have been an imposing sight for BJ, surrounded by eight people. But the attention didn't upset him; either he was accustomed to the sight of doctors in the hospital or he hadn't fully recovered from his convulsions.

"Hi, BJ," Alex called out.

BJ answered with a groggy "Hi" and fondled a toy clock in his crib.

"How's he doing, Louise?"

The head nurse looked briefly at her clipboard. "He's had no further convulsions since his admission. He ate breakfast and is taking medication orally."

For the benefit of the group, Alex condensed two volumes of the child's chart into thirty seconds. "This is a boy with a difficult-to-control seizure disorder that began just before his first birthday. He came in yesterday with a prolonged left-sided convulsion."

"How old is he?" Casey asked.

Alex looked directly at the medical student. "Why don't you tell me?" he asked. Casey didn't know how to respond. "Exam-

44

ine him and tell me his developmental age," Alex continued. "See if you can find any abnormalities on exam."

Casey impulsively reached for her reflex hammer, but realized reflexes were the last thing she would check. Then, while the others watched, Casey painfully performed her neurologic exam in front of an audience. Thrusting her stagefright aside, she reviewed in her mind the outline of developmental milestones for where to begin. She chose language.

"What's your name?"

"BJ."

"What do you have there?"

"Toy."

"What kind of toy is it?"

"My toy."

"What do you do with the toy?

BJ suddenly reacted to the pressure of the group surrounding him. "I want Mommy!"

Alex moved his eyes from BJ to Casey. She took a few breaths and continued.

"Where are your hands?"

BJ reluctantly lifted his hands, then identified other body parts as Casey quizzed him. He did a good job on his ABCs, but Casey couldn't engage him in more than two-word sentences.

The head nurse helped. "I know from past admissions—he's not much of a talker."

"Do you want to go for a walk?" Casey asked the boy and, without waiting for an answer, she lifted BJ from the crib and placed him on the floor. He ran a few steps, then grabbed the toy clock Casey dangled in the air. Casey placed him back in bed, then handed him paper and asked him to draw something, but the best he could do was a crude circle.

Casey had finished the developmental evaluation, and she reached for her ophthalmoscope to begin examining cranial nerves.

"You don't have to check his fundus and optic nerves," Alex said. "Just check eye movements, coordination, strength, and reflexes."

Alex watched Casey perform a clumsy but adequate exam.

45

She had trouble checking for the Babinski reflex; when she stroked the bottom of BJ's foot he invariably withdrew it, making it impossible to tell whether his toe went up or down.

"Are you through, Casey?"

She nodded and began to answer when Alex interrupted.

"What's his developmental age, Jim?"

Both the pediatric resident and Casey were surprised that Alex questioned Jim after Casey had examined the boy, but Jim collected his thoughts while he looked at BJ and examined the child again in his mind. "I would say between three and four years old."

"Which one, three or four?" Alex asked.

"Three."

"Mo, what's his developmental age?"

"Four."

"Louise?"

"I know how old he is."

"Not his chronological age, Louise, his developmental age."

"I'll say three."

Alex next queried the dietician and the two physical therapists, who were flustered but managed to say either three or four.

Casey admired the way Alex had involved everyone in the question. Her eyes caught his and he seemed to smile as he asked, "Casey, what's the difference between a three- and a four-year-old?"

"Well, in terms of language, a three-year-old answers in three-to-four-word sentences; a four-year-old, in four-to-five-word sentences. A three-year-old should be able to copy a circle, a four-year-old can copy a square. A four-year-old can hop better than a three-year-old and can undo buttons.

"During the exam you got him to say a few words, recite his ABCs, and identify body parts. What level is that?"

"About two and a half."

"Right. You couldn't evaluate motor skills apart from walking, and all he did with the crayon is scribble. His writing was at the level of two to two and a half years. From what we've seen, there's no evidence he's functioning higher than two and a half

46

years. That doesn't mean he can't under different circumstances; perhaps when his mother's here or he is fully recovered from the seizure. He'll need formal psychological testing during this admission. When he was tested here at age three, he functioned at a level of two. He just turned four a month ago."

"What about his seizures?" Mo Corning asked.

"I don't know why he has seizures. His Dilantin and phenobarb levels from yesterday were a bit low and I've increased them. He's getting an EEG this morning."

"I didn't find much abnormal on his exam," Casey added, "though I wasn't sure whether his toes went up or down when I stroked the bottoms of his feet."

"After his convulsion, both toes went up," Alex said. "Later, only the left one. Something is probably wrong with the right side of his brain." Alex walked over to BJ, and, gripping him tightly at the ankle so he wouldn't withdraw, gently stroked the bottoms of his feet. The right toe went down, the left one went up.

Alex continued. "No one can figure out what's wrong with BJ, and it's been a terrible ordeal for his parents." Alex looked at his bright medical student. Maybe he could channel some of her energy into helping BJ. "Casey, why don't you take BJ as your patient? Mo, be the resident on the case and countersign her orders. Casey, this afternoon you can examine him in detail, talk to his parents, and review his old chart. We'll have this morning's EEG results by then and I'll discuss the case with you."

They walked into the next room.

"How's Tony this morning?" Jim Wellander asked as he stared at the eight-year-old boy lying in front of him.

"No real change," Louise answered.

"Any problems?"

"No."

The boy lay on his side with a pillow between his knees to prevent pressure sores from developing where the knees pressed together. One of the physical therapists lifted the boy's legs. They were both stiff.

The dietician examined the tube coming from the boy's nose.

47

It was taped back onto his forehead. "He's taking his tube feedings with no difficulty," she announced. "His caloric intake is good."

"I know," Jim replied. "His caloric intake is good, his urine output is good, his blood pressure is good, and he's had no more seizures. The only problem is his brain."

Anthony Zancanelli was a eight-year-old with encephalitis. Six months previously he had had a fever, followed by personality changes, then seizures. When he was brought to the hospital, he was comatose. Inflammatory cells were found in his spinal fluid, and he was given massive doses of antibiotics, but didn't improve. His infection was not bacterial meningitis, which affects the coverings of the brain, but viral encephalitis, which attacks the brain itself. There was no treatment for viral encephalitis, and although his parents felt guilty they hadn't brought Tony to the hospital earlier, it wouldn't have helped. In fact, Jim Wellander wished the family had never brought Tony to the hospital. The doctors only saved a dying child at a stage when the child no longer existed.

"I think he might have moved his arms this morning," Louise said, trying to sound optimistic.

Jim looked at her skeptically, then put his hand on the boy's chest and pinched the skin. Tony groaned and did move his arms, but very unnaturally. Both arms straightened at the elbow and turned in, palms facing out, and at the same time, his legs turned in.

"Is that what you saw?"

Louise didn't answer.

Anthony Zancanelli's strange movements were actually low-level reflexes, responses generated by the brain stem. The frightening way his arm and legs responded to pain gave no evidence of higher brain function. He hadn't attempted to move the painful stimulus away, he just turned in both arms and legs and groaned. To emphasize his point, Jim pressed hard on the boy's forehead, and again Tony responded with groans and the identical arm and leg movement.

One of the physical therapists turned to Alex. "Is there any chance of him recovering?"

"I don't think so."

"Have you ever seen anyone recover from this much brain damage?" Casey asked.

"No, but I've only been a neurology resident for three years," Alex said.

"I talked to one of the pediatric neurologists on the staff," Mo Corning added. "He can't remember a child with this much damage from encephalitis and no improvement over six months who recovered and was normal."

"What about the boy last year who was in coma for nine months and recovered?" Louise asked.

"That was different," Alex answered. "It was a case of head trauma with less damage than Tony. And even though he was in coma for nine months, there were consistent signs of slight improvement all along. Tony has never changed."

Jim looked at Louise. "I guess I shouldn't say this, but maybe we should just let Tony die in peace."

"How do you propose to do that?" Louise answered immediately. "You can't stop feeding him, he's not on any medications except for anticonvulsants, and he's not on a respirator."

Jim's only reply was to restate the situation. "Tony comes from a family with four other children. They are Italian, Catholics from Thompson Street in the Village. His parents are becoming more and more confused by Tony's illness. The father still seems to hope the boy will recover, but the mother's not as sure. She's afraid her boy will never be the same. They pray a lot. I think God should answer their prayers and let the boy die."

"That doesn't mean we should let him die," Louise insisted.

"But we're the ones who saved him—a doctors' triumph," Jim said. "We won't let him die, and now there's no way to make him recover."

The thought of not doing everything possible for a patient was alien to Louise. She became a nurse in order to treat, to heal. In addition, as a nurse, major decisions about patient care were not hers; that wasn't the nurse's role and it wasn't a role Louise wanted.

Jim Wellander enjoyed making decisions. As a doctor, as a pediatrician, he made them continuously: start a child on anti-

49

biotics, admit a child to the hospital, decide how much fluid and electrolytes a baby with vomiting and diarrhea needed. In Tony Zancanelli's case, Jim felt a decision of nonsupport had to be made. A decision that admitted the fruitlessness of keeping alive a child who no longer had a chance of living. It bothered him to see Tony's parents suffer. It upset him that doctors could try to save a child but then couldn't let a child die when the "saving" was incomplete. He felt guilty for what his colleagues had done.

Alex's beeper went off. He stepped into the corridor, asked the secretary to answer his page, then returned to the group. "Jim, there's nothing we can do for Tony now. We had to treat him when he first came in. As Louise said, he's not on a respirator, so he's not dependent on us for every breath. He's only on anticonvulsants. If he were on a respirator, we could consider turning it off. Then we wouldn't be prolonging life artificially. All we're doing now is feeding him. If we stop that we'll be starving him to death."

"Dr. Licata." A nurse appeared from the front desk. "There's a phone call for you from a Mrs. Papineau. She said you saw her girl last night in the emergency ward. I told her you were on rounds, but she says it's urgent that she talk to you."

Alex asked Mo to continue rounds without him and stepped into the hall to pick up the phone.

"This is Dr. Licata."

"Yes. You saw my daughter last night, remember?" Mrs. Papineau didn't give Alex time to answer. "She's not doing well this morning. She seems to be very nervous. She's twitchy."

"Have you given her the medication?"

"No, I haven't had the time to get to the drugstore yet."

"Well, why not? Maybe you wouldn't have had to call me if you had." The conversation rekindled the hostility that had developed between Alex and Mrs. Papineau the night before. "Has she had another convulsion since I last saw her?"

"No."

"How did she sleep?"

"Pretty.good, I guess."

"Then I think it would be best if you got the prescription filled as soon as possible. Start her on two tablets, one now and one this afternoon. Call me tomorrow morning and let me know how she's doing." After listening to Mrs. Papineau's hesitant OK, Alex hung up the phone and then realized he had acted out the oft-repeated physician's cliché: "Take two aspirins and call me in the morning."

When he returned to rounds, he found Mo Corning holding a cute little girl in an orange dress while her mother and father stood smiling nearby.

"This is the girl with ataxia, Alex."

"Is she ready to go home?"

"She better be, she's all dressed up and her parents are here."

Alex nodded to the parents. "Let's see her walk."

"I can run," the girl said with a big smile. Mo put her down and they watched her skip down the hall, then run back to her father.

"There's no unsteadiness at all now," Alex said. "When she came in she walked like a drunken sailor. She was really ataxic. Are the medications straightened out, Mo?"

The mother answered. "Yes they are, one pill twice a day instead of three."

The girl was a normal six-year-old, brighter than most children of her age. She had been on medication for seizures since age three, and as she grew older the medication was increased to keep up with her weight. However, the latest increase was too much, and she had begun accumulating excess anticonvulsants in her body. Gradually she became sleepy, acted strangely in her kindergarten class, and began having trouble walking. Her parents were certain she had a brain tumor. It took only one day after her hospital admission to discover that her "brain tumor" was caused by toxic levels of medication in her bloodstream.

Alex leafed through her chart, which included Casey's history and physical exam neatly written in two colors of ink on five pages. Casey had listed eight possible diagnoses; the fourth one was overmedication. It should have been higher on the list.

As she spoke to the parents, Alex watched Casey. She was dressed in a white skirt and a simple blue blouse. The pockets of her white jacket were stuffed with a small black notebook containing pages of neatly written notes, a crumpled hospital

51

admission form, a reflex hammer, a tuning fork, an ophthalmo-scope, and a stethoscope. Her small brown eyes darted about, full of energy. The longer Alex looked at her, the prettier she seemed. He knew she was a good student and he looked forward to seeing what she did with BJ's case.

The pace of rounds quickened as the chart rack was pushed to the infants' room. Only one of the babies was on the neurolog-ical service, a nine-month-old boy with hypotonia, a muscle weakness. He was first brought to a doctor when his parents realized he was slow to sit, then was admitted to the hospital for diagnostic tests. The child was in no distress but at nine months still could not sit up. In his case, rounds consisted of deciding which tests would be performed and coordinating when they would be done.

Hypotonia could be secondary to a defect of the brain, spinal cord, nerves, or muscles. The challenge to the physician was to discover the location of the primary defect.

"Mo, give me one cause of hypotonia," Alex said.

"Werdnig-Hoffman disease."

"Jim, another."

"Atonic cerebral palsy."

"Casey."

"Degenerative disease."

Alex frowned. "That's not very specific." he paused. "But I'll accept it." Another pause. "And I'll say myasthenia gravis."

The group was familiar with Alex's games. At first, students and residents resented the "quizzes," but eventually they had grown to enjoy them. This particular game was like a spelling bee; if you couldn't think of a disease, you were "out," and the others continued until only one person remained. Alex usually won, although today Mo Corning was victorious with "myo-tonic dystrophy."

"Alex, let me ask you a question," Jim broke in. "Of all the diseases we've just mentioned as a possible cause of hypotonia in this infant, how many can we do anything about?"

Alex didn't answer immediately. He looked at Louise Kidner and sensed she liked the question even less than he did. It wasn't the first time he'd been asked this particular question; nor was it the first time he'd been confronted with the neurologist's ability to diagnose and inability to treat.

"We can't do much about very many," Alex said simply.

"Which ones *can* we do something about?" Jim persisted.

"Well, there's myasthenia gravis and muscle weakness secondary to certain antibiotics."

"Any others?"

"None I can think of offhand."

"The child has already tested negative for myasthenia," Jim said, "and we know he is not on antibiotics. Why continue searching for a nontreatable cause?"

Mo Corning, offended by Jim's attack on his newly chosen speciality, entered the discussion. "It's important for the parents to know. Uncertainty about a child's health is very difficult. Even if the diagnosis is bad, that's easier to live with than not knowing what's wrong. Besides, some of the diseases are inherited and might be prevented in future children."

Jim knew Mo Corning was right and didn't pursue the conversation. But Mo understood Jim's question. One of the most frustrating things for a doctor was the search for the cause of a disease, knowing that none of the possibilities were treatable.

As they moved on toward the adolescents' section at the end of the hall, everyone's mood improved. Whenever possible, children of similar ages were put in the same room, and the room they were entering was occupied by two thirteen-year-old girls, both named Susie. They were called Susie K and Susie W. Everyone liked "the room of the Susies." In contrast to much of the ward, here were two patients with whom the doctors could talk and interact. Equally as important, their condition was improving, and the doctors had participated in the girls' treatment and recovery.

Susie K, who suffered from the Guillain-Barré syndrome, had come to the hospital with walking difficulties and was rapidly becoming weaker. Her condition, an acute inflammation of the nerves, progressed in one week to almost total paralysis, and she had needed a respirator to help her breathe. Yet, in the course of her three-month stay, she had slowly begun to recover and was already walking with two canes. Unlike polio, for which it had

53

often been mistaken, this form of childhood paralysis usually left no motor weakness, and Susie K's prognosis was excellent. Alex reminded the group that before the polio vaccine, children who "miraculously" recovered from polio and left their iron lungs often had the Guillain-Barré syndrome. Susie K had been in the hospital for over three months and was a veteran on the neurology floor.

Susie W had been in the hospital only two weeks. Her diagnosis was Syndenham's chorea, the neurologic form of rheumatic fever. Her illness began with fidgeting and loss of attention in school; punishment only seemed to make her symptoms worse. Soon she had involuntary abrupt movements of her hands and arms, facial grimacing, and severe difficulty in walking. Susie W was sick for almost three weeks before it was diagnosed that her movement disorder was a complication of a recent strep throat infection. In the hospital, the jerkiness in her arms and legs had begun to subside and her grimacing had grown less apparent. Although there was no evidence of heart damage, she would be taking penicillin for several years to prevent cardiac involvement. This was a happy stop on the rounds, and the group entered the room full of greetings: "Hi, Susie K"; "Hi, Dr. Licata"; "Hello, Louise"; "Hi, Susie W"; "Hi, Dr. Wellander"; "Hello, Dr. Corning"; "Hi, Casey."

Mo reached into his pocket filled with brain drawings and articles, pulled out a single sheet, and began, "Okay, Susie W, here's how you'd have been treated a hundred years ago." He read from one of the original articles on Sydenham's chorea: "Conserve of Roman wormwood, conserve of orange peel, conserve of rosemary, Venice treacle, candied nutmeg, candied ginger, and syrup of lemon juice."

"What's Venice treacle?" Susie K asked.

"I don't know," Mo confessed.

"No wonder you're only a first-year resident," Casey teased.

"Be careful, Casey," Alex warned, "I don't know either."

One of the physical therapists helped Susie K to her feet and watched her walk while Jim examined Susie W. There was a happy, almost carnival atmosphere in the room; BJ Balsiger and Tony Zancanelli seemed more than a few rooms away. Alex ended the merriment by announcing: "The schoolteacher's coming this afternoon. You girls had better get to studying."

After a chorus of goodbyes, the group filed back into the hall.

"Two more to see," Mo informed Alex. "The five-year-old with the cerebellar tumor and the kid with the drop attacks."

They spotted the boy with the cerebellar tumor being led down the corridor by his mother. Although his first symptom had been difficulty in walking, it was clear that unlike the little girl in the orange dress, his ataxia was not due to overmedication. Instead, it was caused by a tumor on the back part of his brain. A week of tests had confirmed the initial diagnosis, and the following morning he would be transferred to neurosurgery and taken to the operating room, where the benign or malignant nature of the growth would be determined.

"How's he doing?" Mo asked the child's mother.

"Oh, fine," she replied, scooping her son up into her arms.

She smiled at the boy and caressed his cheek with her finger, oblivious to the group surrounding her. She had been told that her son had a brain tumor and had accepted the verdict. She didn't want a busy hospital ward or a group of doctors on rounds to spoil the little time she might have left with her boy. The chances were good that the tumor could be removed without much brain damage, and that her son would live a normal life, but she didn't allow herself the luxury of expecting it. It was too nice a thought, too much a deeply felt dream to be allowed to surface in her own brain. As he looked at the boy, Alex decided not to quiz those on rounds about brain tumors. It would not only upset the mother, it would mean infringing on the time she was spending with her son.

"Anything we can do for you?" Alex asked her gently.

"Not really," she said quietly.

"Mo, is everything set for tomorrow?" Alex knew the answer, but asked the question for the mother's benefit.

"The surgeons will write preoperative orders tonight and he'll go to surgery tomorrow morning at eight."

There was nothing more to say. Alex managed a feeble "OK," Louise mumbled something about when lunch would begin, and Jim just nodded. Mo grasped the woman's arm briefly and whispered, "Good luck." The mother brushed the boy's hair with her hand and smiled at her son. Rounds moved down the hallway.

"We don't have time to review tumors of the posterior fossa," Alex said as they walked. "But remember, they are the most common tumors of childhood and often can be cured by surgery." No one was listening and Alex didn't care.

A few yards from the nurses' station, a group of children was gathered at a small table in the hallway. Some were being fed, some were playing, and others were just watching, but few were quiet. Division 17 was not noted for its serenity. Two children were in carts, a common mode of transportation at the Children's Hospital. The wooden carts were constructed with two small wheels in front and two large ones in back, which allowed a child strapped in by a "seat belt" to propel himself along with his hands, wheelchair style. The "go-carts" were often used by older children to race up and down the corridors.

For the children eating breakfast, the floor was competing with the table for possession of the food. It appeared to Alex that the floor was winning, even though one tiny girl tried to lift soggy cereal from the floor back onto the table, an endeavor viewed with chagrin by the aide who was feeding her.

On both sides of the table were bassinets containing children with hydrocephalus, or water on the brain. These hydrocephalic infants lay quietly, their eyes following the activities about them. The nurses always put them out into the hall to give them something to watch. Their heads filled with water because blocked cavities in their brains didn't allow normal circulation of fluid. The fluid was constantly produced and had nowhere to go. The head grew larger as it filled with crystal-clear fluid, and the brain became thinner from the pressure of the water. Tubes had been placed to shunt the fluid around the blocked cavities, but in these two children, the hydrocephalus was so severe that the shunts couldn't help the irreversible brain damage.

"Here comes Clark Kent!" Jim Wellander called as he prepared to lift up the last child to be seen on rounds.

Clark Kent's name was Clark Gatewood, but his propensity for dashing down the corridors in the role of Superman had earned him his nickname. Once a sympathetic nurse had draped a towel over his back and fastened it in front with a safety pin like a Superman cape. Now the cape was part of his daily wardrobe, and the task of arranging it had recently been taken over by the two Susies.

"You're the only Superman I know that flies around with a football helmet," Casey teased him, and Clark responded by jumping away from Jim, spreading his arms, and "flying" down the hall and returning.

"He's also the only Superman I know with sudden crash landings," Mo added.

Clark was a four-and-a-half-year-old boy with a rare form of epilepsy which caused drop attacks, or akinetic spells. His seizures consisted of a brief loss both of muscle tone and of consciousness, lasting from one to three seconds. During a seizure he often fell to the floor, and because of this he always wore a football helmet. His seizures had recently increased in frequency, and he had been hospitalized while doctors tried him on a series of different medications. They had been so successful that after two weeks in the hospital his spells had decreased from fifteen attacks a day to only three or four. As he improved, it became more and more difficult to stop him from running down the corridor, and on one occasion a drop attack had resulted in a bruised shoulder. After threats by the personnel to take away his cape and sequester him in a go-cart unless he slowed down, he now walked down the hallway instead of flying. Luckily for Clark, his seizures hadn't interfered with his development and he was a normal four-and-a-half-year-old.

Jim Wellander enjoyed caring for Clark, and took an almost personal pleasure in his improvement. There was a nicely constructed table in the boy's chart with a daily account of his attacks, dosages of medication, and EEG results. "He should be ready to go home pretty soon," Jim said as he handed Alex the boy's chart.

Alex turned the pages and nodded.

"How many attacks is he having that we never see?" Casey asked.

"When he first came in we'd find him on the floor," Louise said, "And other children would tell us Clark was falling again. That hasn't been happening for the last few days."

57

"There's no drowsiness or sleepiness after his attacks," Jim added. "He just gets up and goes on as if nothing happened. I remember learning in medical school about seizures: shaking of arms and legs, falling to the ground, foaming at the mouth, loss of urine and feces, and then sleep. I don't think I've seen one convulsion like that since I've been here."

"There's another way to test for small, unnoticeable attacks," Alex said. He picked up the boy and grasped him under the armpits. "When he first came in, if I held him like this I would feel small lapses in muscle tone. Some were large enough to develop into actual drop attacks, others I could only feel by holding him. I can't feel any now."

Alex handed the helmeted and towel-caped boy to Jim, who also held him under the armpits. Jim then handed the boy to Mo and Mo handed him to Casey, who almost dropped him. All agreed with Alex's observation.

"When are you going to send him home?" Mo asked.

"If he continues to do well, by the end of the week. I'd like to get one final EEG on him in a few days."

Alex put the boy's chart back into the rack and asked if there was anyone else to see on the ward. Both Mo and Jim looked through the 3 x 5 card files they kept in their coat pockets and shook their heads.

"Louise, can we leave?"

Louise nodded. Alex asked the dietician and physical therapists if they had any questions. They said no, and thanked him for rounds, even though he hadn't included them.

"Let's go to the newborn nursery," Alex said as he led Casey, Mo, and Jim up the four flights of stairs to the seventh floor. The nurses' station was just outside the nursery. Checking the chart rack at the nurses' station, Alex told them Baby Girl Carlson's story, then invited them to look through her chart. Nothing more had happened during the night, he pointed out, and an EEG was done that morning.

As they entered the nursery, they were immediately surrounded by the sound of beeping heart monitors. Alex found Baby Girl Carlson's incubator, picked her up, and examined her. Her exam was normal. Alex used her case to lecture on the probable causes and treatment of seizures in the newborn. Jim, as the pediatrician in the group, reviewed general medical problems of newborns and then rounds were over.

It was 9:45 A.M. In the fifteen minutes before the ten o'clock EEG conference, Jim wrote orders back on division 17, Alex checked the X-ray department for skull films, and Mo and Casey visited the coffee shop.

The EEG laboratory at Children's Hospital was big. Surrounding the four rooms where the EEGs were performed was a central conference room where they were read. The staff consisted of three doctors and four technicians, plus the two or three doctors always rotating through. Enormous amounts of paper were used to perform EEGs; in fact, some tracings were as thick as telephone books. No tracings were thrown away. First they were stored in the EEG unit, then transferred to a large warehouse across the street.

For the neurologist, the EEG was a lucrative part of his practice. It was a noninvasive, safe procedure and an important part of his evaluation. A practicing physician in twentieth-century America knew that money was not made merely by seeing patients. The doctor needed a gimmick, a test to perform, a procedure to carry out. People, and more important, their insurance companies, would pay more and would pay more willingly for a procedure than for the doctor's time with a patient. Because of this, surgeons made more money than pediatricians. Neurosurgeons made more money than neurologists. The operating room, the radiology department, and the laboratories made the most money for the hospital. It was the logical extension of a technical, gadget-oriented society.

Casey entered the EEG unit on her way to the conference and stopped to watch a child being tested. Almost two dozen electrodes were attached to the child's head, recording the electrical activity of the brain on a large roll of paper that passed under eight pens. When the child became sleepy, the technician banged her pencil on the table to rouse him, and Casey could see an immediate response in the jerking pens. When the child finally was allowed to drift off, the waves became higher and slower. As she passed through the room, she saw another child being asked to breathe deeply a hundred times while the recording was in process, and a third child lying quietly while a flashing strobe light pulsed in front of closed eyes and was reflected immediately in electrodes attached to the occipital, or visual, part of the brain.

A group of people had already gathered for the conference when Casey arrived. One of the EEG unit doctors sat in the front of the room, ready to begin the job of turning the pages of the EEG tracings. The tracing itself sat on a wooden stand designed like the music stand on a piano. The EEG unit doctor would sit with his back to the other doctors, slowly turning the pages, as if he were assisting a concert pianist.

"How many tracings today?" Alex asked.

"Twelve."

"I'd like to make sure we see BJ Balsiger, Baby Girl Carlson, and Monte Burrows," Alex said.

"They're all here."

Eli Lassiter walked into the conference room. He was a staff neurologist at Children's Hospital, and March was his month to supervise the neurology ward. He was called the "visit." Alex didn't know where the term visit originated, perhaps it was someone who visited the ward without having his home base there. Eli's home certainly wasn't the ward; he spent most of his time in the laboratory, doing research. Eli's supervision took the form of meeting with the neurology residents daily to discuss the children on the ward. He examined the children, reviewed the charts, and wrote small progress notes. The visit had a delicate task; he was responsible for the care of each child, but left most of the treatment and decision-making to the residents. He relied heavily on Alex to keep him informed and to warn him about children who weren't doing well. The only children Eli didn't supervise were the occasional private patients of other staff neurologists.

BJ Balsiger's tracing was the first EEG placed on the stand. Alex sat in the front row, with Casey and Jim on either side so he could explain what was happening to both at once. BJ's previous tracings formed an imposing pile on the table.

Alex gave a brief history as the EEG unit doctor turned the pages of the first tracing. "This is a four-year-old boy with an uncontrollable seizure disorder. He's developmentally retarded.

He came in yesterday with a prolonged left-side convulsion but is better this morning, no more seizures since admission. His Dilantin and phenobarb levels were low. He's also on Diamox, valproate, and the experimental drug, GP 7744."

"There's no question the tracing is abnormal," the EEG unit doctor said: "There is slowing and some abnormal discharges coming from the right temporal area."

"We think something is wrong on the right side of his brain because his left toe is abnormally extensor," Alex said.

As more pages were turned, it became apparent that the abnormalities were not confined to the right side of the boy's brain.

"Can we look at his previous tracings?" Eli Lassiter asked.

"In these older tracings there also are abnormalities on both sides, but the right side isn't as prominent as in today's tracing."

Eli turned to Alex. "What are you going to do with him?"

"I don't know. He's stable now, but I think he needs more extensive studies. He's already had a CAT scan, arteriography, and even pneumonencephalography. Maybe they should be repeated. Medication doesn't seem to be helping. Nolan Magness took care of him the past two years. I'll ask him to join us for rounds tomorrow and we'll present the case to you. Casey is going to work the boy up this afternoon."

"Sounds good," Eli said.

"Baby Girl Carlson."

The EEG conferences reminded Casey of an auction. Names were called out by the doctor turning the pages, then one of the doctors in the "audience" who knew the case responded, as if making a bid. Again, it was Alex who opened the bidding.

"This is an infant I saw over the weekend. She's a newborn whose mother had a difficult delivery. A spinal tap was bloody. She had seizures yesterday but is fine this morning. She's on phenobarbital."

As the pages were being turned, Alex explained to Casey and Jim that the criteria for evaluating newborns with seizures were considerably different from those used for older children. Since the newborn brain was not yet fully developed, the patterns were more primitive. Interestingly, a newborn EEG with little evidence of seizure activity on the brainwave carried a poorer prognosis than one with more intense electrical activity.

"There are nice seizure discharges here, and the background activity is well developed," Eli Lassiter said.

"I never thought a seizure discharge could be nice," Jim mumbled to Alex.

"Monte Burrows."

"He's a boy I saw in the EW on Sunday," Alex said again. "Generalized seizure, normal exam."

"His EEG is normal as well."

"Clark Gatewood."

"He's a boy on the ward with drop attacks," Jim responded, "doing better."

"His EEG has improved as well."

Eight more names were called out and hundreds more pages turned.

"What are those?" Alex whispered to Mo as the pages flashed by.

"It looks like spikewaves, although they are pointing down rather than up."

"Normal or abnormal?" Alex asked immediately.

Mo hesitated for a second. "I'd say abnormal."

"Wrong, they're normal. They're called fourteen- and six-per-second spikes and they're seen in young children, usually during drowsiness. It was thought they occurred in children with behavioral disturbances, especially aggressive behavior. That myth was destroyed after some controlled clinical trials."

Mo jotted down the information in his small black notebook. It was already 11:00 A.M., and Alex was surprised his beeper had gone off only once the entire morning. Mo, Casey, Alex, and Jim gathered around Eli Lassiter.

"I'm going to the ward and briefly check some charts," Eli said. "How are the children doing, Alex?"

"No real problems. The only new admission was BJ Balsiger, and we'll show him to you tomorrow. The girl with the over-medication went home today. The boy with the posterior fossa tumor goes to surgery tomorrow. Tony Zancanelli is unchanged, and the infant with hypotonia continues to get his battery of tests. The two Susies are still improving, and Clark Kent Gatewood will go home this weekend if his drop attacks don't start up again." Alex glanced at his notebook. "We have one admission this afternoon, a patient of yours named Charlotte Quinn, with temporal lobe epilepsy. Mo, why don't you work her up? We can present her tomorrow, Eli, along with BJ Balsiger."

Since there were no scheduled activities for the remainder of the day, people's time would be spent talking to parents and caring for patients. Casey would spend the afternoon with BJ Balsiger and his parents while Mo worked up the new admission. Jim would talk with Tony Zancanelli's parents, and if he was lucky, have time for reading. Alex would be available to help and to teach; he would also cover the emergency ward as neurologic consultant.

When Alex's beeper went off, he was almost relieved. "I was ready to put some new batteries in," he said. "It's been too quiet this morning."

The caller was a Mrs. Burrows, the mother of a boy Alex had seen in the EW on Sunday with a seizure, who had a normal exam.

"Yes, Mrs. Burrows, in fact I just saw his EEG and have already checked his skull X-rays. That's right. Both are normal. Nothing to worry about. Just continue to give him his medication and keep your appointment in the seizure clinic. You can call me anytime. You're welcome. Goodbye."

Alex took Monte Burrows' card from his pack of 3 x 5 cards and placed it in a small notebook; he assumed he wouldn't be hearing from Mrs. Burrows again, and he was right. Monte's card would be moved to Alex's home file, where Alex kept a record of all the patients he had seen. Heather Papineau's card remained with his 3 x 5 cards. He was sure he would hear from her mother again.

At noon Alex walked home for lunch. Mellissa, attending to a crying and wet-diapered Kristen, greeted him with a perfunctory kiss. Elizabeth had just returned from preschool and was

63

demanding a peanut butter sandwich, and Mellissa tried to maintain relative calm as Alex looked through the mail. Nothing interesting.

"What happened to the child you went in to see last night?" Mellissa asked.

"Heather Papineau? I sent her home. Her mother called again this morning. I think she's a bit too worried."

"Mothers usually know when to be concerned about their children," Mellissa said simply. She had laid Kristen on the floor and begun to change her.

"But mothers aren't doctors," Alex said. If I did everything a mother told me to do with her child, the child would get worse, not better, medical care."

"On the other hand," Mellissa reminded him, "doctors aren't mothers. Sometimes doctors forget how close a mother is to her child, and she's usually the first to realize something is wrong."

"Mellissa, I don't need a lecture on how to care for patients. Besides, I thought you liked me at home. Were you glad I had to leave last night?"

"Alex," Mellissa said in the same tone she had been using with her children, "obviously, I wasn't happy to see you leave last night. But it wasn't such a major event. It's your job, isn't it?"

Alex mumbled something under his breath.

Mellissa looked up at him, and for an instant their eyes met. "It was nice last night," she smiled, "even if you had to leave."

Alex nodded.

"But that still doesn't mean I like your night call," Mellissa added, "or your medical journals or listening to talk about neurology when we go out. Last night you told me you were sorry, but you wanted to be a doctor. Well, I'm sorry too, Alex, but I wanted to marry you." Mellissa touched her hand to the apron she was wearing. "I'm still glad I did," she said quietly.

Alex should have taken his wife into his arms, but he didn't. He still had his hospital jacket on, and his hand touched the beeper that hung from his belt. Alex didn't like the thought of

Mellissa "putting up" with his medicine, even though he knew she would have rather not married a doctor.

They sat down to lunch.

"Don't forget we're going to the film series tonight," Mellissa said, "with Nolan and Judy Magness." Mellissa's eyes caught Alex's. "It'll be a chance to be together, away from the kids."

"Right," Alex said. "And I want to tell Nolan about an old patient of his we're presenting to Eli Lassiter tomorrow on rounds. I'd like Nolan to come."

He thought he saw Mellissa, almost imperceptibly, sigh.

Mo Corning sat with Dr. Edgar Quinn, Quinn's wife Rhoda, and their daughter, Charlotte, discussing Charlotte's coming evaluation and treatment for a seizure disorder. Charlotte's father was a pediatric radiologist who worked for a major private hospital in Queens, and who had also trained at Children's Hospital. His daughter was a sixteen-year-old high school junior who had been having seizures for the past two years. The convulsions weren't severe enough to interfere with her school work or daily activities, but they were persistent and difficult to control. Charlotte would be a private patient of Eli Lassiter's. Fine, Mo thought. Eli is the visit this month anyway, and patients who were the relatives of physicians could be difficult to handle.

This was Charlotte's first admission to Children's Hospital. She had been diagnosed as having temporal lobe, or psychomotor, epilepsy, and of all the epilepsies, temporal lobe was probably the most unusual. Psychomotor seizures took many forms that did not involve twitching or convulsing movements. A psychomotor seizure might consist of a simple repetitive movement such as twisting the button on a shirt, or it could be a more "purposeful" act like walking to the window and opening it. Often temporal lobe seizures involved movements about the mouth, such as smacking the lips or sucking, but sometimes they were nothing more than a blank stare. Some doctors felt that there was an association between temporal lobe epilepsy and violent or aggressive behavior. Certainly, personality disturbances were commonly seen in patients with temporal lobe epilepsy.

Although most of Charlotte's past history was outlined on previous hospital summaries, Mo decided to take down his own version; he hoped it would be a fresh view, and he might uncover a new fact or a clue about the origin of the girl's seizures.

"In retrospect, I guess it first started in the summer after she finished ninth grade and was getting ready to enter high school," Charlotte's father began. "There were periods of time when she would stare into space and not seem to hear us. We thought she was just daydreaming. In August there was a strange episode when we were eating at the backyard picnic table. She suddenly cried out, threw her glass, stared with a frightened look, then slumped to the ground. We tried to arouse her, but she didn't wake up for two or three minutes. All she could remember was a weird feeling in her head that scared her."

"Do you remember that, Charlotte?" Mo asked.

"Not very well," the girl answered almost diffidently. "All I know is I was sitting there and had this strange, scary feeling."

"Did you ever have it before?"

"No."

Charlotte was a quiet girl. She was also a big girl, tall and stocky, though not fat. Her face had a shy look, and her eyes turned away as though her face were trying to hide from her body.

"We took her to my internist, who examined her and did some blood tests," the father continued. "He ordered an EEG. Everything was normal. He didn't know what happened, but since she was herself again and didn't have any more episodes, we decided just to watch her."

"Was the EEG a sleep or a waking one?" Mo asked.

"Waking."

Mo wasn't surprised. People with temporal lobe epilepsy often had normal waking EEGs, and it was only during sleep that abnormal discharges were seen. He made a mental note to get a sleep tracing while Charlotte was in the hospital.

"She started school and was doing fine, but in late fall she had another episode. It happened at the kitchen table. It was very

66

similar to the first only this time she knocked her food off as well."

"Did she fall again?"

"Yes, and there was a period when we couldn't arouse her. This time she was admitted to the hospital. She had skull films, a CAT scan, and a sleep EEG. There were some definite abnormalities in the temporal area and a diagnosis of temporal lobe epilepsy was made."

"Does anyone else in the family have epilepsy?" Mo asked.

"No." The doctor glanced at his wife, who also shook her head no.

"Any problems around brith? Did she ever bang her head when she was a child?"

This time the mother spoke. "Her delivery was normal and her development normal. When she was nine she fell from a horse, hit her head, and was unconscious for a few minutes. They observed her in the hospital overnight, but she did fine and there were no problems."

"Any headaches?"

"Not really." The mother looked to Charlotte, who shrugged her shoulders in agreement.

Mo checked the hospital summary of her EEG report: "Mild but definite left temporal abnormalities."

"She was placed on Dilantin," Dr. Quinn said, "and did well over the next six months. No staring and no further episodes. She did develop some acne, and the Dilantin was switched to phenobarbital. That first made her drowsy, but then she got used to it."

"How did she do in the tenth grade?"

"Fine—a B student."

Mo studied the next hospital summary. "It appears she got into trouble again last summer."

"Yes, that's when her French episodes began."

"French episodes?"

"Well, she would be sitting, when her head would suddenly turn to the right, both hands would start moving about, and then she'd mumble something that sounded like French. We tried to talk to her during an attack, but she didn't respond. When it was over she would cry and then ask to go to sleep."

"How often did this happen?"

"About twice a week, and she was readmitted to the hospital. Amazingly, the EEG had improved. It was almost back to normal. She was changed to another medication, Mysoline, and then settled down again with only a rare episode."

"Did she have any episodes during school?"

"Just once."

"What prompted her current admission here?"

"We don't think she's improving as much as she should be, and we'd like to see a more definitive investigation." The wife nudged her husband, and Edgar Quinn half-whispered to Mo that they would like to talk with him alone. Mo excused himself and went to the nurses' station.

He returned a few minutes later. "Charlotte, I'll want to examine and talk to you in a few minutes, so why don't you go with the nurse to your room and put on a hospital gown?"

"Mom, are you coming?" The girl seemed uneasy.

"No, dear, I'll stay with your father to be sure Dr. Corning gets all the information he needs. I'll be with you soon." Grudgingly, Charlotte left the room.

"Dr. Corning," Edgar Quinn began, "some very frightening things have been happening in the last couple of weeks. That's why we brought Charlotte to the hospital. We didn't want her to hear because we didn't want to upset her."

Rhoda Quinn seemed to brace herself as her husband began the story.

"The first episode was last Wednesday in school. The teacher said Charlotte stood up, began sobbing, threw her books all over the floor, ran out of the room, and collapsed. At first they couldn't arouse her, and when she woke up, they took her to the school nurse."

"Did she lose her urine during the attack? Was her dress wet?"

"Not that I can remember," Rhoda Quinn answered. "But the worst happened Friday evening. We were sitting in the living room when Charlotte came down and began what looked like one of her French spells. She turned her head, began mumbling something that sounded like French. But then she began tearing her clothes and flung herself to the floor."

68

Edgar Quinn held on to his wife's hand. Rhoda looked away. "Then she began fondling herself, first her breasts and then her genitals. She was smiling. Then she started crying and went limp. I carried her up to her room and placed her on the bed. She lay there for about fifteen minutes, then woke up. She asked what happened and we told her she had had another spell. She got up and we spent the rest of the evening watching television and then playing a card game. She seemed all right and there haven't been any problems over the weekend. Either my wife or I have been with her all the time. I called Eli Lassiter and he said he would be happy to admit her today and see what's going on."

Mo could see the strain in their faces. It was only the second time they had told the story. It wasn't that long ago, Mo thought, that people with epilepsy were thought to be possessed by the devil and were ostracized from society. Some epileptics were felt to possess mystical or magic powers. Without knowing the workings of the brain, the way its electricity could misdirect itself, these conclusions were understandable. "Sexual seizures" were rare but had been reported. Mo believed they were compatible with the diagnosis of temporal lobe epilepsy. He tried to remember where he had read about sexual seizures. He wanted to bring the reference to rounds tomorrow.

"Are there any other children in the family?"

"No, Charlotte is an only child."

"What kind of person is she?"

"She's a quiet girl," the father said. "I think it's because physically she's so big. But she has no problems interacting with other teenagers. She has friends and is quite active. What do you think, Dr. Corning?" Edgar Quinn was aware he was talking to a first-year neurology resident, but he was asking as a father, not as a doctor. Besides, he knew from his own hospital experience that it was often the intern or resident, not the staff physician, who finally made the appropriate diagnosis.

Mo thought for a moment, then answered. "It sounds as if she does indeed have temporal lobe epilepsy. What you described was a seizure with sexual overtones. I don't think it's any more frightening or significant than a seizure with convulsive movements of the extremities and loss of feces. Remember, there are many different types of epilepsy. There are reports of people who have seizures triggered by light, music, or even by reading. Temporal lobe, or psychomotor, seizures are known for the associated bizarre behavior."

Mo's explanation comforted Charlotte's parents, who were relieved that their daughter's spell hadn't shocked him.

"I can't say what the cause of the seizures is," Mo explained, "but it probably relates to her fall from the horse. Perhaps a small scar developed in her brain and is now serving as a focus for her seizures. Of course, I'll need to examine her and see if there are any positive physical findings."

"What if she has a seizure on the ward?"

"Actually, Mrs. Quinn, I hope she does," Mo told her. "It would help to actually see one of these episodes. It's safer for her to have a seizure on division seventeen than at home."

"What kind of tests will you be running?" Dr. Quinn asked.

"Dr. Lassiter will decide, but certainly she'll have a sleep EEG. We may try to provoke a seizure during the EEG and we may use a special electrode that's put in the back of the nose. She'll have skull films and repeat CAT scan. I'm not sure whether Dr. Lassiter will want a spinal tap immediately and whether we will be doing arteriography. Probably not. It depends on what the other tests show."

Mo felt a sense of accomplishment. His conversation with the Quinns had clearly erased some of the strain from their faces.

"Well then, we'll go down to the coffee shop and let you spend time with Charlotte. When will Dr. Lassiter see her?" Dr. Quinn asked.

"Later this afternoon."

Mo looked forward to having Charlotte Quinn as his patient. Not only was she a challenge, but she would provide him with a chance to learn at first hand about one of the rarer types of epilepsy. He was convinced they would help Charlotte; it was only a matter of confirming the diagnosis, reassuring the parents, and finding the appropriate combination of medicine by serial measurement of anticonvulsant blood levels. Stuffing the hospital summaries in his white jacket, he stepped into the hall and over to the nurses' station.

It was quiet on the ward. Casey was sitting behind the desk poring over BJ Balsiger's chart. Mo didn't see Jim, but knew he would soon appear because the Zancanelli family was visiting Tony and would want to speak to the boy's doctor. Mo was looking forward to a relatively uninterrupted hour of examining and talking to Charlotte, so he grabbed his black bag and walked down the corridor toward her room. She was in the adolescent section in a private room next door to the Susies. When Mo arrived, he found her standing in the hall talking to Susie W.

"Hi, Charlotte—can I talk to you?"

She nodded.

Big as Charlotte was, she seemed petite next to the large round figure of Mort Corning. She sat on the edge of her bed and Mo filled a nearby chair.

"How are you feeling?" he asked, trying to be friendly.

"Fine."

"Do you know why you're here in the hospital?"

"Sure, because of my seizures."

"Tell me about them," he urged.

"What do you want to know?"

"Well, what are they like?"

"I only know what my parents tell me."

"What do they tell you?"

"They say when I have a seizure I move my arms and hands and sometimes will knock something over." Charlotte looked away. "Then I fall down."

Mo bent toward her. "Can you tell when you're going to have one?"

The girl looked down at her hands. "I usually get a strange sensation in my head or sometimes a funny feeling in my stomach."

"What does it feel like?"

"I can't describe it." Charlotte was clearly not a good historian. She didn't volunteer information and her answers were short and imprecise. She spoke slowly, softly, and when she spoke she didn't look directly at Mo.

Mo persisted. "Did you ever miss part of a conversation or watch television and suddenly find that the show was farther along than you remembered it?"

71

"Yes, sometimes."

"How often?"

"I don't know."

"Once a day? Once every three days? Once a week? Once a month?"

"About once a week."

Mo sat back in his chair. "Did you ever look at something and see it getting larger and smaller?"

"Sometimes."

"When?"

"When I'm tired and my eyes hurt."

Mo rubbed his hand over his balding head. "Did you ever have the feeling when you were doing something that you'd done it before or experienced it at another time?"

"What do you mean?"

Mo was asking about the déjà vu, common to temporal lobe epilepsy. Everyone has experienced the sensation of "being there before," but in temporal lobe epilepsy, these feelings might reach frightening proportions. It was clear to Mo that he would learn little by pursuing the question with Charlotte.

"Can I examine you now?" Mo pulled the curtains that surrounded Charlotte's bed and performed a general examination. Blood pressure. Heart. Lungs. Abdomen. All were normal. Although somewhat tense during Mo's exam, the girl seemed relieved that the questioning was over.

He then began a careful neurologic exam. First, mental status evaluation, tests of memory, abstraction, recall, orientation, general knowledge, and simple logic. Charlotte didn't seem to mind the mental tests, though some of the questions sounded silly to her. She even smiled when he asked her to tell him two ways she thought an orange and an apple were similar. Mo felt her mind was agile and concentration good.

Then cranial nerves. Mo tested her visual fields very carefully, hoping to find a specific defect that would implicate one of her temporal lobes, since the visual fibers ran through the temporal lobe. Normal. In fact, almost the entire neurologic exam was normal: strength, coordination, reflexes, sensation. Nevertheless, Mo was convinced that the response of the right toe when he stroked the bottom of the foot was different from the left. He called it abnormal; in fact, it was the only finding on her entire exam that was abnormal. Mo would use that finding, combined with the history and previous EEGs, to support his contention that Charlotte had a defect in her left temporal lobe.

As he was leaving her room, Mo realized that Charlotte wasn't overly concerned about her seizures or hospitalization, and attributed it to good parental support and understanding.

Back in the corridor, Mo walked to the nurses' station and sat down next to Casey.

"Casey, I just saw a great case. A girl with temporal lobe epilepsy. What a weird story! Alex is going to love it."

Casey smiled politely, still immersed in reviewing BJ Balsiger's chart. She thought Mo was too enthusiastic about the patients' diseases and not enthusiastic enough about the patients themselves.

A few yards away, Jim Wellander and the Zancanelli family gathered around Tony. Little was said. The mother, Luciana, sat at the boy's side and held his limp hand in hers. The father, Richard, stood quietly with the teenage daughter who accompanied them.

The stillness bothered Jim, and he felt a compulsion to talk. He launched into a monologue, laced with long pauses between the sentences. No one looked at him while he spoke, and he seemed almost to be talking to himself.

"There's been no change in Tony's condition," he said. "His blood pressure, heart, and lungs are fine. Though he can't eat, we're feeding him through the tube that goes from his nose to his stomach, and he's getting the right amount of calories. His brain function is minimal. There's been no improvement or worsening as far as I can tell. I don't think he can hear us; he's still in a deep coma. There's no evidence he's in pain or is suffering."

Suddenly Tony's arms moved involuntarily against his thighs and his palms twisted outward, taking with it his mother's hand, which still grasped his.

The father looked expectantly at Jim. "I think that's just a reflex movement, Mr. Zancanelli. I'm afraid it doesn't mean anything." Jim could see that the father didn't believe him, and

73

looked at Tony's mother. She nodded her head slowly and lowered her eyes, admitting that Jim was probably right.

Jim didn't know what to do. Impulsively, the resident moved to the boy's side and called Tony's name. There was no response. Then Jim bent down, put his mouth next to Tony's ear, and called the boy's name again. Still no response. Finally he almost shouted into the boy's ear. "Tony, Tony, can you hear me?" But the boy continued to lie perfectly still.

Next, Jim straightened up and placed his hand on Tony's chest. "I'm going to pinch him," he warned the parents. Trying to appear gentle while applying a painful stimulus, Jim slowly turned the boy's skin. Tony responded as he had before by straightening his elbows, arms and legs turning inward. But this time his motor activity was accompanied by a soft groan.

When he heard Tony grown, Mr. Zancanelli started, and without thinking, the father yelled his son's name. But the boy remained silent. Then, in imitation of Jim, the father put his hand on Tony's chest and hesitantly began to pinch him. After a few seconds the boy groaned as his arms and legs again turned inward. The father pulled away his hand as if he had received an electric shock. Tears filled his eyes and the mother cried. Their teenage daughter continued to stare at the floor.

"I'm sorry," Jim said. They stood for a moment at the bedside, then Jim escorted them from the room.

"Let's sit down," Jim said and led them to a reception room adjoining the nurses' station.

"What does all that mean?" the father asked with a dazed expression on his face.

The mother answered. "It means that we've lost our son."

Their daughter cried. "What's going to happen to him?" the father continued.

"I don't know," Jim confessed. "He has severe brain damage and isn't improving."

"Is there a chance he might wake up?" the father asked.

"There is always a chance, but it's very remote. Even if he does wake up, I doubt he'll ever be normal."

"Why don't you just let him die, then?" the mother asked tonelessly, as if she were thinking out loud or speaking to herself.

74

"Luciana, how can you say that!" Richard Zancanelli sat upright in his chair and didn't attempt to hide his anger. He looked at Jim in a way that apologized for his wife's comment.

"It's a difficult situation," Jim said. "We did everything possible to treat him when he came to the hospital, but we couldn't stop the brain infection. It's passed now, but we're left with a severely damaged child. There's nothing to do but continue to support him and pray."

Silence.

"Do you believe in miracles, doctor?" the father asked.

Jim thought for a minute. "To be honest, Mr. Zancanelli, in Tony's case I don't."

Mr. Zancanelli looked to his wife.

"Richard, I'm sorry," she said. "I don't believe in miracles either. I believe in God's will, and for some reason he wanted to take Tony from us. We have three other children. If God is merciful, he will let Tony die in peace." She was on the verge of tears, but she didn't cry.

Richard Zancanelli sat back in his chair. "What are we supposed to do, doctor?"

"There's nothing to do," Jim answered softly. "We'll continue to support Tony and perform any tests that are needed. If his condition remains the same after a couple more weeks, he'll be transferred to a chronic care hospital."

"For how long?" the mother asked.

There was only one answer Jim could give. "Until he either recovers or develops a complication like pneumonia and . . . passes away."

The father took a deep breath, put his forehead into his palm, and closed his eyes.

No one moved. Then his wife spoke. "I think we'd better go," she said.

Jim walked into the nurses' station and joined Casey and Mo. Mo was writing up Charlotte Quinn's history and the results of her exam. Casey was finishing reviewing BJ Balsiger's chart.

"What a shitty case," Jim grumbled, half to himself.

Mo looked up. "Who, Zancanelli?"

75

"Yes. I don't think I can take talking to his parents again." Mo didn't respond. He was thinking about Charlotte Quinn. Casey just nodded.

"Jim, you look somber," Alex said as he walked into the nurses' station.

"Alex, I don't care what you say—something's got to be done about Zancanelli. It's not fair to his family."

"We talked about it this morning. Do you have something new to suggest?"

"I don't know," Jim said, realizing there was nothing he could add. He studied the beeper that hung from his belt, then replaced Tony's chart into the rack. "I'm going to the library to read," he said, clearly upset, and headed for the stairwell.

Alex turned to Mo. "Have you finished with the new admission?"

"Charlotte Quinn? It's a great case, Alex."

Casey left to examine BJ Balsiger and talk to the boy's parents, and Alex sat down next to Mort Corning.

"Charlotte is a sixteen-year-old girl with temporal lobe epilepsy," Mo said. "She's been reasonably well controlled until recently." Then he told Alex about Charlotte's "French" episodes and about the seizure with sexual overtones. Alex listened quietly; he didn't become as excited about Charlotte's case as Mo had expected.

Mo tried to generate enthusiasm. "I think there was an article in one of the neurology journals about sexual seizures. If I can find it, I'll bring it in for you tomorrow."

"I know the article," Alex said. "It was four years ago."

Mo reluctantly took out his notebook and Alex gave him the name of the journal.

"Can I see her?"

They walked to Charlotte's room and found the girl lying in bed, reading a magazine.

"Charlotte, this is Dr. Licata," Mo said. "He's the neurology chief resident here at Children's Hospital."

Charlotte didn't know what that meant, but smiled anyway.

"Nice to meet you, Charlotte," Alex said. "I'd like you to sit up in bed for me, please." He took off her shoes and gently stroked the soles of her feet. Both toes went down. Unlike Mo,

76

Alex didn't think the right toe was abnormal. He looked at Mo with a questioning face, but Mo just shrugged his shoulders.

Alex lifted Charlotte's chin and stared directly at her. "Charlotte, show me what happens to your hands during one of the spells when you speak French."

Charlotte began to lift both hands, looked at them, then put them at her side. "I don't know," she said. "I don't remember the spells."

Alex quickly finished his exam and they left her room. Walking back to the nurses' station, Alex turned to his first-year resident. "Mo, I have a feeling her seizures aren't real."

Mo was visibly shocked.

"There may be something wrong with that girl," Alex continued, "but I don't think it's temporal lobe epilepsy. Her response to medication has been erratic. The EEG is getting better rather than worse. She isn't as worried about her attacks as she should be. I certainly didn't find anything abnormal on her exam and I think she was ready to show me what she does with her hands during a seizure."

Mo became defensive. "Alex, are you trying to tell me everything that's happened to this girl in the past two years is fake? She did have an abnormal EEG, you know."

"Mo," Alex continued, "the girl needs help, whether the seizures are real or not, and there may be evidence she's had real seizures in the past. But if the seizures she's having now aren't real, if they don't represent abnormal electrical activity in her brain, you could treat her with anticonvulsants for the next twenty years and she wouldn't improve."

Mo didn't answer.

"I've stated the case against temporal lobe epilepsy to make this point, Mo. Include hysterical seizures as one of your main alternative diagnoses. If you can prove her seizures aren't real, you'll be able to stop them with psychiatric help. Mo, you have to decide whether she needs anticonvulsants or a psychiatrist."

"How do you propose I do that?" Mo answered slowly.

"You're a doctor," Alex said and slapped him on the back. "You've told me how great a case it is. See if you can figure it out."

As he looked at his first-year neurology resident, Alex realized he had been harsh, even melodramatic, but he felt Mo needed it. Mo's failure to consider hysterical seizures was a major omission. Even if the seizures turned out not to be hysterical, it was too important a possibility to ignore.

"Mo, what does Eli Lassiter think of her?"

"I haven't spoken to him."

"Good," Alex said as he fingered his reflex hammer. "Don't tell him I think her seizures are hysterical. When we present Charlotte on rounds tomorrow, I want to see how he reacts to her." Mo nodded and Alex left the nurses' station.

Casey Lilstrom was sitting with BJ Balsiger's parents in the boy's room. She had just completed an extensive neurologic examination of BJ and, with his mother's help, could now determine the child's developmental age more accurately than she could on morning rounds. Casey knew he was retarded, and estimated that at four years he functioned at a three-year level. Formal psychological testing done the next day would confirm her impression. Since his admission, BJ had no further seizures, and his mother seemed happy as she balanced him on her lap. Casey knew that the Balsigers didn't relish retelling BJ's story, especially to a medical student, but she also knew that each hospital admission offered them hope that something new might be found.

"BJ had an EEG this morning," Casey said. "We reviewed it at the EEG conference. It was abnormal and there was a defined focus on the right side."

"That makes sense," Dennis Balsiger said. "His seizure yesterday was left sided." BJ's father knew that the right side of the brain controlled the left side of the body, so any discernible logic in his son's convulsions seemed a hopeful sign.

"What are the plans for this hospitalization?" Florence Balsiger asked.

"BJ will be presented at rounds tomorrow," Casey answered, trying to ignore the Balsigers' slight annoyance at the fact that she was a medical student. "I'm sure we'll decide to perform more studies."

"Is Dr. Licata around?" the father asked as they placed the boy back in bed.

"Let's walk to the nurses' station and check," Casey said as they left the room. Halfway down the corridor, they met Alex, who invited them back to the desk for a brief talk. After they were gone, Alex picked up BJ's previous three volumes, while Casey took the chart from the boy's current admission and they went into a neighboring room to discuss the case.

"What do you think, Casey?" Alex asked as he reread his own note from BJ's current hospital admission.

The medical student recounted the salient points of BJ's history. Alex knew the history and only half listened. Instead, he found himself staring at Casey's face. It was a pretty face, Alex thought, and it grew prettier as he watched it. Especially her eyes. In some intriguing way, he felt drawn to them.

There had never been anyone except Mellissa since his marriage, and he had no desire for an affair. But that didn't mean that Alex didn't look at other women. His eyes wandered from Casey's face to her slender body in its wrinkled white skirt, blue blouse, and short white doctor's jacket. Her breasts small. Her legs narrow. Alex wondered what her hair was like when it was down and falling across her shoulders.

"That's the history," Casey summed up. "I don't think there are any clues in it, just a long story of an uncontrollable seizure disorder."

"How about the physical examination?" Alex asked reflexively.

Casey outlined her exam in some detail as Alex's thoughts wandered again, this time to Mellissa. Mellissa was larger than Casey, with a fuller face, a rounder body, and bigger breasts. Mellissa's face was prettier but not as subtle as Casey's, and Alex felt one could stare at Casey's face longer than Mellissa's without losing interest.

Alex was ready to dismiss the comparison from his mind when a thought entered his head that he couldn't brush aside— he wondered what it would be like to marry another doctor. Someone who also read medical journals, who understood what night call meant, and who wouldn't mind hearing medicine

79

when they went out. Funny, the thought had never occurred to him before. Certainly such a marriage would be narrow, but medicine made one's life narrow anyway.

Casey realized Alex was preoccupied with something else and stopped her discourse. "Alex, you're not listening."

"Sorry, Casey," he smiled. "I let my mind wander. I guess because I'm so familiar with BJ's story and examination. What were his positive neurologic findings?"

Casey looked at her notes. "His slow developmental milestones and the left upgoing toe."

"I agree. Now let's talk about his seizures. How do you classify seizure disorders, and where in that classification would you put BJ?" Alex had no trouble returning to his role of chief resident. He had asked these questions of countless students. Casey was happy to see Alex's animation and enjoyed the privilege of having him teach her. Alex was considered one of the best teachers among the residents.

As Casey outlined her views of epilepsy; Alex interrupted, challenged, demanded logic. He surrendered little information and forced Casey to produce most of the facts even though she didn't understand their relationships. Casey enjoyed the exchange and learned considerably in the fifteen minutes they reviewed epilepsy. There were scribbled sheets with crude drawings of the brain and even a few voluntary twitches of Alex's extremities that Casey localized to the appropriate part of the brain.

"Now that we've gone over a classification of seizure disorders, are we any closer to understanding BJ Balsiger?"

Casey thought for a moment. "Only that BJ's seizures are not of any one type; they're not easily classified."

"What does that mean to you?"

"More than one part of the brain is involved."

"Precisely. I think BJ has a diffuse brain disease, but I just don't know what type. Even though he had a left-sided convulsion and we now have a focal abnormality on EEG, I don't think we'll find one single cause like a brain tumor. But we'll still have to perform a complicated study to look for one. I don't know what else to do."

"Try to find a new combination of anticonvulsants," Casey suggested.

"We have to do that anyway."

Alex paused, thought a moment, then spoke quickly. "Casey, maybe you can solve BJ's problem. Make an extensive review of the processes that affect multiple areas of the brain and cause seizures in a child BJ's age. See if anything fits. If you find it, it may not be good news for the parents, but it'll be an answer and at least the parents won't have to live with the uncertainty and the false hope that BJ will be normal one day—a hope that as parents they can never let die." Alex had already thought of several possibilities, but none seemed appropriate for BJ. He knew the compulsiveness of a medical student might bring a new idea, and besides it was a good exercise for Casey.

Casey liked the challenge. It gave direction to her studying and the chance to solve a mystery, to find an answer, and perhaps even to help a family.

It was four o'clock and the fantasy of marrying a doctor still played in Alex's thoughts. He found himself asking Casey to join him in the snack shop for coffee.

They sat in a booth that afforded some privacy in the midst of a noisy roomful of doctors, parents, children in go-carts, and nurses.

"Tell me about yourself," Alex said, not wasting time.

Casey didn't show surprise, just laughed and replied, "You first. Tell me about yourself, Alex."

Alex was caught off guard by her answer. Being chief resident offered no immunity from verbal sparring.

"I'm married, with two little girls," Alex began, "and right now I'm looking for a job in private practice."

"What does your wife do?"

Alex thought it was a dumb question. What does any woman with two little children do?

"She used to work in an advertising firm, but now she just watches the kids. They're twenty-one months and four."

"Where are you looking for jobs?"

"In New England. My wife's family's from Connecticut and

she'd like to be near them. My mother and older sister live in Chicago."

"Did you ever think of staying in academic medicine? You're a great teacher."

"I've thought of it, but I think the major contributions in academic medicine are made by those with a specific research interest."

"Why couldn't you go into the laboratory and learn how to do research?"

Alex didn't answer. She had asked the question so easily, and the logic of the question was clear.

"Anyway, you make more money in private practice," Casey added.

Alex shrugged his shoulders.

"I was married once," Casey volunteered. "For two years in college. It was nice, very romantic, but the wrong time and probably the wrong person. I went to Smith and he went to Amherst. He wanted to move to California and be a writer. I wasn't ready to give up medical school, and he didn't like the idea of my going to school for another six or seven years."

Alex watched Casey's eyes as she spoke; they became larger. Once again her face became prettier the longer he stared at it. He hesitated for a moment and then spoke.

"Casey, we've got similar backgrounds. My wife almost didn't marry me because I was going to be a doctor. In fact, we broke up for over a year when I was accepted at medical school. Her father's a doctor and she didn't want another one in the family. I guess we loved each other too much to stay apart."

She laughed. "You wife was smart."

"Do you have a boyfriend now?" It was a blunt question and Alex was surprised at himself for asking it, but Casey answered easily, as if she expected it.

"No one in particular. I don't have much spare time." She was about to start a new sentence, but then hesitated. She stared for a moment at her fingernails. Then she leaned forward and put her hand on Alex's. "Alex," she said, "talk to me about medicine."

"About medicine?" Alex said with a flush as he looked at the hand that touched his.

"Yes!" Casey said excitedly as she took her hand away. "What does it mean to be a doctor?"

The flush from Alex's face was gone as he thought about her question. As he looked at her face and saw her eyes slowly widen, he began to formulate an answer. As he did, he too became excited.

"Casey," Alex said, "to be a doctor, one must separate illness from patient. A line must be drawn between the person and the disease. A doctor can't suture a laceration over the eye of a screaming child without viewing the child as an object. Illnesses must be viewed in terms of organ system involved, in terms of differential diagnoses, in terms of the tests needed to solve the problem." Casey stared at him intently as he spoke. "The doctor must be immune to the sight of blood, blasé in the face of feces and vomit, unexcited when viewing a convulsion, and unflinching when talking to a patient disfigured and made grotesque by illness. And so, the doctor must examine a rash, a tumor, or an infected wound—not a person's rash, or a person's tumor, or a person's wound. But then," he said, waving his finger in the air, "after the doctor examines the rash, or the tumor, or the wound, after examining the object, the doctor must cross back over the line."

Now Casey was completely caught up in Alex's excitement.

"The doctor must then ask: Who is the patient? What does the patient feel? How is the patient affected by the illness? After asking these questions, the doctor then must integrate: Could the patient's own psyche be affecting the illness? Will treatment and diagnosis affect the patient? Sometimes the doctor must polarize totally in one direction—the person doesn't matter, the doctor says, the illness demands treatment. Other times, the doctor polarizes in the opposite direction—the patient shouldn't be treated; it is not the right thing to do."

Alex stared directly into Casey's eyes. "Casey," he said, "it is the dance of the physician—back and forth across the line he dances. It is the art of medicine; it is clinical judgment; it is being a doctor."

Casey took Alex's hand and squeezed it. This time Alex squeezed back.

Alex's beeper went off.

"Division seventeen, Dr. Licata, 3540."

It was Mort Corning. "Alex, I'm on duty tonight," Mo said. "Anything I need to know about BJ Balsiger? I saw Casey's writeup in the chart. Have you talked to her about him?"

"I just finished. We're in the coffee shop. We'll be right up."

On division 17 they reviewed BJ's chart and orders.

"When are you on night duty this week?" Mo asked Casey. Medical students took night call with the residents. It was a chance to see cases as they came into the emergency ward, to be the sole beneficiary of any teaching the resident had to offer, and to help out with the night work on the ward, usually referred to as "scut work."

"Tomorrow," she answered.

"I'll be on tomorrow night," Alex said half to himself.

Casey looked at him and smiled.

Alex watched Mellissa speaking to Nolan and Judy Magness at the Prince Street Bar in SoHo. Over red wine and burgers, they were discussing the evening's offering at the film series. Mellissa's green eyes, full lips, and round face were beautifully framed by her fresh blonde hair. But as he gazed at his wife, Alex began to see the outlines of Casey's face. He imagined Casey's eyes growing wider as he watched them. It was the first time that Alex had looked at his wife and had the image of another woman in his mind.

"Alex, you're staring at me," Mellissa said, almost accusing him.

"What's wrong with that?" Nolan added, a bit surprised at Mellissa's tone.

"Alex usually doesn't stare at me like that," Mellissa said simply. She knew Alex—his habits, his mannerisms, the way he interacted with her. Alex's stare was something new; she hadn't felt it before.

"Nolan, will you be able to come to rounds tomorrow?" Alex asked as he poured Nolan another glass of wine. "We're discussing BJ Balsiger."

"Sure. I doubt I'll have anything to add, but I'd like to participate in any decisions about his future care."

"What will you be doing next year, Mellissa?" Judy Magness was asking.

"Alex is looking at job offers in Connecticut and Maine."

Nolan watched Alex's face tighten.

"Nolan," Alex said, "the closer I get to private practice, the less attractive it seems."

Nolan's eyes shifted to Mellissa. She obviously wasn't pleased with Alex's words and acted as if she hadn't heard them before.

"What makes you say that?" Nolan asked.

"I'm going to miss the university, and though I'll be treating patients and practicing neurology, I'd like to be involved in research, make a real contribution, discover something."

"You mean you'd like to become famous," Mellissa said.

Silence.

"Most people doing research don't discover much," Nolan said.

"They also don't make much," Judy added.

"When did you get this urge to do research?" Nolan asked.

"It isn't an urge. I've been thinking about it as I've gotten closer to private practice."

"If you're serious about it, we could get you a two- or three-year fellowship in one of the labs," Nolan said.

Mellissa's eyes darted to Nolan. "How much do these fellowships pay?"

Nolan paused a moment before answering. "About the same as what Alex is making now."

"What made you go into research, Nolan?" Alex asked.

"I've always liked research. I spent my summers working in the laboratory."

"That sure doesn't sound like you, Alex," Mellissa said, and the conversation shifted back to the film series.

Later, as they drove home by cab up the East Side Drive, Mellissa moved close to Alex and rested her hand on his leg.

"Alex, that wasn't fair," she said.

"What do you mean, Mellissa?"

"You know what I mean. Bringing up the idea of doing research for the first time while we're out with Judy and Nolan

Magness. You've never even talked to me about it. Alex," she said, "you're not serious, are you?"

Alex didn't answer Mellissa's question. "I was just thinking out loud," he said, "but since we're talking about fair, it wasn't exactly fair for you to say that I wanted to do research just to become famous."

"You could never be happy in research," Mellissa said. "You've never liked the lab and you love taking care of the patients. I know you'd like to discover a cure for some incurable disease, but that's a fantasy. Alex, we have a family. We've got loans to pay back. If you go into research, you'd be training for another three years. Besides, I want to go back to school. We need money for tuition and babysitters. It's my turn, you know."

The cab was pulling off the drive and heading toward the Medical Center complex. "Alex," Mellissa said quietly, "I couldn't take three years of your being a research fellow now."

Alex put his arm around his wife and she moved closer. He knew he wasn't being fair to her, and maybe it made no sense for him to go into the laboratory, but that didn't mean that at this moment those weren't his honestly felt thoughts. Soon the cab was stopped in front of their apartment and he paid the driver. Now he had other thoughts, thoughts just as honestly felt. He wasn't thinking about Mellissa and he wasn't thinking about doing research in the laboratory with Nolan Magness. His thoughts turned to the hospital and to being on call the next night. They turned to Casey. It was one of the rare times in his life that he was actually looking forward to night call.

TUESDAY

8:00 A.M. The boy with the cerebellar tumor was being wheeled into the sterility of the operating room. His mother kissed a bald head, shaven clean for the brain surgery, and began her long vigil. In the operating room itself, the ritual began. The boy, already drowsy from medication, was placed in a sitting position so that the back of his neck and the cerebellar tissue beneath it could be exposed. Masked faces watched as he was covered with green sheets and plastic tubing stuck into his arm. Then, clear fluid injected into blue veins brought deep sleep; another tube placed down his throat into the windpipe delivered oxygen and the anesthetic gas that kept him asleep. The anesthesiologist sat at the machine that mixed the gases, periodically inflating a small blood pressure cuff that circled the boy's arm. With a nod from the surgeon, the scrub nurse pushed a tray of sterile instruments near the boy's head and helped the surgeon put on sterile gloves and gown. Finally, the large wall clock slowly began to record the first of six hours that would be needed for the operation.

Brain surgery can be one of the most delicate operations. It requires minimal trauma to brain tissue, careful control of bleeding, and exquisite care to excise only that tissue which must be removed. Yet, after cutting away the skin overlying the skull, brain surgery begins with a drill. Now the sound of a hand-held drill, virtually identical to a carpenter's, filled the operating room. Gloved hands held the sterile bit against the back of the boy's skull, and the bit began to eat away at the bone underneath. The smell of burned flesh was added to the sound of the whining drill. The drill abruptly stopped; having cut through bone, it automatically shut off, engineering insurance that bone and not brain would be penetrated by the bit. A total of four holes were drilled.

Now it was time to saw. A metal wire was passed between two of the holes, and pulled taut; as the surgeon pulled the wire back and forth, its tiny teeth cut into the bone and soon the wire exited from beneath the skull, the two holes were now connected by a line. More sawing and the other holes were connected; a piece of bone, a bone flap, had been cut away; when the operation was over, it would be put back in place. Soon, the underlying brain would be exposed, but first its coverings, the meninges, were dissected away. It was the infection of these coverings that caused meningitis. Now the brain was visible, a pulsating gray mass, rising and falling with each beat of the heart; twenty-five percent of all blood pumped from the heart went to the brain.

Brain surgery involves sucking, not cutting, for jellylike tissue is not easily cut with a knife. The surgeon began sucking away cerebellar tissue and found the tumor mass underneath the swollen left cerebellar hemisphere. A small piece of the tumor was sent to the pathologist for a verdict. It was he who would tell the surgeons how the cells looked under the microscope, what type of tumor it was, and how long the mother could expect her boy to live.

8:00 A.M. Rounds were starting on division 17. Mo Corning had spent a relatively uneventful night in the hospital, finishing his writeup on Charlotte Quinn and reading the references Alex had recommended on sexual seizures. Casey Lilstrom had spent the evening preparing a long, detailed list of diffuse diseases of the brain that caused seizures in children BJ's age. Like Alex, she was looking forward to night call. Louise Kidner had spent the evening at home, while Jim Wellander went to see a movie.

"Let's start with Charlotte Quinn," Mo suggested, but as they all moved to the silver chart rack in the middle of the hall, Alex pulled him aside.

"Don't tell anyone I think Charlotte's spells may be hysterical," Alex said. "I want to see how the others react to her."

"Sure," Mo agreed, and he began to tell Charlotte's story. His large figure dominated the group. His white pants and jacket were wrinkled and his pockets bulged with the ever-present black notebook, drawings of brain pathways, and articles. The article on sexual seizures Alex had mentioned to him was already copied and in one of his pockets. He intermittently ran his hand over the top of his head and through his nonexistent hair.

Casey wore a clean white skirt; the blue blouse she wore on Monday was replaced by a green one. Her small frame seemed even smaller because she wasn't wearing her white jacket. She looked tiny next to Mo, but appropriate next to Jim. Alex studied her face, lines and angles rather than curves, a bit of lipstick, but otherwise no makeup. Her hair was neatly piled on the back of her head and fastened with a simple green clip that matched her blouse. Her eyes fixed on Mo, then jumped around the circle. When they came to Alex, they stopped and widened. She expected Alex to be looking at her and he was. A touch of color came to her face. Alex smiled and looked away.

Jim Wellander wore slacks rather than white pants, and no white jacket. A few note cards filled his shirt pocket, his stethoscope hung around his shoulders, and a reflex hammer was neatly tucked under his belt. He intermittently straightened his horn-rimmed glasses and then blinked with both eyes. Louise's red hair was her most prominent feature, a nurse's uniform topped with bright red. She held a clipboard and listened intently to Mo's discourse on Charlotte Quinn.

Alex was a cross between Mo and Jim. Like Mo, he wore white pants and a white jacket, but he was smaller and less disheveled. He was the same height as Jim but heavier. After smiling to Casey, Alex peeled his wire-rimmed glasses from each ear, wiped them, and set them back on his broad nose. By then, Mo had finished his presentation.

"She hasn't had any seizures since her hospitalization, and she's on Mysoline," Mo concluded. "Her neurological exam is normal apart from a right upgoing toe, though Alex thought it was normal."

"She's been very cooperative on the ward," Louise added, "and is already friends with the two Susies."

"Has she been tried on Tegretol?" Jim asked.

It was a logical question. "No, but that's definitely the next drug I want to use," Mo told him.

Jim turned to Alex. "What do you think?"

Alex hesitated. He didn't want to discuss treatment until he was certain Charlotte was having real seizures. "I'm not sure. I'd like to know more about her seizures; I'd like to see one myself. Whatever the case, I wouldn't change medications until we have an EEG."

They walked the short distance to her room and found Charlotte sitting in bed eating breakfast.

"Hi, Charlotte," Mo greeted her warmly. "I've brought some of the other doctors to meet you. Do you mind if we interrupt your breakfast?" Charlotte couldn't say no, and her unfinished breakfast would be picked up by one of the dieticians while she was being examined. She wasn't bothered by the group of people that surrounded her; in fact, she seemed to enjoy the attention.

Mo performed a brief neurologic exam, during which Alex noted Mo's difficulty in demonstrating an abnormal response in the right toe.

Once back in the corridor, Mo asked Alex's opinion of the exam, but Alex deflected the question to Jim.

"I don't think there's anything significant on her exam," Jim responded. "I don't think the right toe is abnormal. She probably has a temporal lobe seizure disorder related to the fall from a horse when she was nine. For some reason the seizures are difficult to control, but I bet she would do well on Tegretol. I've never even heard of seizures with sexual overtones before this case. Maybe the parents aren't telling the truth. I think it's mandatory that they be interviewed in detail."

"But she started having seizures five or six years after her fall from a horse," Casey broke in. "Don't seizures after head trauma usually occur within two years of the injury?"

"Usually," Alex answered her. "But they can occur later."

Suddenly a scream came from Charlotte's room. They rushed back to find her on the floor, hands jerking at her sides. She was vocalizing what sounded like French, and her nightgown was pulled up over her hips, exposing bright red panties. Louise ran over to cover Charlotte, but Alex stopped her.

"Don't," he ordered, and Louise stepped back as Mo reached for an airway that was taped to the side of her bed.

"Don't do that either—let's just observe."

After twenty seconds, Charlotte stopped jerking; her hands lay still on the floor. She moaned softly. They stood and watched, intermittently glancing at Alex for a cue. He gave none for three minutes. He stared at her intently, occasionally checking his watch. The moaning stopped. Alex knelt, looked at her panties for a moment, then covered her. He lifted her eyelids. Her eyes were in midposition, fixed straight ahead in an empty stare. He turned her head from side to side; her eyes remained in midposition. Then he stroked the bottoms of both big toes; they went down. He pinched her on the shoulder. A slight moan.

Charlotte, get up!" Alex yelled.

Everyone watched. No response.

"Mo, help me lift her back into bed." When that was done, Alex checked her head for bruises, lifted the side rails on the bed, and left the room.

"Why did you just stand there and watch?" Louise asked sharply as they stood in the hallway.

"I know it seemed cruel, Louise, but remember, it's important to observe her seizures carefully," Alex said. "That's why she's in the hospital. She wasn't in respiratory distress and had already fallen, so she was in no immediate danger. Even if we had been watching her fondle herself, the observation would have been crucial. Jim thinks the parents might not be telling the truth."

"It wasn't a sexual seizure," Jim said, "except for the nightgown lifted over her hips. She did utter something that sounded like French, though."

"It wasn't a typical temporal lobe seizure either," Alex added. He looked at the first-year neurology resident. "What do you think, Mo?"

"Seizures take many forms, expecially temporal lobe disorders. I think she started as a temporal lobe spell, then generalized to a major motor seizure with jerking of both upper extremities."

"What about the vocalization, the French sounds?" Alex asked.

"Part of the temporal lobe discharge."

"But that happened while both arms were jerking. Shouldn't a generalized seizure cover up temporal lobe activity?"

Mo didn't answer. "Let's see how she's doing," he suggested instead.

Casey touched Alex's arm as they re-entered the room and whispered, "You think that was a fake seizure, don't you?"

Alex nodded.

"Charlotte, can you hear me?" Mo asked.

She moaned.

"Open your eyes."

She opened her eyes slowly and turned her head from side to side. "What happened?"

"You've had a seizure; everything is all right."

"Where am I?"

"In the hospital. Does anything hurt you?"

"No."

"What do you remember?"

"After you left the room I had a horrible feeling in my head; the next thing I knew I was lying in bed with the side rails up."

"Do you remember anything else?"

"No."

"Rest in bed now, we'll talk later."

Alex thought Mo's questioning was superficial, based on the still unproven assumption that Charlotte had indeed had a temporal lobe seizure.

"Should we change her medication?" Mo asked him.

"Let's not do anything until later this morning when we discuss her with Eli Lassiter on visit rounds."

Alex's beeper went off. He called the page operator, certain it was Mrs. Papineau calling about her daughter Heather. It wasn't an outside call, it was the emergency ward. Alex listened as he watched Jim Wellander pick up Clark Kent Gatewood.

"We've got a little girl down here you saw a few days ago. She continues to have problems urinating. She says it hurts when she goes to the bathroom. A urine culture came back negative."

The story made little sense to Alex, but he didn't interrupt.

"This morning something new happened."

Alex waited for the girl to have a seizure.

"After she got up, she told her mother she wasn't feeling well, then went to the bathroom and passed bloody urine."

The voice stopped. Alex hesitated for a moment, then said, "What else?"

That's it."

"When did she have her seizure?"

"She's never had a seizure."

"Then why did you call me?"

The doctor in the emergency ward was upset. "Don't you take care of children who pee blood anymore?"

Alex thought for a second, then smiled to himself as he made the diagnosis. "This is Alex Licata, neurology. You want urology, not neurology!"

Jim was reviewing Clark's chart, checking the daily account of his attacks, dosages of medication, and EEG results, and was happy to find there had been only one drop attack the previous day. Jim lifted Clark and held him under the armpits. "He passes the armpit test." He handed the boy to Alex. Alex agreed. "Okay, Superman," Jim said. "Keep it up and you can fly out of here this weekend." In response, Clark giggled and flew off down the corridor.

"Okay, on to the Susies," Alex announced.

The two Susies sat on one of the beds in their room and played checkers. As usual, the doctors' visit was as much social as it was medical. Susie K pointed to the two canes propped against the bed. "I can walk with only one of those sticks now," she said proudly, the proved it by hobbling about the room with a single cane.

Susie W sat quietly in bed; the jerkiness in her arms and legs was barely visible. Alex turned to her. "Stick your arms out," he said. With her arms extended, the involuntary twitches of her fingers, produced by Syndenham's chorea, became apparent. Alex tried to stress Susie W. "How much is seven from a hundred?" he asked.

"Ninety-three."

And seven from ninety-three?"

"Eighty-six."

"If you had five dollars and bought seven newspapers, each costing twenty-five cents, how much change would you get?"

Susie became agitated. She grimaced and the twitching in her hands extended to involve her arms. She tried to camouflage her involuntarily movement by disguising it as brushing her hair or wiping something from her gown. She still hadn't answered the question.

"Take your right hand and put it on your left ear," Alex ordered. She slapped the side of her head.

"Now, don't pick up your left hand but take the middle finger of your right hand and put it on your nose." She hit herself in the face.

Alex took both of her hands and held them in his. "Susie, I've purposely excited you to see how much jitteriness I could create. You still have many of the movements, but you're much improved."

"When can I go home?" she asked anxiously.

"Hopefully this weekend," he smiled.

"What's wrong with that new girl, Charlotte?" Susie K interrupted.

"Seizures," Mo said simply.

"They sure are strange," Susie W chimed in.

"How do you two know?" Alex asked.

"She was telling us both last night," Susie K said.

"What did she say?" Alex's spirits rose. Susie K can provide some real data, he thought.

"She said that the doctors haven't been able to figure out what's wrong with her. She told us about these episodes when she talks French, really strange."

"Did she mention anything else?" Alex asked the other Susie.

"No," the girl said. "But she doesn't think the doctors are going to help her. That was when I told her how much the doctors have helped me."

"What do you think of her?" Alex pressed.

"She's a nice girl," Susie W told him. "Funny, she doesn't seem worried by her seizures."

The cerebellar tissue had gone from the operating room to the pathologist, where it was placed in liquid nitrogen. The frozen tissue was stained and mounted on a glass slide, and then the pathologist adjusted the coarse, then the fine dials on his microscope. He fingered the microscope with as much authority and experience as the surgeon fingered his knife, and soon the invisible cells came alive under the microscope. It was an easy slide to read. Cerebellar astrocytoma, a benign brain tumor of childhood. This kind of tumor could be removed and would not seed to other parts of the brain or spinal cord. He immediately phoned his results to the surgeon, who smiled; the boy would be saved and the surgeon fulfilled.

One of the beauties of surgery was its ability to cure, to heal, to repair, all in one dramatic moment. It was active intervention by human hands rather than passive monitoring of a natural process. If the tumor had been a medulloblastoma, the boy would have been doomed. The surgeon could attempt removal of a medulloblastoma, but he knew tiny remnants would grow, spread to other parts of the nervous system, and in two years the boy would be dead. His efforts at the operating table would be meaningless; he might have prolonged life briefly, but that's not why he had become a surgeon. A good case for any doctor was a patient with a life-threatening illness that the doctor could cure. Unfortunately, there weren't enough good cases in the hospital.

On division 17 the chart rack stood next to one of the infants with hydrocephalus, eyes floating on water, staring listlessly at the world. In the adjacent room, Jim Wellander held the nine-month-old infant with muscle weakness.

95

"We still haven't found a reason for his hypotonia," Jim said to Mort Corning.

"But you're going to try," Mo said, alluding to their conversation the previous day on rounds.

Jim didn't argue. "He's getting a muscle biopsy tomorrow, Mo. If that's negative, he's got idopathic hypotonia."

Idiopathic, cause unknown. All tests negative. The doctor doesn't know why or how or what. A negative diagnosis, an unknown process, a problem for someone to solve and become famous. A burden the patient must bear.

Tony Zancanelli hadn't changed. His stiff body and unresponsive brain gave little indication of life, although food and medication continued to be pushed through the tube in his nose and into his stomach. The group stood over his bed, but only mentioned him in passing.

"Tony's the same," Jim announced simply.

Louise nodded.

"Who else do we have to see?" Alex asked.

"We haven't seen BJ yet," Casey suggested.

Alex shuffled his 3 x 5 cards. "I guess that's all. Eli Lassiter will be here for visit rounds at ten. We can present Charlotte to him and discuss BJ. Nolan Magness will be at rounds too. When he was a resident he took care of BJ."

Tony Zancanelli's silent presence didn't stop them from discussing ward business. Doctors on rounds often discussed a case in front of the patient. "Do you mind if we discuss something about your case?" the doctors would ask, and patients rarely said no though they often misinterpreted the discussion. Even worse, the doctors might say, "Don't worry, we're not talking about you." For Tony Zancanelli it didn't matter what happened at his bedside. Nevertheless, Tony's heart beat faster this Tuesday morning. His body temperature had risen slightly and that rise was reflected in his heart rate. The clipboard Louise carried listed his temperature as 99.8. It was a rectal temperature and not abnormal enough to deserve comment. Yet, it was one degree higher than it had been the previous five days. No one touched Tony that morning on rounds.

BJ hadn't had a seizure since entering the hospital, and by now he had recovered from the effects of Sunday's prolonged

96

convulsion. He was playful, more verbal, and interested in his surroundings, but still only a three-year-old brain in a four-year-old body.

Alex looked at Casey's neat six-page multicolored workup on BJ. She had read through all three volumes of his history, examined him, and talked with his parents. Somehow she had managed to condense all that information on both sides of the 3 x 5 card she was now holding.

"Don't review his entire history now," Alex interrupted as Casey began reading from her card. "We'll be presenting BJ on visit rounds."

"I checked BJ before rounds and didn't find anything new," Casey said. "In fact, now both toes are downgoing. Normal. After his formal psychological testing this afternoon we'll have to decide what other studies he needs. We saw his EEG yesterday. Anything else, Louise?"

"He spent a restful night," the nurse told her. "But his parents haven't stopped asking the nurses questions. Since he hasn't had any seizures, we'll let him go to the playroom this morning."

In Casey's pocket was a folded piece of notebook paper she used to make a list of processes that could affect multiple areas of the brain and cause seizures in a child BJ's age. She had faithfully executed the assignment Alex gave her. The list was long, all inclusive, but rarely pertinent. It contained diseases that were only seen in tropical climates, processes already ruled out, illnesses that didn't resemble BJ's, and some diseases that didn't even cause seizures. Yet, on the list was BJ's diagnosis.

"I've made a list of processes that might cause seizures in a boy like BJ," Casey said, extracting the folded piece of notebook paper from her pocket. "It's long and many of the diseases are obscure." She handed the paper to Alex.

Alex quickly ran his finger down the list. It was complete, too complete. Obviously, Casey had done her homework, but nothing particular struck his eye. Still, he felt the need to commend what had clearly been an arduous job. "We'll go over this list in detail later," he told her. "It'll be invaluable as a touchstone for the seizure discussion. Maybe it'll even help us come up with some new ideas about BJ." He was pleased to see her smile at his comment and without thinking he winked at her. "It's nearing ten," he then told the group. "Eli Lassiter soon will be here for visit rounds."

Visit rounds gave the staff neurologist a chance to monitor patient care on the ward, ensure that no errors were being made, and participate in major decisions. Furthermore, it gave the staff neurologist a chance to teach, enlighten intern, resident, and student, and provide the perspective of his clinical experience. Obviously the success of visit rounds depended on who visited. A staff neurologist who spent his time in the laboratory doing research had little new clinical information to offer. Visit rounds served more to keep him in touch with clinical neurology than to teach the house staff. A staff neurologist who spent time seeing patients brought more to visit rounds. He had seen more cases, knew more clinical pearls and tidbits of medicine the house staff would scramble to pick up and put in their black pocket notebooks.

Exactly at ten, Eli Lassiter arrived at the nurses' station. He was thirty-eight years old and had been in the neurology department at Children's Hospital for five years. His field was developmental neurobiology, and most of his time was spent in the laboratory. Eli Lassiter studied mouse brains, how neurons took their position in the developing brain, the sequence in which new layers of nervous tissue appeared, and the age at which different parts of the brain matured. Time spent on the hospital wards and in clinics seeing patients had been minimal. Unfortunately, productivity in the lab had also been minimal and the few papers he had were not important ones. It was the time for him to be promoted from assistant to associate professor, and most people didn't think he'd make it in academic medicine. Alex expected him to leave New York at the end of the year, either to take a position at a smaller university or to go into private practice.

Eli Lassiter was tall, thin, and nervous. A full head of hair, streaked with gray, sat like a mop on his narrow triangular face. Whether sitting or standing, he constantly shifted his weight or busily fingered the pockets of his lab coat. He never seemed comfortable.

Nolan Magness walked onto division 17. He was Eli Lassiter

six years earlier, having finished his neurology residency, and just beginning the lab work that would start his career in academic medicine. Nolan's interest was neurochemistry, and Alex felt he would succeed. Nolan, unlike Eli, was already productive after only a year in the lab.

Nolan sat next to Eli in the small conference room adjoining the nurses' station. Nolan's straight black hair was combed flat and his features were obscured by a full black beard that he intermittently pulled with his left hand. "If possible, I'd like to discuss BJ Balsiger first," he said. "I'm in the middle of an experiment in the lab." If Eli Lassiter hadn't been the visit, Alex was sure that Nolan would have stayed for rounds, but everybody knew Eli's rounds were not the best.

Now it was Casey's turn. Referring to her 3 x 5 card, she told BJ's story in its entirety. As she spoke, Eli, then Nolan, leafed through her workup in the chart. After her presentation, Eli began the ritual of visit rounds. First he asked Casey what she thought.

"The boy has an uncontrollable seizure disorder and is developmentally retarded," the medical student began. "After his last seizure there were focal neurologic signs that have since disappeared. I've done a lot of reading and even made a huge list of processes that cause seizures, but I have no idea what's wrong," she confessed. Realizing BJ was a difficult case with no obvious diagnosis, Eli didn't force Casey to commit herself. Instead, he asked Nolan about BJ, searching for other ideas rather than quizzing.

"We shouldn't disregard the possibility of a slow-growing tumor," Nolan stated. "I know—he's had arteriography and even pneumoencephalography before and they've both been normal, but that doesn't rule out an infiltrating tumor."

Casey looked at her list. Infiltrating tumor was listed under "rare causes."

"Furthermore, he needs another CAT scan. His last one was two years ago."

Computerized Axial Temography, the CAT scan, was a technological breakthrough in neurologic diagnosis, devised not by a doctor but by a physicist and an electronics engineer who won the Nobel Prize for their discovery. It was administered by placing the patient's head in a giant X-ray machine connected to a computer. After the X-rays passed through the skull, they were deflected at various angles by the brain, then millions of the deflected rays were analyzed by the computer, which then presented an actual picture of the brain. By adjusting the machine, the brain could be viewed at different angles, and by adjusting the computer, the picture could be made darker or lighter. The beauty of the technique was that no more X-ray exposure was needed than for a simple skull film. Other techniques for visualizing the brain were potentially dangerous and more time consuming. The advent of the CAT scan was making previous diagnostic studies, such as injecting dye into the blood vessels for arteriography or injecting air into the brain cavities for pneumoencephalography, obsolete.

Nolan spoke with authority about the need for further tests on BJ. His confidence made a complicated problem appear simple and made Eli more comfortable. Eli, continuing with the visit ritual, asked Alex's opinion.

"There's no question that BJ needs another CAT scan," Alex began, "but I doubt it'll show anything. A slow-growing tumor would be located in one part of the brain, but the pattern of his seizures and his EEG suggest diffuse, not localized brain disease. Nolan, what would you do if the CAT scan's negative?"

Nolan hesitated. He hadn't considered that possibility seriously. "He would need repeat arteriography."

Alex persisted. "And if the arteriography is negative?"

"I don't know. There's nothing else to do. Continue to manipulate his medications, I guess."

The problem was now in focus. BJ needed a CAT scan and arteriography to rule out a tumor, despite the likelihood that the tests would be negative. Even if there was an infiltrating tumor, it would be incurable. The best that could accomplish would be to let the parents know what was happening to their son.

"What medications would you put him on?" Alex asked.

Nolan didn't know.

Eli was uncomfortable again. He continued the ritual, quizzing Mo and Jim, who had little to add. Now it was his turn. At best, Eli would have an idea or course of action no one had considered, but Eli realized this was impossible. Even the most experienced clinician would have had little to add about BJ. As his hands fingered the edge of his labcoat, he also knew he had little to add about infiltrating tumors or BJ's medications. And so, Eli Lassiter talked about the only thing he knew, developmental neurobiology.

"It's very interesting," he began, "that when isolated mouse neural tissue is placed in tissue culture at different stages in development, this tissue acquires certain potentials and loses others. I've studied them in detail by cell-membrane surface changes. The developing nervous system represents a dynamic process; what was true at one time during development has changed at a later stage. However, even though the nervous system has the potential for change, it can't regenerate itself."

What a bunch of crap, Alex thought. Why doesn't he just say he's got nothing to add. No one expects a revolutionary thought on BJ. Alex was angry. A four-year-old boy, developmentally retarded, with uncontrolled seizures and parents struggling to deal with their child's unknown disease, sat in a hospital bed. His case was presented to the visit in great detail by a medical student who spent hours laboring over three volumes of hospital chart. The visit, in turn, discusses brain cells from mice placed in test tubes.

"What does developing mouse brain have to do with BJ Balsiger?" Alex asked, clearly upset.

Silence.

Mo thought Alex was wrong to attack Eli, even though the attack was appropriate. "I was reading about seizure types in children," Mo said. "They often appear and disappear depending on the developmental stage of the child's brain. Has anyone looked at the electrical excitability and potential for seizures activity in the brain cells of these mice, Eli?"

Eli was grateful for Mo's support. He shifted his weight and tried to relate developing mouse brain to epilepsy and to BJ Balsiger. Finally he had finished. "Time to examine the boy," he said.

BJ was brought in from the playroom so Eli could examine him. The boy's small teeth were buried in gums that had swollen from anticonvulsant medication. The large doses of anticonvulsants were also reflected in his dull eyes and expressionless features. Most children on seizure medication looked and acted normal, but BJ was not like most children.

Eli examined BJ and taught the basics of the pediatric neurologic examination. Casey and Jim learned, while Mo watched impatiently. Alex thought that Eli's examination was well done; it was clear he hadn't forgotten that basic neurologic skill.

Normal. An abnormal child with a normal exam.

"I feel he should be presented at grand rounds on Thursday," Eli suggested.

The first constructive comment Eli's made all morning, Alex thought.

"It would be important to have the CAT scan done by then, and if that's negative, the arteriography," Eli continued.

"We'll do the CAT scan tomorrow morning and schedule him for arteriography in the afternoon," Alex said. It would be difficult coordinating both tests on one day's notice, but it could be done.

"I'll get permission from the parents this afternoon," Casey told Eli, who was in the process of once again shifting his weight from one foot to the other.

"Fine," Eli said. "Who was on duty last night?"

"I was," Mo answered. "It was quiet. The only admission was your patient, Charlotte Quinn."

The hollow metal instrument made a hissing sound as air was sucked through it. It was connected by a rubber hose to a suction apparatus on the wall of the operating room. The tumor within the cerebellum was well encapsulated and the surgeon thought he could remove it completely. The hissing stopped when the metal instrument was placed against the tumor mass. Dabbing the tumor as one might stick a toothpick holding a piece of cheese into a party spread, the surgeon carefully sucked out tissue. Tiny bits of tumor clogged the metal hole, then were pulled into the tubing and finally came to rest in the bottle attached to the wall. There was blood as well. When a point of bleeding was identified, no matter how small, the surgeon placed the tip of a silver instrument, like the end of an icepick, on the bleeding point and stepped on a pedal near his right foot. A short buzzing sound, and the area he touched sizzled, burned black from a wave of electricity; blood coagulated and the bleeding stopped. Suck out a piece of tissue. Burn a tiny bleeding point. Again and again. The surgeon watched his ritual through magnifying spectacles suspended from a band that circled his head. The slightest movement of his hand appeared a clumsy thrust when viewed through the spectacles.

It was time to discuss Charlotte Quinn. In the conference room, Eli listened carefully as Mo described in detail Charlotte's two-and-a-half-year history of seizures, her most recent "French" episodes, and the sexual seizure. Besides being· responsible for Charlotte in his role as the visit, Eli was the girl's private physician. After the embarrassment of BJ Balsiger, he was glad to be confronted with Charlotte's problem, which he viewed simply as temporal lobe epilepsy, and which he felt could be controlled by a few drug manipulations.

"We had just finished talking to her," Mo recounted, "when we heard a noise coming from her room. She was lying on the floor, making noises that sounded like French. Then she had a tonic-clonic convulsion with arms twitching. When it was over she was unresponsive. After she woke up, she didn't remember the episode. She wasn't incontinent and her examination after the seizure was normal."

Alex was astounded to hear Mo describe Charlotte's episode; it seemed like a different event from the one he had witnessed. Mo's description left no doubt that Charlotte indeed had a seizure. Mo said the speaking of "French" came before the movements of the arms; Alex felt they happened at the same time. Mo described the jerking of the arms as tonic-clonic movements, a classic epileptic phenomenon. Alex viewed the jerking of the arms as a strange motor pattern, not at all typical for epilepsy. Finally, Mo didn't mention that Charlotte lay there with nightgown above her waist, exposing her red panties. It was a hunch, but Alex thought it too much a coincidence that Charlotte had had an episode on the ward while she was wearing red panties.

Alex didn't want to contradict Mo publicly. Yet, he didn't want Eli to be misled by Mo's account. If Charlotte was having hysterical seizures, no amount of anticonvulsants would cure her. Before Mo's description of Charlotte's episode, Alex didn't want to reveal his skepticism; he wanted to see if Eli had similar suspicions. Now he felt he had to say something.

"Eli," he said, "after hearing Charlotte's story and observing the episode this morning, I think her convulsions may be hysterical."

Eli didn't react. Louise and Jim were surprised. Only Casey seemed comfortable with the suggestion.

"The sexual seizures she's having are really bizarre," Alex continued. "This morning during the episode she was wearing red panties and had her nightgown pulled above her hips." Alex moved forward on the edge of his chair. "The vocalization and arm twitching happened simultaneously, and the twitching wasn't typically tonic-clonic in nature; in fact, the legs weren't even involved." Alex's right hand waved in the air as he counted off each point with a finger. "Furthermore, she didn't bump her head or hurt herself when she fell, she didn't bite her tongue, and she didn't lose urine or feces." He sat back in his chair. There was a brief silence.

"I'm hesitant to diagnose hysterical seizures in this girl," Eli began. "We all know temporal lobe epilepsy can take the strangest forms. She's had an abnormal EEG in the past. Remember, her father's a physician and has observed her convulsions himself. We would be in big trouble diagnosing her as hysterical if she wasn't."

"I'm not saying we should diagnose her as hysterical; I'm saying hysterical seizures are a possibility," Alex retorted.

"I wouldn't even consider them a possibility until she's had an adequate trial of anticonvulsants."

"That could take months," Alex said, once again sitting on the edge of his chair.

"Yes, even years," Eli answered, unruffled by Alex's concern. Eli was certain he was right and Alex was wrong. Furthermore, after being intimidated by Alex over BJ Balsiger, he was more than happy to argue with Alex over Charlotte Quinn.

"Alex," Eli suggested amicably, "before we discuss this further, let's see the girl."

Charlotte was sitting on her bed, chatting with the two Susies. Alex thought they might have been discussing Charlotte's seizures, but all conversation stopped when the entourage of doctors appeared.

It was the third time Alex had visited Charlotte in less than twenty-four hours. He studied her carefully. She was a big, shy girl, who avoided eye contact by constantly looking down at her hands. She was rather plain and had an almost masculine body. With her large arms and shoulders, almost nonexistent breasts, and chunky legs, she best resembled a Russian peasant working the fields.

"Charlotte, I'm Dr. Lassiter," Eli said as he walked over to her and shook her hand. "Your parents asked me to check you."

"Hello," she offered noncommittally.

"You had a seizure this morning?"

"Yes."

"Tell me about it."

"I don't remember," she said and lowered her gaze to her hands.

"Was there a warning?"

"A funny feeling in my head."

"What was it like?" Under the stress of her resistance, Eli was beginning to shift his weight.

"Hard to describe," she said tersely.

"What language do you study in school?"

"Spanish."

Charlotte's unwillingness to discuss her seizure forced Eli to examine the girl after he'd been in the room for only two minutes. Both toes were downgoing and her exam was normal. Eli would have liked to spend more time with Charlotte, but there was no reason for the group to stay in her room. The entourage moved back to the conference room to discuss the case.

"She's a strange girl," Eli mused. "Withdrawn, afraid to communicate. Altered behavior patterns occur in temporal lobe epilepsy, and, unfortunately, may not improve when the seizures are controlled."

"Why did you want to know what language she studied?" Jim asked.

"If these French episodes were hysterical, she'd probably be studying French in school," Eli said.

Alex cringed at Eli's reasoning. "You think there's no possibility her episodes are hysterical?" Alex demanded.

"There's always a possibility. but I'll bet they're real."

"What are you willing to bet?" Alex challenged.

"A fifth of whiskey," Eli said without hesitating.

"You're on. How will you prove they're seizures?"

"The sleep EEG tomorrow. It will show typical discharges of temporal lobe epilepsy." Eli smiled confidently. "How will you prove they're hysterical, Alex?"

"That's my problem."

Eli asked the others. "Mo?"

"They're real."

"Jim?"

"Real."

"Louise?"

Real."

"Casey?"

"Hysterical."

After the shuffling of 3 x 5 cards, each person reported on his other patients to Eli and visit rounds ended.

The cerebellum is composed of two lobes connected by a central structure called the vermis. A giant hole had been sucked into the left cerebellar hemisphere of the boy; little of the actual cerebellar tissue remained. Unlike bone, gut, skin, hair, liver or blood, brain didn't regenerate. The cerebellar tissue was gone forever. Yet, unlike other parts of the brain, one could function without a lobe of cerebellum, especially a child. Although the cerebellum was responsible for balance and coordination, when he recovered, the boy's balance and coordination would be normal. A rare treat for the neurosurgeon, suck out brain and still have a normal child.

Casey and Alex sat in the crowded hospital cafeteria, surrounded by white pants and jackets, children in wooden carts, and a steady stream of doctors scampering to the wall phones.

"You don't like Eli," Casey said. It was both a question and a statement.

"I think he's a weak part of the neurology program," Alex said

106

honestly. "His clinical skills are nonexistent, and he really hasn't done much in the laboratory."

"Nobody knows what's wrong with BJ—why should he?"

"He shouldn't, but he doesn't need to waste our time with that mouse crap. Besides, he's wrong about Charlotte, plain wrong. Part of it's Mo's fault."

"You really think they're hysterical seizures?" Casey asked.

"They can't be real. You yourself said they were hysterical."

"I know, but I don't count," she said with a smile.

"Why not?"

"I have no experience. Anyway, I like siding with you."

Alex didn't know what Casey meant, but he liked the way she said it. He looked straight at her. She stared back.

"I think Eli was being difficult about Charlotte because I gave him a hard time with BJ," Alex said, then paused. "Why do you like siding with me, Casey?"

"Why did you ask me to lunch?"

"There's nothing wrong with the chief resident eating lunch with a student."

"I didn't say anything was wrong."

"You haven't answered my question."

"You haven't answered mine either." Casey lifted her eyebrows and her small brown eyes widened. She smiled, then laughed. "You're the chief resident," she said. "Give me a differential diagnosis of the possible reasons I like siding with you and then figure out why you asked me to lunch."

Alex was silent. He continued eating.

"Well, I'll tell you why I like siding with you," Casey said. "Because I respect your ability as a neurologist, and of all the people up there, I know you'll be right."

"I don't believe that," Alex said.

"How about because you're going to give me a grade and I want to build up extra points?"

No response from Alex.

"How about I feel a tremendous physical attraction toward you and am trying to figure out a way to get you into bed?"

"I'll pretend I didn't hear that."

"Ok, let's change the subject." Casey put her hand on Alex's;

this time a flush didn't come to Alex's face. "Tell me about medicine," she said with a smile.

"We did that yesterday," Alex said, giving her hand a squeeze.

"I know, and I loved it."

"Do you *really* want me to talk about medicine again?"

"What else would a chief resident and his student talk about at lunch?"

Alex was more than happy to shift the conversation, to retreat to the familiar. "Casey, the other day I got a page from the EW, and the resident said to me, 'Alex, I've got a three-year-old boy down here who had his first seizure tonight.' When I heard that I thought about offering a twenty-dollar bill to the first doctor who called me about a case and didn't begin with 'I've got,' or 'I have.' Casey, doctors are possessive about their patients. Instead of saying, 'There is a patient here with convulsions,' they say, 'I have a patient with convulsions.' It's a trait of the physician and I'm not exempt. After all," Alex said with a wink, "I *am* a doctor." Casey smiled. "If the doctor has a unique case, the doctor takes credit. And do you know what?" Alex said, picking up his spoon and pointing it at Casey. "Colleagues don't condemn the practice, they perpetuate it by adding their compliments. And the doctor apologizes if he has to ask another physician to see an uninteresting patient, even if it's obvious that the patient needs evaluation."

Casey looked at Alex. Her eyes were as wide as they had been in the past two days. "Alex, I like you," she said softly.

Alex looked at her cautiously. "I like you too, Casey," he said slowly.

"I guess that answers why we are eating lunch together," Casey said with a flourish.

Alex would have loved to sit in the cafeteria and talk to her for the entire day, but as he looked at her, he shifted uncomfortably in his seat. What would he say to her now? As he looked at her face, the image of another woman came into his mind. "Casey," Alex said slowly, "I'm married. I have two children."

Casey was silent.

"I'm sorry," he said. Impulsively, he picked up his tray and left the cafeteria.

Casey wasn't sorry. Her impulse was to follow him, but she didn't. Instead, she finished eating, then walked up to division 17.

Alex walked out the main entrance of Children's Hospital. He had no destination, but he walked briskly, his feet driven by the disquiet in his mind.

For many married men there were other women—because the freshness of the marriage had grown stale, or more simply because the marriage didn't work; often it was nothing more than circumstance and the attraction of two people of the opposite sex. For married women the same rules applied. Nevertheless, in the five years of Mellissa and Alex's marriage, there had been no one else. For Alex there had been fantasies, fantasies triggered by the movement of another woman's hips as she walked, and thoughts of how it would be to move with them in bed; by the bouncing softness of another woman's breasts and of how it would be to hold them; by the beauty of another woman's face and of how it would be to caress it. But for Alex, never the desire to act. Not until Casey.

She was right to ask Alex why he had invited her to lunch. There were other female medical students, many were prettier than Casey, but Alex had never invited them to lunch, or stared at them, or looked forward to being with them on night call. But there was never anyone whose eyes he had watched widen and who he had told about medicine like Casey.

Maybe his attraction to Casey was because he was afraid of private practice, and his wanting to do research wasn't real. But Alex did have honest feelings about doing research. He wanted the challenge and he wanted the chance. He knew he could do better than the routine of private practice. Casey understood that.

No, Casey wasn't beautiful; she was lovely. And wonderful to be with. But Alex was married, and he realized he was getting too deep. He knew what he had to do. He had to stop.

Casey Lilstrom sat in the small conference room on division 17 with BJ Balsiger's charts stacked on the table in front of her between two dictating machines, but she was neither reading nor dictating. She was thinking about Alex. She was not upset with him, only disappointed. He obviously liked her, but he was afraid.

Casey had grown up in Topeka, Kansas, one of five children from a comfortable upper-middle-class home. Her father was a contractor and her mother was a housewife who was proud of her role. Casey was as bright as she was fiercely independent, and, by high school, it was clear that Topeka was too small for her. She decided to head east, ultimately taking a scholarship from Smith.

Casey was not classically pretty. She was small-boned, with brown hair, a thin, triangular face, narrow lips, and cold brown eyes. Yet, if one looked at her for a long time, her eyes seemed to widen, they grew warmer and softer, and when this happened, her face became unquestionably prettier. It was as if her eyes controlled a secret energy, a hidden beauty, something that poured out from them and spilled onto her face. Not everyone reacted to Casey's eyes, but enough did that there were boyfriends in high school, suitors in college, and a two-year marriage that ended just before she started medical school.

The marriage, to an English major at Amherst, had been idyllic for a while. They lived on borrowed money in an apartment halfway between the two campuses, romantically isolated from an interfering world. Yet, the romance evaporated with graduation. Casey's desire to be a doctor in the East clashed head-on with her husband's dreams of being a California writer, and so they were divorced. The divorce was less painful for Casey than for her husband. There would always be men to love, but only one chance to attend medical school, so she got a scholarship for medical school and took another loan to cover living expenses in Manhattan.

The first two years in New York were difficult. Medical school began with basic science courses and exams, not with delivering babies, treating heart attacks, or watching surgery. Not until the third year did Casey get exposure to patients, which she found physically more demanding but mentally more stimulating.

Casey dated and, when it suited her, went to bed with her partner. She missed the companionship of marriage but felt the lack was more than compensated by the challenge of medical school. Still, in New York her eyes remained small and cold; no one had seen them widen and felt their warmth pour out onto her face, no one until Alex. Casey could feel Alex reacting to her. It had made her blush on rounds and led to her placing her hand on his in the cafeteria. But he was a man who respected his marriage, and his delight in her clearly disturbed him. She could tell that Alex was frightened; he wasn't ready.

Casey shifted BJ Balsiger's chart from one hand to another. Her first impulse was to forget Alex, but it had been so long since a man reacted to her as Alex did. And the way he looked at her made her realize how lonely the three years had been. She wanted to pursue the relationship, but was afraid it might be the wrong thing to do.

As she sat, unseeing, before the stack of charts, Casey made an abrupt decision, identical to the one Alex was making as he walked outside the hospital, to stop.

2:00 P.M. The boy's head was wrapped in white bandages, the bone flap put back in place, and the endotracheal tube pulled from his windpipe. He breathed on his own. The bandages were soiled with blood over the area of surgery, and for the rest of his life, whenever a skull X-ray was taken, there would be four translucent holes, holes drilled when he was too young to remember, but no tumor underneath. Green sheets, previously draped across his shoulders and lap, were now removed. Because the operation was performed with the boy sitting, removal of the sterile sheets was like removing the sheets draped across the shoulders of a man in the barber's chair. Instead of sweeping up hair, the nurse picked up the remaining blood-soaked sponges and tallied them in a final sponge count. The mother greeting her son in the recovery room; emotionally numb from the experience, it was hard to believe her son had now been returned to her normal.

On division 17, Casey spoke with BJ's parents. BJ had been in the hospital for three days without a seizure and Dennis and Florence Balsiger were hopeful that something might be found to help him. Their initial skepticism about dealing with a medical student was erased by Casey's interest and her rapidly acquired knowledge of BJ's history, and they welcomed the enthusiasm and the freshness she brought to BJ's problem.

"BJ'll be going shortly for psychological testing," Casey began.

"Did they present him on rounds this morning?" Dennis Balsiger asked.

"Yes, and Dr. Magness came specifically to help evaluate BJ." Casey thought Nolan's presence would add to the impression that everything possible was being done for BJ, but Florence Balsiger wasn't impressed.

"Dr. Magness could never figure out what was wrong with BJ," the mother said.

Casey wanted to remind her that no one else, including BJ's current doctors, could figure out what was wrong with him, but she remained silent.

"Is BJ going to have more tests?" the father asked.

"Tomorrow morning he'll have a CAT scan." Casey explained the intricacies of the machine that would outline BJ's brain and its cavities. "If the CAT scan is negative, we would like to perform arteriography in the afternoon."

"He's already had arteriography," the mother objected.

"I know, but that was two years ago. We'd like to repeat it."

"What if that's negative?" the father asked.

"Whatever the results, BJ will be presented at grand rounds on Thursday."

Twice before, Florence Balsiger had accompanied BJ to the large amphitheater where an audience of doctors listened to BJ's story, but these visits had never produced an answer. "Are you going to try any new medication?" the mother asked.

"Not until after the tests. By the way, I'll need you to sign a permission form for the arteriogram." Casey brought a standard form, put BJ's name on it and the words "cerebral arteriography." Dennis Balsiger read the form:

1. I hereby authorize and consent to the performance upon BJ BALSIGER the following procedure CEREBRAL ARTERIOGRAPHY.

2. I further consent to the performance of any other operation or other procedure, preceding, during, or following the above-mentioned procedure which the physician in charge

deems necessary for the purpose of preserving my child's life or health.

3. I also consent to any such procedure being witnessed by students in the health sciences in connection with their educational program.

4. The effect and nature of the procedure to be performed and the possibility of complications and unforeseen consequences have been fully explained. No warranty has been made as to the results that may be obtained.

DENNIS BALSIGER
Father
witness: CASEY LILSTROM

Dennis Balsiger had signed many forms for BJ. So had scores of other parents for their children. Forms to allow the sticking of a needle in their child's back. Forms to allow the taking out of their child's appendix. Forms to allow the cutting open of their child's heart. Forms to allow the drilling into their child's skull. Forms to allow the cutting off of their child's leg. Forms to allow the removal of the organs from their dead child's body so an autopsy could be performed.

As Alex walked onto division 17, he spotted Casey standing in the hallway talking to the Balsigers.

"Oh, there's Dr. Licata," Dennis Balsiger called out.

Alex heard the remark and felt compelled to join the trio, despite his discomfort at being with Casey. He tried not to look at her.

"I've been explaining the various tests we've planned to Mr. and Mrs. Balsiger, Dr. Licata." Casey's matter-of-fact tone bothered Alex almost as much as hearing her call him Dr. Licata.

"We've got a busy schedule for him," Alex said, "CAT scan and possible arteriography tomorrow, then grand rounds on Thursday."

"Do you think anything will come of it?" the mother asked.

"To be honest, no. But we've got to keep trying." Alex gave the unpleasant truth purposely. He felt there had been too much false hope for BJ's parents. Then he spoke to Casey. "Dr. Lilstrom, I'll be talking to you later this afternoon." And, with-

113

out looking at her, he turned and went upstairs to the newborn nursery.

Alex leafed through Baby Girl Carlson's chart and noted that she had had no more seizures and was doing nicely. Inside the nursery, next to an incubator, a woman stood uncomfortably in the white gown she was forced to wear and looked at her child.

Alex washed his hands and put on a similar gown. "Is this your baby?" he asked gently.

"Yes," Mrs. Carlson answered.

"I'm Dr. Licata, the neurologist who's been evaluating her."

"How's she doing, doctor?"

"Didn't your husband tell you?" Alex was surprised.

"He said everything was all right, but he never worries about the kids and I just can't take his word for it."

"You can this time, Mrs. Carlson," Alex reassured her. "Her EEG showed good prognostic signs and she's done well in the hospital."

Baby Girl Carlson's mother smiled.

Alex took out the infant's 3 x 5 card. He placed it on top of the incubator and began to scribble some notes.

The mother looked over his shoulder and said, almost shyly, "Her name's Ruth Jean now."

Without looking up, Alex crossed off the words "Baby Girl" and wrote above them, "Ruth Jean," then put the card back in his pocket. "Ruth Jean. Certainly an improvement over Baby Girl," he said, smiling.

Anthony Zancanelli's heart beat quickly. It wasn't because he was excited to be with his visiting family, but because tiny organisms were growing in his lungs. Their presence caused an elevation in body temperature and the raised temperature resulted in a faster heartbeat. The family sat at the bedside watching Tony and looking at each other, something they had done daily since their son entered the hospital. Jim Wellander joined the parents in Tony's room and spoke with them briefly. After Monday's long discussion and the realization that Tony's chances for recovery were practically nonexistent, there was little to say. Jim reported that Tony's condition hadn't changed, even though the doctors who stood at his bedside at morning rounds had discussed a different case and no doctor's hand had touched his body. There was no reason to suspect Tony was different, but on this day he was. It would become obvious at night when a thermometer stuck into his rectum by a nurse would read 102.5.

Returning to the nurses' station, Jim took Tony's chart from the silver rack and wrote a brief daily progress note that Tony was unchanged. Mo Corning sat next to him, looking through Charlotte Quinn's chart.

"Mo, I don't have anything more to say to the Zancanellis," Jim said with a combination of anger and frustration.

"Don't worry, Jim," Mo said offhandedly. "Just give them the support they need and wait."

"Wait for what?"

"You know. Until he dies or until you rotate off the service. How much longer do you have?"

"Two weeks. But hell, that's a crappy way to look at a case, Mo."

"What else can you do, Jim? You can't cure him and you can't kill him. All you can do is wait. You're lucky you only have to follow him for two more weeks. If he were my case, I'd have to follow him for the next three months."

"But how long do his parents have to follow him, Mo?"

Mo Corning didn't answer. For the freshman neurologist, medicine was technical. He needed to know pathways in the brain, differential diagnoses of neurologic problems, names of obscure neurologic diseases, and doses of anticonvulsant medication. Facts were paramount and had to be learned and classified in either black or white. Facts couldn't be gray, because if they were gray, they were difficult to classify. Patients were viewed as diseases, and the greater the variety of diseases Mo saw, the more neurology he learned, the better neurologist he would become. He didn't learn neurology by caring for one comatose child, or by seeing the same disease over and over, or by treating someone without nervous system dysfunction. When he finished his neurology residency and was more secure in his technical knowledge, he would view a patient as a person

115

with a disease rather than as a disease that happened to occur in a person.

When Jim Wellander began his pediatric internship, he had been like Mo, caught up in the technical aspects of treating sick children. But he grew out of it quickly, quicker than Mo. As a pediatric resident rotating through neurology, it wasn't his task to learn all of neurology, only to gain a broader exposure to neurologic diseases. Jim liked to philosophize, to think about the gray areas Mo tried to avoid. For him, neurology was a backward specialty, localizing areas of the brain that didn't work but not being able to do anything about it.

Charlotte Quinn's parents appeared on division 17 and went straight to her room. Edgar Quinn took time from his work as a radiologist to be with his daughter. They found Charlotte sitting on her bed reading a movie magazine.

"I had a seizure this morning, Dad," Charlotte said nonchalantly.

"What was it like?"

"Like the other ones, I guess. I don't remember much."

"Were the doctors here when you had it?" her mother asked.

"Yes."

"What did they say?"

"They asked questions and examined me."

Communication between Charlotte and her parents was strained, especially now. While Charlotte didn't seem bothered by her seizures, her parents were frightened by them. After small talk with their daughter, Edgar and Rhoda Quinn met with Mo Corning.

"I haven't spoken to Eli Lassiter yet," Edgar Quinn said. "What did he think of Charlotte?"

"He thinks it is a matter of medication control; her exam is normal."

"But she just told us she had a seizure this morning," the father said, a bit concerned.

"Yes, we all observed it on rounds." Mo wondered how Charlotte had described it to her parents. "It was a generalized convulsion lasting a couple minutes. There were no focal features and she was fine afterward."

"Was there anything unusual about the seizure?" Rhoda asked tentatively.

"If you're worried about sexual overtones," Mo said, "the answer is no. It was just a run-of-the-mill seizure."

"Does she have any tests scheduled?" Edgar Quinn asked. He took Charlotte's chart from the rack and began to thumb through it. "How do you plan to manipulate her medication?"

"She'll have a sleep EEG tomorrow morning, and, depending on what that shows, she may be started on Tegretol."

Edgar Quinn stopped abruptly as he looked through his daughter's chart. His lips tightened and his face grew red, then pale. "What's this about Charlotte's seizures being hysterical?"

At first Mo didn't respond, then he glanced at the chart. "That doesn't mean anything," he managed to say.

"Doesn't mean anything? Why doesn't it? It says right here that a sleep EEG will be done Wednesday morning to rule out the possibility of hysterical seizures." Charlotte's father pointed to the bottom of the page. "Dr. Corning, the note is signed by you."

Mo tried to brush aside Edgar Quinn's question. "It was just something brought up on rounds," he said, and took the chart away from Charlotte's father.

"Who brought it up?" Edgar Quinn demanded.

"Alex Licata, the chief resident."

"What did Dr. Lassiter say?"

"He thinks the seizures are real and disagrees with Alex."

"Does anyone agree with Alex?"

"Only the medical student."

"I want to talk to Eli," the father said angrily. "Right now."

Mo had no choice but to call Eli's lab. He handed Charlotte's father the phone. "Eli, this is Edgar. I'm on division 17, talking to Mo Corning. I just found out there was a discussion this morning that Charlotte's seizures might be hysterical. What's going on?"

"The chief resident brought up the possibility," Eli said. "Don't get upset. I think there's no chance her seizures are hysterical. I actually had an argument with him on rounds."

"I still want to talk to him, Eli. He can't do this to Charlotte."

"Wait until tomorrow, Edgar. She's having a sleep EEG in the morning; that'll settle the issue. The EEG should show the seizure discharges, and then we can begin manipulating her medication. Don't you remember when you were a house officer? The chief resident often thinks he has to propose a different diagnosis for the sake of argument."

"But not with my daughter."

"After the EEG, there'll be nothing to argue. Believe me."

"I hope so."

Charlotte's father was satisfied with Eli's explanation. Although he understood the position of the chief resident, he was angry with Alex for trying to make his daughter's case more interesting by bringing up an obscure diagnosis. Besides, Edgar Quinn didn't want *his* daughter to have hysterical seizures. Nevertheless, as he walked down the corridor to meet his wife, he realized he hadn't asked Eli Lassiter what would happen if his daughter's EEG was normal.

4:00 P.M. Two people pushed a cart down the corridor, then through large swinging doors, and finally onto division 17. They were dressed in green. A tiny figure lay in the cart, his arm connected by plastic tubing to a bottle of sugar water that hung on a pole above him; he was pushed into the critical care room on division 17. Nurses were there to greet the boy minus his cerebellar tumor. They lifted him from the cart to his bed, transferring the tubing and IV bottle with him. They took his blood pressure, pulse, and checked the bandage circling his head. The anesthesia and recovery room records were incorporated into his ward chart and a new list of medications entered in the order sheet. One of the women at the bedside was his mother; she clutched her son's hand in hers. The boy was awake. He looked up at his mother's face and asked when he was going to have the operation. His mother closed his eyes with her fingertips and told him it was all over.

"Hi, Mellissa, are you coming to the hospital for dinner?"

"I guess so."

118

"Bringing the girls?"

"Sure. Cheaper than a baby-sitter. What time do you want us?" she asked cheerfully.

"It's four-thirty. How about an hour?"

"Okay. Have you recovered from last night?"

"What do you mean?" he asked.

"You acted sort of strange. All those crazy ideas about doing research."

"I think I'm over that."

"I hope so. See you in an hour." She sounded relieved, even warm.

Mellissa was worried about Alex. She had known something was different when he had looked at her so intensely in the SoHo bar. His stare had bothered her more than his misgivings about private practice. His professional wavering she attributed to anxiety about leaving the womb of residency, but his stare implied something personal, something different about the way Alex was reacting to her.

Alex had mentioned to Casey that he would discuss BJ Balsiger with her in the afternoon, but he was afraid to talk to the medical student. In a complete reversal of the previous night's anticipation, he was sorry to be on night call with her. It would be better never to see her again, never to be tempted, never to look into her eyes and watch them widen. He knew if he didn't go back up to division 17, he wouldn't have to meet with her. He decided to spend as much of the evening as possible at home; meanwhile he spent the afternoon at the library reading medical journals until it was time to meet his family.

Casey sat on division 17, not expecting Alex to appear, but waiting anyway.

Dinnertime. Mellissa, Elisabeth, and Kristen waited for Alex. Mellissa was anxious to have dinner with Alex, to watch the way he reacted to her. Alex sounded better on the phone, no trace of what had bothered him the night before, but Mellissa would know only when she was with him. Within minutes after Alex arrived and distributed family kisses, Mellissa could tell that he was different. He was more polite, his tone was gentler, he was more relaxed. Alex looked at Mellissa's face but didn't stare.

Casey walked into the cafeteria. She spotted Alex and his family and tried to avoid them, but as she walked to her table, Alex looked up and saw her.

"Hello, Casey," he said reflexively, in a tone that identified more than it greeted.

Casey nodded, managing a weak smile.

"Who's that?" Mellissa asked.

"A medical student rotating through the service," Alex said blandly.

Casey sat at a nearby empty table.

"Why don't you ask her to join us?"

"She's just a student, Mellissa. I don't know her very well. She probably has some reading or work she's anxious to do. I doubt she'd want to sit with us and two small girls."

Mellissa glanced again at Casey. She sat alone, a small, almost frail figure. Mellissa walked over to Casey. Alex grimaced. He turned to see Casey, food tray in hand, following Mellissa toward him.

The conversation was mundane. Casey made appropriate remarks about the two girls and Mellissa asked her how she enjoyed medicine. Casey complimented Alex on his ability as physician and teacher. Mellissa lamented that she was ready to return to work. Casey said she liked medicine. Mellissa mentioned current events. Casey spoke about the weather.

Alex was silent. He ate slowly, determined to prevent any interplay between himself and the medical student. He felt confined. Casey was at his side and Mellissa sat across from him; the juxtaposition of two people that confronted him in his mind had become real. They had somehow jumped from his mind and materialized next to him.

"It should be a quiet night," he said to Mellissa. "I'll come home with you after we finish dinner. They can call me if they need me."

Casey didn't react.

"You mentioned you were on duty tonight, Casey." Mellissa turned to the medical student. "What'll you do if nothing happens?"

"Read in the library, I guess."

Mellissa noticed Alex was no longer relaxed. His voice cracked when he spoke and he sat on the edge of his chair.

Casey looked at Alex and Mellissa. She did not want to see Alex with his wife and two children. It made Alex a different person. It took him away from her.

Suddenly a voice cried out over the hospital intercom, "Dr. Licata, stat, emergency ward, Dr. Licata, stat, emergency ward!"

Alex jumped from his chair and ran from the cafeteria, calling his goodbyes as he ran. He was rarely paged over the hospital loudspeaker; even urgent messages arrived via beeper, and only a true emergency demanded voice paging. The word "stat" in the operator's page meant "immediately." As he ran to the emergency ward, he assumed the case was either a child in continual, uninterrupted seizures, called status epilepticus, or perhaps a child with raised intracranial pressure, pressure so high it threatened immediate death by compressing vital respiratory and cardiac centers in the brain stem.

By the time Casey realized what had happened, Alex was gone from the cafeteria. She excused herself from Mellissa and chased after him. Mellissa sat with two children and two trays of food that would never be eaten. At that moment, she wished she were Alex's student, running after him to the excitement of the emergency ward instead of his wife, wandering home with two children at her side.

As she ran down the corridor, Casey felt a wave of exhilaration. That is why she stayed in the hospital for night call. Unlike Alex, she didn't postulate what was in the emergency ward, she simply looked forward to the awaiting drama and the chance to learn something. The next day she would tell a fellow student about the great case she saw in the emergency ward and her colleague would be jealous.

Alex was far from exhilarated as he ran down the corridor. Unlike Casey, he was responsible for treating the awaiting case. While Casey would observe, Alex would have to act, and, too often, death accompanied an acute neurologic emergency. Having once heard the crying of parents who had just lost their child, his exhilaration was permanently transformed into dread.

It was not difficult to recognize an emergency in the hospital: people ran toward it, others exited from it, still others stood near it, trying to watch. Tonight it was in room 7.

Alex pushed his way into the room "It's an eight-year-old, who came in about thirty minutes ago in status epilepticus," the pediatric resident told him. "We gave her some Valium and that seemed to slow the seizures, but they didn't stop. So we gave her more Valium and the seizures got worse. Now, she's beginning to have trouble breathing."

"Has she had seizures before?" Alex asked.

"Her mother's so upset we can't get a history, but it would appear she has. The girl has a record here, but the chart hasn't come up yet."

The eight-year-old was in a state of continuous convulsive movements, with both arms and legs jerking, eyelids and mouth twitching. The nurses had strapped her to the examining table so she wouldn't fall. Alex checked for lateralizing or focal features to the convulsion, but found none. The violent jerking didn't predominate on one side or in one extremity. Her head wasn't turned to the side, but her eyes were rolled up and back. The girl was becoming cyanotic, with a blue color staining her lips, and her fingernails and hands turning a dusky gray. Alex was worried by the severity of the convulsions and surprised by the lack of a response to Valium.

Casey entered the room and ran to Alex's side. "It's an eight-year-old in status," he told her. "Valium hasn't helped and she had respiratory difficulties." Alex's description was a "bullet," the essence of a case, described in minimal words.

Next Alex asked for Dilantin; it was a good anticonvulsant and it didn't suppress respirations. He sat at her side and slowly injected the medicine into her IV tubing. It took almost fifteen minutes to inject the medicine, and Alex waited another fifteen minutes. No response.

"Can you tube her?" Alex asked the resident, and when the resident hesitated, Alex turned to the nurse. "Call anesthesia, stat," he said. "She needs phenobarbital and maybe more Valium, but we can't give her the medicine unless we're prepared to intubate, in case she stops breathing."

Almost immediately, the hospital loudspeaker cried out again, "Anesthesia, stat, emergency ward, Anesthesia, stat, emergency ward!" People in other parts of the hospital heard the two stat pages and felt blessed that they were not in the emergency ward. Later they would ask what happened. Some would ask directly, "Did the child in the emergency ward die?"

"How much does she weigh?" Alex asked.

"Sixty, maybe sixty-five pounds," the resident replied.

"Let's see," Alex calculated mentally. "Two-point-two pounds to a kilogram, call her sixty-six pounds, that's thirty kilos. I want to give her five milligrams of phenobarbital per kilogram. I'll need 150 milligrams of phenobarb."

The anesthesiologist had just arrived, and Alex told the nurse, "Give her half of the 150 mg IM and I'll give the rest IV." The nurse injected seventy-five mg of phenobarb into the girl's buttock, while Alex slowly gave the other half intravenously.

Everyone watched. There was a slight reduction in the severity of the seizures. Then the girl stopped breathing. The anesthesiologist pushed air through her mouth and nose with a special bag, then prepared to intubate her. He grabbed a silver metal blade connected to a handle; on the tip of the blade was a small light. The instrument was shaped like an L, the handle forming the upright part of the letter and containing the batteries for the light. He pulled back her head and stuck the blade down her throat, pushing the tongue aside as he went. Next, he attempted to pry open the girl's windpipe, or trachea. He searched for the epiglottis, a flap of tissue that covered the trachea, by flicking the blade with his wrist, but it wasn't easy. Finally he succeeded in lifting the epiglottis and the trachea came into view, guarded by two vocal cords. Now his job was to pass a rubber tube between the vocal cords and into the trachea so oxygen could be blown down the tube directly into the lungs.

Although the convulsive movements had lessened, they made the intubation difficult. "I see the vocal cords!" the anesthesiologist shouted, and with one fluid motion he passed the rubber endotracheal tube deep into the girl's throat. The people in the room, who had bent over in identification with the bent-over anesthesiologist, straightened up when he did. He began to blow oxygen into the endotracheal tube.

Alex watched carefully. When the girl's color didn't change, he grabbed his stethoscope and put it to her lungs. Unsure of whether or not he heard air moving, he placed the stethoscope over the stomach. He heard a bubbling sound.

"The tube's in the esophagus!" Alex cried. "You're blowing air into her stomach." In his mind, Alex visualized the two pipelike structures in the throat, the trachea and the esophagus. The former led to the lungs, the latter to the stomach. When a person ate, the trachea was closed off by the epiglottis and food went down the esophagus. When a person breathed, the trachea was open.

The anesthesiologist yanked out the endotracheal tube and started again. Everyone in the room bent over. He pushed the tongue to the side, lifted the epiglottis, visualized the vocal cords, and thrust the tube down the girl's throat for a second time. This time when he blew oxygen down the tube, Alex heard air filling the lungs.

"You're in," Alex said. Everyone straightened up. A bag was attached to the endotracheal tube, and the girl's chest rose and fell each time the anesthesiologist squeezed the bag.

"What's her blood pressure?" Alex asked.

"One hundred over sixty."

"Good." He looked at his watch. "We'll see how she does for the next ten minutes, then decide on further medication." Although the girl wasn't breathing on her own, and the convulsive movements continued, Alex left the room. Casey followed.

Casey admired Alex's performance. It was hard to imagine one day she would be the physician in charge of an emergency. She knew it would happen; Alex was once a student like her. Yet it seemed so far away.

Outside the room Alex saw a woman frantically waving her arms, crying, and calling his name all at once. "Oh, my God," he whispered to himself. "It's Mrs. Papineau. That girl in there is Heather Papineau." His stomach suddenly felt as if the lining were turned inside out, and his legs felt both heavy and light as they propelled him toward Heather's mother.

"It's your fault!" she screamed. "You wouldn't see her, you wouldn't put her in the hospital, you kept talking to me on the phone, telling me not to worry. Now she's going to die."

Alex didn't know how to respond.

The nurses tried to restrain the mother. "I don't know how, but you'll pay for this! What kind of doctor are you? Give her some medicine, you said. *Well, she got the medicine and look what happened!*" Heather's mother was in a total frenzy as the nurses led her into an adjoining room, with Alex in their wake. He tried to talk with her, to soothe her, to learn the circumstances surrounding Heather's convulsions, but meaningful dialogue with the mother was impossible. The only history available was from the rescue squad, who reported that the woman had returned home from shopping to find her daughter in a state of continual convulsions.

Heather's chart appeared. Alex carefully read his note of Sunday night. It was straightforward, containing no obvious mistakes, but Alex knew he had not been a compassionate physician Sunday night. Called away from lovemaking, he had been more impatient, perhaps more careless, than usual. He searched his mind for a mistake in judgment or treatment, but, although he could find none, he envisioned a hostile woman blaming him for the brain damage, or even for the death, of her daughter. He realized there was nothing to do but treat the girl and hope, and tried to fight off the hollow, sinking feeling that permeated him as he walked back to room 7.

"What's that all about?" Casey asked.

"I saw this girl Sunday night. The mother wanted her admitted, but I didn't think she needed it."

"Did she?" Casey rose from the desk to face him.

"No." Alex looked directly at her. "I'd do the same thing again." The tension between them had disappeared. Alex was grateful for a comforting face, for an ally, and was glad Casey was there.

Heather's convulsive movements hadn't stopped, and Alex forced himself to think about Heather in different terms. Besides the girl's underlying convulsive disorder, there could be a complicating factor, something that made her seizures difficult to control.

"Have we sent blood for sugar and electrolytes?" he asked the pediatric resident.

"Yes."

"Make sure they do a calcium, BUN, and liver function tests as well." He turned to the nurse. "Give me some fifty percent glucose." Low blood sugar might be making the seizures impossible to control, in which case a quick injection of concentrated sugar water would stop them. Alex injected the sweet, sticky solution into the girl's vein via the IV tubing and watched. No effect. A blood sugar drawn prior to Alex's injection later returned normal, confirming Heather's lack of response to 50 percent glucose.

"Let's draw blood gases to make sure she's getting enough oxygen." The blood gases would test how well the respiratory therapist had ventilated Heather with the large black rubber bag she intermittently squeezed with both hands.

The resident filled a glass syringe with a few drops of heparin, which would prevent the red cells from clotting. Red cells carried the oxygen and carbon dioxide that would be measured. Almost all blood tests were drawn from a vein; blood gases were drawn from an artery. The resident felt for the pulsing femoral artery in the girl's groin. He put both his middle and index fingers on the pulsing vessel, an inch apart. The target was between his fingers. He plunged the needle straight down into the girl's groin. It was like searching for oil. The pressure in the artery was so great that when it was punctured by the needle, blood shot into the syringe, pushed up the plunger, and filled the barrel. The pediatric resident hit the artery on the first try. Alex watched bright red blood force its way into the syringe; it looked like she was getting enough oxygen.

The syringe was stoppered to prevent air from entering, placed in a bag of ice to maintain a constant temperature, and sent to the blood-gas lab for immediate assay. A nurse applied pressure to the girl's groin for five minutes to prevent extravasation of blood from the artery.

Alex noticed a decrease in the severity of the seizures. Now waves of hard convulsions were followed by gentle twitching of extremities and face. Since the endotracheal tube had been inserted, there was no need to worry about anticonvulsants depressing her respirations. Only two things concerned Alex now—blood pressure and the possible damage the prolonged convulsions might have on the girl's brain. Blood pressure was OK, but the seizures continued.

"Let's give her some more Dilantin," Alex said. He calculated the dose on the basis of what he had given her previously and on her kilogram weight. He wanted the medication in the high therapeutic range. Dilantin and phenobarbital were the two most commonly used anticonvulsants, and in combination with Valium, there were few seizures Alex had not been able to stop.

Results of blood tests began to return, indicating that the blood gases were good: oxygen was appropriately high, but the carbon dioxide was low. That meant the respiratory therapist was ventilating the girl too quickly, and Alex told the therapist to give fewer breaths per minute. Sugar, potassium, chloride, sodium, BUN—all were normal. Calcium and liver function tests had yet to return. Still no clue as to why she had such prolonged seizures.

"She has a fever, Dr. Licata," the nurse said urgently.

"How much?"

"It's 39.7."

"That's over 104."

"Maybe an infection triggered her seizures," Casey suggested.

"What was her temperature when she arrived?" Alex asked the resident.

"Normal."

"I bet her fever is caused by the convulsive movements of her muscles," Alex said, "but we're forced to check for a source of infection." He checked her ears—normal. Lungs sounded clear, and a chest X-ray taken to check the position of the endotracheal tube showed no evidence of pneumonia, even though it was a poor quality film due to her convulsive movements.

"We'll have to cath her and check the urine," Alex said. The girl's legs were held apart, pubic area cleaned, and a catheter passed through her urethra and into the bladder. Yellow urine filled the tubing and emptied into the attached bag. A balloon was inflated on the end of the catheter to prevent it from falling out of the bladder. Heather Papineau now had a tube coming from between her legs, two tubes connected to each arm for the IV fluids, and a tube coming from her throat.

Alex lifted the back of her head to check for the presence of a stiff neck; perhaps the girl had meningitis. It was supple. Still, Alex knew he had to do a spinal tap to be certain. It would be disastrous to overlook an infection of the brain or its coverings as a cause of her seizures. Furthermore the tap could show blood, a signal of bleeding in the brain, or occlusion of tiny superficial vessels.

Doing a spinal tap was not without a risk, for if there was a large collection of blood or significantly raised pressure inside the skull, removal of fluid from the lower spine might upset the equilibrium of the system. That in turn could lead to pressure on the brainstem and possible death. Alex lifted the girl's eyelids with his finger, trying to visualize the optic nerve with his ophthalmoscope. The nerve to the eye was a direct extension of the brain, and in the case of raised intracranial pressure, the optic nerve was often swollen and blurred. It was almost impossible to see into Heather's eyes, because they jerked back and forth in rhythm with her convulsions, but Alex was patient. Every few seconds, the optic nerve flashed briefly into view. It was a pretty sight, like a gold sun against a red sky. After a half dozen glimpses, Alex was convinced the nerve head was perfectly round, didn't budge, and had distinct margins. No evidence of raised pressure: he would do the spinal tap.

"Get me a lumbar puncture set. I'm going to do an LP."

Realizing the difficulty of sticking a needle into the spine of a convulsing eight-year-old, Alex decided to inject more Valium to quiet her down. Yet, after only a small amount was given, her blood pressure began to drop. He had already stopped her breathing with large doses of anticonvulsants, and was now at the stage when further IV doses of Valium affected blood pressure. He couldn't allow the blood pressure to drop.

"I'll have to hit a moving target," Alex decided as Heather was gently rolled on her side so as not to disturb the endotracheal tube in her throat. Alex put on sterile gloves and cleansed Heather's lower back, first with an iodine solution, then with alcohol. As her body convulsed under his gloved hand, he palpated the lower back to identify the bony prominences of the spine and the gaps between them. He needed to thrust the needle into one of the gaps, parallel to her hips, and direct it in such a way that if the needle were long enough, it would exit from her umbilicus. No local anesthesia would be needed, for the girl felt no pain. Alex first pushed the needle under the skin, stopping just before the spinous processes. He held the needle loosely as the back gyrated beneath his gloved hand. He drew an imaginary line in his mind from the needle to her spine and watched the angle of the line change with her movements. When the angle was right he quickly thrust the needle deep into her back and let go of the needle. Now her back moved with a needle stuck from it. He pulled out the stylet, a needle within the needle, and watched. Clear fluid began to drop from the end of the needle. There were sighs and one-word compliments from those watching, the equivalent of a small round of applause. Alex held a test tube under the dripping needle, following it around as the girl moved. After about fifty drops were collected, he quickly pulled the needle from her back and placed a Band Aid over it.

When he held the tube to the light, the fluid looked clear. In the small emergency ward laboratory, Alex placed a few drops under the microscope. There were no cells. No white cells, no evidence of infection; no red cells, no evidence of bleeding. No cells and no clues. The remaining fluid was sent to the laboratory for culture, sugar, and protein.

Alex was ambivalent about the results of the spinal tap. If it had shown something, he would have had a diagnosis. Yet the possibilities, either bleeding or infection, were bad for the girl. With a normal LP, her chances were better.

Alex thought out loud. "She's had maximum doses of phenobarbital and Dilantin. I can't give her more Valium because it lowers her blood pressure. Let's draw blood levels to make sure she has enough Dilantin and phenobarb on board. Meanwhile we'll give her some paraldehyde."

Paraldehyde was a safe drug for status epilepticus, though rarely the drug of choice. It was given to Heather in a solution that was squirted into her rectum, from where it would be absorbed. Soon everyone in the room would know the girl had been given paraldehyde. The medicine had a very characteristic odor, and much of it was metabolized and blown off by the lungs. As they breathed for her, the room would smell from paraldehyde.

"It's time to make a seizure chart," Alex said to one of the nurses. "We'll need an exact record, otherwise we won't know if the girl is improving or not." He took a hospital record form of crosshatched lines, like graph paper. Each large box across the paper would represent an hour, each small box going up the paper, the length and number of seizures. On top of the form there was room for medication, blood test results, and procedures. It was 8:00 P.M. He would see how Heather did during the next hour, after which she could be given more anticonvulsants.

Alex's beeper went off. He was being called to division 12, where a boy had suddenly developed a severe headache and passed out. A neurologist was needed to evaluate him, but Alex couldn't leave the emergency ward, so he asked Casey to see the case, then report back to him. Not only was she happy to help, she was thrilled by the chance to evaluate a case on her own. "Of course," she said warmly to Alex, and he watched her narrow figure work its way down the aisle and out the emergency ward. He was glad she was on duty. He would need her help.

Mrs. Papineau sat in the lobby of the emergency ward, close to the place where BJ Balsiger's parents had sat on Sunday morning. Their son had also been in room 7 with seizures, but BJ's convulsions had been controlled with a single injection of Valium. Heather was not so lucky.

Dreading the encounter, Alex escorted Heather's mother into an adjacent conference room and asked her to sit down.

"She's doing a little better, Mrs. Papineau," Alex began.

"Why didn't you admit her to the hospital on Sunday night?" Heather's mother was still angry, but fortunately no longer hysterical.

"I didn't think she needed admission. I've carefully reread my note from that evening and thought about Heather's case several times," Alex stated firmly. "I would do the same thing again."

"You shouldn't be allowed to practice medicine if you refuse admission to children who later come into the hospital with uncontrollable convulsions" she said angrily.

Alex was tense but tried not to show it. "Mrs. Papineau, if I've offended you or have been impolite to you, I apologize. We can talk about my ability as a physician later. Now, the most important thing is to stop Heather's seizures. Is there anything you can tell me about how she felt today that was in any way out of the ordinary?"

"You're just a resident aren't you, Dr. Licata?" Mrs. Papineau asked.

Alex bit his lip, then managed a feeble "Yes."

"Isn't there a staff person or someone above you who supervises?"

"Dr. Lassiter is the staff neurologist for the hospital this month."

"I want you to call him." Once again she began to get agitated. "I want him in the hospital tonight. *I want him to see my daughter.*"

Alex didn't respond. The last thing he wanted was to call Eli Lassiter.

Heather's mother, sensing that Alex was hesitating, began to plead. "Dr. Licata, I'm a sick woman myself. I'm under psychiatric care. I've been in a great deal of emotional stress ever since Heather's birth. She has no father, but I decided to keep her and raise her myself. I don't know what I'd do if she died or became brain damaged. You've got to help me." She slowly put her head in her hands.

Alex tentatively touched her shoulder. "I'm going back to see how Heather's doing. I'll call Dr. Lassiter immediately afterwards."

Heather's mother didn't look up.

9:00 P.M. The first hour was now recorded on Heather's seizure chart. Twelve seizures in one hour, one every five minutes. They lasted thirty to sixty seconds and were generalized. She was breathing on her own now, exchanging air through the tube that came up from her throat and out her mouth. The tube was taped in place, white adhesive formed crisscrosses as it traveled from her nose, across her mouth, and under her chin. Humidified, oxygenated air was blown in front of the tube.

"Eli, it's Alex." Reluctantly, Alex kept his promise to Heather's mother. "I've got a girl down here in the EW in status that I want to talk to you about." Alex told Heather's story, replete with medical slang and jargon. It was almost in a different language. He described Heather's visit to the emergency room on Sunday night and his argument with her mother. Yet, he emphasized the mother's psychiatric history and hysteria in the emergency ward and glossed over his own rudeness and lack of patience. He knew Eli would have to see the girl that night.

Eli was not gentle with Alex. In a way, he was happy to hear of Alex's difficulties, which elevated his own position. Still, he wasn't happy about coming to the hospital late at night; few doctors were. He asked Alex many basic questions about Alex's plans for Heather. Some were so basic that Alex felt it was insulting to ask them of a chief resident. Yet he had no choice but to answer. Eli agreed to arrive at the hospital before midnight.

Alex's beeper went off. It was division 17.

"Dr. Licata, Charlotte Quinn just had a seizure," a nurse told him excitedly.

"What happened?"

"We don't know, we found her on the floor in the hall."

"Was she convulsing?"

"No."

"Any movements at all?"

"No, she just lay there."

"What's she doing now?"

"We put her back to bed."

"Is she awake?"

"Yes, she's talking to us. Says she doesn't know what happened, but her head hurts her."

"Any bruises on her head?"

"Not that we could find."

"Keep her in bed and I'll be by to check her later."

"What if she falls asleep, Dr. Licata?"

"What do you mean?"

"We have orders to keep her up most of the night. She's supposed to have a sleep EEG in the morning," the nurse reminded him.

"I want her to get that EEG in the morning. Don't let her sleep. Make her watch television or something."

It didn't sound like a seizure to Alex, but it was possible that

132

Charlotte could have bumped her head and might need a skull X-ray.

Meanwhile the blood levels of Heather's anticonvulsants returned from the lab. Both Dilantin and phenobarbital were in low therapeutic range. Alex decided to push them. He gave another slow IV infusion of Dilantin through the tubing in Heather's right arm plus an intramuscular injection of phenobarbital in her right buttock.

Blood pressure was stable, respirations spontaneous, but seizure frequency was unchanged. Blood calcium returned normal. There was nothing further to do but wait and watch.

Alex's beeper went off. The call was from division 17. "I just talked to division seventeen," he told the operator.

"I know, Dr. Licata, but they want you again."

What's Charlotte Quinn done now? Alex wondered.

"Dr. Licata?" It was the nurse he had talked to only minutes before. "It's Anthony Zancanelli—he's got a fever."

"How much?"

"It's 38.2."

A little over 102 rectally, Alex thought. Close to 101 orally. Probably from a urinary tract infection or something starting in his lungs. "What are his vital signs?"

"Blood pressure is 130 over 80 and pulse is 120."

Tony's rapidly beating heart had finally declared itself.

"I'll check him when I see Charlotte Quinn," Alex said. "How's she doing?"

"Watching TV."

"Does her head still hurt?"

"Yes, but we can't find any bruises."

"I'll be by as soon as I can," he told her, then returned to Heather Papineau.

10:00 P.M. Alex sat in room 7 and stared, almost transfixed, at Heather. It was a variation on the picture of a doctor at the turn of the century sitting at a child's bedside in a darkened room with a small gaslight burning, blankets heaped on the tiny body, a rag on the child's forehead, a woman in a long apron-clad dress standing next to a basin of water, and the doctor's bearded chin resting on his palm as he stared intensely at the feverish child.

Alex sat in a brightly lit room, surrounded by women in short white dresses, watching a child with tubes coming from almost every orifice, medication being pumped into the tiny body, and ripples of convulsions passing through the child's body every five minutes.

Alex's beeper went off again. Was he the one who'd said tonight would be quiet? "It better not be division seventeen," he told the operator.

"It's division twelve, Dr. Licata."

"Alex, it's Casey. I've finished seeing this boy on division twelve, the one with the severe headache who passed out."

"Subarachnoid hemorrhage?" Alex guessed.

"Not quite. First of all he didn't pass out. Only a funny feeling in his stomach. Second, he doesn't have a headache; it's more of an earache."

"Otitis media," Alex said.

"That's it. He's got an inflamed eardrum!"

"Who was the moron that called a neurologist?"

"It was a nurse's aide that told the nurse about the boy. The nurse called the doctor, who told her to call a neurologist. He never even saw the child."

"Better an ear infection than something in the brain," he told her. "We've got enough to do. I'll come up there and counter-sign your note, then we can go to division seventeen. Charlotte Quinn had one of her spells and may have hit her head; Tony Zancanelli is running a fever."

Before he went upstairs, Alex checked on Heather, who was stable, even though her seizure frequency hadn't changed. He gave her more paraldehyde per rectum and drew a second set of anticonvulsant levels he hoped would return by the time Eli arrived. When he walked out to speak to Heather's mother, he was surprised to find her mood had changed drastically; from a frenzied, agitated state, she was now somber, even quiet. Now, she displayed a total lack of animation, as if her body had been drained of all its energy. It frightened Alex that her mood had changed so dramatically in such a short period of time. No wonder she sees a psychiatrist, he thought.

On division 12, Alex looked briefly at the boy with the

134

"headache." Casey was right, it was an ear infection, and he countersigned her overly elaborate two-page workup. If Alex had seen the boy, he would have written: "Child with otitis media, neurologic exam normal, no evidence of neurologic dysfunction."

They walked to division 17, chatting easily. By the time they arrived, Alex had told Casey about his talk with Mrs. Papineau, his phone conversation with Eli, and the staff neurologist's impending visit.

Charlotte Quinn, with orders not to sleep, was sitting at the nurses' station. She could recount nothing about her latest episode. When Alex checked her, he found her neurologic exam was normal, with no evidence of a scalp bruise. Nevertheless, Charlotte was complaining of a headache, so Alex decided to get skull films. He knew he was practicing defensive medicine, but did it for several reasons: because Charlotte's case was controversial; because her father was a doctor; and because he didn't want to invite trouble by not doing an X-ray, even though the chances of finding a fracture were minimal at best. He left her at the nurses' station, immersed in a paperback romance.

Anthony Zancanelli indeed had a slight fever. Alex looked at Tony's chart; the last note read "unchanged." He checked Tony's ears and throat, lungs, heart, and abdomen, finding nothing abnormal apart from the rapidly beating heart. He ordered a urine culture, two blood cultures, and aspirin for fever over 103.

"What if he develops a severe infection?" Casey asked. "Would you treat him?"

Alex paused. "It's not easy to withhold treatment for an infection in a big hospital like this."

"It would be a shame to keep him alive," Casey said. "Pneumonia is the natural way children like Tony die."

"We'll have that philosophical discussion when he develops the pneumonia," Alex said. "Jim Wellander's his doctor and Jim will not want to treat him."

11:00 P.M. They sat quietly for a few moments on division 17 before returning to the emergency ward. Alex stared at Casey. She could tell he was reacting to her again. She tried to act

135

neutral, but couldn't hide her pleasure. She smiled at him; her eyes widened.

He put his hand to her face and gently touched her cheek, and she put her hand on his.

"Don't let Eli upset you when he comes to the EW," Casey said as she softly caressed Alex's hand.

"I'll tell you something, Casey," Alex said quietly. "I only wish I knew what was wrong with Heather Papineau."

WEDNESDAY

It was after midnight. Eli Lassiter had arrived at the emergency ward on schedule and joined Alex and Casey in room 7. By now, four hours had been charted on Heather's seizure sheet, and the spells had slowed, but only minimally, to thirty-to-sixty-second convulsions every seven minutes. A second set of blood levels for Dilantin and phenobarbital had returned in the high therapeutic range. Alex retold Heather's story while Eli examined the convulsing girl. Amazingly, her examination was almost completely normal. The only abnormality, two upgoing toes when Eli stroked the bottoms of her feet, was common in children during a convulsion; it meant little.

These were not visit rounds, and Eli wasted no time with academic games in discussing Heather's case. "Alex, I have no idea why this girl's seizing."

"Neither do I," Alex admitted.

"Exam is normal. Spinal fluid is clear. All the matabolic parameters—glucose, sodium, calcium—are normal, and now she's getting anticonvulsants in the high therapeutic range. Luckily you were able to intubate her so we didn't lose her because of a respiratory arrest. We can give more Valium but I doubt it'll help. I would push the paraldehyde, though."

"Did we send a magnesium level?" Casey asked.

"No, but that wouldn't be done until tomorrow anyway," Alex said.

"Make sure they do one," Eli said. Since arriving in the EW, Eli had directed all his attention to Heather, but now it was time to deal with Alex, and Eli immediately asked him the question Alex knew he would have to answer. "Alex, why didn't you admit the girl when you saw her Sunday night?"

"She didn't need admission," he said firmly. "She had a seizure that evening and some local doc sent her with a note that she had to be admitted. I send five children a week from the EW with stories like hers. They get anticonvulsants, an EEG, skull films, and an appointment for seizure clinic."

"Why was the mother so upset, demanding that I see the girl tonight?"

"Evidently the child was born out of wedlock and the mother cares for the child herself. There may be some maternal guilt involved," Alex said. "Furthermore, the mother is emotionally labile. Here in the EW, she's gone from hysteria to almost being mute. She told me she's under psychiatric care."

Eli's tall figure dominated the trio. "You're telling me the mother is emotionally unstable and her relationship with her daughter is not a healthy one. I accept that." Eli didn't have the edge of a long lab coat to maneuver between his nervous fingers, so he pulled at his belt buckle instead. "Furthermore, you say Heather is no different from countless other children we see and send home. Fine. But the facts are, no matter how crazy the mother is, her daughter lies before us in status epilepticus, convulsions which we can't control despite massive doses of medication, and we have no idea why. Is there something you might have missed in the history? What did the mother say on the phone when she called you yesterday?"

Casey watched Alex. His face was drawn. Tiny wrinkles on his forehead, kept there by the excitement of the situation, flattened, as if the energy had been drained from them. Although he'd been expecting Eli's question, it was difficult

138

nonetheless. Alex knew he had not made a mistake in not admitting Heather on Sunday night. Yet, the facts remained: he had seen a girl in the EW and refused her admission, only to have her return in status epilepticus. Maybe he had missed something. But what? Granted he had been irritated at being called to the hospital just when he had finally gotten into bed with his wife, but even if he had seen Heather in midafternoon, he wouldn't have admitted her to the hospital. He had been rude to the mother, but the rudeness hadn't precipitated the girl's seizures. Something else must have happened.

"Eli," Alex answered slowly, "of course I could have missed something, but I don't think I did. Yesterday, when the mother called, she hadn't even bothered to fill the anticonvulsant prescription. I ordered her to go to the drugstore and get the phenobarbital at once."

Eli didn't react. He empathized with Alex's predicament and knew Alex was caught up in circumstance, but he couldn't bring himself to sympathize with the resident. Eli, too, had been caught up in his own circumstances—lab work not successful, clinical skills rusty—and Alex had not been easy on him during rounds.

They went to talk with the mother.

"This is Dr. Lassiter, Mrs. Papineau—he's the staff neurologist I mentioned to you. This is Dr. Lilstrom, a student on the neurology service."

"What do you think, Dr. Lassiter?" the mother asked. Mrs. Papineau was no longer excited or overly subdued. In fact, she looked and spoke quite normally. "Why has this happened to Heather?"

"I don't know," was all Eli could say.

"I'm very upset with Dr. Licata," she said, as if Alex were not standing next to her. "If he'd admitted Heather on Sunday night, she'd be all right."

Alex's jaw tightened as he waited for Eli's response.

"I've spoken at length to Dr. Licata and reviewed Heather's case in detail. There was no reason to admit her on Sunday. We send many children like Heather from the emergency ward each week." Eli would not speak against Alex, both because as staff physician, he supported the house staff and because he agreed with Alex's handling of the case. Alex was thankful for Eli's response.

Mrs. Papineau realized accusations were now of little help. "What are you going to do with Heather, Dr. Lassiter?"

"We'll put her on division seventeen in the critical care room and try to bring her seizures under control. There's no evidence of neurologic damage, and once the seizures stop, she should be all right. Then, hopefully, we'll be able to find out why this happened. Mrs. Papineau, is there anything you can tell us about Heather, any detail you might have overlooked before?"

"Nothing more than I've told Dr. Licata."

"Heather does well in school? She's never had seizures or blackout spells before? There's no one in the family with seizures?"

"Not in my family. I don't know much about the father's side. She does fine in the special school she attends."

"Special school?"

"Yes, she's in a school for slow learners, as I told Dr. Licata."

Both Eli and Casey were startled. Alex had never mentioned Heather's learning problems. The mother had mentioned it Sunday night, but Alex brushed it aside; he had made no note of it in the chart.

Eli shot a surprised look at Alex, then turned back to Mrs. Papineau. Alex's jaw tightened again. "How long has she been in the special school?" Eli asked the mother.

"Since first grade. They say she has a learning disability."

Now that a flaw in Alex's history had been discovered, Eli was forced to reask a large number of questions, to actually retake the medical history. Alex did that frequently with a medical student, but rarely was it done with the chief resident.

Alex knew that when a second doctor took a history, he often discovered something new. It was a classic phenomenon. The ward visit or chief resident was told a key piece of information the parent didn't mention during the prolonged initial history-taking. The first doctor would mutter to himself, "Why didn't

140

you tell me that?" Yet, in Heather's instance, the mother only repeated what she'd told Alex Sunday night. Then Eli uncovered a more important part of Heather's history. The girl had had meningitis at age two.

"Does the special school explain something about the seizures?" the mother asked.

"That and the meningitis may explain why Heather had her seizure on Sunday night," Eli replied, "but it doesn't explain why she's having prolonged seizures today."

As they left Mrs. Papineau and walked back to room 7, Eli immediately turned to the chief resident. "Jesus Christ, Alex! How in the world did you miss a meningitis at age two and the fact that she goes to a school for slow learners?"

"I don't know," Alex said weakly. How could he tell Eli what happened on Sunday night?

"And you're the chief resident," Eli said. "Who knows what else you missed on Sunday night?" Eli thought out loud. "It's clear the meningitis resulted in the learning disability and an increased risk to develop a seizure disorder; the problem is, that doesn't explain why we can't stop them." Alex's lack of history added a strange unknown to the case, but Eli could think of nothing to do but monitor Heather's convulsions.

"Should we anesthetize her?" Alex asked tentatively. General anesthesia would stop the convulsive movements of her body, though it might not stop the abnormal electrical discharges in her brain that caused the seizures.

"It's too early. Vital signs are stable and we have control of her airway. I would opt for watching her through the night, continue with Dilantin and phenobarbital, get blood levels, and push paraldehyde."

"How about steriods?"

"I wouldn't start cortisone until the morning," Eli said. He looked at his watch, then at Alex. "And I bet tomorrow we find that Charlotte's EEG is abnormal."

Alex remained silent. There was nothing for him to say, no explanations he could give. And at the moment, nothing he could do to dispel the uneasiness that grew inside him.

Eli returned briefly to Mrs. Papineau, then left the emergency ward.

1:00 A.M. Five people—an escort, a nurse, a respiratory thera-pist, a medical student, and a doctor—surrounded Heather Papi-neau as she was wheeled onto division 17. Her bed was steered into the critical care room and placed next to the boy recovering from brain surgery for his cerebellar tumor. The boy had been awake since late afternoon and was trying to sleep amid the noise of a room that was always awake.

Heather had to be transferred from the emergency room bed to the bed in the critical care room. The beds were placed next to each other and the sheet on which she lay freed from the mattress. Three people leaned across the empty, critical care room bed and grabbed the sheet; three people held the other side of the sheet. The IV bottles and tubing were transferred to poles on the empty bed, the urine collecting bag and its tubing moved, and the respiratory therapist stood at the head of the bed guarding the endotracheal tube. One nurse called out, "One, two, three, go!" and Heather was transferred to her new bed. It was a job well done, for Alex had seen urinary catheters, IV lines, chest tubes, and endotracheal tubes torn from their orifices during such transfers.

Alex spoke to the nurse who would care for Heather during the night. He explained the seizure chart, clarified medications, and ordered blood tests to be done during the night and in the morning. Alex had thought of asking Casey to write the brief admitting note in Heather's chart, but it was after one o'clock in the morning, and it would take her too long; so he did it himself.

Heather would spend the night convulsing every five to ten minutes despite anticonvulsants that saturated her body tissues. She would not regain consciousness. Her heartbeat, blood pres-sure, respirations, and blood tests would be within normal range. Aspirin, given via rectal suppository, would help control her elevated temperature. At 8:00 A.M. on morning rounds, she would look exactly the same as she had six hours previously, when Alex left the critical care room to write the admitting note in her chart.

"What's wrong with that girl?" Charlotte Quinn asked Alex as he left the critical care room.

Alex was about to tell Charlotte to get into bed, but then he remembered she had to be kept awake for the sleep EEG.

"She's having problems with seizures, Charlotte," he said.

"Why's she in that room?" Charlotte had closed her book and was looking at him.

"The seizures aren't under good control."

"Could that happen to me?"

"What do you think?" he asked, almost challenging her.

"Mmm . . . I don't think so."

"Why not?"

"My seizures are different. I would never let that happen."

"You mean you can control your seizures?" Alex looked directly at the girl.

Charlotte was silent.

Alex persisted. "Why couldn't it happen to you, Charlotte?"

"My seizures are different," she repeated and walked away.

Alex might have been sloppy in dealing with Heather Papineau, but the more he observed Charlotte Quinn, the more he was convinced her spells were not real.

He sat down to finish his note, and Casey joined him.

"Why do you think Heather's in status?" she asked.

"I don't know."

"Will she be all right?"

He paused. "I hope so."

"Alex, how could you have missed the history of meningitis and her learning disability?" Casey looked him straight in the eye.

Alex smiled.

"Why the smile?"

"Do you really want to know?"

"If you really want to tell me."

"Okay. Let's make a final check of the ward, then you can walk me down to the hospital entrance."

The ward was quiet except for activity in the critical care room. Charlotte Quinn was talking to one of the nurses in the hall. Tony Zancanelli's pulse had slowed and he wasn't feverish. "They probably gave him some aspirin," Alex said to Casey. Heather Papineau was unchanged. Alex spoke with Mrs. Papineau, who now stood outside the critical care room. He found the mother subdued, relieved by the vision of Heather surrounded by medical personnel.

Alex and Casey left division 17 and waited for the elevator. When it finally came, it was empty.

Unlike most people on elevators, they didn't look at their shoes or the flashing floor numbers above the door. They looked at each other. No barriers now, Alex stared intently into Casey's face. The angular face with no makeup and brown hair piled on the head behind it was beautiful. Casey's eyes were as wide as Alex had ever seen them; they almost exploded onto her face. Alex moved his hand toward Casey and she stepped closer to him. Finally, he took her into his arms and they kissed. It was a wonderful kiss. When the elevator door opened they were still embracing. Luckily it was one-thirty in the morning and they walked hand in hand down the empty corridor.

"I was screwing my wife," Alex said.

"What?"

"Sunday night. When I got called to see Heather. I was in bed with Mellissa. There was absolutely no reason for me to even go to the emergency ward. It really pissed me off."

"But you were on duty, Alex. You knew you could get a call."

"Sure, and if it had been an emergency, I wouldn't have minded; just an occupational hazard. But a routine seizure, hell. Even if I had known the history I wouldn't have admitted her."

They walked outside in the direction of Alex's apartment house, the drone of a compressor from the nearby power plant filling the night. They walked with their arms around each other; each of their arms was tucked snugly underneath the other's white hospital jacket. They walked naturally, easily, as if they had been close for years.

"What are you going to do about Heather Papineau and Eli Lassiter?" Casey asked.

"I don't know," Alex said. "What can I do?" Alex could feel Casey's honest concern for him, and he held her even closer.

"Just my luck Charlotte's EEG will be abnormal tomorrow," Alex added as they approached his apartment house.

"Don't worry about it, Alex."

But even the joy of his newborn intimacy with Casey couldn't dispel his unease. He had made mistakes early in his medical training, but they had never bothered him; they were the honest errors of learning. Heather was the first patient he had cared for who might actually be harmed by one of his mistakes.

"But it wasn't a mistake!" Alex said out loud.

"I know it wasn't, Alex." Casey knew exactly what he was thinking.

Then Alex thought about Charlotte and his wanting to spend a few years in the laboratory. He could feel a pain in the upper part of his back; an aching sensation. He knew what it was—he was scared. The last thing he wanted to do at that moment was to leave Casey.

"Casey," Alex said. "Hold me. Hold me as tight as you can."

BJ Balsiger's head was engulfed by a giant sphere. Next to the hard table on which he lay, a computer was ready to analyze the X-rays that would be shot through the boy's head. The CAT scan was turned on, and it began to analyze the millions of tiny deflections imposed on the X-rays by BJ's brain.

In another room, Charlotte Quinn lay sleeping on a softer table, with almost two dozen tiny electrodes pasted to her head. As she slept, thin steel pens poured their ink onto the rolling paper, shifting when the electricity shifted in her brain. After an hour's recording, a pile of paper as thick as a phonebook would be generated, and etched onto the paper there would or would not be tiny blips from the electrodes that recorded the electrical activity of the temporal lobes: no blips, no evidence of temporal lobe epilepsy.

Wednesday's rounds came quickly for Alex. He had been called hourly throughout the night and into the morning with Heather Papineau's blood test results, changes in blood pressure and breathing habits, and variations in type and frequency of seizures. Now he stood at her bed, eyeing the seizure chart. No change. She was still having one seizure every five or ten minutes, lasting thirty to sixty seconds. Blood levels of anticonvulsants were in maximal therapeutic range. Alex retold Heather's history to Jim, Mo, Louise, and Casey, including his own failure to learn the girl's past history. Mo and Jim sympathized with Alex; each could remember a time they had missed something in a child's history. Besides, Heather's history of meningitis didn't seem related to her continual seizures. Nevertheless, they could tell it bothered Alex. Alex looked briefly at Casey and for an instant their eyes met. For them nothing else was needed. Thank God you're here, Alex thought to himself. Then he returned to Heather Papineau.

"Jim, take her as your case," he said.

Everyone watched as Jim examined Heather. His neurologic exam was weaker than his general exam, but he called both normal apart from the two upgoing toes.

"Find a source for her fever?" Alex asked.

"No."

"You're sure the spinal fluid was normal?" Mo Corning asked.

"Yes," Alex responded. Everyone watched Alex, waiting for a pithy statement, a new direction to take, a diagnosis no one else had considered, but he disappointed them. "I don't know what's happening to this girl," he said. "Mo, this is no academic exercise. A girl's seizing in front of you—what would you do? Louise, you've seen many children with seizures on division seventeen. Any ideas? Jim, did we overlook something? Casey, check the list you made for BJ Balsiger. Does anything fit Heather?"

Casey pulled the list from inside her lab pocket and scanned it. Louise put her hand on her chin and looked up. Jim didn't react. Finally Mo spoke.

"I'd stop her seizures with general anesthesia."

"What if she starts seizing again when the anesthesia wears off?" Alex countered.

Mo didn't answer.

"How long would you put her under? A few hours? A day? Two days? Prolonged general anesthesia can be dangerous." Mo shrugged his shoulders. Alex had made his point. "It's not a bad idea, Mo, but it's premature."

"What would you do, Alex?" Mo asked.

Alex may not have known what was wrong with Heather, but he knew what he'd do. "First I'd continue to search for the cause of her status, check metabolic parameters, watch for localizing

146

neurologic signs. Second, I'd make sure she doesn't get into trouble, either cardiovascularly or respiratory-wise." Alex thought for a moment. "I don't see how an arteriogram or CAT scan could help us."

"What about an EEG?" Jim asked.

"Not a bad idea. It'll only show the convulsions, but it might give us a clue about which medications to use."

"Could she be developing cerebral edema?" Mo asked.

"Yes. Status sometimes causes brain swelling," Alex agreed. "Let's give her some steroids to treat that possibility."

"What anticonvulsants is she getting?" Casey asked.

"Dilantin, phenobarb, and paraldehyde."

"How about valproate?"

"I'd be afraid to give it IV, and since she can't swallow, she can't take it by mouth."

"We could put down a nasogastric tube to get it into her stomach," Louise suggested.

"Right. And we won't have to worry about putting the tube into her lungs by mistake because she has a tube down her trachea already," Alex said.

"Shall I get an NG tube?" Louise asked.

"Sure, go ahead."

"What will you do if we can't stop her seizures and we can't find the cause?" Mo asked.

"Then I'd try general anesthesia. If we're lucky, the seizures won't start up again when the anesthesia wears off."

"Okay," Mo said. "Steroids, NG tube, valproate, EEG, anticonvulsants, and wait."

Casey looked at Mo. "You sound like a football quarterback."

Mo smiled.

"Steroids. I'd give her four milligrams of Decadron IV every four hours," Jim suggested, then he turned to Alex. "What did Eli say about her?"

"He didn't have anything to add. He wants to wait before we try general anesthesia. He was really upset with me for not taking a good history."

"Remember the boy with the cerebellar tumor?" Louise

147

interjected. "Here he is, sitting up in bed, watching television and wondering when he can go home. It was an astrocytoma; they got it all out."

"I wouldn't mind seeing Heather sitting up in bed ready to leave," Alex said.

Tony Zancanelli's fever had risen to 102 rectally. Jim had just heard about the fever and was checking the chart for his previous notes. They were one-word notes that read: "Unchanged." Jim knew the fever meant infection. It also meant a chance for Tony to die. He didn't want to save Tony from a natural infection, and felt it his duty to prevent the boy from being treated. A strange duty for a physician.

"When did he get the fever?" Jim asked.

"They called me last night," Alex said. "I couldn't find anything. We drew some blood cultures and sent off a urine."

Jim looked at the urine emptying from the catheter, a piece of tubing pushed through the boy's penis into his bladder. It was clear, no obvious infection, so the source of Tony's fever was probably the boy's lungs. Jim placed his stethoscope on the boy's chest, but could hear only a few crackles intermixed with normal breath sounds.

"I don't find anything on exam," Jim said.

"Should we give him antibiotics?" Louise asked.

"No, I don't want to treat an infection until I know what it is. If we give him antibiotics now, a resistant organism might grow."

"How about a chest X-ray?" Mo asked.

"Not now, his lungs sound clear."

Alex looked at Casey. They were not surprised by Jim's inaction. Alex could have insisted on treatment or a more vigorous investigation, but he agreed with Jim's approach.

Jim wrote a detailed note on Tony's chart, ordering aspirin suppositories every four hours to mask the fever that would accompany any severe infection that developed. "We'll get preliminary results of the urine and blood cultures this evening," Jim said, ending the discussion, and they moved down the corridor toward the two Susies.

"How do you feel this morning?" Alex asked Casey as they walked.

148

"Fine. One of the most exciting nights on call I've had."

"A lot of students think neurology's boring."

"Depends on the chief resident," Casey smiled.

As usual, Susie K and Susie W provided relief from the other patients on the neurology service, and the group left them in a better mood.

Next they discussed the nine-month-old hypotonic, floppy infant, who lay outside the operating room waiting for a muscle biopsy. A piece of muscle would be taken from the boy's thigh and examined under the pathologist's microscope to discover why the child was weak.

"We'll see the muscle biopsy tomorrow at brain cutting," Mo said.

"Watch it, Mo!" Alex said with a smile. "The staff doesn't like to call it brain cutting. We're supposed to call it the neuropathology conference."

"For me, it'll always be brain cutting," Mo said.

"I know. Where's Clark Kent?"

Louise looked at her clipboard. "Down in X-ray."

"The easiest way to make rounds," Jim said, "is to schedule all the kids for tests in the morning, then you don't have to see them. Today we've missed Charlotte Quinn, BJ Balsiger, the infant with hypotonia, and Clark Kent Gatewood." They all laughed.

Eli Lassiter walked onto the ward, looking confident and relaxed. He was anxious to see Charlotte Quinn's EEG, certain it would be abnormal, and BJ Balsiger's CAT scan, which he hoped would be abnormal. Heather Papineau's seizures bothered him, but he knew everything was being done and he couldn't help enjoying the fact that they were a thorn in Alex Licata's side. "Let's look at Heather first," Eli suggested.

The graph of her seizures hadn't flattened in the past ten hours. After examining Heather briefly, Eli turned to Alex. "What are you doing for her?"

"She's getting IV steroids and Valproate via NG tube. She'll get an EEG later today. We're monitoring anticonvulsant levels and metabolic parameters. If she doesn't stop, we may have to try general anesthesia."

"Sounds good."

149

"What do you think's wrong with her, Eli?"

"I'm not sure, perhaps a metabolic derangement."

"Which one? We've checked everything, they're all normal."

"Let's see how she does today." Eli had expected Heather's seizures to have diminished by morning, and, like Alex, didn't know why they continued. But he had other things on his mind. "Time to check Charlotte Quinn's EEG," he announced.

"Do you want to hear about the others on the ward?" Alex asked.

"Are there problems?"

"Not really. Tony Zancanelli has a slight fever."

They left Louise on division 17 and walked to the EEG unit. Mo and Jim spoke about Heather's prolonged convulsions and the chance that they might cause brain damage. Eli talked with Casey about her ultimate plans in medicine. Alex walked alone, the problems of the ward flashing through his mind.

Charlotte Quinn's EEG lay on a table in the main reading room of the EEG unit. A card with the technician's interpretation was attached to its first page, and Eli could have looked at the bottom line to see whether the technician had checked "normal" or "abnormal." Purposely he turned the card over without looking, anxious to interpret the EEG himself. He began to turn the pages while Alex looked over his shoulder. Of their group, only Eli, Alex, and Mo understood the EEG. Jim and Casey idly watched the undulating lines pass, occasionally interrupting Eli with a question.

"So far I haven't seen anything," Alex commented.

"I agree, but look, she hasn't fallen asleep yet," Eli said, pointing to the trace.

Soon the lines began to change configuration, as the brainwaves became deeper, slower, and more undulating.

"Now she's getting drowsy," Eli said.

Alex carefully scanned the two lines that recorded electricity from the temporal lobe. If there was evidence of temporal lobe epilepsy, tiny blips or spikes would interrupt the smooth flow of these lines. There were other, larger, interruptions on the tracing, but when Mo asked about them, Alex told him they represented normal eye movements or muscle twitching.

150

Alex saw it first. He didn't say anything, but there was an occasional spike over the left temporal area. Initially, he thought it was only the electrical activity of the heart, projected up to the head and appearing on the EEG, but he calculated the rate of the spikes; it was obvious the rate was not the regular eighty-per-minute pace of Charlotte's heart. It was a more erratic electrical discharge, one compatible with the diagnosis of temporal lobe epilepsy.

Finally Eli reacted. "There's something abnormal in the left temporal area. Wouldn't you say, Alex?"

"Let's see what she does in the other leads," Alex said half-heartedly.

When the leads changed to record electrical activity of the temporal lobe from a different perspective, the abnormality became more apparent. Now Mo saw it. "No question, there's something going on in the left temporal lobe," he said.

Casey watched Alex. She would have known Charlotte's EEG was abnormal just by looking at his face.

"We bet a fifth of whiskey, didn't we?" Alex said to Eli. "What kind do you want?"

"Makes no difference—let Mo buy it and you can reimburse him."

What must Eli think of me now? Alex wondered. Not a mature clinician, but a cocky resident who couldn't recognize a temporal lobe seizure in one patient and who didn't know how to take a history from the mother of another one.

Casey came up to Alex as they left the EEG unit. "We'll talk at lunch," Alex said as he gave a tug on her white jacket.

On the way to check BJ Balsiger's CAT scan, the conversations began again. Eli talked with Casey, this time national politics and women's lib, while Jim and Mo discussed medications they would now use to control Charlotte Quinn's strange temporal lobe seizures. They were impressed by the value of a sleep EEG; if Charlotte's EEG had been done while she was awake, no abnormality would have appeared. As before, Alex walked alone, this time brooding about Charlotte Quinn. Although there was no question that her EEG was abnormal, he still had doubts about her seizures. Yet, he realized Eli might be right, temporal lobe epilepsy could take the strangest forms.

Alex didn't mind losing the whiskey. He had lost bets about patients and their diagnoses before, but he hated losing to Eli Lassiter, especially since he was certain that Eli was just lucky.

Once in the X-ray department, the radiologist in charge was summoned to interpret BJ Balsiger's CAT scan.

"Is there something in the left frontal tube?" Eli asked.

"No."

"Is there an asymmetry of the lateral ventricles?" Mo wondered.

"No."

"Why is there a difference in the density of the right and left parietal lobe?" Jim asked.

"Artifact."

"Is the size of the third ventricle normal?" Casey asked.

"Yes."

"No abnormalities, not even a question of an abnormality?" Eli asked.

"Right. Perfectly normal."

"Looks like he gets an arteriogram this afternoon," Casey said.

"I was sure we'd see something abnormal," Eli said as he fingered his lab coat.

"They can't all be as easy as Charlotte Quinn," Alex said with a noticeable hint of pleasure in his voice.

"Or as easy as Heather Papineau," Eli answered immediately.

"It's a shame mother nature hasn't been more cooperative for you," Casey said as she sat with Alex in the hospital cafeteria for the second day in a row.

Alex smiled a half-smile and shrugged his shoulders.

Casey looked straight into his eyes. "Are you all right, Alex?" she asked gently, a bit concerned.

He took her hand and gave it a squeeze. The first time Casey had touched his hand, he had almost blushed; now it was so natural.

"I've never been through this before," Alex admitted. "I didn't mean to get into a direct confrontation with Eli over two cases, but that's what's happened. He must think I'm a real moron. Shit, Casey, no one would have admitted Heather Papineau to the hospital, believe me. And Charlotte—how could I have screwed that one up?"

"Is that all that's bothering you, Alex?"

"You know that can't be all, Casey." He looked away from the female medical student who was rotating through the neurology service. "I'm tired," he said. "They called me every hour last night to give me reports about Heather Papineau. You can imagine how well I slept in between calls. We do have to talk, Casey. We both know that, but right now just sit with me."

"I wouldn't want to be sitting anywhere else."

Alex took a deep breath and sat up in his chair. "Have you figured out what's wrong with BJ Balsiger, yet?" he asked a bit more animated.

"No," Casey said. "Do you think BJ's arteriogram will show something?"

"I predict BJ's arteriogram will be normal," Alex said with a trace of his former cockiness. "Nothing of substance will be said at grand rounds tomorrow, and he'll leave the hospital without a diagnosis."

"That's pessimistic," Casey said.

"It's realistic," Alex countered.

Casey took out her list. As she reached into her pocket, Alex thought of his arm under her white jacket. "We haven't discussed these diseases in detail, yet."

"You've got over two dozen diseases on that list; it would take two months to discuss them in detail," Alex said.

"What if I read a disease and you tell me why he can't have it?" Alex agreed. Casey began to read from her list, and Alex answered without hesitation. His answers fell into one of four categories: BJ was too old, BJ was too young, a test for the disease had proved negative, or the disease was untreatable and could only be diagnosed at autopsy.

"Alex, I bet we've mentioned his disease."

"Maybe. It's certainly a comprehensive list. You must have taken it from the largest textbook of pediatric neurology you could find."

"It means we'll only have a diagnosis after BJ dies."

"Or one of the tests was negative when it should have been positive."

"Would you repeat all the tests?" she asked him.

"We're repeating some now—arteriogram, EEG. If there's a simple test that can be repeated, I would."

"O.K. Now that we've solved BJ Balsiger," Casey said, "how about Heather Papineau?"

"I wish I knew. We've done everything to stop her seizures short of general anesthesia. It's important not to panic and do something that could hurt her. There's no evidence of brain damage, but we won't know for sure until she wakes up."

"What if she never wakes up?"

"Dies?"

"No, keeps on seizing."

"That won't happen," Alex told her. "People live with continual partial seizures of an extremity, but not continual generalized seizures."

"Will she need the general anesthesia?"

"Can't say. Maybe the steroids will help her."

"Alex, please don't let Eli upset you about Heather. Remember it's not your fault she's in status epilepticus."

"I know. Anyway, Eli was just lucky that Charlotte's EEG was abnormal."

"Could Charlotte's seizures still be hysterical?"

"Yes, but first she'll need a trial of anticonvulsants. That'll take months. By then who knows where I'll be?" That was the hardest question for Alex and he couldn't help saying it. Casey kept her promise; she stayed to her discussion of medicine.

"Where will Tony Zancanelli be?"

"Hopefully he'll be dead."

"What did you think of Jim's performance at rounds?" she asked.

"Pretty good. I would've done the same thing. We can't be too vigorous with Tony."

"Some people might say we're withholding medical care," she suggested.

"Not at this stage. Jim's only waiting to see if Tony's fever represents an infection."

"But Jim's masking the fever by giving aspirin."

154

"Aspirin will mask a low fever, but if Tony really gets sick, it won't make a difference. Then we'll decide whether to treat him."

"You're so nonchalant about him, Alex."

"Tony's a permanently brain-damaged child with no hope for recovery who may be developing a secondary infection. If he wasn't in the hospital, how do you think a child like Tony would die? He'd die from an infection. I've got live people on the ward to worry about," Alex said as he stared into Casey's eyes. "Heather Papineau, Charlotte Quinn, BJ Balsiger. And you."

"I thought you didn't want to talk about that."

"I didn't. But I can't help thinking about it."

"It was nice last night, Alex."

"I know."

"I didn't want you to leave me," she said softly.

"I felt the same way."

"Was your wife awake when you came home?"

"Mellissa was asleep," Alex said, and when he heard himself say his wife's name, he knew it was time to end the conversation and return to division 17.

Alex had barely had time to speak to Mellissa since running from the cafeteria the night before. He had kissed her at two o'clock in the morning when he finally crawled into bed, but when the phone began ringing with hourly reports about Heather, Alex took the phone from the bedroom and slept on the couch so Mellissa wouldn't be disturbed. In the morning, Mellissa knew Alex had had a difficult night and she wished they would leave her husband alone, let him be with his family where he belonged. At breakfast, Alex didn't want to talk about the girl they kept calling him about during the night. Mellissa understood. She also knew that tonight Alex would be so tired he would only want to sleep. He deserved the sleep, she thought. Soon it would be over. Maybe she would make him one of his favorite dinners.

BJ Balsiger's parents sat in his empty room on division 17. The sheets on the boy's bed were fresh, tucked tightly under the mattress. Toys belonging to the hospital had been neatly arranged on the floor by Florence Balsiger. A teddy bear, brought from home, sat alone on the bed next to the pillow. If BJ's parents would have taken the teddy bear and left, there would be nothing about the room unique to BJ.

Casey Lilstrom entered the room.

"They told me BJ was down having an arteriogram," Dennis Balsiger said. "That means the CAT scan this morning was normal."

"Right—nothing on it except the picture of a normal brain."

"Do you know what the arteriogram showed?" the mother asked.

"No, it should be done shortly."

"I'm sure it'll be normal," the father said.

"Why?" his wife asked.

"If they were going to find something abnormal about BJ's brain besides the EEG, they would have found it a long time ago."

"New things turn up, Dennis, a test that was negative before could turn positive."

"BJ's problem is too complicated, Flo. He was born too early. Like polio, before the vaccine there was no treatment; if a child got polio bad and was unlucky, he lived in an iron lung; if he was lucky, he died. BJ is lying in an iron lung."

"Don't say it, Dennis."

"I can't help it."

"But don't believe it, Dennis."

"I'm sorry, Flo."

"Aren't you going to wait for the results of the arteriogram?"

"They'll be normal."

"And grand rounds tomorrow?"

"Nothing new will be said."

Casey looked at Florence Balsiger's face. It was expressionless. BJ's mother sat motionless in her chair, her body tense. Casey shifted to the father; his weatherbeaten face was relaxed, serene. His body molded itself into his chair like a person sitting on a large pillow. His wife barely communicated with her chair, like a round stone on a table.

"Dennis, have you given up hope?"

156

Her husband didn't answer.

"I haven't. Even if I have to be alone, I'm not going to desert BJ."

The father sat up in his chair, leaned forward, and took his wife's hand. "What are you going to do different than me, Flo?"

His wife didn't answer.

"Give him medications, take him to the doctor, give permission for more tests? Play with him, send him to a special school, love him?"

She pressed his hands to comfort him.

"I'm going to do all those things, Flo, and whatever else we have to do. But our son is lying in an iron lung. He missed his chance for the vaccine, Flo. He missed it."

The mother's body stiffened even more. "Don't give up hope, Dennis. Don't leave me alone."

The couple sat in silence, holding onto each other, oblivious to Casey's presence. The silence was interrupted by the noise of wheels and the shaking of metal bars. BJ was wheeled into his room. An IV bottle was connected to his arm, a bandage pasted over his groin where the catheter had been inserted for arteriography. He was transferred to his bed by a nurse who accompanied him from arteriography. She checked the bandage for bleeding, then began to wheel the empty bed from the room. Casey grabbed BJ's chart from the moving bed and began to look through it.

"Anything there about the arteriography?" the mother asked.

Casey found a scribbled note from the radiologist: "Four-vessel arteriography performed without complication, no abnormalities seen." Casey purposely didn't react to the note.

"Nothing here in the chart, Mrs. Balsiger. I'll call radiology."

Casey left the room. At that moment she couldn't tell them that the arteriogram was normal. Besides, she wanted first to check with the radiologist; perhaps he had seen a subtle abnormality that would appear in the final interpretation.

She phoned the radiologist only to find the arteriogram was indeed normal. She tried to coax doubt from him but he was

157

firm about his interpretation and saw no reason to expect an abnormality on the final reading.

Casey returned to the parents. "I just called the radiologist. He said the arteriogram was normal."

"Is that the final reading?" the mother asked.

"No, but he doesn't expect to discover anything when he checks the films later." Casey left BJ with his parents and walked slowly to the nurses' station.

It was early afternoon. Heather Papineau continued to convulse despite the valproate and steroids, and her seizure chart was monotonous in its graphic display of her convulsions. Luckily there were no problems with blood pressure, heart rate, or respiration.

A technician rolled a portable EEG machine into the critical care room and began attaching electrodes to Heather's head, no easy task given the frequency of the seizures and the many other machines surrounding the girl.

Mo, Jim, and Alex stood at Heather's bedside. Mo looked through Heather's chart as Jim examined the seizure record and Alex stared at the girl. Between seizures, Mo performed a quick neurologic exam, tapping elbow, wrist, knee, and ankle with his rubber hammer to test reflexes. He lifted each limb and let it fall to check for differences in muscle tone that might betray an underlying paralysis. He pushed back the girl's eyelids, aimed his light into her eyes to check pupillary reaction, and rotated her head to test eye movement. Finally he took a key from his pocket and stroked the bottoms of her feet. Both toes went up.

"Except for the upgoing toes, I still don't find anything on her exam," Mo said.

"No change in the seizure frequency either," Jim added. "She's sure getting a load of anticonvulsants."

Alex tapped the girl's reflexes but he didn't watch for the response. He tapped to occupy his hands while he thought, an oblique form of communication with the girl. Unfortunately, nothing new came to his mind.

"I can't get a recording," the technician said.

Alex looked at the EEG. It was a disorganized splash of ink

that covered the entire record, making the paper totally black. The pens that responded to impulses from the electrodes were very sensitive; muscle movement during a seizure generated enormous amounts of electricity and obliterated any impulses coming from the brain. It was impossible to record cerebral electricity while the girl seized.

"What does it show between seizures?" Alex asked.

"I don't know. I shut off the machine to clean the ink when she started to convulse."

"Turn it on just after she finishes a seizure."

The EEG between seizures showed diffuse, large, slow waves, a typical interseizure pattern. There were no localizing features.

"Mo, how long before she starts seizing again?" Alex asked.

"About two and a half minutes." Mo had been monitoring the spells on his wristwatch and found they occurred at six-minute intervals.

"Let us know when we get closer."

"One minute," Mo said.

The slow wave pattern didn't change.

"Thirty seconds."

Still no change.

"Fifteen seconds."

"There it is!" Alex shouted.

Heather began seizing and the pens once again splashed ink over the entire record. The technician stopped the machine and they examined the tracing.

"Fifteen seconds before she convulses, there's a buildup of electrical activity," Alex pointed out. "The slow wave pattern disappears, there are sharp waves, then fast activity just before the seizure and the obliteration of the record."

"What does it mean?" Jim asked.

"The buildup occurs on both sides and is symmetrical. That means there isn't a single focus that's triggering her seizures; it's a diffuse abnormality affecting the entire brain. That's why we don't find any abnormalities on exam. This speaks against a focal process and supports a generalized, or metabolic, derangement."

"Do we treat her differently?" Jim asked.

"I don't think so," Alex said.

"What about Zarontin?" Mo suggested. "It's one of the few classes of anticonvulsants we haven't used, and it often helps nonfocal, generalized seizures. We could put it down her nasogastric tube."

"Should I finish the EEG?" the technician asked.

"No, that's enough," Alex decided.

"But I can't turn in only two minutes of record," the technician protested.

"Turn it in and if anyone gives you trouble, have them call me."

"Should I start the Zarontin?" Jim interrupted. "She's already getting Dilantin, phenobarb, paraldehyde, valproate, and steroids."

"Maybe we're giving her too much medication," Mo said. "Some people seize *because of* their anticonvulsants."

"It's true, but it's rare," Alex commented. "Anyway, it's too early in Heather's course, and her anticonvulsants are still in therapeutic range. She is getting a lot of meds, though. How about stopping her paraldehyde and adding Zarontin?"

"Sounds good," Mo agreed. "When will you go to general anesthesia?"

"I'd do it tomorrow," Alex told him, "but it depends on Eli. Anesthesia doesn't like to put kids under for seizures. He'll need to contact them this afternoon and convince them for tomorrow."

Heather's mother joined the three doctors at her daughter's bedside while the EEG technician unpasted electrodes from the girl's head.

"Mrs. Papineau, this is Dr. Corning and Dr. Wellander, two other doctors here on the neurology ward helping to care for Heather."

The mother nodded. "How's she doing?"

"About the same. Her seizures haven't slowed down, but her blood pressure and breathing are under good control. She may get general anesthesia tomorrow if she's not better."

Mrs. Papineau watched on as the girl began another convulsion. The muscles in her arms and legs contracted violently as the abnormal burst of electricity passed through her brain.

"Dr. Licata, I want to ask you something," Mrs. Papineau said. "Do you think it's possible Heather's problem is in her muscles instead of her brain?"

"What do you mean?"

"During the convulsions it's the muscles that twitch and contract. Her head doesn't even move."

"But the brain controls the muscles," Alex told her. "We recorded abnormal brainwaves on the EEG when she had a convulsion."

"You're sure?"

"Positive. Believe me, if there's one thing I know, it's that Heather's problem is in her brain, not her muscles." Alex was struck by Mrs. Papineau's misconceptions about seizures. It was easy to understand how people once thought epileptics were possessed by the devil.

"Something else, Dr. Licata. Why were you so mean to me Sunday night?"

"I didn't realize I was mean to you," Alex forced himself to say.

"You were. Now you're not mean; you're a different doctor."

"I apologize if I was mean, Mrs. Papineau."

"Why do people have to be mean to me?" The woman's mood changed suddenly; she began to cry. "See what it's done to my little girl. I tried to help her and raise her but people won't let me; they accuse me." Mrs. Papineau's cheeks were now wet with tears. "Even the doctors are against me. Now she'll die or have brain damage and it won't be my fault, it'll be yours and everyone else's!"

Alex led the sobbing woman from critical care to a nearby waiting room, then asked Louise to sit with her while he returned to Heather's bedside.

"That mother has real psychiatric problems," Alex told the residents. "I was afraid for a minute she would become psychotic."

"It'll be a lot easier for her when Heather's stopped seizing," Jim said.

"Speaking of seizures," Mo interjected, "were you surprised Charlotte's EEG was abnormal this morning?"

"Do you think I bet bottles of whiskey for nothing?" Alex said, raising his eyebrows. "Believe me, Mo, nine out of ten girls with stories and seizures like Charlotte's don't have abnormal EEGs. Eli was just lucky."

Louise Kidner burst into the critical care room. "Come quick, Charlotte's having another seizure."

"Are you sure it's nine out of ten, Alex?" Mo said.

A large group—children, nurses, nurse's aides, dieticians—had gathered outside Charlotte's room. Alex ordered them away.

Charlotte lay still on the floor, dressed in pajamas and a hospital gown. She was still. Mo bent over to lift her back into bed.

"Don't touch her," Alex ordered. "I want to watch."

"We went through this yesterday, Alex. We've already established she has an abnormal EEG and real seizures. Let me put her on the bed so she doesn't hurt herself."

"Mo, I said don't touch her! Stand up and leave her alone!"

Mo was surprised at Alex's tone, but obeyed him.

Suddenly Charlotte began to vocalize, first in nonsense syllables, then in words that sounded French. Alex asked Mo and Jim if they understood French. Neither did. Then Charlotte began jerking. First both arms jerked at the same time and her legs were still, then the pattern changed to arms and legs together, then only legs. Finally she lay still.

"Have you seen enough Alex? Can I put her in bed now?"

"Let her be, Mo," he insisted.

When the seizure cycle resumed, Alex bent over and lifted her eyelids. Her blank eyes stared straight ahead. He thrust his hand toward her face. She didn't blink.

"Charlotte, I want you to stop this and get back into bed!" Alex shouted into the girl's ear. No response. "*Charlotte—did you hear me? Back in bed!*" he cried.

Still no response.

Alex looked at Mo and Jim, who shook their heads as if to say, sorry.

"Don't worry, Alex. I'm not going to touch her," Mo said. "You can watch as long as you want."

Louise Kidner appeared at the door. "Alex, Charlotte's father is here. What should I tell him?"

"Tell him his daughter is having a seizure and if he wants, he can come to her room."

Edgar Quinn appeared almost immediately. "What's happening?"

"Charlotte's in the midst of a seizure."

"Has she hurt herself?"

"No."

Both arms and legs were moving.

"What did her EEG show this morning?" the father asked.

"Seizure discharges from the left temporal lobe," Alex said.

"So you were wrong."

"I was wrong about the EEG," Alex said carefully.

Charlotte was now quiet. Her father bent over and asked Mo to help lift his daughter back into bed. Alex didn't want the girl moved, but now it was impossible to interfere.

"Okay, Alex, let's leave the room," Jim urged after the girl had been safely placed on her bed.

"I'd like to watch her until she wakes up."

"I'll stay with you," Edgar Quinn said.

Charlotte had begun speaking "French" again. Alex wished that he or one of the residents or Dr. Quinn understood French.

"Watch closely," Alex said to Dr. Quinn. "Tell me if anything's different from the spells at home. This is the third time she's done it," Alex added. "First verbalization, then extremity twitching."

"She never did it more than once at home."

Now a new pattern was developing. Only her right arm and leg shook, while the left side was still. Then, with her left arm she began to fondle herself, first her breasts, then her genitals.

"Thank God my wife's not here," the father said, as he looked away from his daughter.

"We've got to get out of here," Alex insisted.

"We can't leave her like this," the father said.

Alex raised both side rails on the bed. "If we don't leave, she'll never stop." He pushed the father into the corridor. "Dr. Quinn, I don't care what the EEG showed this morning, that wasn't a real seizure; the more we watched, the worse it got. Let her quiet down before you go back into the room."

163

The father stood in the corridor, uncertain whether he should go back into the room, then decided to follow Alex down the corridor.

Eli Lassiter walked onto division 17 and joined Jim, Mo, and Casey at the nurses' station. Alex and Edgar Quinn arrived, enlarging the group to six.

"Did you hear about Charlotte's EEG?" Eli asked the father.

"Yes, Alex told me it was abnormal."

"That ends the hysterical seizure possibility. We'll start her on Tegretol right away."

"Would you continue her present meds?" Mo asked.

"Yes. I don't want to add and take away a medicine at the same time. It creates two rather than one variable."

"Charlotte's just had another seizure," the father said. "This one was longer and more involved than seizures she's had at home. There were overt sexual overtones."

"Don't let it bother you," Eli said as he put his hand on Edgar Quinn's shoulder. "That's why she's in the hospital."

"Eli," Alex said, "I watched the seizure she just had very carefully; I think it was hysterical."

Eli laughed. Even Mo and Jim were surprised at Alex's statement, and Casey merely hoped Alex knew what he was doing. Edgar Quinn understood Eli's laughter, and he himself was becoming angry with Alex. He felt it was time to leave his daughter alone.

"We have a girl with previously documented temporal lobe epilepsy," Eli said. "An increasing seizure frequency, even in the hospital, and a clearly abnormal EEG. What would you like me to do," he asked with a trace of disbelief in his voice, "stop all her medicines? What if she goes into status epilepticus like Heather Papineau?"

Alex didn't answer.

"Why do you think the seizure we witnessed was abnormal?" Mo asked. "You tried to stop it by telling her to get back in bed, but that didn't work. In the middle of her spell you pushed open her eyelids and thrust your hand at her face, but she didn't react."

"I know temporal lobe seizures take strange forms," Alex

164

said, "but there is a certain logic and order to the brain and Charlotte violated that order during her seizure. The separate shaking of her arms and legs doesn't make sense. It's all right for both arms and legs to shake—that could be a generalized motor discharge. But for only her arms and then only her legs, that doesn't fit anatomically. It means both sides of the brain were involved in the seizure, but only the parts controlling the upper extremities and then only the parts controlling the lower extremities. Someone can have a Jacksonian seizure, which starts with a finger shaking, then spreads to involve the hand, then the arm, then the arm and leg on one side, and then both sides. But to start in both arms, then spread to arms and legs and to finish with the legs alone, that's someone who doesn't know how the brain works trying to imitate a seizure. Mo and Jim, you left before the sexual overtones started. For that, she shook on one side and fondled herself with the other hand. I suppose I could accept that. But then she switched sides. She shook on the opposite side and used the free hand to fondle herself. How could she move from one side to the other without having a generalized convulsion? She had three spells in a row and stopped only when we left the room."

"How do you account for her abnormal EEG?" Jim asked.

"There's nothing to account for. She has an abnormal EEG. In fact, she probably has temporal lobe epilepsy. People with real seizures can have hysterical seizures as well. If I'm right about Charlotte, then all the medicine in the world isn't going to help her."

"I think they're real seizures," Eli said, "and first she needs a trial of anticonvulsants."

"How long will that take?" Alex asked.

"At least a month, maybe two."

"That means she won't be in the hospital," Alex said, beginning to build his case.

"Right. She'll be at home."

"And she may have these spells at home or at school."

"I suppose."

"That means her parents can't let her go to school for two months."

Eli paused. "OK, Alex. Let's say there's a chance her seizures are hysterical. How could you prove it? Her EEG is already abnormal."

Alex was ready. "One of the features of hysteria is the marked suggestibility of the patient. What we do is tell Charlotte she's going to have a seizure and see if she acts on the suggestion."

"Great," Mo said. "We have one girl on the floor we can't stop from seizing and another we'll tell when she's supposed to start seizing."

"How will you suggest it?" the father asked. "and how will you know she wouldn't have had a seizure at the moment anyway?"

"Good question," Alex said. "We'll have to inject her with something she believes causes seizures. Then we can see whether she convulses immediately afterwards."

"What are you going to inject?"

"Sugar water."

"It's risky," Eli said. "I don't like deceiving the patient."

Mo agreed. "Besides, what if she has a reaction to the injection?"

"From sugar water?" Jim asked.

"I'm not suggesting we stop anticonvulsants," Alex said. "She needs coverage whether or not these spells are hysterical. But, if we can prove they're hysterical, intense psychiatric help will bring them under control. Positive evidence that the seizures are hysterical can only be obtained now, while she's in the hospital."

Everyone looked at Edgar Quinn, aware that the decision would be his. He was a doctor, who understood the situation, as well as a father, who had to live with Charlotte for the next two months. Dr. Quinn resented Alex's intrusion as much as his diagnosis, but he understood the chief resident's logic and actually admired Alex's persistence. On the other hand, Edgar Quinn did not want his daughter to have hysterical seizures, and she did have an abnormal EEG.

Charlotte's father turned to Eli. "I can't tell you whether I want you to provoke a seizure with a fake injection," Edgar Quinn said finally. "I must see Charlotte and talk to my wife."

* * *

Rhoda Quinn arrived to join her husband in the waiting room and was told the story. The mother's face tightened and she rubbed her hands together as if to protect herself from the details she didn't want to hear. She asked no questions, only listened, and when her husband asked her opinion, she replied simply, "Let's see Charlotte."

Charlotte lay on her side, hands tucked underneath her pillow, knees drawn to her belly, eyes staring emptily at the corridor she could see through the open door. The side rails on her bed were up, but they didn't bother her, for she had raised her head on the pillow so the metal bar didn't interfere with her view.

Her parents tried to hide their apprehension as they entered the hospital room. "Hi, Charlotte," the mother said, bending over and kissing her daughter on the cheek. "How are you doing today?"

"Don't you know I had a seizure?"

"Your father told me," the mother said. "Remember, that's why you're in the hospital, to get these spells under control."

Edgar looked at his daughter and wondered if she had been awake during the last episode, if she had even been aware that he was standing there, watching her? "What was the seizure like?" he asked innocently.

"Like the others. I got this funny feeling in my head and the next thing I knew I was in bed with the side rails up."

"Was it worse than your other spells?"

"The same," she said sullenly, lowering her eyes.

"You mean you can feel something during the seizure?"

"No, it felt the same before I started and when it was over."

"Charlotte, are you frightened by these spells?" her father asked her.

"No. I'm in the hospital; they should be able to cure them. Are they going to give me a new medication?" She was playing with the top sheet, folding it back and forth.

"The doctors will have to decide that, dear."

"How long will I be here?"

"I don't know," he replied as Rhoda Quinn moved closer to her daughter.

"Charlotte, is there anything bothering you? Something you haven't told us?"

The girl, seemingly surprised by her mother's question, answered with a flat "No" in a tone that didn't invite further questions.

Still, the mother persisted, "Are you sure?"

This time a pause. "Sure, Mama. Why should anything be wrong?" Charlotte hadn't used the word "mama" since she was ten.

Rhoda caressed her daughter's forehead. "Anything we can get for you before we leave?"

"No, Mama, I'm fine." And she settled down in the bed, turning away from them.

Rhoda and Edgar Quinn sought out Alex, who explained to Mrs. Quinn his reasons for thinking Charlotte's spells were hysterical, as well as his plans for the fake injection. He saw no danger in the plan. The mother mentioned her daughter's use of the word mama. The father didn't know what it meant, but Alex viewed it as a form of regression, something common in hospitalized children. The mother was upset by it. She didn't want her daughter at home on yet another round of anticonvulsants, when anticonvulsants might not be the answer to Charlotte's difficulties.

To Charlotte's father, however, hysterical seizures meant his daughter was emotionally unstable, a reflection on her parents. Perhaps if they took her from the hospital on a new anticonvulsant, went on vacation, and tried to support her emotionally, she might overcome any psychological problems that existed. Besides, if the spells weren't hysterical, the new anticonvulsant alone might stop them.

"When would you do it?" the mother asked tentatively.

"I'll talk to Charlotte this afternoon and make the injection tomorrow."

Edgar and Rhoda Quinn moved a few yards from Alex to discuss their daughter's condition in some privacy.

"I don't think we should go ahead with it," the father said.

"Why did she call me 'Mama,' Edgar? That's not like Charlotte."

"I don't want any more meddling," the father said angrily.

"She's already had an abnormal EEG. Don't be fooled by Alex Licata, Rhoda, he's only a resident on the case. Besides, why should they play games with our daughter?"

Rhoda Quinn put her hand on her husband's arm. "I know you don't want the seizures to be hysterical, Edgar. I can understand that. But if that's what they are, we'll have to confront it—if we ever want her to get better. I don't care what she has, I just want her to get well."

"So we'll try some new medications, Rhoda, and the spells will quiet down. I know they will."

"Edgar, I do not want her at home if there is any possibility at all that her seizures are not real," the mother said emphatically.

"I'm a doctor, Rhoda. You know I wouldn't do anything to harm Charlotte."

"Well, I'm her mother, Edgar, and I don't want her having seizures at home." Rhoda Quinn looked directly at her husband. "If you agree to stay home for two months and take care of her, Edgar, then I'll agree. We won't have the injection."

Edgar Quinn didn't have to answer.

Eli Lassiter and Alex Licata were standing at Heather Papineau's bedside when Alex told him about the Quinns' decision to proceed with Charlotte's injection. Eli was surprised; still he had no choice but to go ahead with the plan. He told Alex he wanted to be present when Alex talked to Charlotte. Edgar Quinn would also be there. The more people the better, Alex thought.

"How long's Heather been seizing?" Eli asked.

"Almost sixteen hours."

"I wish she'd stop."

"Me too."

Eli and Alex were equally uncomfortable with Heather. They had manipulated her medication in every possible way, but she continued to seize without even a hint of slowing down. Luckily, breathing and blood pressure remained under control and there was no gross evidence of neurologic damage. The animosity between the two doctors was now overshadowed by the gravity of Heather's problem and their own helplessness. Even if Alex had somehow been negligent, it was Eli's responsibility as ward visit to stop the girl from seizing. They checked and rechecked anticonvulsant blood levels, a myriad of other blood tests, and bacteriology culture slips. Everything was in order.

"Heather's mother's a little crazy," Alex said. "If something happens to her daughter, I hope she doesn't sue me."

"If it reassures you at all, she'll probably sue me, too."

"What about general anesthesia?"

"It's the only thing left," Eli said. "We'll have to do it."

"OK. I'll contact them and set it up for tomorrow morning," Alex told him. "Maybe we'll be lucky and she'll stop by then."

"It's unlikely. By the way, an EEG will have to be done during the anesthesia," Eli said. "She'll be paralyzed; it's the only way to monitor her seizures."

Alex called anesthesia, who balked at anesthetizing a child with seizures, but when Eli took the phone and demanded to speak to the head of the department, arrangements were made. Heather would be taken to the operating room at 10:00 A.M., placed under anesthesia for six hours, then returned to division 17. Alex next called the seizure unit to reserve a technician and portable EEG machine for the operating room.

A cast of seven characters walked into Charlotte's room. Alex, Mo, Jim, Casey, Eli, Louise, and Charlotte's father, accompanied by the silver chart rack.

"I think it's good to make afternoon rounds periodically," Alex said to Dr. Quinn. "The morning can be very hectic. How's Charlotte doing, Mo?"

Mo was unsure of his role, aside from Alex's instructions to "pretend we're on rounds and talk naturally." He was now looking to Alex for a clue.

"How's she doing?" Alex repeated.

Finally, Mo shrugged his shoulders and began. "Not too well. Her EEG this morning was abnormal and she had a seizure this afternoon."

"Her lab work?"

Mo thumbed through the chart. "No abnormalities thus far."

Alex took out his reflex hammer and began pounding on Charlotte's arms and legs. He examined her for five full minutes, performing as many variations of the standard neurologic exam as he knew, variations Charlotte had not encountered before.

"Dr. Lassiter, this is a very difficult case, would you agree?" Alex asked.

"Yes," Eli managed.

"Especially after the EEG results this morning."

"I haven't seen results like that for a long time," Eli said, almost smiling. "What should we do?"

Alex was happy to force Eli's participation, and gave the neurologist credit for his willing performance. "You're an expert on these types of seizures and this particular EEG pattern," Alex added. "In the talk you gave last month, you mentioned a new medicine that's used in these cases."

"I'm glad you remembered," Eli said, as if there actually had been such a lecture and a medicine.

Jim couldn't resist getting into the act. "Is that the medicine they had a big article about in *The New England Journal of Medicine* last week?"

"Yes," Alex said. "It works simply. The medicine is injected into a person's vein and it causes them to have a seizure. It works one hundred percent of the time. By causing a seizure, then carefully observing it, one can decide which medicine to use for treatment."

"Is it painful?" Edgar Quinn asked, wanting to reassure his daughter.

"No. It's absolutely painless. Casey, after rounds call the pharmacy and make sure they've got it. The medicine doesn't have a name yet; it goes by number LW-245."

Charlotte was listening intently to a conversation designed solely for her own ears.

"Do you understand what we've been talking about?" Alex asked the girl.

Charlotte nodded.

"Fine. Don't worry, I'll explain more tomorrow when we do the test. If you think of any questions, you can ask me before we start. Nothing will hurt. I'm convinced that by doing this test

171

we'll be able to control your seizures." Despite the charade about a nonexistent medicine, Alex was telling the truth: the test was indeed being done to decide on the best course of treatment for Charlotte's seizures.

"Who else do we have to see?" Alex asked. "How about the two Susies?"

They walked into the adjoining room for an afternoon visit. It was the first time in three months Susie K had witnessed afternoon rounds by a full complement of doctors.

Richard and Luciana Zancanelli sat, as they had every afternoon of the last six months, in Tony's room. Today, the father sat in a chair against the wall at the foot of the bed, and the mother was at Tony's side with the boy's hand in hers. The mother noticed her son's hand was warm but didn't realize he had a fever. The half-year ordeal had been painful for them and for their four other children. Time, both in thought and hospital visits, had been taken from family and given to their comatose son. Conflicts began to develop between husband and wife, between parents and children, and the family was approaching the limit of its emotional resources. Each parent prayed for God's intervention to solve the dilemma. The father prayed for a miracle to cure his boy. The mother prayed for her son's death.

Louise and Jim stood at the nurses' station. "His fever's 102.5 rectally again," Louise said.

"I'll check him."

"His parents are in the room."

"Good. I want to talk to them."

"Why do you think he has a fever?" Louise asked.

"I don't know," Jim said.

"I bet it's his lungs," Louise said. "Why don't you get a chest X-ray? Maybe he should be started on antibiotics?"

"Is he bringing up sputum?"

"No."

"When he does, send some for culture and sensitivity."

Louise thought it strange Jim didn't order a routine X-ray. Whenever any child on the ward had an undiagnosed fever, a chest X-ray was one of the first tests ordered. But Jim would not yield to her pressure, and his plan was to delay treating Tony for as long as possible. Jim knew that once treatment was started, it was almost impossible to stop; it was much easier not to initiate treatment at all.

As he walked toward the room, Jim thought of situations when he put children on respirators, and turning off the machine meant taking away life. It was far easier never to put a nonviable child on a respirator. But the fallacy of that logic was obvious to him: the doctor often didn't know who was viable. Nevertheless, Jim knew that Tony was not salvageable, and the approach to Tony was well defined in the young doctor's mind; no shades or hues to complicate the situation.

"Hello, Dr. Wellander," the father said as Jim entered the room. "How's Tony doing?"

"About the same," Jim answered reflexively, even though Tony wasn't the same.

"Our daughter couldn't come with us today," the mother said. "She's busy this afternoon."

"You know it's not that, Luciana." The father turned to Jim. "She's tired of visiting Tony, Dr. Wellander, and we didn't want to force her to come."

"Actually, there is a new development," Jim told him. "Tony has a slight fever."

The mother put her son's hand down and felt his forehead. "He *is* warm. What does it mean?"

"I'm not sure. Maybe nothing. Sometimes children with brain damage develop fever because the brain's temperature-control center has been damaged. On the other hand, it might be the beginning of an infection. We've taken cultures and done blood tests, but so far they've been negative.

It was the first change in Tony's condition in weeks. Both parents realized something would happen to their son one day. Was this that day or just a false alarm?

"When will you know what's happening?" the father asked.

"By the weekend."

"Tony's very ill and his chances for recovery are small, we know that," the mother said, then stopped and looked tentative-

173

ly at her husband before continuing. "This fever he's developed—could it be the beginning of a complication that might lead to his death?"

At first Jim was astonished to be asked the obvious question so quickly and succinctly by Tony's mother. Then he realized that the issue of Tony's death was on the parents' minds constantly and it took little to transform the thought into verbalization.

"The answer is yes."

"Is that true for fever from brain damage and from infection?" the father asked.

"Yes, either one could be fatal."

"If it's an infection, couldn't you treat it?" the mother asked.

"Depends on the type of infection."

"If it's brain damage, there's no treatment?"

"Right."

The parents wanted to know what the chances were of their son's dying, but Jim wasn't sure he should ask the parents directly about Tony's death. He did know from previous discussions that the mother was more pessimistic about the boy's survival than the father. Because of the parents' questions and because Jim wanted support for his nonaggressive treatment, he decided to confront them.

"Do you want Tony to die?"

The mother spoke first, as though it had been a question she had answered a hundred times. "No mother wants her son to die, doctor. But no one wants their son to suffer, and certainly not to live the way Tony's living. I'll tell you honestly, I would be relieved if Tony died, and I think it would be the best for him."

"It's not what we want," the father insisted. "It's what the Lord wants. He knows what's best. I'm praying for a miracle to bring Tony back, but I too would be relieved if Tony died."

It's not God so much as yours truly, Jim thought. He didn't relish his mission, but he wasn't going to shrink from it by treating Tony vigorously. That course was morally unacceptable to Jim.

"I have your home phone number. I'm on duty tonight, and I'll call you if anything develops," he told them quickly.

"Thank you," the parents said.

Jim walked from the room with the image of Tony's parents in his mind. He had been watching them since his rotation on division 17 began, and this was the first time he detected a look resembling hope on their faces.

"Why do you think Tony has a fever?" Mo asked as Jim walked into the nurses' station.

Jim simply shrugged.

"I bet he's got pneumonia," Mo continued.

"How about abnormal temperature regulation from his brain damage?"

"Possible, but not likely. Don't worry," Mo assured him. "I wouldn't treat him for a pneumonia either. You're doing the right thing."

"What did you think of Alex's performance with Charlotte?" Jim asked, changing the subject.

"Not bad."

"I believe him. I bet her spells are hysterical."

"You didn't think so before," Mo said. "I still think they're real."

"At least I have one convert to my point of view," Alex said with a smile as he entered the nurses' station and sat down next to Casey.

"Quite a show this afternoon," Casey said. "Why did you do it?"

"Because I don't believe the seizure I saw was real. I can't let her be treated as a true seizure disorder if they're hysterical."

"Have you ever done this injecting business before?"

"No, but when I started in neurology, my chief resident did. It actually worked, and the patient was subsequently cured with psychotherapy. Casey, don't forget you're presenting BJ Balsiger tomorrow at grand rounds. Be sure to get there early to put his workup on the blackboard."

"Right, Chief!"

Alex smiled and stepped on her foot. "Call Nolan Magness to remind him to be there."

Casey didn't move her foot. She stared at Alex, her eyes widening. She saw a flush develop in his face. Then, suddenly, he began to pale.

Alex held up his right hand and spread his fingers. He could only see four of them. Turning back to Casey, he watched the right side of her face begin to blur.

The warm feeling he'd experienced when she stared at him changed into a sick feeling. He stood up and walked to the window, staring at blurred buildings. White, shimmering, zig-zag lines seemed to radiate from the center of his vision and move toward the periphery. They became larger and more numerous and soon filled his entire field of vision. He closed his eyes, but still saw them in gray. He was virtually blind.

Alex sat down and rubbed his eyes, the sick feeling in his stomach spreading to the rest of his body. He felt cold, his hands were clammy, and his head began to throb, especially over the left eye.

"Alex, what's the matter?" Casey was frightened.

"I'm getting a migraine. Hell, I haven't had one for three months." He opened his wallet and took out two pills wrapped in cellophane.

"What's that?"

"Cafergot. It's supposed to stop the headache. They don't really work for me, but I keep hoping." He attempted a grin.

Jim joined Alex and Casey. "What a classic! A neurologist getting a migraine! Was that a prerequisite for getting into the residency program?"

Alex's vision began to clear and his headache became worse. The sickness that centered in his stomach and radiated to the rest of his body begged to be vomited up, but Alex struggled to hold back.

"Jim, I'm going home to sleep," he mumbled. "You're on tonight, so call me if there are problems. Watch Heather Papineau closely. She's going for general anesthesia tomorrow if her seizures don't slow. Remember, morning rounds start tomorrow at seven-thirty so we can get to grand rounds on time."

As Alex stood up and began to walk from the nurses' station, he squeezed Casey's arm. "See what happens? I look at you and I get a migraine."

176

"You didn't get one last night on the elevator," she smiled.

Alex walked toward his apartment. At first the afternoon March air was refreshing, then it made him sicken. He succumbed to the nausea and vomited, which helped his stomach but made his head throb more. When he opened the door to his apartment, Mellissa was surprised to see him. She put her arms around him and began to kiss him, but he drew back.

"I've got a bad migraine, Mellissa. Help me get into bed."

Within minutes, Alex was curled into a ball, his left temple positioned against the pillow to numb the throbbing above the left eye. Fighting waves of nausea and intense pain, he waited for sleep, trying not to think of the pain. Because his headaches usually began with loss of vision and shimmering scotomata, he could remember exactly when they started, counting change in a restaurant, reading an article about hydrocephalus, bowling, watching the news. Now, looking at Casey as her eyes widened.

Alex was home, but Mellissa was still alone. She put his favorite dinner back in the refrigerator. She fed the girls supper, refereed their squabbles, bathed them, and put them in bed, then peeked into the bedroom to check Alex, who was asleep. She sat passively in front of the television, not distinguishing between the commercials and the movie that was showing.

11:30 P.M. Alex was still asleep. He woke up briefly when Mellissa slipped under the covers, then fell immediately back to sleep.

The phone rang. Alex woke up and reached for the receiver.

It was Jim Wellander. "Sorry to bother you, Alex. Tony Zancanelli's fever has risen to 105."

With news of Tony's fever, Alex was wide awake. He got up and walked into the kitchen, where the conversation wouldn't disturb Mellissa. "So Tony's got a real fever now? Why did you call?"

"What should I do?"

"What do you want to do?"

"Nothing."

"I agree."

"But the nurses are giving me a terrible time. They want me to get a chest X-ray."

"Did any of his cultures come back?"

"I called the lab. The blood and urine cultures are negative. The sputum cultures are no good. They were contaminated."

"The aspirin isn't holding his fever?"

"I've doubled the dose."

"What do his lungs sound like?"

"Terrible. I'm sure he's got a roaring pneumonia."

"Fine. Don't do anything."

"Do you know which nurse is on? The old one, the one who should've retired twenty years ago. She keeps asking me why I don't do something for the boy's infection. She's afraid he'll miss his chance for recovery."

"He doesn't have an IV does he?"

"No."

"Start an IV and put something benign in it, like potassium. Tell the nurse that the potassium is important for possible electrolyte disturbance caused by fever and may help any infection. She won't know the difference. Add Tylenol to the aspirin to control the fever. Order a chest X-ray for tomorrow morning and tell the nurse that I don't want any antibiotics started until the sputum culture comes back in the morning."

"The sputum culture was contaminated, Alex. It won't come back in the morning," Jim reminded him.

"I know. That'll give the pneumonia a chance to develop. By tomorrow after grand rounds, he should be very sick. And then, with Eli in attendance, we can make an open decision not to treat him. If there are any problems, have the nurse call me directly. How's Heather?"

"No change."

"Still seizing at the same frequency?"

"Like a clock."

"How are her vital signs?"

"Good."

"She'll need general anesthesia tomorrow. Make sure blood is sent in the morning for anticonvulsant levels."

Alex left the kitchen and walked back toward the bedroom.

Mellissa was sitting in the living room. "I thought you were asleep," he said.

"The phone woke me and I heard you in the kitchen. How's your headache?"

"Better, thanks."

"Do you have to go back to the hospital?"

"No, just a question about one of the kids on the floor with a fever." Alex turned and headed toward the bedroom.

"Where are you going?"

"Back to sleep."

"You've just slept six hours and we haven't talked for two nights. What's the rush?"

"I've got to get up early tomorrow. Grand rounds."

"Alex, you only have to get up a half hour earlier because of grand rounds. Sit down. Let's spend a few minutes together before you're gone for another day."

Alex sat on the couch in the living room, opposite Mellissa. He was in his underwear, she was in her nightgown. The apartment was dark save for the living room light.

"How are things at the hospital?" she asked.

"Pretty good."

"How's the girl with seizures that kept you up last night?"

"Still seizing."

Silence.

As Alex stared at his wife, he became dizzy. It wasn't only the nausea from his migraine, it was the thought of what awaited him in the hospital. Heather Papineau. Charlotte. Eli. Casey. Mellissa could tell Alex was distraught. She moved next to him and put her arm around his shoulder. He was surprised by the gesture, but he moved closer to her. Soon his head rested in her lap, and she gently rubbed her fingers on his temples.

"What was the phone call about?" Mellissa asked.

"Nothing. Just a child with a fever."

"Then why did they call you?"

"It's complicated, Mellissa. The child is permanently brain damaged and we're trying not to treat him."

"Is that what's bothering you?"

"Why should something be bothering me?" he said sharply.

179

Mellissa didn't answer. She knew Alex wasn't feeling well and there were problems at the hospital. He needed her support, not an argument. The residency would soon be over. She would get her chance. She would demand it. But now was not the time for that.

"Please don't worry about it, Alex," Mellissa said softly as she leaned over and kissed him on his forehead. "It isn't worth it."

Alex stared up into Mellissa's green eyes. Her blonde hair hung straight across her cheeks, almost touching his face. Pulling her toward him, he kissed her deeply. His impulse was to tell her everything, but he knew he couldn't. Instead, they walked together to their bedroom and made love. For once, the phone didn't ring.

THURSDAY

Tony Zancanelli's heart raced faster than before, over two beats a second, 150 beats per minute. On Wednesday, his heart rate had been 72. His heart could be seen beating through his thin chest wall; it pushed his left breast up and down so fast that the chest wall quivered rather than moved in an identifiable rhythm. Jim Wellander put his stethoscope over the boy's heart; the stethoscope itself began to move up and down on the boy's chest. The sound of Tony's heart was too loud for Jim; he loosened the ends that stuck in his ears. When Jim listened to a child's heart, he heard two heart sounds, and each of those sounds was composed of two others. Thus, he heard three and often four parts to each heartbeat, depending on the child. But Tony's heart was beating too fast for fine auscultation; the heartbeats came so close together that they sounded as one. All Jim heard was one loud pounding sound, over and over.

Air moved in and out of Tony's lungs faster than before. On Wednesday, his respiratory rate was twelve times per minute; it was now over twenty. There was a gurgling sound as the air moved, and Jim was certain it represented the boy's pneumonia.

The lungs were beginning to fill with bacteria and pus, and the air moving through the liquid infection created the gurgling sound. Jim put his stethoscope to the boy's back; no need to instruct the child to breathe with an open mouth, so breath sounds were more audible. Tony was panting like a dog. Jim heard wet rales, or gurgling, on both sides of the chest.

Alex, Casey, Mo, and Louise were watching Jim examine Tony; a heaving chest overlying a pounding heart. When he saw sweat begin to form on the boy's forehead, Alex suggested the IV be adjusted to supply the extra water needed to prevent dehydration due to the fever.

"Definitely something going on in his lungs," Jim said.

"Do we treat it?" Mo asked.

"No," Alex said.

"How can you decide that without knowing what it is?" Louise asked.

"The decision doesn't relate to what's causing Tony's fever," Jim said as he turned to face her. It relates to how vigorously we want to support him. It's fine to feed him through a tube in his stomach, to give him aspirin for fever, to turn him in bed and provide a special mattress so he won't get bedsores, but when he gets a natural complication of his illness, it's not right to treat him. You should have seen his parents yesterday. I told them Tony had a mild fever; they immediately wanted to know how serious it was. For the first time, there was a look of hope on their faces."

"Did you ask them if they wanted to withhold treatment in case of pneumonia?" Casey interjected.

"That's not their decision, and it's an unfair question. I would never ask them to make such a guilt-laden decision. They have enough guilt already. But they both said they'd be relieved by Tony's death and that his life was in God's hands."

"Not that I think you should treat him," Mo said, "but aren't you taking his life into your own hands by not treating him?"

"No," Jim argued. "By not treating him, I'm leaving his life in God's hands. I'm not interfering."

"Assuming there's a God, of course," Alex said.

Not one of the group believed Tony should be treated, but

Louise Kidner was the most uncomfortable with the decision. In nurses' report, she would have to say Tony Zancanelli has a fever and possible pneumonia. What if one of the nursing students asked why they weren't doing anything for him? And if they wanted him to die, why replace lost fluids with an IV? It was easier to let someone die peacefully in a small private hospital than in a large medical center.

Each felt uncomfortable leaving Tony's room, despite the certainty with which they spoke of his nontreatment.

Casey wished Tony would die immediately; it bothered her to watch, even though she knew he wasn't suffering. Jim thought of Richard and Luciana Zancanelli and what he would tell them. He decided to tell them everything possible was being done for their boy and that the fever came from brain damage, not pneumonia. He didn't want them to live with the thought that their son might have survived if the doctors had treated him. Then Jim remembered the autopsy. He must do his best to get permission for one when the boy finally died.

Alex had watched many hopelessly ill children die when the doctors decided no further treatment was warranted. He thought of their pale bodies, arms and legs frozen in the last position they occupied prior to death. Nurses methodically detached tubes, and a sheet was neatly tucked under the child's chin so the family could view the body. Alex knew death was final, but he *felt* it only when he actually saw it. Treatment never helped then.

"Have the ward clerk call his parents," Jim told Louise.

"Continue with the present regimen," Alex said. "NG-feeding, IVs, anticonvulsants, aspirin, and Tylenol. No chest X-ray or blood tests. I'll see Eli in a half hour and tell him what's happening. He can check on the boy after grand rounds."

"What if he has a cardiac arrest?" Louise asked, knowing the answer but wanting official word.

"Page me," Jim said. "Don't call an arrest, obviously we don't want to resuscitate him."

"Okay. Heather Papineau's next," Alex said as they entered the critical care room.

The frequency of Heather Papineau's seizures hadn't

changed. No evidence of infection had been found, and her fever was now ascribed to the intense muscle activity of her seizures.

Mo scanned the seizure chart, which had grown to three pages since Tuesday night. "I can't figure out why she doesn't stop." He ran his hand through his thinning hair. "We've given her every anticonvulsant possible, her metabolic parameters are normal, and there's nothing dramatic on her exam. Between Heather, Charlotte, and BJ, we're not exactly winning the gold medal for treating seizures."

"Look, Mo," Alex said. "You know that only the most difficult cases are hospitalized. In the clinics there are hundreds of children with seizure disorders perfectly controlled on phenobarb or Dilantin."

"Heather goes for general anesthesia at ten," Jim reminded him.

They all looked at the girl. She appeared peaceful between convulsions. The endotracheal tube was still down her windpipe, and an IV in each arm. In only two days, her hospital chart had swelled to the size of other children's charts after two weeks.

"What if the general anesthesia doesn't work?" Casey asked.

"I don't know," Alex confessed.

"Maybe she has a subdural collection of blood or other space-occupying lesion that isn't showing up on exam," Mo suggested.

"We'd have to do an arteriogram or CAT scan to find out," Jim said. "And that's impossible now. We can't keep her head from moving long enough."

"But she won't be moving during anesthesia," Alex added.

"Why not?" Mo said. "Let's do the CAT scan while she's under. A CAT scan's not dangerous at all."

"Not bad," Jim agreed. A CAT scan was difficult to arrange at the last minute, but he could manage it with help from both Alex and Eli. The decision to do the CAT scan temporarily relieved the frustration they all felt of having nothing to offer Heather besides general anesthesia. No one mentioned what would be done if the CAT scan was negative.

184

"Where's the boy with the cerebellar tumor?" Mo asked as they left the critical care room.

"He's back on the floor. Doing fine," Louise announced happily.

"Maybe you should study neurosurgery instead of neurology, Alex," Jim chided.

As they approached the nurses station they spotted BJ Balsiger in a go-cart, waiting with his parents for the trip to the hospital amphitheater for grand rounds. In the wooden go-cart with BJ lay his teddy bear and the hospital chart. Florence Balsiger's efforts were reflected in BJ's freshly washed face and neatly combed hair.

"BJ will be the first case," Alex told the Balsigers.

"How long will the rounds take?" Dennis Balsiger asked.

"They start at eight-thirty. Dr. Lilstrom will present BJ's history, then one of the doctors will examine him. His case should take about fifteen minutes. After the exam, you and the nurse can wheel him back to division seventeen."

"Won't there be a discussion of his case?" the mother asked, and when Alex nodded, continued: "We'd like to stay and listen to it."

"Of course," Alex said.

Rounds moved to Charlotte Quinn's room. "Good morning, Charlotte. How do you feel?" Mo asked.

"Fine," the large girl replied shyly.

"Any more spells?" Alex asked.

"I don't think so."

"Any questions about the injection you'll be getting later today?"

Reluctantly, she looked at Alex. "Will it hurt?"

"Do you feel any pain when you have a seizure?"

Charlotte shook her head.

"It'll be exactly like that. Mo"—he deliberately turned to the resident—"I plan to give her the injection early this afternoon. The pharmacy promised to have the medication ready around lunchtime, but why don't you check when we're through here?"

"Sure thing," Mo said.

They stepped into the corridor. "What happens if she has a

seizure a few minutes before we plan to inject the sugar water?"
Mo asked.

"If her seizures are hysterical, she'll wait until the injection to
have another one."

The remainder of rounds went quickly. The hypotonic infant
showed no ill effects from his muscle biopsy; he would leave the
hospital after the microscopic slides were interpreted. The two
Susies continued their day-by-day improvement. They still
didn't understand why the doctors had made rounds the previous afternoon. Clark Kent Gatewood's drop attacks remained
at a sufficiently manageable level so that after two more days of
observation and a final EEG he would be sent home.

Medical amphitheaters differ from conventional auditoriums
in that there is no stage, and the seats rise precipitously around a
central area. At Children's Hospital, neurology grand rounds
were held in a turn-of-the-century medical amphitheater where
young doctors and eager students had watched from above as
the professor performed actual surgery or examined patients for
the onlookers. The walk up from the floor of the amphitheater
was a steep climb whose only diversion was the imposing pic-
tures of bearded doctors on the surrounding walls. These physicians had practiced medicine at Children's Hospital decades
before; some had become famous and their names would be
recognized at any medical amphitheater in the world, while
others had remained obscure, known only to the young doctors
who couldn't escape the portraits as they sat in the amphitheater.

The seating pattern at grand rounds seldom varied. Professors
and senior physicians sat in the front row, accompanied by the
visiting speaker; other physicians sat directly behind; and students, interns, and residents were spread out in the higher rows.
Alex preferred the heights, since, if the case was boring, he
could read the medical journal he always brought and not be
spotted. Today, however, he sat in the front row, next to Casey,
who was to present BJ Balsiger.

BJ waited in the hallway outside with his mother and the
nurse. His father sat inside, waiting to hear the presentation,
which he would later report to his wife.

Before beginning, Casey had filled three blackboards with BJ's history. Now she took to the podium, note cards in hand, a tiny microphone around her neck.

"Brian James Balsiger," she began, hoping her stagefright wasn't evident to the audience, "is a four-year-old boy who's been followed at Children's Hospital since he was eleven months old for a difficult-to-control seizure disorder. His fifth and current Children's Hospital admission was for a prolonged convulsion that was predominately left sided and was stopped with IV Valium. He's had no further seizures during his week of hospitalization."

Nolan Magness only half-listened to Casey's presentation as he read the blackboards for the results of the CAT scan and arteriogram he had urged be done. They were normal. Nolan sat back in his chair, puzzled. Like Eli, he had been certain that at least one of the tests would be abnormal. Now he didn't know what he would do for BJ. He did know, however, that he was no longer BJ's primary physician, that he no longer bore the responsibility of caring for a child with no diagnosis and difficult-to-control seizures. One good thing about residencies, Nolan thought, tough cases were left to someone else when the residency was over. That wasn't true in private practice. Nolan's thoughts wandered to the laboratory.

"BJ's first seizure occurred when he was eleven months old," Casey continued, her nervousness beginning to subside. "It was a generalized convulsion with no focal features. Birth history was normal and developmental milestones were normal. He smiled at three months, sat at six months, and was beginning to walk at eleven months. There is no family history of a seizure disorder."

Eli Lassiter liked Casey's concise, well-organized presentation of what was clearly a complicated case. Still, he found no surprises either in her monologue or on the blackboard behind her. Before rounds, Alex had told him about Tony Zancanelli, and Eli had concurred that the boy should not be treated, agreeing to write a note in Tony's chart after grand rounds. And he had to admit he was looking forward to Charlotte Quinn's injection; he thought Alex was foolish for his persistence, and felt certain Alex would be proven wrong. As he looked at the

187

backs of the heads in the first row, Eli thought of his own career and what had gone wrong; nonproductivity in the lab, withering of his clinical skills. He wondered whether he should have gone into private practice. If he had, he'd be richer and wouldn't be subjected to the hassle of looking for another job. Of course he could still leave academic medicine and enter practice, but he wasn't sure he had the courage.

In a spiral notebook, Mo Corning was copying down pertinent information from the blackboard and Casey's presentation. The cover of his notebook was titled "Grand Rounds." Each week he took detailed notes of the cases and discussion. Yet, as he wrote, he didn't think it was a mechanical maneuver. Mo was busy learning patterns, formulas, hard facts about neurologic disease. He hadn't reached the stage where a soft fact didn't bother him, where he could synthesize in his own mind without depending on the structure of a textbook. He looked forward to Charlotte's upcoming injection but was uncomfortable because he couldn't find a precedent in the medical literature. He didn't know why, but he was confident that Heather's seizures would stop, and he had absolutely no idea what was wrong with BJ Balsiger.

As Casey was describing BJ's third hospital admission, Jim Wellander thought about Tony Zancanelli. Nothing could push the comatose, feverish child from his mind. He wondered what Eli had said when Alex told him of their decision not to treat. He thought about Tony's parents and the relief they would feel when their son finally died. He thought of what he would say to them and how he would approach getting permission for an autopsy. At autopsy there would be inflammation, evidence of an encephalitis, nothing more. Jim didn't care about BJ Balsiger, but he did care about Heather Papineau; he was afraid when she finally stopped seizing, she would no longer be a normal child.

"A repeat spinal tap, arteriography, and pneumoencephalography were negative," Casey was saying. "His EEG remained normal with diffuse changes and without one particular focus. He was discharged from the hospital and new drugs added to anticonvulsant regimen. . . ."

Eight medical students from other hospitals sat in the back row. They were a motley group, both physically and intellectually. Some were dressed in white pants and jacket, others in streetclothes; some took notes on Casey's presentation, others dozed; some understood seizure disorders, others were sloppy and naive in their conceptualizations. BJ's father scanned the faces of the large group of doctors that listened to Casey's presentation, hoping that someone might have a new idea about BJ. The sight of a dozing medical student bothered him.

Sitting in the front row was a visiting professor whose job it would be to examine BJ and discuss his case. Having read through Casey's notes on the blackboard and listened carefully to her presentation, he knew immediately there was no obvious diagnosis. Still, he would have to provide twenty minutes of an organized and informative discussion, during which his audience would expect a "new twist" or the unearthing of a forgotten point. The visiting professor shifted through the various talks he could give on seizure disorders; he had done it so often. Always required to discuss a wide variety of topics, the talks were like tiny cassettes in his mind, ready to be played. The cassettes were updated as new advances were made; some tapes were better than others. If his cassettes were better than another professor's, it would be because they were heavily colored by rich personal experience and an innate gift for clinical judgment.

But the visiting professor's cassettes were like the material in a textbook, not something unique in his mind. His discussion would be a regurgitation of pages from a book.

"After the ketogenic diet," Casey said, "BJ was followed in the seizure clinic and begun on a variety of experimental medications. Their numbers and formulas are listed on the board."

Sitting next to the visiting professor was a true professor, an elderly physician in his seventies who had treated children with neurologic problems for a half-century. There were no cassettes in his mind, only a wealth of clinical experience. More important, intuition and a sense of clinical judgment that made his diagnoses right more often than wrong. His expertise was the result of treating children until adulthood and then caring for the next generation. Luckily, his mind had remained sharp, the years of experience had not been wasted on a decaying brain.

"On the day of his current admission BJ had a prolonged left-sided convulsion preceded by three shorter convulsions and was brought to the emergency ward," Casey was concluding. "The seizures were controlled with IV medication, and since his hospitalization five days ago he's had no more seizures."

Alex Licata sat four seats away from the old professor, watching Casey intently while he mulled over his problems on the ward. Casey didn't look at Alex, her eyes were fixed on her note cards. Alex was pessimistic about BJ's future, and doubted a diagnosis would be made while the boy was alive. He was relieved that Tony Zancanelli was about to die; nonetheless felt uneasy about the comatose child, a feeling that would disappear only when the tubes were pulled from the boy's body and the sheets pulled over his head. Charlotte Quinn's problem didn't bother Alex as much as the antagonism that had developed between himself and Eli Lassiter. Charlotte's seizures *had* to be hysterical, at least the ones Alex had witnessed. But even if they weren't, Alex's conscience would be clean; he hadn't succumbed to the pressure. It would have been much easier to say nothing and give Eli his bottle of whiskey. But Alex knew that if Charlotte's seizures were hysterical, he wouldn't stop them by treating Eli with a bottle of whiskey. He would only stop them by giving her a fake injection. Heather Papineau did bother Alex. He felt helpless in not having more to offer the girl except general anesthesia. He felt betrayed by the medication that saturated her brain but was unable to stop her convulsions, medication that seldom had betrayed him in the past. And he felt tricked by his Sunday-night encounter with the girl's crazy mother.

Still, Alex's underlying mood was a happy one, happy because of his encounter with Casey. It was exciting, fresh, and he felt surprisingly little guilt. It happened naturally, something he tried to stop but circumstances forced upon him. His love for Mellissa and his responsibility to his two girls seemed separate from his affection for Casey, even after making love to Mellissa

190

the night before. For Alex, Casey lived in a different world than Mellissa. Alex didn't seriously consider what his feelings for Casey implied for his family.

Forcing his thoughts back to Casey's presentation, Alex heard her finishing: "During this hospitalization, blood levels of anti-convulsants have been adjusted to therapeutic range. The results of the other blood tests are on the board. The EEG continues to be abnormal, with diffuse changes. CAT scan and repeat arteriography have both been normal. Psychological testing during this admission shows that at age four he is functioning at the level of a three-year-old."

Dennis Balsiger winced when he heard Casey describe his son's retardation. An intellectually normal child with seizures, or diabetes, or heart disease, or even cancer, was not as bad as a mentally retarded child. A retarded child could be more an animal than a person, but still a human being who thought, no matter how primitively, and felt, and could love and be loved. Guilt permeated the father's thoughts. Genetically he must in some way be responsible for BJ's condition; even worse, he couldn't avoid feeling hostile toward BJ because the boy had failed to be a normal son for his father. The father sighed deeply and briefly stroked his forehead, then his weatherbeaten face with the splash of acne across his nose and cheeks.

Returning to her seat next to Alex, Casey received a complimentary pat on the thigh, and she smiled, acknowledging his presence for the first time since her presentation.

Eli Lassiter watched the visiting professor rise. He was a slim, handsome man of forty, who had retained the same youthful appearance he had had in medical school. He was bright, energetic, productive in the laboratory, and adequate with patients. Now, as head of his own neurology program, he proved to be a good administrator. Others his age had turned down his position, feeling they were too young. Eli watched him enviously. Eli was only a few years younger.

"After listening to this fine presentation," the visiting professor began, "it's obvious BJ is a difficult case. The workup and treatment has been excellent. Before my discussion, let's see the boy."

BJ was wheeled in by his mother and a nurse.

"I'd like to have the mother sit here with the boy on her lap."

Florence Balsiger sat in the middle of the amphitheater with BJ and his teddy bear. Without exception, the people in the front row smiled at the boy. BJ didn't react, but his mother smiled back at the faces in the first row, then at those that rose high above her.

"How's BJ been doing?" the visiting professor asked. He held the tiny microphone in his hand, then moved it over to the mother.

"He hasn't had any more seizures in the hospital, but there doesn't seem to be a medication that controls his convulsions for long." She articulated her words clearly.

"How does his development seem to you?"

"He's slow."

"BJ, what are you holding?" the professor addressed the boy, who answered softly, "My teddy bear." The front row smiled.

He was asked the same question again, only this time with the microphone pushed to his lips. "My teddy bear." All the faces in the amphitheater smiled.

"Do you see your daddy here?"

BJ didn't respond, but his mother whispered to him and shifted him on her lap to the right side of the amphitheater.

"Hi, Daddy, you're over there!" Everyone smiled.

BJ wasn't needed for the discussion of his case at grand rounds, but his presence was important. Without him, the case was a mere exercise; with him, the case was a real problem that existed.

"Can we see him walk?" asked the professor.

The mother took BJ's hand and together they walked across the front of the amphitheater. "Now let's see him run." The visiting professor lifted up BJ and placed him a few yards from his mother. The boy ran to her arms. "As you know," the professor addressed the students, "running is one of the best tests of brain function in a child. It tests for weakness, incoordination, spasticity, and abnormal movements." BJ then sat on his mother's lap while the visiting professor quickly tested reflexes, eye movements, and hand coordination.

"I've seen enough. Is there anything else someone wants me to check?" Silence and a few negative head shakes from the front row. "Thank you, BJ, your mommy will take you back to bed now."

"Byebye," BJ said, loud enough to be heard without the microphone, and everyone smiled.

As the nurse wheeled BJ back to division 17, Dennis and Florence Balsiger remained in the amphitheater for the discussion.

The visiting professor put the microphone around his neck. "We have a four-year-old child with uncontrollable seizures and psychomotor retardation. All tests have been negative apart from the EEG. There is no evidence of a metabolic disturbance or an inborn error of metabolism. Conventional anticonvulsant medication has not helped and even some of the newer experimental medicines have failed. His doctors have been unable to make a diagnosis, and after listening to a fine presentation and seeing the child briefly, I can't make a diagnosis either."

Florence Balsiger, who had been sitting toward the edge of her chair, now sat back.

"Nevertheless, the search for new anticonvulsants is the only way these children will be helped, and I'd like to discuss one of these areas of research." The visiting professor switched on one of his cassettes and began a discussion of biochemical changes in nerve cells during seizures and current theories about pharmacological control of convulsions.

He spoke for thirty minutes, even drawing a multitude of diagrams on the board after erasing Casey's neatly outlined history of BJ's course. When the cassette was over, there was still time for questions. Nolan Magness asked about biochemistry; someone in the front row, about current directions in epilepsy research.

When Eli Lassiter had been confronted with BJ's problem, he spoke about mice; now the visiting professor spoke about nerve cell biochemistry. Alex thought that he was honest in stating at the onset that he had no diagnosis for BJ and that the talk on epilepsy certainly showed why he was a professor at forty. Nevertheless, Casey had filled the board with BJ's history, the boy was paraded before a gallery of doctors, and BJ's parents sat in the amphitheater.

Alex stood up. "If you were taking care of BJ, what would you do at this point?" he asked.

"I've forgotten about the boy, haven't I?" The visiting professor said. Then he hesitated before he spoke; there was no cassette he could utilize. "All diagnostic procedures have been done; the only avenue is anticonvulsant manipulation. Unfortunately, there aren't many medicines left to try. I know of research at the National Institutes of Health at Bethesda; there's a new experimental drug which will soon be ready for clinical trial. I could get it for you."

Florence Balsiger's spirits lifted, but her husband seemed skeptical. He thought the answer to BJ's problem was a diagnosis, not a new experimental drug.

Alex didn't sit down. He turned to the old physician who sat four seats away. "Dr. Hollsworth, what do you think of this boy?"

The "true professor" spoke slowly and softly so that only those in the front row could hear. "I'm afraid there's nothing to do but manipulate medication. I'm not sure what his diagnosis might be. I'd like to examine him myself sometime."

Grand rounds, case one, over. A five-minute break and then case two.

Casey intercepted BJ's parents at the amphitheater door.

"I'm very disappointed with the grand rounds," Dennis Balsiger said. "All the trouble to bring BJ here and the doctor discussed fancy research. The other doctors didn't get a chance to say what they thought. You didn't need BJ for all that."

"I'm sorry," Casey said. "But he did say he'll make the new experimental drug available to us."

"They should save the experimental drug for guinea pigs."

"Dennis, it's not Dr. Lilstrom's fault."

"Let's go back to division seventeen," he said.

Alex appeared at Casey's side. "They're mad, Alex, and I don't blame them."

Alex placed his hand lightly on her back and escorted her into the hall. "I have an idea, Casey. There's one test BJ hasn't had

194

and it probably has a better chance of yielding a diagnosis than the CAT scan or arteriogram. It's the Hollsworth test."

"Hollsworth test?"

"Sure. We'll present BJ to Dr. Hollsworth tomorrow at visit rounds. You heard what he said when I asked him about BJ. He wanted to examine the boy himself sometime. Do you know how Dr. Hollsworth examines children? He puts them on his knee and jiggles his keys in front of them. The old guy has seen more kids with seizure disorders than all the doctors in the room together. And he's made more diagnoses with his keys than we have with our reflex hammer, ophthalmoscopes, and CAT scans."

"Did you ask him?"

"Yes, and he agreed. Save your cards for an abbreviated presentation tomorrow."

Grand rounds, case two. A case from one of the adult hospitals, a woman with a stroke.

Casey and Alex moved to one of the back rows. Instead of listening to the case presentation, they wrote notes to each other.

When shrill beeps pierced the amphitheater, no one reacted; the sound of a beeper during rounds was common. Jim Wellander pressed the tiny red button to quiet his beeper and walked up to the back of the amphitheater. As he waited for the operator to answer, he noticed Alex and Casey writing notes to each other. It was division 17.

"This is Dr. Wellander, did you want me?"

Jim slammed down the phone and rushed to Alex.

"It's Tony Zancanelli, Alex."

"He died?"

"No, he's seizing."

Within minutes Alex, Jim, and Casey stood at Tony's bedside. The boy was in the midst of a generalized seizure, his feverish body convulsed, his eyes rolled up so far into his forehead that only the whites were exposed.

"What should we do?" Jim asked.

"Call Louise. Tell her to bring some Valium," Alex said. "We can't let him seize."

Louise soon appeared with a syringe.

Jim cleaned the rubber tubing on Tony's IV with an alcohol swab and prepared to inject the medicine.

"That's not Valium," Mo Corning said.

"What are you doing here?" Jim said. "How do you know this isn't Valium?"

"I saw the three of you leave rounds after Jim's page. Valium is pale yellow, that fluid's crystal clear."

Jim looked at Louise. "He's right about the color," she said. "I must have drawn the medicine from the wrong vial."

The two of them went to the nurses' station. "It was Digoxin, here's some Valium," Louise said.

"We may not have stopped his seizures, but we would have cured any heart failure," Jim said.

When they returned to Tony's room, he had stopped seizing.

"We would have given him Digoxin, his seizure would have stopped, and no one would have known the difference," Mo said.

"We didn't need to use Digoxin; sugar water would've done it," Alex said.

"For that matter, a brief prayer would have sufficed," Casey said.

"I remember a child whose cardiac arrhythmia we thought we cured with propranolol, only to find he never received the medicine," Jim added.

"Give him some IV Dilantin," Alex said, "to make sure he doesn't start again. With his fever, the Dilantin he had on board was not enough."

Heather Papineau was wheeled into a small operating room, with a nurse, Jim Wellander, and Mo Corning accompanying her. The technician from the EEG unit and the portable EEG machine were already there. Heather had been rushed from division 17 to the operating room immediately following a seizure so she wouldn't have one in the corridor. Promptly upon arriving in the operating room, she convulsed.

Because an endotracheal tube was in place and Heather already had an IV attached to each forearm, no preparation was needed for anesthesia. First, a fast-acting barbiturate was injected. Heather was already unconscious, but the barbiturate was administered because of the next drug, succinyl choline. Succinyl choline was a paralyzing drug. Although it didn't affect the brain, within minutes every muscle in Heather's body would be incapable of contracting. If succinyl choline was given to a conscious child, he would become paralyzed while awake. Unable to move, unable to breathe, unable to blink, unable to yell out, the child would immediately feel the need for oxygen but would be unable to gasp. Within minutes he would begin to suffocate.

The anesthesiologist breathed for Heather, squeezing a bag attached to the endotracheal tube, each squeeze pushing air into her lungs. She received oxygen, then a gaseous anesthetic. Next, the EEG technician began pasting electrodes to the girl's head, still sticky from previous pastings. Her muscles, blocked by medication, would be inert for the first time in two days, unable to respond to the abnormal brain signals. The succinyl choline wore off quickly, but it wasn't the artificially induced paralysis that would help Heather, it was the gaseous anesthetic that would stop the abnormal waves of electricity from flowing through the girl's brain. The brain cells would be given a rest, the cycle of seizure discharges broken, and, hopefully, when the anesthetic was removed the cycle would be ended.

The electrodes were in place and the steel pens began pouring their ink onto the flowing sheet. The brainwaves were slow and rhythmical, forming the typical interseizure pattern. Then, suddenly the pattern changed. The pens flew up and down, scratching against the paper, banging against each other. They traced out a seizure unhampered by muscle activity. Instead of the incoherent splattering of ink, there were continuous, high sharp waves traced out by each pen; the abnormal electricity engulfed the entire brain.

The scratching and banging of pens stopped and the slow rhythmical waves resumed.

"That's the picture of a seizing brain without a body to react to it," Mo said, then told the special nurse assigned to Heather to note the seizure on her chart.

"What happens now?" Casey asked.

"We increase the anesthesia and try to stop the seizures."

"How much anesthesia is needed?" Jim asked.

"I don't know," Mo told him. "There's only a certain amount that can be given before the cardiovascular system becomes depressed and she has problems with heart rate and blood pressure. The question is, can we depress her brain enough to stop the seizure activity without depressing the heart?"

"There's only one way to find out," the anesthesiologist said.

Heather's convulsing arms and legs were now replaced by the scratching and banging together of eight steel pens. Their sound filled the room with each seizure; the seizures continued on the same schedule. The anesthesiologist increased the amount of gaseous anesthesia he pumped into the girl's lungs and Heather's special nurse faithfully charted the noise of the steel pens.

"I agree," Eli Lassiter said. "The Zancanelli boy shouldn't be treated."

"He's had a recurrence of his seizures," Alex said, "probably related to his fever. We've given him extra Dilantin."

"Do the parents know?"

"They've been called."

"I'll write a note in the chart."

"What will you say?"

"His fever appears to be related to his brain damage and a complicating viral pneumonia."

Alex looked at him directly. "You know we don't have a chest X-ray or sputum culture."

"Don't worry, he'll probably expire sometime this afternoon or early evening," Eli said.

Alex handed Tony's chart to Eli.

"So when do we inject Charlotte Quinn?" Eli asked.

"This afternoon at two."

"How's Heather Papineau?"

"Her seizures continued during the night, and right now she's getting general anesthesia. She'll also get a CAT scan this afternoon."

"I still don't know how you missed the history of meningitis, Alex."

"Come on, Eli, you know that has nothing to do with her seizures."

"How do I know if I don't know why she's seizing?"

"Don't worry, Eli. I'll figure her out. In fact, I'll figure her out before you do."

"Like you figured out Charlotte Quinn?" Eli said immediately. Boy, was that stupid, Alex!"

"What?"

"The fake injection. Charlotte's father's really mad. Did you know he has strong family ties to the administration here at Children's?"

"Don't worry about me, Eli," Alex said firmly. "There's no chance that Charlotte Quinn's seizures are real."

"And what kind of recommendation do you think I can give you? You've messed up Heather Papineau and you're about to make a grave error on Charlotte Quinn."

"We're doctors, Eli. I don't know about you, but I'm trying to make a diagnosis on Charlotte."

"We already have a diagnosis," Eli said. "It's called epilepsy."

"I've asked Dr. Hollsworth for rounds tomorrow," Alex said, realizing it was time to change the subject. "He's going to examine BJ Balsiger."

"Fine," Eli said dryly and left Tony's room.

The amount of anesthesia blown into Heather Papineau's lungs was increased, blood pressure and heart rate remained stable. Heather's special nurse thought the noise from the steel pens had diminished. Finally, after two hours of anesthesia, electrical silence accompanied the artificial stillness of Heather's muscles. The EEG showed continuous, slow, rhythmical waves uninterrupted by sharp discharges. Quiet at last.

"How long will she be kept at this level of anesthesia?" Casey asked.

"I can't do it for more than four hours," the anesthesiologist said.

"She has a CAT scan scheduled at four."

"Fine. We'll decrease the anesthesia then."

"What about the EEG?" the technician asked.

"Keep it running until she goes for her CAT scan."

Alex and Casey ate lunch together. It was an encounter they both wanted. They needed to be with each other, to talk, to exchange intimacies. For now it was only the cafeteria that provided that chance.

"Alex, aren't you glad Heather Papineau came to the hospital?"

"Why?"

"Without her our relationship would've ended."

"I'll tell that to Mrs. Papineau the next time I see her."

"Alex, has Eli said anything more about Heather?"

"That guy's such an asshole, Casey! He started telling me about Charlotte's father knowing people in the hospital administration, and then he told me *he* wasn't going to give me a good recommendation. Does he think I'm a medical student?"

Casey fidgeted in her chair.

"I'm sorry, Casey, I didn't mean that."

"But you have to be careful, Alex. If you're wrong about Charlotte and something bad happens to Heather, you could be in trouble."

"Casey, I know I'm not wrong about Charlotte. Believe me."

Casey looked at Alex and her eyes began to widen. How could she not believe him?

Alex felt a rush of blood to his face. Mellissa was a thousand miles away.

Casey leaned forward. "Come to my apartment for dinner tonight, Alex." She pulled a 3 x 5 card from her pocket and wrote on it. "Six-thirty. Here's the address." She stuffed it in Alex's pocket, where he kept all his cards with patients' names and hospital numbers.

Alex was silent.

"Will you come?"

"Let's get back to the ward. In a little while Charlotte gets her injection."

* * *

Richard and Luciana Zancanelli arrived on division 17 accompanied by a teenage daughter, and instead of entering Tony's room as they had in the previous months, went straight to the nurses' station. Louise Kidner explained Tony's condition, then ushered them into his room. Tony was on his side. He was no longer resting peacefully. His breathing was labored, gurgling sounds came from his throat, and beads of moisture formed on his face.

Tears came to the mother's eyes. Though she felt a sense of elation when the phone call came announcing Tony's deterioration, seeing her son was painful. She turned to her husband. "Do you think he's suffering?"

"Probably not, with all the brain damage."

Tony's teenage sister wiped the sweat from her brother's forehead, then placed a small metal cross around his neck. "Is Tony going to die?" she asked her parents.

"It's possible he may. We have to talk to the doctor," her father told her.

"It's in God's hands," the mother said. Before Tony's fever and seizures, the mother had hoped for her son's demise, while the father prayed for a miraculous recovery. Now, with death imminent, it became harder for the mother to lose him, easier for the father to give up hope and accept the inevitable.

Jim Wellander walked into the room with the boy's chart open in his hands. He glanced at it, nodded to the parents, and went directly to Tony's bedside. Questions on the parents' lips waited while Jim examined their son. Hand on wrist, feeling the pulse; stethoscope on the chest, listening to heart and lungs; and reflex hammer on the extremities, making arms and legs jerk.

"Tony is very ill," Jim said. "He's developed a high fever and this morning he had convulsions, probably related to the fever. He's been evaluated by Dr. Lassiter, the staff neurologist; he thinks Tony's deterioration is related to brain damage and perhaps a complicating viral pneumonia."

"Is he suffering?" the mother asked.

"No," Jim answered empathetically. "Even though he looks uncomfortable with the fever and labored breathing, he feels no pain. There is no suffering."

"What are his chances?" the father asked.

"Very bad. He could expire at any time." Jim chose the word "expire" rather than "die." It wasn't as final to expire as to die.

"Is there anything to control his fever?"

"He's getting aspirin, Tylenol, fluids, and Dilantin."

"Is there something we should do?"

"There's one thing. The postmortem examination." Jim avoided the word autopsy. It wasn't as bad to have a postmortem examination as an autopsy.

"Do you mean an autopsy?" the mother asked.

"Yes," Jim mumbled.

"I don't want an autopsy," the father said adamantly. "He's suffered enough. Let him die in peace."

Jim knew it was common for families to feel the dead person suffered during an autopsy. The autopsy was viewed as a violation of the body, a body which somehow could suffer even when it was no longer alive.

"But the autopsy is extremely important," Jim said. "It will help us understand Tony's illness; apply the knowledge to someone in the future with a similar problem." Jim wanted the parents to agree to an autopsy prior to the boy's death because Mo Corning was on duty that night. If Tony died then, it would be harder for Mo to get autopsy permission; he didn't know the family as well.

"Can we still have a regular funeral after an autopsy?" the mother asked.

"Definitely."

"What does the body look like?"

"There's only a scar on the abdomen. Like surgery. You won't see the scar at the funeral."

"Well, then, what do you think, Richard?" Mrs. Zancanelli looked to her husband.

"If it helps someone else, we have to do it," he decided. "Tony would have wanted it."

Families also postulated what the dead person would have wanted. One never got an autopsy if the person said before he died, "No autopsy." But without the autopsy, the doctor was without a judge. He had treated a patient who then died; in a sense the doctor had failed. What really caused death? Was the wrong diagnosis made, wrong treatment given? Jim expected Tony's autopsy to show two things: inflammation of the brain and pneumonia.

The operating room was quiet save for the sound of the respirator that filled Heather's lungs with oxygen and anesthesia. The pens on the EEG machine still traced their pattern quietly; there were no more bursts of electricity from the brain, causing the steel pens to scratch loudly on the paper or bang into each other. The nurse could only sit and watch. She glanced from the monotonously gliding pens, to the respirator, to Heather's seizure chart, and back again to the EEG. Two o'clock. In two more hours Heather would be taken for a CAT scan.

They were all gathered near the nurses' station—Alex, Jim, Mo, Casey, Eli, Louise, and Edgar Quinn. Alex handed Louise a vial of 5 percent dextrose in water. She placed the sugar water on a small medication tray with an alcohol swab, two 10 cc syringes, a tourniquet, and two Band Aids.
"How much are you going to inject?" Eli asked.
"A full ten cc's, slowly. I'll inject a cc per minute."
"Is there anything you want me to do?" the father asked.
"Just observe," Alex told him.
"What if she has a seizure during the injection?" Mo asked.
"We'll watch it carefully, compare it to her other spells."
They found Charlotte talking to the two Susies, explaining the upcoming injection in detail. The two Susies listened, fascinated.
"Girls, you'll have to leave," Louise said. "Charlotte's having a special test."
"We know. Good luck, Charlotte," Susie W said.
Charlotte sat quietly in bed, her large legs dangling almost to the floor. She certainly isn't nervous, Alex thought as he pulled a chair next to her bed. He didn't know whether to interpret her discussion with the Susies as positive or negative evidence for hysterical seizures. At first he thought it supported hysterical spells. Charlotte enjoyed being an epileptic; she bragged about

it to her friends. Yet her talk might be a defensive maneuver to protect herself from ridicule.

"Do you have any questions about the test?" Alex asked.

"How long will it last?"

"The injection takes ten minutes."

"You're sure it's not painful?"

"No more than having blood drawn in the morning."

"Is it okay, Dad?"

Edgar Quinn nodded. He had no choice.

"I'll explain the test once more," Alex said, "then we'll do it. Okay. This is a special medicine. When it's injected into people who have seizures, it will cause a seizure. If it is injected into a normal person, nothing happens. By injecting it and observing a seizure we can decide on medication and treatment. Any questions?"

"What if you inject the medicine and I don't have a seizure?"

Alex paused. He looked at Eli and at Charlotte's father.

How are you going to answer that one? Eli wondered.

"Don't worry," Alex told Charlotte. "Because your spells are real, I know you'll respond to the medicine."

Eli motioned Alex and Edgar Quinn outside. "Be back in a second, Charlotte," Alex told her as they walked into the hall.

"That was a stupid thing to tell her," Eli said.

"Why?"

"No matter what happens, we'll have to tell her we lied. If she really has seizures, she won't respond to the fake injection and we'll have to tell her. If she does respond to the injection, we'll have to tell her the test was a ploy."

Edgar Quinn waited for Alex's answer, disturbed by Eli's analysis.

"If she doesn't respond to the injection," Alex said, "I'll look at the bottle and say it's the wrong material, or it's past the expiration date. We'll tell her we're postponing the test and never do it again. If she does have a spell with the sugar water, she'll have to be confronted anyway. I won't tell her we injected a fake medicine, only that the seizure we witnessed wasn't real and that we want to begin psychiatric evaluation."

Charlotte's father and Eli grudgingly accepted Alex's explanation and they re-entered the room.

The curtains were drawn around Charlotte's bed, and the girl lay on her back. Alex sat in a chair at her bedside with Louise standing next to him holding a tray with sugar water, syringe, swab, and tourniquet. Louise held up the vial, showed it to Alex, then turned it upside down. Alex filled the syringe with air, stuck the needle through the rubber stopper on the vial, and pushed air into the vial. This made withdrawal of fluid from the vial easy. He put a tourniquet around Charlotte's biceps and watched the veins in her forearm fill with blood. He wiped her arm with an alcohol swab and waited for the alcohol to dry. Then he quickly plunged the needle into a vein. Charlotte winced.

Alex pulled slowly on the plunger of the syringe. Dark blood billowed into the clear water and changed the 5 percent dextrose-water into maroon. Alex had demonstrated that the needle was intravenous. He released the tourniquet; he did not want to impede the flow of material he was about to inject. He took off his watch and placed it on the bed. It was difficult to administer the water at the slow rate of one cc of fluid per minute without the aid of a second hand.

"Are you ready for the injection, Charlotte?" Alex asked.

"I feel a little funny."

"In what way?"

"Hard to describe."

Alex felt her pulse. A bit fast, but strong.

"Go ahead, inject it," Charlotte said.

"I'm starting now. The injection will take ten minutes; tell me if you feel anything."

The second hand swept past the six as Alex began to inject the first cc. He waited one minute. Charlotte lay still, her eyes fixed on the ceiling. The others in the room stood equally as still, their eyes fixed on her.

Still no reaction. Alex injected the second cc. Another minute passed.

He injected the third cc.

"How do you feel?" he asked.

205

No response from the girl.

"Charlotte, can you hear me?"

Quiet.

Alex snapped his fingers in front of her face. She didn't blink. He turned to the onlookers. "I think the injection worked— she's going to have a spell." Alex pulled the needle from Charlotte's vein, applied pressure with a swab, then covered the injection site with a Band Aid.

Charlotte began to talk. It was "French."

"Turn on the tape recorder, Louise." The nurse pressed the button on Alex's cassette recorder. "Now we'll find out what she's been saying." The others watched, transfixed by the scene. Edgar Quinn slowly shook his head. Mo muttered to Jim that he wouldn't have believed it if he hadn't been there. Louise watched with her mouth open. Casey smiled quietly to herself. Eli Lassiter's face betrayed no emotion.

Charlotte had finished speaking. Now her extremities began to shake in the same pattern Alex had witnessed before, first arms, then arms and legs, finally legs alone. Then she lay still.

Thank God there were no fondling movements, Edgar Quinn thought as Alex put the side rails up and led the onlookers from the room.

The monotony of Heather Papineau's EEG continued: slow, undulating waves uninterrupted by seizure activity. Blood pressure and pulse remained stable despite the deep anesthesia that had successfully sedated her irritable brain. It was three o'clock, one more hour until the anesthesia would be lightened and the girl taken for her CAT scan. The special nurse would be happy then, she would have something to do; it would be her responsibility to monitor vital signs. The anesthesiologist would be equally as relieved; his anesthesia had been effective in controlling the seizures and there were no complications.

"Alex, you proved your point," Mo said animatedly.

"I thought she would have the spell immediately after I began injecting," Alex said, "but it took a couple of minutes."

"She said she felt funny just before you started the injection. What do you think that meant?" Jim asked.

"I don't know."

"What if it was the beginning of a seizure?" Eli asked.

"What do you mean?"

"How do we know that by chance Charlotte wasn't starting a seizure before you gave her the injection?" he persisted.

"You must be kidding, Eli."

"I'm serious. I'm as interested as you are in finding out whether her spells are hysterical, but something was happening to that girl before you injected the water. I'm not convinced the spell we witnessed was hysterical."

Jim turned to the tall, nervous staff neurologist. "Eli, if we discount that spell, we have nothing."

"Are you ready to tell the girl her spells are hysterical, discontinue drug manipulation, and begin psychiatric care?" Eli shot back. "What if we're wrong?"

Everyone looked to Alex. "Eli's point is valid," Alex said without hesitation. "There must be no doubt that Charlotte's spells are hysterical before we begin psychiatric treatment. If she hadn't responded at all today, we would've had our answer. Because she had a seizure after not feeling right, we can't rule out the possibility that she was going to have a bona fide convulsion just before my injection. I think her spell today was hysterical, but maybe that's not good enough."

"What do you suggest," Eli asked, "another injection?"

"Precisely, only this time while she's attached to an EEG machine. If her spell is fake, there'll be no abnormalities on the EEG prior to her convulsion. I'd go a step further. I'll tell Charlotte that since we've caused a seizure, we'd like to inject another medicine while she is having a convulsion to make her stop."

"What will you inject?"

"Dextrose in water both times, only there will be two different-colored vials. I bet we can start and stop a seizure by injecting sugar water. With the EEG running, there'll be no dispute as to what happened."

Alex looked at Eli, then at Edgar Quinn. It was Charlotte's father who spoke first. "When will you do it?"

"Tomorrow afternoon."

"We have no choice," Eli said.

"What about the tape recording?" Louise asked.

"I'll have to find someone who speaks French. If she has any French books at home, Dr. Quinn, bring them to the hospital."

Alex, Eli, and Edgar Quinn returned to the girl's room. She was awake, sitting up in bed.

The father took her hand. "How do you feel?"

"Fine, Papa." Charlotte hadn't called her father "Papa" since childhood.

Alex performed a quick neurologic exam. It was normal. He explained what had happened after the injection and told her of the test scheduled for the next day. She accepted the information passively and was willing to cooperate.

It was four o'clock. Heather Papineau's prolonged general anesthesia was over. The EEG electrodes were removed from her head, leaving paste-filled hair behind. The level of anesthesia was lowered enough to keep her unconscious but not enough to prevent seizure activity from beginning again. She remained paralyzed; abnormal electrical discharges from her brain could not be translated into a convulsion. With the EEG disconnected, there was no monitor of seizure activity; the success or failure of anesthesia would be known only when the medication that paralyzed her muscles had worn off. That would take an hour, enough time for a CAT scan without the danger of a convulsion during the X-ray. The anesthesiologist, his machine, and the special nurse followed Heather to the CAT scan. Her head was placed in the giant sphere and the X-rays began flowing through it; the computer analyzed the deflections and printed a picture of the girl's brain. Normal.

Late afternoon on division 17. A time that usually found Tony Zancanelli's family home. Today they sat in his room. His condition hadn't changed since morning, feverish with labored breathing but no further convulsions. The mother, father, and daughter sat at the boy's bedside, staring at him and exchanging glances. Two of them would leave the room for fifteen minutes; one always stayed. Jim Wellander entered the room to examine the boy, then told the parents that there had been no change in

Tony's condition, still critical. Should the family stay or go home? If something happened, when would it occur? Jim didn't know, but unless they felt strongly, he advised they go home. They would be called immediately if there was a change. The mother wanted to stay. It didn't matter that there was no place for her; she would stay in the boy's room; she would sit on a chair. She didn't expect to sleep. The father encouraged her to come home. She refused. Finally a compromise was reached. She would stay until ten o'clock, when her husband would return and take her home. Certain that her son would die by ten, Mrs. Zancanelli wanted to be at his bedside when it happened.

Dennis and Florence Balsiger stood in the corridor talking to Casey. They were still bitter about grand rounds, but Casey tried to console them, emphasizing the importance of Dr. Hollsworth's visit the next day. Neither of the parents was impressed. There had been too many doctors and too many opinions. Casey mentioned the new experimental drug that would be given to BJ. The mother was encouraged, the father disdainful. Casey was depressed after talking to the Balsigers. She felt helpless; medicine and its miracles had failed this couple and their son. To them, Casey represented a company that had produced faulty merchandise, hadn't fulfilled its contract, promised something it couldn't deliver. She took out her list and once more reviewed it. Still, nothing fit. If Alex showed up for dinner, she would ask him to go over the list with her again.

Heather Papineau was being transferred back to her bed in the critical care room of division 17, while Alex, Mo, Jim, and Casey looked on. Her muscles were still paralyzed and she still needed help breathing from the respirator.

"When will we know if the anesthesia worked?" Alex asked.

"She's still paralyzed. The medication should wear off in another thirty minutes," Mo answered.

"Could she be seizing right now?" Casey asked.

"Sure," Alex said, "but with no muscles to react we'd never know. In fact, there's only one part of the neurologic exam you can do with someone who's totally paralyzed. What is it?"

Mo answered. "Not reflexes; there has to be a muscle contraction for the response. Not sensation; even if the child could feel, he couldn't move or talk to let you know. How about the corneal reflex?"

"Wrong. The child wouldn't be able to blink," Alex said. "It's the pupillary response. The smooth muscle responsible for pupillary constriction can still respond." Alex held open Heather's eyes and aimed his flashlight at her black pupils, which immediately became smaller. "That's the shortest neurologic exam you'll ever do; hers is normal."

"Her CAT scan was normal too," Jim said.

"What happens if the medicine wears off and she wakes up seizing?" Casey asked.

"Nothing to do but wait," Alex said. "If she's still seizing tomorrow morning, we'll have to resume anticonvulsant manipulation. If that doesn't help, I don't know."

Louise entered the critical care room. "Alex, Mrs. Papineau wants to talk with you."

Alex walked to the parents' waiting room. Mrs. Papineau's hair was disheveled and she wore the same clothes as the day before. No makeup, nervously smoking cigarettes, she spoke in halting, disjointed sentences.

"She's had a test. Another day and how's she doing?"

"The special X-ray test was normal," Alex said. "The general anesthesia was successful in suppressing her seizures. We're waiting for her to wake up. Then we'll know if the seizures will start again."

"Start again? Why should they start? They've stopped."

"That was only because of the anesthesia."

"Only because. Here in the hospital and not getting better."

"We're doing everything possible."

"But she's not getting better."

Alex led the distraught woman to a chair. She fumbled with her cigarette, unsuccessfully trying to put it in an ashtray. This woman's decompensating, Alex thought. Maybe he should call the psychiatrist who cared for her.

"Mrs. Papineau, who is the psychiatrist you've been seeing?"

Her face became red and her lips tightened. "Don't bother me. Don't start that."

"Then you should go home and get some rest."

"Rest? Home? I'm staying with my girl. Until she wakes up. I've got to talk to her."

"Heather won't be able to talk to you. She may begin her seizures again."

"You want me to leave. I'm not leaving my girl."

Alex didn't want to upset her more. Besides, she had the right to wait. Perhaps Heather wouldn't wake up seizing and the mother could talk to her. He left Mrs. Papineau huddled on a chair in the waiting room.

Alex found Mo, who was on night duty, at the nurses' station. "Did Jim tell you about Zancanelli before he left?" Alex asked.

"Yes. We're waiting for the boy to die. Jim spoke to the parents this afternoon. They're ready to give permission for an autopsy."

"Good. Heather Papineau's mother's still in the waiting room. She's very unstable emotionally; you know she's being treated by a psychiatrist. Heather's seizures have finally gotten to her. I told her she could stay here; she wants to talk to Heather, but try to get her to go home as soon as possible."

Alex extracted his file cards from his pocket and was beginning to flip through them when he came across Casey's address. He paused just long enough for Mo to notice.

"What is it?" the resident asked.

"Mo, do me a favor. Cover for me until nine o'clock."

"But you're not even on. I am."

"I know. But just in case something happens. Trade beepers and sign out to me. Your calls will come to my beeper, which you'll answer. My calls will also come to my beeper, but there shouldn't be any. If you need to reach me, have the page operator call me on your beeper."

"Sounds complicated. Who are you hiding from?"

Alex didn't answer.

"Okay, I'll do it," Mo agreed. "If I can understand it. But what if someone wants you and gets me?"

"Tell them I'm busy and take a message. If it's urgent, call me."

"All right," Mo said.

"See you about nine," Alex said as he grabbed his coat, walked to the stairs, and then down to the lobby.

He called home from a phone booth near the hospital's main entrance. "Mellissa. Listen, I won't be home until after nine."

"Why?"

"Mo Corning's supposed to be on night duty, but something personal came up and he asked me to cover for him. I have to do it. I owe him for covering me on Elizabeth's birthday."

"Oh, Alex, I made dinner!"

"I'm sorry, really. I'll grab something in the cafeteria."

Alex knew that Mellissa wouldn't argue. She couldn't. In the past, his absences had always been related to the hospital, and she had come to expect them. Her pressuring him to go into private practice was partially due to her wanting them to structure their own lives. Now, without her even suspecting it, he was threatening that structure in a way that medicine never could.

Alex decided to walk the eight blocks from the hospital to Casey's. He wasn't hungry, but his stomach churned with a combination of anticipation and anxiety that was best diagnosed by a nonmedical term, "butterflies." Before he knew it, he was standing before a row of graystones, many with plant-filled bay windows. He studied the "40" written in small, pale-gold letters on the glass above an entrance for a few moments before walking up the steps and ringing the bell.

Casey wasn't certain that Alex would show up, but hoping for the best, she had prepared dinner and set a candlelit table near the bay window. She took down her hair, brushed it, and changed into jeans and a T shirt. As she worked in the kitchen, she remembered the dinners she'd cooked for her husband. Even if Alex didn't arrive, there was joy for her in the anticipation and preparation.

A harsh buzzer rang in the apartment. Only 6:15. Too early for Alex, but she went ahead and pressed the intercom button. "Who is it?"

Downstairs, Alex heard a voice which didn't sound like Casey's issuing from the tiny box above the apartment buzzers.

"Casey? It's Alex, Casey."

Casey couldn't restrain a grin of pure pleasure. Not only had he arrived, but he was early. "Come up!" she yelled into the intercom, as another buzzer sounded, unlocking the door to the apartment building. Alex pushed open the door, then began the walk up six steep flights of stairs. His heart, already beating rapidly, pounded even harder from the physical exertion.

Casey stood by the banister on the sixth-floor landing, watching Alex's figure grow larger as he slowly circled upward. Only when he was next to her did she realize how nervous she was. "I wasn't sure you'd come," she said shyly.

"It was an impulsive decision," Alex said, panting, but with a smile on his face. He followed her into the apartment and studied her as she took his coat. In jeans and a T shirt she looked even slimmer. He followed the movement of her small breasts, unrestrained beneath the T shirt, as she placed his coat on a chair, and his fantasies about the hair that was always pinned to the back of her head were fulfilled as he watched it rippling down her shoulders. The pleasant smell of her perfume was an added surprise. A warm feeling grew in Alex's body and almost erased the queasiness in his stomach and the fatigue in his legs.

Casey's chief resident was transposed unchanged from division 17 to her apartment. A beeper hung from his belt and he stood before her in his short white hospital jacket, complete with 3 x 5 cards in his pocket. She quickly removed the white jacket and slowly walked toward him.

The triangular face stared into his and her eyes widened as they had two nights previously in the hospital elevator. He gently touched the side of her face and she moved up against him. It was a long kiss and an even longer embrace.

"I'm so glad you're here," Casey whispered.

"I wanted to be with you," Alex said simply. "But," he added with a grin, "I almost didn't make it up those stairs. That's some hike!"

"I'll try to make it worthwhile," she smiled. "Come. I'll show you around."

Casey's one-bedroom apartment consisted of a small kitchen and a large living room with a bay window, looking south toward the glittering skyline. In one corner of the living room, which held a desk, bookshelves, and a stereo, Alex could identify Casey's courses and her hospital rotations from the volumes on her shelves. The desk was piled with neurology texts.

"You've been studying hard."

"I want to impress my chief resident."

"You already have."

"Alex, BJ Balsiger's parents were really upset by grand rounds this morning and I can't say I blame them. I tried to pacify them by emphasizing the experimental drug we'll be getting for BJ and Dr. Hollsworth's visit tomorrow. But they're used to promises that never materialize. Could we go over my list one more time? Maybe we can come up with something."

At first they sat across from each other on the sofa, Casey reading from her list. But soon their feet were up, and Casey's head nestled on Alex's shoulder. The discussion of each particular disease was interrupted by a kiss, sometimes the gentle touching of Alex's lips to Casey's, other times a harder kiss, almost an uncontrolled one that threatened to end their discussion. But whether it was the circumstances of the "neurology rounds" that Alex and Casey were conducting on Casey's sofa, or the complexity of BJ's case, Alex and Casey were still unable to identify on Casey's list the disease that mirrored what was going wrong in BJ's brain.

"Time for dinner," Casey said finally.

"That's why I'm here," Alex said with a smile. "Anyway, that's what the invitation said that was written on my 3 x 5 card."

Elizabeth refused to put on her coat, so dressing Kristen was twice as difficult. Finally, Mellissa had both girls ready to go out. They rode the elevator to the lobby, then made the three-block walk to Children's Hospital. After a brief delay in which the girls insisted on riding the bicycle merry-go-round in the lobby, they all headed for the cafeteria. Mellissa expected Alex would be there, but if not, she could always page him. Even if he was too busy to eat with them, she would at least have gotten the children out of the house. Alex wasn't in the dining room, and when Mellissa saw Mo Corning she was confused. It was five after seven. Alex had said he was covering for Mo until nine. Yet Mo was there and Alex wasn't. Mellissa stood for a moment, trying to figure out what had happened, then abruptly grabbed her two girls and left.

* * *

Alex and Casey were sitting at the candlelit table by the window, hypnotized by the line of moving light from passing cars which snaked a path down the avenue as far as they could see.

Casey took Alex's hand into hers and held it. Unlike the cafeteria, it didn't have to be a quick squeeze; there was nothing to force her hand away, nothing to prevent her fingers from slowly caressing the back of Alex's hand as long as she liked.

"I was so excited with Charlotte's injection," Casey said.

"I just knew I had to be right," Alex said.

"But isn't there still a chance that it could have been a real seizure?"

"Sure, there's a chance. But don't worry, Casey. I'll prove it wasn't real with the second injection tomorrow when we have EEG monitoring."

"Alex, don't be too cocky," Casey said. "Even if you're right about Charlotte, you've got to be careful with Eli."

Alex didn't say anything. He knew that Casey was right but he didn't care. "Casey, to be honest, I'm more worried about Heather Papineau than about Charlotte. Charlotte's not in any danger."

It was quiet. Neither of them spoke for over a minute. Then Casey took Alex's hand into both of hers. "What do we talk about now?" she asked quietly as she stared at Alex's hand.

Alex put his hand to her chin and lifted her face so he could see her eyes. They were wide, their brown color had somehow turned soft, and they were pouring out to Alex as they never had before.

"I think neurology rounds are over," Alex said softly. "No need to talk anymore."

They both stood up and he took her freely into his arms. His hands moved under her T shirt as hers roamed inside his shirt. When Alex lifted Casey to carry her into the bedroom, her long, straight hair almost brushed the floor.

In bed, they were each other's now. Alex was surprised how easy it was for him to make love to Casey, how natural it was to tangle himself in her arms and legs. Thoughts of his lovemaking with Mellissa flashed through his mind. Mellissa was heavier when she was on top; her breasts didn't flatten and disappear

215

like Casey's when she was underneath. Casey was much easier to turn than Mellissa. But these thoughts quickly passed and then Alex was only with Casey.

For Casey, there were comparisons as well. Her husband and her college nights returned. Alex's chest was more hairy, his kisses more gentle. Casey thought of the times she and her husband had come together, and she remembered her first orgasm. But like Alex, these thoughts passed and then she was lost in his embrace.

She took Alex's head into her hands. "I want you now, Alex," she moaned. "Please—I need you inside me."

Alex rose up over Casey and they were one. There was nothing else in the world for them at that moment.

When it was over, Alex floated off into another world. He didn't know where it was; he only knew it was wonderful. Then he found himself wanting Casey again, and he was ready, something that rarely happened so quickly with Mellissa. Casey took Alex in, and they frantically pushed into each other. Now they were totally out of control.

Shrill beeps filtered into the bedroom.

Alex and Casey didn't hear the beeping until they had finished and lay spent in each other's arms.

"What's that?" Casey asked.

"I think it's my beeper."

"I thought Mo was on call tonight," she said, beginning to disentangle herself.

"He is, but we switched beepers and he signed out to me."

"He what?" Casey looked puzzled.

"Just to make sure my wife couldn't reach me."

When the beeps continued, Alex sat up. "Mo said he'd call only if it was an emergency. I'd better find out what he wants."

Alex got out of bed, walked into the living room, and called the hospital.

"Could you page Dr. Corning, please?"

"I'm sorry. He's signed out to Dr. Licata."

"Oh, right." Alex forgot the switched beepers. "Okay, page Dr. Licata."

Alex's beeper went off. Mo pressed the tiny red button on it and answered the page.

"Alex"—Mo sounded harried—"your wife just called. She wants to talk to you. She's mad!"

"What'd she say?"

"When I answered the page, she said that I was supposed to be signed out to you. I told her you'd be back in a minute. She asked where you were; I told her I didn't know. She didn't believe me. Where the hell are you, anyway?"

"I'll be on the ward in a couple minutes."

"Good. And listen, after you settle your family problems, will you please talk to Heather Papineau's mother? She's worked herself into a frenzy. By the way, Heather's seizing again."

Alex held the dead receiver in his hand, staring into the darkened apartment. Finally he forced himself to hang up and begin dressing. Casey's naked figure appeared in the bedroom doorway. She looked at him but said nothing.

"I think my wife knows I'm not at the hospital," Alex said. "Heather Papineau's seizing again and her mother may be going crazy right on the ward. I've got to leave."

"I don't expect you'll be able to come back," Casey said quietly.

Alex paused in the middle of buttoning his shirt, walked over, and took her in his arms. They held on to each other for over a minute until Alex took Casey's face into his hands and gently kissed her.

"It was beautiful, Casey, wasn't it?"

Casey put her fingers to his lips. "Do you love me, Alex?"

Alex stared into her widened eyes.

"I love you, Alex."

The warm feeling burned its way through Alex's body.

"I love you, Casey."

Alex ran the eight blocks back to the hospital. He walked onto division 17, red-cheeked and puffing, to find Mo at the nurses' station, where they exchanged beepers and notified the page operator.

"Thanks, Mo. I've got to get home."

"What about Mrs. Papineau?"

Alex had already picked up the phone and was dialing.

"Hi, Mellissa, it's Alex."

"Where are you?" she demanded angrily.

"At the hospital."

217

"Come home this instant!"

"Give me a few minutes. There are some problems on the ward I have to solve." Alex took the receiver from his ear. "Mo, I've got to get home. She hung up."

"What about Mrs. Papineau?" Mo repeated.

"You talk to her." Alex looked at his watch. "It's eight-fifteen, visiting hours are over in fifteen minutes."

"One day you'll tell me what happened tonight, OK?"

Alex slapped his large, balding, first-year resident on the shoulder and dashed from the ward.

The walk home from Children's Hospital was much too short for Alex. He tried to collect his thoughts. What did Mellissa suspect and why did she call him at the hospital? If he was lucky, one of the girls was sick. How would he explain where he had been? He could say he'd been doing a spinal tap. Or talking to an hysterical patient. But in that case, Mo would have known where he was. And why was Mo in the hospital if Alex was covering for him? Alex allowed himself to focus briefly on his evening with Casey as he rode the elevator up to the fourteenth floor.

Mellissa sat woodenly on the couch, an unread newspaper on her lap. When Alex was on duty, she never suspected he was anywhere except the hospital. Yet she couldn't explain Mo's eating dinner in the hospital cafeteria at 7:00 P.M. and then answering Alex's beeper. Mellissa hadn't told the page operator to page Dr. Licata; she had given the operator Alex's beeper number. She hoped for an explanation she could believe.

"Sorry I'm late, Mellissa." Alex attempted to make his kiss more than perfunctory, but she resisted.

"Where were you Alex?"

"At the hospital."

"What was Mo doing there if you were covering for him?"

"Maybe some work he forgot to do. He didn't tell me why he wanted me to cover."

"Alex, why did Mo answer your beeper?"

No reply.

"Alex, the girls and I went to the hospital tonight. We wanted to surprise you for dinner. I saw Mo Corning eating in the cafeteria. I didn't know what to think. When we got home I

218

paged you and Mo answered the page. He didn't know where you were. Just said you'd be back shortly. Alex, I gave the operator your beeper number, not your name. Why was Mo carrying your beeper?"

Alex visibly paled, but still didn't speak.

"Okay, Alex. I'm going to ask once more and I want the truth. Were you at the hospital?"

Alex managed a feeble "No."

"Then where were you?" A red color began to fill Mellissa's face and her hands trembled.

When he still didn't answer, Mellissa shouted, "*Where the hell were you, Alex?*"

"At a girl's apartment."

Mellissa stepped back. The color left her face. Her voice fell. "What were you doing there?"

"Dinner."

Mellissa stared at her husband. She felt the loneliness of hundreds of nights alone deep in her bones. Dinner with one, then two little girls pounded in her head.

"What did you do after dinner Alex, screw her?" she yelled.

Alex buried his forehead in his palms.

"Did you screw that girl, Alex? *Did you?*"

"Yes, I screwed her."

"How many times has it been? How many girls has it been?"

"The first time. She's the only girl."

"Who is she, a nurse?"

"No, a medical student."

"What's her name?"

"Casey. We ate dinner with her Tuesday night, remember?"

The phone rang; Alex moved quickly to answer it.

"Alex, it's Mo. I don't care if you're in the process of a divorce, you've got to come to the hospital right away! Heather Papineau's mother appears to be having a psychotic break. She refuses to leave the parents' room and she won't talk to anyone but you."

"I'll be over," Alex said quietly.

Mellissa didn't move.

"You're not going to believe me," Alex said, "but I've got to go to the hospital."

"Alex, why did you have to do it?" Mellissa asked, not with tears in her eyes but with a deep sadness that had taken over her face. "Don't you realize we almost made it? Only a few more months and we would have been home free. Oh God, if we could've only made it a few more months."

Alex moved slowly toward the door.

"I'll be back in half an hour," he said weakly.

Alex was numb as he walked back to the hospital. He didn't want to go to the hospital and talk to Mrs. Papineau. He wasn't even sure he wanted to return to Casey's, and he was afraid of what awaited him at home. Why did he have to get caught? How stupid it was to switch beepers. But he wanted to be with Casey so badly, and it was so wonderful! Hell, he knew a lot of the doctors who cheated on their wives. They never seemed to get caught. At this very moment there had to be a doctor in bed with a nurse in an on-call room somewhere. But Alex was unable to categorize his thoughts further; he was too confused. As he approached the hospital, he watched an ambulance pull up to the emergency room and the attendants frantically rush a child through the large swinging doors. The sight of the ambulance calmed him, and he realized how lucky he was to be returning to the hospital, to the familiar, to the problems he always had been confident he could solve. And so, as Alex Licata walked onto division 17, he welcomed the task of quieting Mrs. Papineau. It would be therapeutic for him as well as for Heather's mother.

Mo greeted him with a sympathetic smile. "Nice to see you, Alex!"

"Okay, Mo. Let's check Heather before I talk to the mother."

"She started seizing again," Mo said as they walked into the critical care room. "At first the seizures weren't as frequent as before, but now they're back to the old pattern."

Alex scanned the girl's seizure chart. Eight hours of blank spaces ended with a pattern of alternately filled-in boxes, indicating a seizure every ten minutes, then every seven minutes, then every five minutes.

"The anesthesia did nothing," Alex said. "We might as well have put leeches on her back and bled her."

"We did get a CAT scan, though."

Alex studied Heather's chart. "Here's the summary, Mo. Anticonvulsant levels in upper therapeutic range, blood pressure and pulse normal, good spontaneous respirations, no evidence of infection, blood chemistries normal, CAT scan and LP normal, and no localizing findings on exam."

"Plus a crazy mother you'd better talk to before it's too late."

Mrs. Papineau was standing in the corner of the parents' waiting room, her arms flying in circles, her voice rising and falling in inappropriate pauses. "Why should I go home?" the woman yelled to the nurse at her side. "Why should I stay here? You'd better not try to hurt me anymore."

As Alex and Mo walked into the room, Mrs. Papineau ran to them.

"Dr. Licata, you've got to help me. They're hurting Heather." A pause. "Are you trying to hurt Heather, too? Don't hit me."

"Mrs. Papineau, no one's trying to hurt you," Alex said. "We're only trying to help."

"What's bothering me? What's bothering me? No, don't touch me. Where's my medicine? Where's my baby?"

"Heather's fine. She's in the hospital, where she's being taken care of."

"The hospital! Why?"

"Do you know where you are, Mrs. Papineau?"

"Of course. Don't touch me. Where's my medicine?"

"Tell us where you are, Mrs. Papineau."

"I'm home. Close the door. Why is it empty?"

"What's empty?"

"My medicine. Why is my medicine empty? I'm going to the store. Don't touch me."

"Mrs. Papineau—" Alex began.

"Watch Heather," the woman said, as if he had not spoken. "She's OK. I'm going to the store."

"What medicine are you talking about?"

"My Thorazine. Dr. Albertson gave it to me. Where's Dr. Albertson?"

"It's not a bad idea, Mo. Let's give her some IM Thorazine." Alex looked at Mo, who shrugged his shoulders.

"How much?" the nurse asked.

"Fifty milligrams."

Alex and Mo held the woman while the needle plunged into her arm and the medication injected intramuscularly. Thorazine was one of the most widely used tranquilizing drugs in psychiatry. It would be absorbed by the muscle, flow back to the heart, then be pumped to the brain. Hopefully, in about thirty minutes it would sedate the disturbed woman. Until then, Alex and Mo left Mrs. Papineau with the nurse. Meanwhile, Alex called the psychiatry resident on duty, who agreed with IM Thorazine administration and who knew a Dr. Phillip Albertson. The psychiatrist's office was called and a message was left with his answering service.

Alex sat in the nurses' station and thought about Heather Papineau's problem. Problem solving is not well understood. It requires more than intelligence. It requires the ability to sift the components of the problem and view them in a different perspective. After thinking about a problem, more thinking is often counterproductive. Let the mind rest, go to a movie, "sleep on it." A problem not actively pursued often settles on the brain in a different way, its solution then obvious. And for Alex, solving Heather's problem was something even more. It was the need to re-establish his equilibrium, to gain control again. He didn't know what would happen with Mellissa and Casey, but he knew he couldn't let neurology slip away from him. If he did that, he was lost. And it might have been this realization that provided the energy for Alex's insight into what was wrong with Heather Papineau. It happened when Mo joined him in the nurses' station and they discussed the uncertain future of the convulsing girl and the probable need for her mother's hospitalization. Suddenly Alex stopped talking. He stared at Mo; a smile came to his face.

"What is it?" Mo asked.

Alex's smile broadened, his eyes lit up, and he clapped his hands together. "I've got an idea."

"What is it?"

Mo could almost see Alex savoring the insight that was creeping through his mind. He was rethinking, re-examining.

222

"Sure," Alex said, half to himself. "That would explain everything."

"What would explain everything?"

"Jesus Christ! We could even treat it!" Alex shouted.

"Treat what?" Mo asked, now impatient.

"The Thorazine," Alex said.

"We've already given her. Thorazine? How do you treat it?"

"Not the mother. The girl."

"Why do you want to give Heather Thorazine?"

"I don't. She's had too much already."

"Alex, we haven't given Heather any Thorazine."

"Of course we haven't. She took it herself. All of it. Her mother's Thorazine. The bottle's empty. That's why the woman's gone crazy."

Mo was astonished. "You mean Heather took her mother's medicine?"

"Exactly. That explains Heather's seizures, the mother's hysteria, and her disjointed talk tonight about medicine and an empty bottle. Heather got into her mom's Thorazine. She probably did it when her mother went to the store or something. When the mother returned, she found the girl was seizing. Don't you remember? When Heather was two she sustained minor brain injury from her meningitis, so she already had an underlying seizure disorder. That's what brought her to the emergency ward Sunday night. Thorazine can lower the seizure threshold in someone with an underlying seizure disorder. In Heather, it triggered status epilepticus."

Alex poked his finger toward Mo for emphasis, presenting his ideas like a debater. "When she came in on Tuesday night there was a drop in blood pressure and problems with respiration that developed after a relatively small dose of anticonvulsants. Now I know why. She was already depressed from the Thorazine. Of course we didn't find anything on CAT scan or LP or on any of our metabolic screens. And that's why her neurologic exam was normal. It wasn't brain damage that caused the seizures, it was an overdose. Why did her mother go crazy tonight? The emotional stress of Heather's hospitalization and not taking medication led to Mrs. Papineau's decompensation."

"What if your theory is wrong?" Mo asked.

"We won't have to consider that possibility for long. Once she quiets down, Mrs. Papineau will give us a history of an empty medicine bottle. A test of Heather's blood will show high levels of Thorazine."

"Why wasn't a toxic screen sent off when she came in?" Mo asked.

"We didn't think of it; we were so sure something else was going on."

"Dr. Licata," the nurse on duty called. "Dr. Albertson's on the phone."

In the course of his conversation with Mrs. Papineau's psychiatrist, Alex discovered she had been hospitalized once before at Bellevue, on the psychiatric floor. Arrangements would be made to transfer her there tonight, where Dr. Albertson would evaluate her. Interestingly enough, he didn't think that the two or three days without Thorazine would make the woman psychotic, for the medication took longer than that to disappear from the body.

The injection had subdued Mrs. Papineau enough that Mo and Alex attempted to obtain a clearer history of the recent events, but it was difficult. She didn't remember finding an empty medicine bottle when she returned from the store and discovered Heather seizing. As Alex pressed his questions in an attempt to get a good history for an ingestion, he realized he was putting words in Mrs. Papineau's mouth and had to stop.

"The mother's not going to give us the answer," Mo said. "We'll have to wait for the blood test. I called the lab; they're sending an extra serum sample they have to the poison control lab. We should have the answer in a few hours."

"Mo, I'm calling the renal fellow, maybe we can dialyze out the Thorazine."

Renal dialysis was for people in kidney failure. The artificial kidney, a hundred times bigger than its natural counterpart, bathed blood in a special solution, to pull out toxic substances the diseased kidney couldn't remove from the body.

Alex thought of the first lecture he had heard on dialysis in medical school and how he could apply it to Heather's case. "Mo, how would you like to hear a little talk on kidney dialysis?" Alex said with a smile.

"Whatever turns you on, Alex," Mo said, enjoying Alex's animation.

"Dialysis means the passage of substances across a membrane with holes so tiny that red and white blood cells and the large blood proteins of the blood are too big to pass through them," Alex said. "However, small, toxic substances pass freely, moving according to the basic physical law that if a substance in one solution is very concentrated, it will pass to a less concentrated solution. During dialysis, the blood passes through a tubing bathed in special solution into which only the small, toxic substances pass. However, there are also small vital substances which could be lost in the process."

"Right. So what do you do then, doctor?" Mo asked with a chuckle.

"Easy," Alex continued. "Any vital substance small enough to pass through the tiny pores is placed in the dialysis solution at its exact concentration in the blood. Because the concentration is equal on both sides of the tubing, it remains in the bloodstream. Thus, the standard dialysis solution contains the same concentrations of sodium, chloride, potassium, magnesium, and calcium as blood. But guess what it *doesn't* contain."

"Thorazine."

"Right."

"That's just great, Alex. But don't forget Heather's got large amounts of anticonvulsants in her blood. You might dialyze those out along with the Thorazine."

"Not if we put anticonvulsants in the dialysis solution. Then we won't lose them."

Alex called the renal resident, who, after a short, intense discussion, wasn't convinced Thorazine could be dialyzed. He refused to begin dialysis until they were certain the girl's blood contained toxic levels of Thorazine. Besides, dialysis couldn't be started until the morning. Alex would have to wait.

It was almost ten o'clock. Mrs. Papineau was in an ambulance on her way to Bellevue by the time Mo and Alex checked Heather once more, then walked back toward the nurses' station. Through an open door, Alex saw Luciana Zancanelli sitting in her son's darkened room, her head lowered, dozing.

"Is Tony still alive?" Alex asked Mo.

"I think so. I haven't heard anything from the nurses."

"The mother could be sitting in that room with a dead son. It looks like she's fallen asleep."

Mrs. Zancanelli woke up when they entered Tony's room. "What happened?" she asked.

"We just came in to check Tony," Mo explained as he approached the bed.

The boy was still alive, but his breathing seemed faster and more shallow. He was still feverish.

The mother looked at her watch. "My husband will be picking me up soon. How's Tony?"

"The same. His breathing may not be as strong."

"How long will it take, doctor?"

"We don't know," Mo told her.

The mother walked over to stroke her son's face, then touched the cross that lay on his chest and kissed his forehead. She straightened up and stood silently staring at the boy. Finally she looked at Alex and Mo. "It's time to go home and be with my family," she announced simply.

Alex walked with Mo to the kitchen on division 17. "I'll treat you to some juice and toast," Mo said. Although a sign on the refrigerator door read, FOOD IN THIS REFRIGERATOR IS FOR PATIENTS ONLY—ADMINISTRATION, Mo opened the door and helped himself to juice, bread, butter, and jelly.

As he sat chewing the toast, Alex's thoughts returned to Mellissa and Casey.

Then he fantasized about just being a doctor. He found himself afloat in a sea of sick children, children whom he cured one by one, and as he did, he cast them back onto the shore. He thought of his own two little girls and a sinking feeling overcame him.

"How bad is it?" Mo asked.

"Bad."

"I'm sorry."

Alex stared at his toast. "It's not your fault. Thanks anyway. See you in the morning."

When he got to the apartment, Alex found the inside latch in place. He didn't want to ring the bell and wake up the girls, so he knocked quietly and called to Mellissa. A moment later she appeared in her nightgown.

"You're not staying here tonight, Alex." Her tone eliminated the possibility of bargaining. She had an answer for "Where should I stay?" but he didn't ask. Mellissa could have slammed the door in his face but she didn't. She still was his wife. She handed him a grocery bag with underpants, change of clothes, and his shaving kit.

"I'm sorry, Mellissa," Alex said.

"Good night, Alex," Mellissa said blandly and she closed the door.

Alex walked back toward the hospital, carrying a large brown paper bag. He found an empty on-call room in the sleeping quarters and phoned Casey. Her voice kindled a now familiar warm feeling in his body. He told her about Mellissa and Heather. They avoided talking about Mellissa and instead relived their evening together, giggling, teasing. Casey invited Alex to spend the night at her apartment, but he refused. He decided to stay in the hospital where it was safe. They would talk tomorrow. Alex called the page operator and told her he was spending the night at the hospital. On a mimeographed sheet listing the subspecialties she found "Neurology" and Mo Corning's name; underneath she wrote, "Alex Licata, extension 5149, wake up 7:00 A.M."

FRIDAY

Jim Wellander stood in Tony Zancanelli's room. He held the boy's chart in his hands and leafed through it. Then he looked at Tony's bed. A bed that previously held the dying boy's body hadn't changed. An IV pole still was in place at the top of the bed and an IV bottle hung from the pole. Tubing ran from the bottle to the boy's arm. The boy's chest, moving up and down rapidly the night before as it took shallow, gurgling breaths, no longer moved rapidly. But it did move. Up and down in a more natural, even rhythm. Tony Zancanelli was alive.

Jim put his stethoscope to the boy's chest. It sounded better. The temperature chart showed Tony was still feverish, but the drops of sweat on his forehead were not as prominent. Shit, the pediatric resident said to himself. What happened? He searched the chart but only found a note written by Mo at 10:30 P.M. "Shallow breathing and fever continue. Condition deteriorating. Parents notified. Will continue to support." There was no record of a new medication or treatment during the night.

Mo Corning walked into the room.

"What happened, Mo? Tony's still alive," Jim said.

"I don't know." Mo was as surprised as Jim was. "When I went to sleep, I thought the ward nurse would wake me up with news of Tony's death, but she didn't. He looked terrible when I checked him before I went to sleep. Did you see my note?"

"Yes. I wonder what happened."

"Nothing," Alex said as he walked into the room. "He got better. Children don't always die when we don't treat them."

"What are his parents going to say?" Jim asked.

"What can they say? The pneumonia probably broke on its own. Before antibiotics, people didn't always die from pneumonia. Especially children. It was the old people who died. They still die from pneumonia, even with antibiotics."

"That's really a shame," Jim said. "His family has no luck."

Casey and Louise entered the room. "Are we starting rounds in here?" the nurse asked. "Isn't that something, Tony's getting better? Maybe his brain will snap out of it, too."

"I doubt it," Jim said and turned to examine the boy. It seemed to Louise that Jim was pinching Tony's chest harder than usual when he checked for a pain response, as if the young doctor were angry with him. There was no response except for reflex turning of arms and legs. "His neurologic status is unchanged," Jim said.

"Is he still feverish?" Casey asked.

"It's 39.4 rectally. Same as yesterday."

"Let's get a chest film," Jim suggested. "Find out what's happening." He took a form from the bottom shelf on the chart rack, filled it out, and handed it to Louise. "Do it this morning."

They left Tony's room. Jim dreaded talking to the boy's parents. He didn't know whether it would be better to call them or wait until they called. But when he thought of the family sitting at home, huddled together during Tony's final hours, waiting for news, he knew he had to call.

The mother answered the phone.

"Mrs. Zancanelli, this is Dr. Wellander, calling from Children's Hospital." He heard the woman whisper to someone in the background, "It's about Tony."

"Yes?" she was fighting to keep her voice steady.

"He's doing a little better this morning."

"*What did you say?*"

"He's doing a little better this morning. He still has a fever, but the breathing is better and he looks more comfortable."

"Doctor, he was so sick last night . . ."

"I know. It may have been a pneumonia that cleared itself."

"You even asked us about autopsy permission."

"Sometimes children have amazing power to heal themselves. We're going to check his lungs with a chest X-ray this morning."

The father's voice came over a second phone. "Tony's not dead?"

"No, Mr. Zancanelli. In fact, he seems a little better this morning."

"How's his brain?"

"There's no change in his neurologic condition. He's just breathing easier."

"I see."

"I'm truly sorry, Mr. Zancanelli. If you'd like to discuss it further, I'll be available this afternoon here at the hospital." Jim slowly put the receiver down, then joined the entourage as rounds moved to the critical care room.

Alex and Casey were exchanging professional pleasantries. Then Casey whispered to him, "We've got to talk."

"I know," he murmured gently. "This afternoon, at lunch."

When they arrived at Heather's room, Eli Lassiter was there. Alex looked to Mo, who was holding Heather's chart. "Toxic levels of Thorazine in serum," Mo announced. "You were right, Alex."

A broad smile blossomed on Alex's face as he told the story of Mrs. Papineau's Thorazine and Heather's overdose. Eli was surprised that a toxic screen for possible overdose hadn't been sent. Still, he was in no position to criticize; he had been involved in the girl's care, and the thought of an overdose hadn't occurred to him either.

"The frequency of the girl's seizures hasn't changed," Eli said. "What about the dialysis?"

"I spoke to the renal people this morning," Mo told him. "They won't dialyze her."

"Why not?" Alex interrupted. "When I spoke to the renal

fellow last night, I got the impression they would dialyze her today if the Thorazine level was high and her seizures hadn't improved."

"I don't think he knew that Thorazine is hard to dialyze out of the blood. Maybe it adheres to the large proteins that don't go through the dialysis membrane and becomes strongly bound in the tissues."

"What are we supposed to do?" Alex asked.

"Continue what we've been doing," Jim told him. "If it's just the Thorazine that's causing her seizures, when the Thorazine level drops, her seizures will end. I'd give her a lot of fluids though, it might help the urinary excretion of the Thorazine."

Alex wasn't satisfied. He called the head of dialysis, who still didn't think dialysis would help and who seemed beyond convincing. Alex felt cheated that his discovery was not to be rewarded with the opportunity for active intervention. They would just wait around and watch her get better. Even if he had never figured out Heather's overdose, she would've gotten better.

"All we're left with is flushing out her kidneys," Alex said.

"How much fluid would you give her?" Mo asked.

"Two or three hundred cc's an hour," Jim said. "She has a catheter in her bladder. We'll measure how much she puts out."

The kidneys are responsible for fluid balance. In a child like Heather with normal kidneys and a normal heart, excess fluid would be excreted by the kidneys. Hopefully, the extra urine would take excess Thorazine with it. Jim remembered medical school and an experiment in physiology. During one twenty-four-hour period, he drank gallons of liquid. During the same period, he peed gallons of urine into large measuring flasks. Firsthand knowledge of kidney function.

Another column was added to Heather's hourly seizure chart: fluids in, urine out.

Alex walked to the nurses' station and called Mellissa. There was no answer. He called again, letting the phone ring for a long time. Still no answer.

It was nine o'clock, and Dr. Hollsworth would arrive at ten to evaluate BJ Balsiger. Alex decided to use the hour to show Eli the other children on the ward.

They began with the hypotonic infant. Jim summarized: nine months old, floppy muscles, unable to sit. His reflexes were preserved, so he didn't have Werdnig-Hoffman disease. He probably didn't have cerebral palsy, because his development was otherwise normal, and he didn't have a neuropathy because his nerve conduction studies were normal and there was no evidence of degenerative disease.

"How about a muscle biopsy?" Eli asked.

"The preliminary report was normal. We'll see the biopsy later this morning at brain cutting."

"Any family history of muscle weakness?"

"None."

"Is he going home tomorrow?"

"This afternoon. Mo will follow him in neurology clinic."

"What do the parents say?"

"What can they say? If they're lucky he'll have normal intelligence and won't be physically handicapped."

Eli picked up the infant and sat him in the crib, but he fell over. The child was like a rag doll. Then Eli handed the child a toy, pulled the rails up on the crib, and left the room.

The hydrocephalic babies had already been put in the corridor. The thin hair covering one of their large heads was tied with a pink bow. The tiny girl's eyes slowly moved from side to side as the chart rack and doctors moved past her and down the corridor to Clark Gatewood.

Clark Kent Gatewood sat on his bed.

"Why aren't you flying around?" Mo asked.

"I want to color," the boy replied. He wasn't even wearing his cape.

Eli listened to the boy's history. Drop attacks, increasing frequency, normal development. Excellent response to manipulation of medication over a two-week hospitalization and home tomorrow.

"I wish there were more kids like him on the ward," Jim said.

Mo put his large hands under the boy's armpits and lifted him up. "He passes the armpit test," Mo said.

233

In the bed next to Clark Gatewood was the boy with the cerebellar tumor minus his cerebellar tumor. As his mother fed him breakfast, Alex noticed she was a different person from the woman who had carried her son up and down the hallway the day prior to surgery. Now she smiled, laughed, and enjoyed talking to the doctors. Mo even thought she was wearing more makeup. The mother watched proudly as her son was tested for evidence of ataxia or paralysis. No evidence of brain damage from the surgery, and the ataxia had lessened.

"Are you ready for the Susies?" Alex asked.

"Is it true I'm going home tomorrow?" Susie W asked.

"If you're good," Mo teased her.

Susie K wasn't happy with the prospect of losing her roommate, especially since they had become good friends. Susie K had been in the hospital for three months, Susie W, only two weeks. Susie K had watched many children admitted and discharged from division 17, and there had been two rotations of pediatric residents before Jim, and two other medical students before Casey.

"Susie W is the girl with Sydenham's chorea," Alex explained to Eli. "She's on prophylactic penicillin. Susie K had a bad case of Guillain-Barré and was on a respirator for a while. You probably remember her from grand rounds a couple months ago. She's getting physical therapy and now can walk with two canes."

"One cane," the girl corrected.

Eli examined both girls. "Why isn't Susie K going home now?" he asked.

"She needs another week of physical therapy," Jim said.

"Can't she get it as an outpatient?"

"I'll talk to her parents," Jim agreed.

Susie K was elated.

"When is the crazy girl Charlotte going home?" Susie W asked.

"Why is she crazy?" Eli asked.

"All those spells she has on the ward. She always talks about them."

"What does she say?"

"She's afraid of them and she doesn't know what's going to

happen to her. She told us about the medication you're injecting. She thinks it's going to help her."

Eli interpreted Susie W's comment as evidence that Charlotte's spells were real. Alex was now more certain than ever
that they were hysterical.

"What time does Charlotte get her next test?" Eli asked.

"This afternoon at two," Alex informed him.

In the next room, Charlotte sat on her bed reading a comic
book.

"How do you feel today?" Eli asked.

"Okay," the girl said. She surveyed the doctors, who stared at
her. "When am I going to have my test?"

"This afternoon," Alex assured her.

"Will it be in the EEG unit?"

"No, we'll bring an EEG machine to the ward."

"You'll use the same medicine as yesterday to start the seizure and another medicine to stop it?"

"Right."

"What if the second medicine doesn't work?"

Alex wanted to say, "Don't worry, it will," but Eli spoke first.
"If it doesn't stop the seizure, we'll let the seizure stop on its
own, like it always does."

"Do you study French in school?" Alex asked.

"Yes."

"You told me you studied Spanish," Eli said.

"That was last year. I switched."

"Do you ever associate anything from your French class with
your 'French' spells?"

"No."

"Okay. Thanks, Charlotte. See you at two."

They stepped into the hall. "Has anyone checked the tape of
yesterday's spell?" Eli asked.

"I haven't had time," Alex admitted.

At ten o'clock sharp, Dr. Hollsworth appeared on the ward.
Four other doctors appeared at the same time, having heard Dr.
Hollsworth would be evaluating a child and wanting to see the
old doctor in action. One of the four was Nolan Magness, who
had been notified of the event in advance by Casey. Florence
and Dennis Balsiger waited with BJ in his hospital room.

"Would you like us to present the boy to you at the bedside?" Alex asked.

"I think there are too many people here," Dr. Hollsworth said to Alex, then turned to the parents. "Please join us in the conference room and help us review BJ's history before I examine the child. There may be questions I'll need to ask you."

BJ's parents joined the large group of doctors in the conference room. Since there weren't enough chairs for everyone, Mo and Jim vacated their seats to make room for the mother and father. Although he was skeptical about a possible repetition of grand rounds, Dennis Balsiger sensed that Dr. Hollsworth might be different. His strange optimism was buoyed by the look of anticipation on the doctors' faces as they waited for Hollsworth to begin.

Dr. Hollsworth sat in the middle of a couch, flanked by Casey and Eli. His suit was more new than old and he wore a tie that didn't betray a collection of neckwear spanning a half century. There were two patches of hair on the back of his otherwise bald head; he wore wire-framed glasses and kept a neatly trimmed mustache. His figure was slim and his gait almost as agile as his youthful mind. The only instrument he carried for the neurologic exam was his reflex hammer. But of course he had his keys. And a set of keys in the hands of Dr. Hollsworth was equivalent to a bag of instruments in the hands of another neurologist.

The old doctor smiled at BJ's parents as Casey began her presentation. He didn't interrupt during the entire monologue, and took no notes, but rubbed his mustache and shifted his eyes around the room, as he listened carefully. At times he focused on BJ's parents, observing their reaction to a particular point in history. When Casey had finished her presentation, Alex asked, "Do you have any questions, Dr. Hollsworth?"

"Does anyone else in the family have a disease of the brain or spinal cord?" Dr. Hollsworth asked the parents. The answer was negative.

"Let's see the boy."

The large group of doctors moved to BJ's hospital room. Two chairs were placed next to the crib, one for Dr. Hollsworth, the other for Florence Balsiger, who would be holding BJ on her lap during the exam.

"How old are you, son?" the old doctor asked.

"Four."

"Do you like to play?"

"Yes."

"What do you play?"

"With my horsie and my teddy bear."

"Who are all these people?"

"I don't know."

"Are they doctors?"

"They're doctors."

"Where's Daddy?"

BJ searched the room and easily identified his father.

"Do you want to play with me?"

"Okay," the boy agreed.

Dr. Hollsworth told Mrs. Balsiger to keep the boy on her lap, then took out his keys and shook them in front of BJ.

"What are these?"

The boy didn't answer, but grabbed for the keys. The old man moved them from side to side as BJ reached out, first with his right and then with his left hand. Dr. Hollsworth watched BJ's hands and fingers grab for the keys, then studied the boy's eye movements as he followed the keys from side to side.

"He's just examined the cerebellum, motor system, and half of the cranial nerves," Alex whispered to Casey.

Dr. Hollsworth next let BJ play with the keys while he quickly tapped on the boy's reflexes. Then he took the keys away from the boy, rose, and stepped to the door. He jingled the keys in the air, calling, "Come get them, BJ." The boy climbed from his mother's lap and ran toward the door. BJ grabbed back the keys, then returned to his mother's lap.

"That's the rest of the motor exam," Alex told Casey.

Dr. Hollsworth's wrinkled hand touched the boy's arm as he examined BJ's skin. Then he ran his hand over the boy's nose and cheeks. Finally he checked the back, abdomen, and legs.

"I know you said the fundi were normal, but I'll have to look at them," Dr. Hollsworth said without looking up. Three ophthalmoscopes appeared in the air, each one yanked from a white lab coat and offered by a different doctor. Dr. Hollsworth idly chose one, then steadied the boy's head with his hand and looked into BJ's eyes. Allowing a few seconds for each eye, he returned the ophthalmoscope.

"It would've taken me fifteen minutes to adequately examine that kid's eyes," one of the doctors said.

"Did you see anything?" Alex asked.

"They're normal," Dr. Hollsworth said. Then he turned to the boy. "Thank you, BJ. We'll leave you alone for a while."

The doctors filed back into the waiting room while Dr. Hollsworth spoke briefly with the parents. They asked to be present when he discussed BJ and walked with him to the conference room.

"He's a lovely child and I can understand why you've trouble treating and diagnosing his condition," the old doctor said.

Dennis Balsiger was bursting to ask, "Do you know what he's got?" But he sat silently. Nolan Magness could see the question in the father's tightened face muscles and the intensity with which he listened to Dr. Hollsworth.

"The boy is developmentally retarded," Dr. Hollsworth began. "Even though there was a large number of doctors in his room, BJ should have spoken more for a four-year-old. And he handled the keys like a three-year-old."

"What's the difference between the way a three- and four-year-old handle keys?" Mo asked.

The old man smiled. "I guess it's not written anywhere. Whatever the case, the remainder of the neurologic exam is normal. There's no evidence of hemiparesis, incoordination, or abnormal movements. I thought I might find something in his fundus, but the eye grounds were normal. All we need now is a Wood's lamp." He turned to Casey. "Could you get one?"

"We checked him with a Wood's lamp a couple years ago," Nolan Magness said. "It was normal."

"I'm sure it was, but let's do it again today."

Everyone except BJ's parents knew the disease Dr. Hollsworth suspected, but, before Dennis Balsiger could ask about the Wood's lamp test, the doctors had filed out of the conference room and walked back toward BJ's room.

"Could you undress him for us?" Dr. Hollsworth asked the mother. "Leave his diaper on."

Casey arrived with a small ultraviolet light called a Wood's lamp. Dr. Hollsworth held the light next to the boy's body and systematically moved it from one area to the other. "Here's one," he said, pointing to an area on the back, "and here's another one on the back of the leg."

One by one each doctor looked at BJ and nodded in agreement. Dr. Hollsworth then showed the areas to BJ's parents—a leaf-shaped, unpigmented patch of skin. It was the "ashleaf" or "white ash" sign, an area of skin that looked like a leaf of white mountain ash, about an inch in size. It couldn't be seen under regular, room light but stood out prominently under the ultraviolet light.

Dennis and Florence Balsiger were elated that a diagnosis had finally been made. "What does it mean?" the mother asked a doctor who stood next to her.

"Tuberous sclerosis," he said quietly.

The parents' joy was to be short-lived: tuberous sclerosis was an inherited disease that caused mental retardation and epilepsy. It not only affected the brain, but many other parts of the body—eyes, skin, kidneys, bones, heart, and lungs. Eventually, the soft gray-and-white tissue of the brain would be replaced by irregular patches of hard, tumorlike nodules. Viewed under the microscope, the orderly arrangement of brain cells would become an overgrowth of scar tissue and groups of large, bizarre cells that some pathologists called "monster cells." There was no treatment for tuberous sclerosis.

Alex wanted to spare the parents the doctors' discussion of BJ's diagnosis, and Dr. Hollsworth concurred. "Stay with your boy," the old doctor suggested. "I want to talk with the doctors about your son, then I'll spend time with you."

"How could we miss tuberous sclerosis?" Mo said to Nolan Magness as they walked back to the conference room.

Nolan shrugged. "We missed it."

"What made you think of tuberous sclerosis?" Eli asked Dr. Hollsworth as they sat in the conference room.

"He reminded me of two other children I've seen with the disease. The diagnosis had also been missed on them until they developed the characteristic rash across the nose."

"But BJ doesn't have the adenoma sebaceum," Jim said.

Adenoma sebaceum was a classic feature of the disease, an

239

acnelike rash most prominent over the nose and cheeks. One could usually make the diagnosis of tuberous sclerosis on the basis of adenoma sebaceum alone.

"I think he's beginning to manifest it," Dr. Hollsworth said. "His nose and cheeks didn't look normal to me, and when I ran my fingers across them, I thought I felt the beginning of a rash. In a few years there will be no question about it. By the way, did you look closely at the father? He has an acnelike rash across his nose and cheeks which is hard to see because of his rugged features. That's who gave BJ the disease."

"Do you think the Wood's light exam was really negative when we tested the boy two years ago?" Nolan asked.

"The ashleaf spots might have been small. He only has two of them now. But they were probably there."

Casey fumbled in her pocket for her list of the possible diseases BJ might have. There it was. Number eight. Tuberous sclerosis.

"He doesn't have the other skin manifestations," Dr. Hollsworth said. "I could find no shagreen patches or café-au-lait spots."

"What are those?" Louise asked.

"The shagreen patches are areas of uneven, thick skin; grayish-green in color, usually found in the lower back. Café-au-lait is French for coffee with milk. Those are blotches on the skin which are the same color as coffee with milk in it."

"What do we do for the boy now?" one of the doctors asked.

"There's no treatment," the old doctor said simply. "His seizures are caused by the multiple areas of scar tissue in his brain. Because they are so small, they didn't show up on any of the studies he's had. No one knows the cause of tuberous sclerosis; it's a genetically determined developmental defect. Should the parents have any more children, there's a fifty percent chance that other siblings will be affected."

"But the father has normal intelligence."

"There are a certain number of people with tuberous sclerosis, normal intelligence, and no seizures. The father's one of them."

"What's going to happen to BJ?" Casey asked.

"He will continue with seizures that are difficult to control, and may develop tumors in his brain or other parts of the body. Sooner or later, both because of retardation and seizures, he'll have to be institutionalized. One of the first cases of tuberous sclerosis was described by a pathologist named Bourneville in 1880. His case involved a girl who began having seizures at age two. When she died at fifteen, the autopsy revealed her brain to be full of small tumors and scar tissue."

Dr. Hollsworth's rounds were over. "I'm glad I don't have to tell the parents," Nolan Magness told Eli as they left the room.

"The old man's really a master, isn't he?" Eli said.

Casey joined Dr. Hollsworth as he went to talk with the parents. Nolan Magness returned to the laboratory.

"It's better not to talk in front of the boy," the old doctor said to the parents. "One never knows how much children understand."

They sat on four chairs in the conference room.

"Your son has a disease called tuberous sclerosis," Dr. Hollsworth began. Casey was happy that of all the physicians the Balsigers had seen, the old doctor was the one to talk to BJ's parents. His seniority and experience conveyed an authority that other doctors couldn't have.

Still, the explanation was painful since the verdict was even more damning than they had expected, especially for the father. He unconsciously fingered the bridge of his nose and cheek after Dr. Hollsworth explained that it was he who probably had transmitted the disease. Parents often felt guilty about their children's illnesses, usually with no cause. Dennis Balsiger's guilt would be based on reality, even though the affliction was probably transmitted from his parents. The father insisted that his parents were normal. He didn't know his grandparents and had no other siblings. Yet, his mother was not an intelligent woman; a simple woman who never completed high school.

Florence Balsiger was thankful they had waited to have more children. Her support of the father was now crucial for the success of their marriage. The bitterness for having married someone who gave her a defective child, and who made future natural childbirth impossible, would have to be suppressed.

For BJ no more expensive diagnostic tests would be performed. The amount written about him in his chart would be substantially shortened. There would be no more long lists of differential diagnoses. "Tuberous sclerosis" would now appear on all his charts. Clinic notes would always have BJ's disease written next to his name.

The new experimental drug would still be tried in an attempt to control the seizures, and anticonvulsant manipulation would be continued. Perhaps one day BJ's seizures would be brought under control, but even that victory would not bring with it the hope of salvaging a potentially normal child; it would simply make his management easier.

By the time the session ended, there were tears in both parents' eyes. Casey's eyes were not dry either. Dr. Hollsworth led them gently from the room. In the hall, having comforted the parents, the old doctor comforted the young student.

Brain cutting was held in the pathology department. Alex, Mo, Jim, Casey, and Eli stood around a stainless steel table, viewing the neatly sliced brains, each on its own tray. The brain is too soft to cut into when first removed from the skull at autopsy and requires two weeks of soaking in a bucket of formaldehyde to become firm enough for a pathologic analysis.

Jim was happy there was no autopsy in progress. The sight and smell of an opened human carcass bothered him; too much a reminder of what he was.

Each of the five wore gloves to protect their hands from the formaldehyde. There were five brains on display, and the pathologist assigned them according to difficulty of identifying the abnormality. The hardest conditions to spot went to Eli and Alex.

They picked up the slices, which were the size and shape of a piece of toast, and began looking for clues.

"Casey, you're first," the pathologist said.

Her brain was easy. Multiple red blotches interrupted the gray-and-white architecture on several of the slices. "This child obviously has had bleeding into the brain," Casey said. "Because there are multiple areas of blood and no discernible pattern, there was something wrong with the clotting mechanism of the blood. I'll say the child had leukemia and died of brain hemmorhage."

"Right. Jim, what do you have?"

Jim's brain was disfigured by a large mass in the frontal lobe. The tissue looked different from the surrounding brain substance. "Looks like a tumor."

"What kind?"

"I don't know."

"It's a glioma." The pathologist then read the case history of a child who had died from the brain tumor.

Mo's brain was a meningitis, the coverings of the brain thickened and bathed in pus. Alex's brain was an infant who died from lack of oxygen at birth. The brain was small, poorly developed, not as much white matter as a mature brain. Eli's brain was puzzling because it seemed normal. He spared himself embarrassment with an honest reply. "I know I'm missing something, but I can't find anything wrong."

"There isn't anything wrong. It's normal," the pathologist said.

The thought of holding a brain in his hand fascinated Alex. A brain studying itself. Emotion, memory, rationalization, all dependent on the masses of nerve cells and their connections. Under the microscope, the appearance of the symmetrical rows of nerve cells offered few clues how the brain worked. Painful impulses from other parts of the body were felt in the brain, yet, the brain itself was without pain. It wasn't connected to itself.

Then there were slides to look at under the microscope: the boy with the cerebellar tumor; a fungal infection; and the muscle biopsy from the hypotonic infant. As expected, it was normal.

On division 17, Heather Papineau's seizures continued, yet there was a minor change. Instead of having a convulsion every five minutes, the girl's seizures occurred at six-minute intervals. The nurse monitoring her spells had been filling the spaces on Heather's seizure chart since the girl's anesthesia, but the regularity of attacks made her less than compulsive in her timekeeping, and the subtle one-minute change escaped her notice.

* * *

In the pathology department, rubber gloves were deposited in the wastepaper backet, and the trays of brains covered with a wet cloth. Before going upstairs with Casey for lunch, Alex called home.

Mellissa answered.

"I tried to call you this morning and you weren't home," Alex said, but she hung up.

When he called back, she answered immediately: "Alex, I don't want to talk to you. Not now, anyway." And he heard the phone click off.

It was the fourth consecutive day Casey and Alex had sat together in the hospital cafeteria. They talked about BJ Balsiger. Casey had pulled out her list and they found tuberous sclerosis as number eight. Together, they recalled how they had rejected tuberous sclerosis because of the normal Wood's lamp two years previously. They talked about Heather Papineau. It was only a matter of time before she would wake up, but they both felt uncomfortable with her, until she was sitting in bed and talking to them. She was still in danger. They talked about Charlotte. At two o'clock she would get her injection. Finally they talked about their night together, and Alex confessed that Mellissa wouldn't see or talk to him.

"What are you going to do?" Casey asked.

"What are we going to do?"

"I don't know."

"I've been thinking more and more about going into the laboratory after my residency," Alex said softly, as if he were thinking out loud.

"You're going to give up being a real doctor?"

"I can do both, Casey. I know I can."

"But look what's happened to Eli Lassiter."

"Nolan Magness seems to be doing all right," Alex said.

Casey put her hand on Alex's. "Alex, when I said I loved you, I meant it. Did you mean it?"

Alex didn't answer immediately, but he didn't take his hand away. He didn't care if someone saw. "It's not easy, Casey. Yes, I love you. I feel something beautiful when I'm with you. But I loved Mellissa once, too. I still do, but it's not as intense and exciting as with you. What would happen to us in five years?"

"Maybe the same. Love changes."

"To be honest, I don't know if I could go back to Mellissa now," Alex said. "There's a whole part of my life she'll never belong to. Casey"—he took both her hands in his—"Casey, you're going to have to give me time."

Luciana and Richard Zancanelli sat in Tony's room, deeply upset. When they had recovered from the shock of their son's survival, they both confided how relieved they had been when they were told Tony was dying. The mother, initially sad at the thought of her son's passing, had left the hospital the previous night, freed of the anguish of having to see her disfigured boy again. She had imagined him in a funeral casket, dressed in a nice suit with his hair combed and a peaceful look on his face. Now the passive suffering, the acceptance of tragedy with which they had lived for so long, was replaced by an anger, directed at the doctors, at themselves, at their son, at God.

Jim Wellander entered the room.

"Doctor, why did you do this to us?" Mr. Zancanelli began. "My wife sat here last night expecting her son to die. We gave him last rites. The family prayed for him. We didn't sleep all night. Now he's better. How can you predict things when you don't even know? Can't a doctor tell when someone is about to die? And if the doctor can't, why tell the family? We've suffered enough; it's not fair."

"We thought he was going to die, Mr. Zancanelli. It wouldn't have been fair to tell you otherwise. We were wrong."

The mother burst into tears.

"I'm sorry," the father apologized. "It's been difficult for us."

As Jim looked at the couple, a hollow, angry feeling grew in his stomach. Not only can't we save people, we can't even predict who'll die, he thought. Once more he thought of the idea he'd had before but always rejected. Now, it was harder to dispel. "I looked at a chest X-ray that Tony had this morning," Jim said. "It shows an infiltrate in his lung."

"What does that mean?" the mother asked.

"It means part of Tony's fever came from an inflammation in

the lung. However, the infiltrate is small, and brain damage contributed to his difficulties. We won't know until tomorrow morning whether he'll survive."

"What are you trying to tell us, doctor?"

"Tony hasn't made it yet."

It was almost two o'clock, and like the previous afternoon, people gathered at the nurses' station in anticipation of the injection. The portable EEG machine was already in Charlotte's room, and the electrodes were being pasted to her scalp.

"Alex, what else do we have this afternoon?" Jim asked.

"Only Charlotte's injection and EEG."

"How about some squash?"

Alex seemed reticent.

"Come on, Alex. I'd really like to play."

Alex sensed that Jim's request was really a demand. "Okay. We'll go right after Charlotte's EEG."

Because there would be two injections, Alex was forced to put an IV in Charlotte's arm. He could stick a needle directly into her vein to start the seizure, but it would be difficult to stick a vein during the seizure. He taped the IV into place and attached it to a small bottle of 5 percent dextrose in water.

"What's in that bottle?" the girl asked.

"Just sugar water." The same thing I'll be injecting to start and stop your seizures, Alex said to himself.

Eli Lassiter and Edgar Quinn joined Casey, Jim, Mo, and Louise in the room. The nurse held a tray with two bottles on it, each bottle covered with a different-colored tape. There were two 10 cc syringes on the tray; the syringes were covered with tape that matched the bottles, and Alex slowly filled each syringe.

"Are you ready, Charlotte?"

"Yes."

"Do you understand the test?"

"Yes."

"Do you have that funny feeling you had yesterday before we started the injection?"

"No. Just go ahead."

The EEG technician turned on the machine, and paper slowly began rolling under the steel pens.

"Charlotte, I want you to close your eyes and relax."

Alex glanced at the EEG tracing; it was normal; symmetrical, 12-cycle-per-second waves were being traced from each pen. There were no irregularities apart from occasional large waves in the frontal leads that reflected muscle activity as Charlotte's eyes moved underneath her closed lids.

"I'm beginning to inject the first medicine," Alex announced loudly. "This is the medicine that caused her seizure yesterday."

He pushed the needle through the rubber IV tubing and began to inject. The EEG technician marked the event on the rolling EEG paper.

The day before, it had taken almost three minutes after the injection for Charlotte to begin her convulsion. Today, in less than thirty seconds, Charlotte began moaning and was soon uttering "French" words. Alex looked at the EEG tracing. It contained no obvious abnormality, but the tracing was masked by muscle artifact and he saw only a few seconds of it as the paper rolled under the pens. The EEG interpretation would come later.

Now the jerking began. First arms, then arms and legs, then legs. Edgar Quinn looked at Eli Lassiter, who stood quietly, his gaze fixed on his daughter.

The shaking stopped, then Charlotte lay quiet, then she began to babble more "French." This time the vocalization was accompanied by her hands moving to her breasts and groin. Louise looked away. Edgar Quinn forced himself to watch.

Everyone in the room except Charlotte jumped as Alex yelled, "Okay—this is the injection to stop the seizure. I'm giving it now!" He purposely held the girl's forearm tightly so she could feel his actions as he began to inject.

Abruptly Charlotte's right hand stopped its rhythmical movement over her right chest and fell limply to her side. The left hand stopped its movement between her legs and somehow lifted itself onto the bed.

"*Charlotte, wake up!*" Alex shouted, and, at once, the girl opened her eyes.

"That's powerful medicine," Jim whispered to Mo. "We should use it more often."

"How do you feel, Charlotte?" Alex asked.

"I feel OK."

"Do you know you had a seizure?"

"I guess so."

"The medicine to stop the spell worked very nicely."

"Good."

"We want to examine the EEG record and then we'll talk to you later."

"Amazing," Eli Lassiter said as they walked back to the nurses' station. "No question that spell was hysterical."

The EEG was easy to interpret: apart from the electrical artifact caused by the girl's movement, the tracing was normal and there was no evidence of seizure.

"Now what happens?" asked Edgar Quinn.

"First, tell your wife we now know conclusively that Charlotte's seizures are hysterical. Then we'll have to confront Charlotte with the truth."

"When?"

"This afternoon, after I talk to the people from psychiatry. If they don't recommend confronting her with the diagnosis, I won't do it. But I think they will." Just then Alex remembered his squash game with Jim. "I'll be back at four. We'll talk to Charlotte then."

Casey came up behind Alex and squeezed his arm. "I'm proud of you," she whispered.

Across Children's Hospital, amid the buildings of the medical complex, was dormitory housing for the medical students, and next to the dormitory a gym, weight room, and six squash courts. The courts were in poor repair, but few people noticed, especially medical students, as they chased the tiny black ball from one wall to another.

From October to May, before the courts became too hot, Alex played squash once a week. He had played intermittently with Jim during Jim's rotation through neurology. Although they were evenly matched, Jim usually won because of his delicate shots in front corners and softly hit balls that died before they hit the back wall. Today, Jim was losing. He hit the ball too hard, making it easy for Alex to wait until it bounced off the back wall and into the center of the court.

Before starting to serve the second game, Alex turned to his obviously preoccupied partner. "Jim, what is it?"

"Tony Zancanelli," he answered without hesitation.

Alex now understood why Jim had been so adamant about the game. For the next thirty minutes, they stopped keeping score; they hit the ball against the wall and talked.

"I don't know how the parents can take it," Jim said. "You should've heard them this afternoon. The mother was so happy that her comatose son was going to die. She already had visions of him lying peacefully in his casket."

"How do you know?"

"The father told me."

"Look, Jim, we've been through this before. There's nothing you can do. You didn't treat the kid's pneumonia."

"There *is* something I can do, Alex. I can make sure he dies tonight." Jim punctuated the disclosure by blasting the ball against the front wall.

Alex stopped, letting the ball bounce past him. "Are you crazy?"

"It's not crazier than *not* treating his pneumonia. It's certainly no crazier than keeping him alive."

Alex didn't know what to say. All he could think of was, "How are you planning to do it?"

"It's easy," Jim told him. "There are many ways, you know that. He's got an IV. All I do is inject something."

"What if you get caught?"

"I won't. I'm on tonight. I'll do it when I check him before I go to sleep."

"Have you ever done this before?"

"No. Have you?"

"No."

Now Alex picked up the ball and blasted it against the front wall. "I can't let you do it," he said emphatically. "It's immoral, it's unethical, and if you get caught you'll ruin your entire career. That's apart from going to jail."

"Alex, I've thought about this and I honestly don't believe it's immoral or unethical." Jim had stopped playing and faced Alex directly. "There's no difference between withholding treatment that will save someone's life and giving him something to end it."

"You're wrong, Jim. One's active and the other's passive."

"We pull respirator plugs on people all the time; if that's not active, what is?"

"But those people have met the four criteria for brain death. If you've forgotten those criteria, let me refresh your memory. One. Total unresponsiveness to external stimuli. Tony doesn't fit. If you pinch him, he moves his arms and legs."

"You know that's a lower-level brainstem reflex, Alex."

I know, but the boy is not totally unresponsive. Two. No movements or breathing. I'm sure you'll agree that Tony breathes on his own. Three. No reflexes. My five-year-old girl could get reflexes from Tony by tapping him anywhere on the knee with a reflex hammer. And four. A flat EEG. Every EEG that boy has had shows electrical activity."

"Alex, I know he doesn't satisfy the four standard criteria. And that we couldn't legally use his kidneys for a transplant. But let me ask you a question. I want an honest answer. You're a neurologist, a brain expert. Is Tony's brain dead?"

Alex was quiet for a moment, then answered. "No, it's not dead. There are brainstem reflexes."

"Alex, I'm not talking about reflexes that a frog and cat have. I'm talking about the human brain. The thing that makes a person. I'm talking about the brain of Richard and Luciana Zancanelli's son. Is his brain alive? Does that boy exist anymore?"

"Okay, Tony Zancanelli's brain is dead."

Jim was quiet for a moment. He again began hitting the squash ball against the wall. "You know, Alex, the doctors got a raw deal. They went to medical school because they loved science and they wanted to heal people. I know, some people are doing it now for the money. But that's not why most do it, certainly not why you and I do it. Then, with the miracles of medical science we devise ways to keep dead people alive. Then the doctors have to be theologians, philosophers, and moralists. Decide who lives, decide who dies. Let them die in subtle ways. Do it passively rather than actively."

250

"That's not right, Jim. There are plenty of theologians and moralists to decide about death and life."

"Bullshit. I've talked to those guys. You know what they say? The doctor decides whether a person has died or not. Their rules were made up before respirators, antibiotics, and kidney transplants. The easiest thing for me to do is let Tony live. You know that. But letting Tony live takes no courage."

Alex was silent.

"There's nothing wrong with trying to save someone," Jim continued, "no matter how hopeless it seems. Initially, you don't know how bad the brain damage will be. But when it becomes obvious that the person no longer exists, there isn't a way to dispose of the body. We have to hope it will die by itself. Alex, what would you do if you were in my place?"

"I've been in your situation before. I've never actively killed someone by injecting them."

"Have you pulled out a respiratory plug?"

"Yes, but only when the four criteria of brain death existed."

"Old people with brain death, they don't live long. But, Alex, a child is different. Remember that girl who drowned on division twenty-seven? She was on a respirator for six months, even though after three months it was obvious her brain was dead. They couldn't take her off because she didn't satisfy the four criteria for brain death. One day someone finally took her off the respirator. What happened? She started breathing on her own. Now she lies like a vegetable in an institution, fed by a tube into her stomach. She could live for another thirty years. Do you know how much that costs? Do you realize the emotional trauma to her family?"

"Jim, don't do it."

"What happens if you arrive on the ward tomorrow morning and Tony Zancanelli is dead?"

"I'll ask you if you got permission for an autopsy."

"That's all?"

"That's all." Alex turned and faced the pediatric resident. "Jim, the decision is yours. I understand your position, but I don't agree with it."

They returned to their squash game.

"What's going on between you and Casey?" Jim asked.

Alex stopped in the middle of a swing. "What makes you ask that?"

"I saw you passing notes back and forth during grand rounds yesterday, like two school kids. You eat lunch with her every day in the cafeteria."

Alex's reaction was so immediate that Jim realized he had stumbled onto a sensitive issue. The chief resident walked to the corner and picked up the squash ball, fingered it momentarily, then balanced it on his racquet. "Can I talk to you about it?"

"If you want. I have the shortest memory in medicine," Jim said, adding, "and I'll take it personally if you agree with me."

Alex smiled, then resumed hitting the ball off the front wall. He began to tell Jim the whole story of his affair with Casey, enormously relieved to be discussing her with someone else.

"From what you tell me," Jim said, "your attraction to Casey was natural. You even tried to stop it. I've never been married, so I don't know how flat a person's relationship with his wife can become after the initial excitement."

"Jim, there's another issue besides the attraction to Casey. This is a chance to escape entering private practice. Mellissa's not prepared for the struggle we'd have if I chose academic medicine. She made that quite clear before I even met Casey."

"Are you sure you want academic medicine, Alex? Do you want to be clinical or in the lab?"

"I wouldn't go into academic medicine and just do clinical work."

"Have you had any lab experience?"

"Not really."

"Good God, Alex! Look what happened to Eli Lassiter," Jim said, echoing Casey's words. "You don't want that. You're an excellent clinician and a good teacher who would probably fail in a lab."

Alex didn't like hearing the word "fail." "But it would be a challenge," he countered.

"Don't forget, you haven't even been able to talk to Mellissa since last night at Casey's. Your wife may have already made the decision for you. She may not want you back."

The possibility of Mellissa's rejection was as distressing as the word fail.

"On the other hand," Jim continued, "even if you're serious about academic medicine, Mellissa may agree to stay with you."

"What about Casey?"

"If you choose her, she won't interfere with your plans either way. Alex, unless you've already decided that under no circumstances will you continue family life, you can't settle anything until Mellissa talks to you."

"What would you do?" Alex asked.

Jim laughed. "That's not a fair question, but if you want, I'll answer it. If you're truly afraid of private practice, if Mellissa absolutely won't stay with you in academic medicine, and if you think your love for Casey and her love for you is real, I'd go with her. If, on the other hand—"

"That's enough—the rest is obvious."

"We both have decisions to make. You, about your life. Me, about someone else's." Jim smashed the ball against the front wall.

"Let's get back." Alex slapped the resident on the back. "I've got to talk to Charlotte Quinn."

Before confronting Charlotte, Alex called one of the psychiatrists, who agreed it was best to do it immediately. Since the test was a trick, she needed to be told. The psychiatrist thought Alex should confront the girl in the absence of her parents, should stress the positive aspects of a long-awaited diagnosis, and avoid the negative issue of her deceptive behavior. He strongly advised against any allusion to the sexual overtones of Charlotte's spells until she had had a more complete psychiatric evaluation.

On division 17 Alex talked briefly with Charlotte's parents and told them of his discussion with the psychiatrist. Louise had found someone who understood French, played them the tape, and learned that Charlotte was reciting French verb conjugations. Evidently those conjugations were underlined in the textbook her father brought to the hospital.

Alex closed the door in Charlotte's room and drew the curtains around her bed. The large girl sat expressionless on her bed, watching Alex arrange the room and place a chair next to her.

"Charlotte, we have your test results. They show that the spells you've been having are not seizures."

"What are they?" she asked tentatively.

"I don't know, but they're not seizures."

"That's not possible," she said, now more assertive. "You injected a medicine that cuases seizures and it did. Then you injected a medicine to stop the seizure and it did. You even had an EEG attached to my head."

"Charlotte, the medicine I injected wasn't a medicine. It was just water."

"Both times?" she asked quietly.

"Yes. And the EEG showed normal brain activity. There was no seizure in your brain when you had the spell."

A strange look appeared on Charlotte's face. It wasn't shock and it wasn't anger. Her mouth was partly opened, the color drained from her face, and her eyes stared nervously at Alex. It was a look of fear. "You tricked me," she mumbled.

The girl's face frightened Alex and he impulsively took her hand. She didn't resist. "It's all right, Charlotte. We're trying to help you. We're not against you."

"All those people in the room. It was all a trick?"

"Yes."

"My father knows?" He nodded.

"Mother, too?"

The girl grasped Alex's hand with both her own and began to cry.

It's better, Charlotte," Alex said, trying to soothe her. "Now that we know, we can help you. I would rather have spells like yours than real spells."

"You would?" She stopped crying for a moment.

"Sure. Once this problem is solved, you may not have to take medicine anymore. If your seizures were real, you'd have trouble getting a driver's license."

"What will my parents say?"

"They'll be happy when you're well again."

Charlotte sat silently for over a minute, still grasping Alex's hand. Then she stopped crying. Suddenly she became animated. She dropped Alex's hand and nervously fingered her hospital gown. For the first time during her hospitalization, she spoke to a doctor in more than three short sentences. Her monologue revealed an immature and insecure sixteen-year-old only child, unable to deal with the pressures of adolescence, whose parents did not take her problems seriously. Charlotte's mind was filled with sexual fantasies, feelings of inferiority about her large, unfeminine body, and reminiscences about the comforts of childhood.

Alex didn't comment during her entire monologue, and afterward said simply, "Dry your eyes. Your parents want to talk with you."

When Alex left Charlotte's room, he was confronted by Eli Lassiter and Charlotte's father.

Edgar Quinn extended his hand to Alex. "I want to thank you for helping my daughter. I'm sorry if I made things difficult for you. You're a fine physician, Alex, and I won't forget that." Edgar Quinn walked into his daughter's room, leaving Eli and Alex alone in the corridor.

Eli put his hand on Alex's shoulder. "Come into the treatment room, Alex. I want to talk to you."

They closed the door to the treatment room and sat together on the examining table. "First of all, Alex, I want to congratulate you. I admire what you've done to diagnose Charlotte and how you finally figured out what happened to Heather. As you probably know, the consensus is that you're one of the best residents we've ever had in neurology. I still don't understand why you missed Heather's meningitis, but those things happen." Eli stopped speaking for a moment. He stared at an IV bottle that lay next to him on the examining table. "Alex," he said slowly, "I've been harsh on you, but I think it's because of my own problems. Things aren't going well for me. I'll probably have to look for another job. Maybe I'm envious of you."

"Forget it, Eli," Alex said with a wave of his hand. "We'll go out and have a drink together. Save you the price of a bottle of whiskey. You know, this isn't an easy time for me either. I've been thinking about private practice, but the closer I get to it, the more I'm afraid of leaving the medical center. Eli, I'm beginning to have visions of doing research, taking the path you've taken."

"Alex, if you want to go into the laboratory, I'll support you fully. The staff will support you, and now you even have an ally in Edgar Quinn."

"What will happen to me in the laboratory, Eli?" Alex asked, and then without thinking added, "Will I wind up like you?"

Eli wasn't bothered by the question. "There's no answer to that, Alex," he said. "It depends on you. Coming into the laboratory means you'll have to prove yourself again. It's a new challenge, if that's what you want. But it's also a sacrifice. It means giving up a lot of the things you've already developed."

"Do you think I could make more of a contribution to medicine in the laboratory?"

"If you're lucky."

It was five o'clock. Alex called home.
Mellissa answered.
"It's Alex—don't hang up."
Silence.
"I'm coming home."
"You're not staying here."
"Where should I sleep?"
"Where did you sleep last night?"
"At the hospital."
"Stay there again."
"Mellissa, we've got to talk."
"I'm not ready yet, Alex."

Alex searched the ward for Casey but couldn't find her. He had talked to her last before going to play squash with Jim. He called her apartment.

"Alex," she answered, "I was just going to call you. I left the hospital early. How was squash?"

"Fine."

"What did Charlotte say when you told her about her spells?"

"She was frightened at first, then she cried. Finally she spilled the beans. She's a mixed-up girl, quite immature."

"Can you come over?"

"I called Mellissa again. She still won't talk to me or let me come home."

"Why don't you stay here?"

Thoughts of another night together brought a warm, exciting feeling to Alex. Besides, until he talked to Mellissa, he couldn't make his decision, if in fact there was a decision left to make.

"What's for dinner?" he asked.

They were together once again. No beepers needed to be exchanged, no other beds needed to be filled that night. Alone at last. They made love, then lay in each other's arms. They dozed. They made love again. They talked.

"I feel sorry for Eli, Casey. I wonder what he was like before he went into the lab."

"Just like you, only not as good," Casey said.

"The week's almost over," Alex said. He gave Casey a kiss. "I hope you've learned your neurology," he said with a smile.

"I've learned a lot," Casey answered seriously.

"Like what?" Alex asked, sitting up in bed.

"I've learned about seizures and about epilepsy," Alex's medical student said. "What I've seen is not a disease of children, it's a disease of parents. The child knows nothing of the attack; the child is unconscious during it and then has no memory of it. The horror, the worry, the suffering, that's all endured by the parents."

"What else, Casey?"

"I've learned how a doctor makes decisions. Too often doctors must give hard answers based on soft facts. And people always feel better when doctors can give them numbers. The operation has a twenty percent chance of succeeding. There's a fifty percent chance of cancer. Doctors always have to make decisions, whether they know the answer or not. Stop a medicine, order a lab test, decide whether something on the physical exam is normal or abnormal. Doctors are trained to make decisions, even if there is no answer."

257

Casey put her hand to Alex's cheek. "And I've learned about myself, Alex. About my love for medicine. But more than that, about my own feelings and how they are still there, ready to be touched, ready to be satisfied. I was afraid they might have been buried by too many medical books. And I've learned about my feelings for you, Alex." Now a tear appeared in Casey's wide brown eyes. "I've fallen in love with you, Alex."

"Casey—" Alex began, but the medical student wouldn't let her chief resident speak.

"Let's enjoy our time together," she said. "There will be plenty of time for decisions. We're good at that you know."

On the fourteenth floor of Alex's apartment house, his wife fed her two daughters, played with them, bathed them, read them a story, and tucked them in bed. Soon she would be ready to talk with Alex, but she didn't know what she would say or how she would react to him. She had accepted one of Alex's mistresses; how could she compete with a seizing child or a boy with a brain tumor? But with time, she would be less willing to grant Alex his medicine. And now his mistress had grown into something that he could hold in his arms. How could she be certain there was still a future for them? Mellissa made herself a drink and watched television.

On the third floor of Children's Hospital, Jim Wellander sat in the nurses' station, wearing his short white lab coat—a coat he wore infrequently but that tonight he had put on immediately after dinner. He needed the pockets of his lab coat to hide the materials he would need when he checked Tony. It was almost midnight. The evening had been quiet, only a few minor problems on the ward. The eleven o'clock nurse's report came and went; the ward was asleep for the night. At this time of night Jim was usually tired, hoping he wouldn't get a call so he could go to sleep. But tonight he was wide awake, and he knew he could wait no longer. It was time to check Tony before going to bed.

SATURDAY

7:30 A.M. Heather Papineau sat up in bed, with blood trickling from her mouth. During the preceding sixteen hours the frequency of her seizures had gradually lessened: every six minutes, every eight minutes, every ten minutes, four times an hour. During the night they stopped completely, and at 7:00 A.M. the girl woke up. Still groggy from the prolonged convulsions, she was not frightened by the strange surroundings, but something did bother her—the tube that had been in her throat for almost four days. She felt the irritation of the endotracheal tube in her windpipe and began coughing; finally she grabbed the tube that stuck from her mouth and pulled it out.

Alex woke in a strange apartment, but knew immediately where he was. The bed next to him was empty. He called for Casey but there was no answer. In the kitchen, he found a breakfast table set for him and a note. "Alex, I had some chores to do and you have some thinking to do. See you at rounds. Whatever you decide, I love you. Casey." He stood at the bay window, staring at a morning jogger on the sidewalk.

259

* * *

On division 17 people gathered for morning rounds. Louise, Mo, and Jim were there when Alex joined them. He could tell nothing from Jim's behavior about the events of the previous night, so he remained silent, waiting for someone else to mention Tony Zancanelli. Casey hadn't arrived yet.

"I have good news this morning," Louise announced happily. "Heather Papineau woke up. Her seizures stopped completely at about two A.M. She pulled the endotracheal tube out herself this morning. Apart from some bleeding from her mouth, she's fine."

They walked into the critical care room to find Heather sitting up in bed, eating breakfast. Alex recognized her as the girl he sent from the emergency ward late Sunday night. Had it been only a week since he'd first seen her? It seemed like years. Heather's only demand was to see her mother. Mo performed a neurologic exam; it was completely normal except for two up-going toes.

"In a day or two her toes will be normal," Alex said. "We're still seeing a residual from the seizures."

"You realize," Jim said smiling, "if you'd admitted her to the hospital on Sunday night, this never would have happened."

"Not this week, anyway," Alex smiled back.

Alex saw a large teddy bear sitting on the floor near Heather's bed, and placed it next to the girl. Heather put her arm around the teddy bear and rested her head against it. Thoughts of his oldest girl flashed through Alex's mind. Just then, Heather's mother appeared in the doorway.

"Mama!" the girl cried happily, standing up in bed.

Mrs. Papineau, now calm, ran to her girl and hugged her, then thanked the doctors profusely. An overnight stay at the psychiatric hospital, an increase in medication, and a chance to talk to Dr. Albertson had stabilized Mrs. Papineau. Dr. Albertson could not refuse her demand to visit Heather first thing Saturday morning.

In another room, Florence and Dennis Balsiger dressed their son and prepared to take him home. There was an adjustment in his medications, and the experimental drug would arrive at the hospital Monday. If the boy had no trouble over the weekend, the new medication would be started on an outpatient basis. If not, he would be readmitted to the hospital.

Dennis and Florence Balsiger thanked the doctors, but unlike previous thank yous, it carried no hope that this hospitalization would be the last and that BJ's problem would be solved.

"Where's Dr. Lilstrom?" the mother asked.

"She hasn't arrived."

"Please thank her for us. She was very kind," Mrs. Balsiger said.

"Also Dr. Lassiter," the father added.

The rounds entourage walked past Tony Zancanelli's room. "Don't forget Tony," Mo insisted. "Just because he didn't die on schedule doesn't mean we still don't see him on rounds."

Tony Zancanelli lay in his bed, still connected to his IV.

"How's he doing?" Jim asked.

"Better," Louise said. "His fever has started to come down."

"What happened?" Alex said, staring at Jim.

Mo and Louise were puzzled by the tone of Alex's question.

"What do you mean?" Jim said. "We talked about it yesterday. Evidently it was a pneumonia that resolved on its own. His chest X-ray yesterday showed an infiltrate in the right lung, but not as bad as I expected."

"I see," Alex said.

In the hallway, Alex cornered Jim. "What happened?" he asked again.

"I couldn't do it."

"You made the right decision."

"Alex, at first I thought I was going to do it. I even put on my short white jacket so I'd have pockets to put things in. But when I walked into his room at midnight just to check him, that's when I realized I couldn't do it."

"Why?"

"A feeling. It was different to rationalize and prepare myself in my mind than to do it. Hell, this isn't why I became a doctor, I said to myself. Funny, now I'm sorry I didn't do it. I hate to face his parents. I'd try again, but it wouldn't be any different." He paused. "Anything new with you, Alex?"

"Mellissa still won't talk to me. I spent the night at Casey's. This morning I'm leaning toward academic medicine. God knows how I'll feel this afternoon."

"Good luck," Jim told him as they walked toward the Quinn family.

Charlotte, dressed to leave the hospital, was sullenly standing next to her parents while Eli Lassiter talked to the father. She would be admitted to the psychiatric wing of the hospital the following week and would continue on standard doses of one anticonvulsant. During her psychiatric evaluation, it would be learned that her first fainting spells were indeed real seizures. Only later did she begin to embellish on her own.

The father shook Alex's hand. "You really helped us."

"He's a good doctor," Eli said and smiled at the chief resident.

"Thanks," Alex said.

The two Susies were escorting the boy with the cerebellar tumor down the corridor. They were both going home, and he would leave the following week. Mo would be following the hypotonic infant in clinic. The hydrocephalic heads watched the Saturday-morning exodus, unable to distinguish the blurred movement from all other blurred movements they had witnessed in their short lives.

Alex's beeper went off.

"Dr. Licata—8425."

Alex dialed the number.

"Alex, it's Mellissa. I'd like to talk to you. I'm at the front desk in the main lobby."

"I'll be right down."

The lobby was crowded, but Alex had no trouble finding Mellissa. He was actually relieved to see her. They stepped out onto the street and then walked a few hundred yards until they stood alone where Alex had stood with Casey three nights earlier.

"It hasn't been easy for me, Alex," Mellissa said. "What are we going to do?"

Alex knew that "give me time" was no longer an acceptable answer. Strange, at this moment he finally felt more time would not make a difference. Earlier in the morning he was ready to go with Casey, but he had made that decision without talking to Mellissa. Now, the reality of his life with his family was inescapable. But why was he drawn to Casey? He had told Casey that he loved her, and he did. She shared a part of his life that Mellissa never could.

Alex watched the movement of people on the nearby street and unconsciously fingered the red button on the top of his beeper.

"Alex," she repeated, "what are we going to do?"

He hadn't even known the words were there until he heard himself answering. "I know what I'm going to do, Mellissa. I'm going to stay in New York and do research."

Silence.

"I want you to stay with me, Mellissa," he said as he stared intently at his wife. "Please. I know it'll be difficult, but at least there won't be night call. And we can take out a loan, get someone to look after the girls so you can go back to work."

"Alex," she said, looking up, "what does that girl mean to you?"

He hesitated, thinking out the answer for himself as well as for her. "What does she mean?" he said finally. "Well, I know what she meant at first. She was someone I was attracted to, not because of something you did, but because of the hospital. Then she was consolation during a very rough time. I like Casey; I respect her. I don't blame her for what happened, and it wasn't your fault, Mellissa, believe me. If anything I blame myself, I blame the system."

"Does she know," Mellissa asked slowly, "that it's over?"

"Not yet."

"She'll be hurt," Mellissa said almost reflexively.

Alex didn't answer. He could never tell his wife that he had told Casey he loved her. For an instant Alex wondered whether it would be worse not to find out about his feelings toward Casey. He didn't want to spend his life fantasizing. But he did love Mellissa. If there were real problems in their marriage, they'd find out.

Alex put his arm around Mellissa's waist and kissed her. He had made his decision, a hard decision based on soft facts. After all, he was a doctor. "Let's go home," he said.

263

* * *

The door to the main entrance of Children's Hospital opened. Dennis Balsiger walked out, balancing his son on his right arm and clasping his wife's hand. The boy's legs dangled in the brisk Saturday air as he explored the world over his father's shoulder. Soon he held a balloon, purchased from the vendor who stood on the corner of Lexington Avenue, in his tiny hand. His mother kissed him and the boy laughed.

"I like it!" the boy said.

"I'm sure you do," the father replied as he lifted his son's shirt and planted a kiss on his belly.

They left the massive medical complex, its machines, its drugs, its charts, its rounds, and its doctors.

In the library of the hospital, amid millions of words written about illness and its treatment, was a paragraph composed by an English neurologist a quarter of a century before. In stilted prose, it described the treatment available for children with BJ's disease: "Faced with a disease whose springs lie buried at inaccessible levels of fetal existence, the observer can only veto marriage into tainted stocks, treat fits (seizures) symptomatically, and ensure that the patient has that home or institutional shelter to which his infirmities entitle him."

Unfortunately for BJ there were other books in the same library, books written only one year previously, books that used less archaic language to convey the identical message. But the pain that BJ's parents felt, the pain that all parents feel who have a child with an untreatable illness, is a shared agony. And it is this helplessness that drives some to understand those instances when nature has gone astray. One day the illnesses would be understood, one day the "buried springs" would bubble up to show themselves. It is only a question of how closely nature has guarded her secrets. It is only a question of time.